A thrumming sounded overhead, coming closer.

Hackles rising, Refit glanced up and saw the wasp-shaped BirdSong JK91 heligyro approaching. The stubby, movable wings under the main rotor were canted up so it could descend.

The FREELancers agent ran for the lake, hoping down there in the uneven terrain he could escape. His legs trembled but he made them work. He knew two more strides would bring him within leaping distance of the dark water.

Then a cone of light surrounded him and bullets clawed at the broken ground. Four rounds hit him in the back and he fell. A warm lassitude crept through his extremities, and he knew he'd been hit with Para-bullets.

Unable to move, he watched the heligyro descend, whipping dust and grit over everything. The men closed in on him, moving like wraiths amid the swirling debris.

Refit watched, unable to close his eyes as the poison wreaked havoc with his weakened system. The enemy seemed to want him alive for now. But he didn't know if that was a blessing or the opening to something much worse.

Other TSR® Books

Mus of Kerbridge
Paul Kidd

Yor's Revenge
Roy V. Young
(available Summer 1995)

Dragons Can Only Rust
Chrys Cymri
(available Fall 1995)

Dragon Reforged
Chrys Cymri
(available Winter 1995)

F.R.E.E.Lancers

Mel Odom

F.R.E.E.Lancers

First Printing: June 1995
Printed in the United States of America.
Library of Congress Catalog Card Number: 94-60843
ISBN: 0-7869-0113-6

9 8 7 6 5 4 3 2 1

TSR, Inc.
201 Sheridan Springs Rd.
Lake Geneva, WI 53147
U. S. A.

TSR Ltd.
120 Church End, Cherry Hinton
Cambridge CB1 3LB
United Kingdom

DEDICATION

This is for my wife, Sherry Lynn.

You gave me friendship and love and trust, and a gentleness I've never known. Before you came into my life, my world had a space in it that knew only storms and cold, hard rock. Thank you for taking me to the beach and showing me sunsets and cotton candy and the joy of holding hands.

I love you, and I'll always be your friend.

ACKNOWLEDGMENTS

I'd like to thank the people who helped make this book possible. First of all, Brian Thomsen, whose friendship and jokes are always appreciated, as well as a similar taste in fiction. Thanks for the trust and the interest, guy. And the "interesting phrase!"

To the support team at TSR: Patrick McGilligan, who helped put the book in shape and was enthusiastic about what we had. For Eric, who steered me along the path. And to Jeff Grubb, who invented the game and allowed me to pick his brain. To Marlys Heeszel, who helped stir the pot and added spice. You couldn't ask for a nicer bunch of folks to work with.

To my agent, Ethan Ellenberg, who keeps me believing in dreams when I sometimes forget.

To M. J. and Todd Brantley, who mistakenly got left out of the STALKER ANALOG book.

To the guys at Planet Comics in Oklahoma City who kept me in information: John Hunter, Mike Kennedy, and Kevin Hooper.

To Leonard Bishop, for suggesting the band's name.

To Darlene and Vern Olson, who kept the lights on for me in Motley, MN.

To Deanna, sister of my buddy, Robert Lynn McDonald, who wears panties most of the time and doesn't mind if her preacher knows. Thanks for the laughs that night, and for asking Sherry and me why the hell we didn't just get married if everything was so peachy keen. (It was, and we did, and we're happy as can be.)

To my children, Matthew Lane and Matthew Dain, who are turning into fine young men I'm going to be proud to call my friends. My daughter, Montana, who can be as vexing to me as Lois is to Clark, and that's only part of why I love her. To my little guy, my best buddy, Shiloh, for believing in heroes just as much as I do.

1

Chicago, Illinois   ***3:54 a.m. CST***
Great Lakes Authority (GLA)   ***0954 Greenwich Mean***
87.7 degrees W Longitude   ***October 24, 2023***
41.8 degrees N Latitude   ***Tuesday***
Assignment: Broken Goblin
Tactical Ops: Recovery, Limited Engagement
Status: Code Yellow

"Okay, team, we've got a green light. Kick Gibney free."
Refit tapped the controls for the Burris transceiver mounted
on his collarbone and stepped farther back into the shadows of
the warehouse.

"Sending her now," a female voice responded.

A few seconds later, a woman stepped from the azure Caleri
sedan parked on DeWitt Place and walked toward the black
van that had pulled up in front of her fifty yards away and
extinguished its lights. No one had moved from the second
vehicle. The chipped and broken faces of the buildings stared
out over the unlighted street.

"Download," Refit called over the Burris.

"I've got 'er, mate. No worries 'ere." Download's words

were strangely soft and sibilant.

Refit ignored them; he'd heard much worse from the other agent. "Prime."

"Go." The answer was totally neutral.

Though practiced at controlling emotions and fears, Refit knew he'd never be as detached as Agent Prime. The lives of two kids were riding on their actions. "The van?"

"Can't get an infrared scan to take," Prime responded. "Maybe they're there, maybe they're not."

Refit watched as Gibney approached the van, less than twenty yards away now. The woman held her arms across her chest and kept her head up, but her steps were quick and short. Not for the first time he considered that his team could have been set up. He booted the Burris up to the secondary frequency, knowing FREELancers Control was monitoring the situation. "Net, can you help us out?"

"Negative, Refit. We have primary visual and audio limited to your frequencies."

Refit was surprised to hear Lee Won Underhill's voice. Usually the FREELancers administrator oversaw only the most demanding assignments. His scarred lips twisted into a semblance of a smile. "Affirmative, Net."

"They told her to stop," the female voice said.

"Roger, C4." Refit stared across the rain-polished streets. Gibney had come to a stop less than ten feet from the side of the van. "Probably eyeballing her to make sure she's not carrying a vid-wire. Download?"

"Still can't confirm the interior of the van."

"Damn," Refit whispered to himself as he watched Gibney standing there so vulnerable.

"Won't mean a thing to them if they burn her down where she stands," Prime said.

"I know." Refit didn't like waiting, but he'd learned to. Sometimes it kept a guy from getting real dead real quick. He was six feet four inches tall, most of the time, and was built broad and sturdy from the hard years as a steelworker in his previous life—before he'd learned he was a metable. His jumpsuit was gray with red piping, but he'd ripped the sleeves off and slit the bottom few inches of his pants seams to show off the hand-tooled cowboy boots he habitually wore. A low-slung leather belt held a Detonics .45 in a tied-down holster. He kept a Crain combat blade in his left boot. Armament was intentionally kept low because the operation was supposed to be covert. Refit didn't think it would stay that way.

The van door opened with a crash that echoed across the street, and two men got out armed with Sandusky X-13 backpack lasers. They kept the firing wands canted upward as they closed on Gibney. She held out a small cylinder.

"Once that cylinder's open," Prime said, "we're blown."

"Maybe worse than you think," C4 put in. "Gibney could have actually put Carter's genetics research in there instead of the dummied disks Underhill gave her. After all, she's protecting her husband and her two kids."

"They're not getting away," Refit promised. He pulled on the battered trench coat he'd worn for disguise earlier while reconning the team's positions, then started out into the street, weaving slightly. "Download."

"Go."

"You get to open the ball, buddy." Refit fisted the Detonics under the trench coat, wishing there were something more lethal than the Para-bullets in the magazine.

"When a man's partner is killed he's supposed to do something about it," Download said. "When one of your organization gets killed, it's bad business to let the killer get away with it."

Refit dimly recognized the words from *The Maltese Falcon*, and the accent was almost Bogie. He knew the other agent had been raiding the old movie vids from the base library again. Download's personality, at times, seemed as fragmented as Refit's scrambled body. He kept moving down the sidewalk.

A zeppelin went by overhead as he walked, its undercarriage

transmitting a vid announcement for Cyborgs Izz Us. Rainbow-colored letters streamed across the bottom of the screen: *Remember, if you're dissatisfied with* any *part of your body, come on down to Cyborgs Izz Us and we'll replace it.* Nick Scemo's signature wrote itself across the screen in lime-green neon immediately following. The lights strobed across the street for an instant.

"Hey, pal," one of the two armed men said. "This here's a private party."

Refit stretched out his empty hand. "Please. All I'm asking for is a little change." He closed the distance to just over ten feet. Gibney looked at him, her face paling visibly. If she'd had any thoughts of a double cross, now she knew it would be a costly move.

"He said beat it," the other man said, taking Gibney by the arm again and moving toward the van.

Refit peered through the gloom and saw Gibney's husband, son, and daughter handcuffed and gagged inside the van. There was no way to relay the bad news to the rest of the team. His anger increased because of his helplessness. He kept his voice neutral. "Just a little change."

"Jeez, will you get a look at this guy's face," the first man said. "Looks like it's been burnt off."

Refit ignored the words. Since the mill accident where he'd been burned over ninety percent of his body, lost both legs, and discovered he was a metable, he'd heard all kinds of comments. His body was just meat, a tool that could be used, and not really him at all. Most people just didn't recognize that.

A few of the figures shifted inside the van, and Refit got a good look at Gibney's little girl: dark brown tresses, an oval face with widely spaced eyes, almost a carbon copy of her mother.

"Get that bum out of here," the van's driver called out.

The first man lashed out with his laser. Refit deliberately didn't block the blow. It slammed against his temple and the shock drove him backward on his butt. For a moment he experienced double vision, but he didn't let the pain touch him.

"Hey," the second man said, "look at his feet. Burnt face or no burnt face, you aren't going to find boots like that on some street beggar."

Refit freed the Detonics .45 from the holster and threw himself to one side of the street as a laser blast cored a ten-inch hole where his head had been. Bringing the pistol up, he fired two rounds into the laser-user's face and watched the man go backward from the impacts. He made his move on the second opponent, hoping Download had a shot.

Chicago, Illinois   4:02 a.m. CST
Assignment: Broken Goblin, cont'd.
Status Upgrade: Code Red

Download lay on top of the warehouse on the east side of DeWitt Place with a H&K PSG-1 sniper rifle hugged to his cheekbone. He had a clear view of the van and saw Refit struggle up from the street surface, the pistol in his hand spitting flame. He held back retaliation because saving Refit wasn't his objective, and Colonel Rance Charles of Australia's Special Forces wouldn't have fired before he had a clear target no matter whose life was in danger.

At the moment he knew that to be a certainty, because a large part of him *was* Colonel Charles. He held the sniper rifle with a firm grip despite the perspiration soaking his jumpsuit and the headache that pounded all the way around his skull.

His real name was Jefferson Scott, and on most days he had to work really hard to remember that. A couple inches short of six feet, he had the rangy build of a baseball outfielder.

He peered through the H&K PSG-1's StarTron night scope, trying to get a fix on the targets inside the van. Mounted on his right shoulder, the Octopus fed Colonel Charles's skills as a sniper from a disk through steel-sheathed fiber-optic tentacles that connected directly to the right side of his brain through implant modules.

He'd downloaded the skill through the Octopus nearly half an hour before the scheduled rendezvous, then spent the time since reliving old arguments Charles had experienced with his unfaithful wife during his military career. The intensity and emotions of those arguments would stay with Download longer than the skills. The agent knew that from personal experience.

His finger caressed the rifle's trigger.

Doc Random, FREELancers Research Operations director, had created the Octopus device but didn't fully understand it. According to him, the ghosts that were left in Download's brain after using a disk weren't possible, and he had suggested psychiatric treatment. Download had passed on the option. These days, he stayed away from shrinks and anyone else who wanted to pick his brain over. There were already enough people in there.

"Download," Agent Prime called over the Burris.

"No," Download said, staying on the van.

"Dammit, we're going to lose them all."

Download ignored the outburst. Prime was more concerned about his success rate than he was about Gibney. Even Dr. Sherman Carter's stolen research took a back seat.

Then a hand came up inside the van, caught for a moment in the thin moonlight. It pointed a small pistol at the three captives in the back of the vehicle.

"I've got a shot," Download said in a calm voice he was aware carried an Australian accent that was not his. His finger pulled the trigger through, and he effortlessly rode out the recoil.

The bullet crashed through the windshield and took the man in the passenger seat in the forehead. Jerking from the impact of the heavy 7.62mm round, the corpse flopped halfway out the window.

Without warning, the van pulled forward, leaving the outside man to deal with Refit and Gibney. Coolly, Download bracketed the van's front wheels and squeezed off two rounds for each. Both tires instantly deflated, but the driver wasn't going fast enough to lose control.

Lee Won Underhill broke in over the frequency. "Broken Goblin, be advised that you have more potential unfriendlies en route. We've picked them up from satellite recon."

Download glanced at the north end of DeWitt Place and saw the three cars streaking toward the firezone. Somewhere inside him, he knew Colonel Charles was smiling. It was something to take his mind off the wife.

Chicago, Illinois   4:04 a.m. CST
Assignment: Broken Goblin, cont'd.
Status: Code Red

Refit threw himself at Dr. Clarice Gibney as she ran toward the van.

The little girl inside screamed, "Mommy! Mommy!" Her words were punctuated by the dull roar of gunfire and the sizzle of lasers.

Catching Gibney in his arms, Refit pulled her to the ground and shielded her with his body. The van took off as they rolled dangerously close to the wheels. Hot exhaust blew across Refit's face, warming the places that weren't completely dead from the burning so long ago.

"My babies!" Gibney screamed.

"Stay down," Refit ordered, searching for the other gunner. He found the man too late. The guy's Sandusky X-13 neatly sliced off the last three fingers of Refit's left hand. Just meat, the patchwork giant told himself as the familiar scent of burned flesh filled his nostrils, ain't you at all. He raised the Detonics and fired three times, the rounds stitching the gunner from navel to chin.

Glancing over his shoulder, he saw the van wobbling off on two flat tires. He issued his orders on the heels of Underhill's warning, registering the headlights that sped toward them.

"Scratchbuilt."

"Yes, sir." John-Michael DeChanza's voice sounded every bit of his fourteen years of age.

"You've got the van."

"Yes, sir." In response, a thirty-five-foot-tall metal monster roused itself from hiding on top of the decrepit, three-story motel at the far end of the block. Man-shaped with a head like a washtub, it crouched for an instant on the edge of the building, the low wall crumbling under its massive feet and raining brick and mortar over a ragged awning in front of a closed sidewalk cafe. Moonlight kissed the sleek silver surface of the man-amplifying powersuit and turned the crimson stripes bloodred. The armament pods on the MAPS's shoulders bearing the grenade launcher and a .50-caliber machine gun looked more artistic than deadly.

Then, with movements that appeared more flowing than mechanical, Scratchbuilt leaped from the top of the building. Refit grabbed for the fleeing woman with his injured hand just as Scratchbuilt thudded to street level with enough force to shake the immediate vicinity.

Refit cursed as his blood made the woman's arm too slick to hang on to. She continued running. He pursued, aware that the other members of the team were in the fray now.

C4, slender and lovely and deadly in her abbreviated silver-and-crimson bikini and thigh-high boots, sprinted into position ahead of Refit and set herself to confront the lead sedan bearing down on them. The headlights splashed over her ebony skin as she crossed her gloved hands before her. Orange-and-yellow incandescence boiled around her palms for an instant, then lanced out at the sedan.

The car's engine exploded, blowing the hood off as flames splashed back over the windshield. Obviously unnerved, the driver pulled hard right and mowed down one of the darkened light poles. Four men pushed their way out of the wrecked sedan as it continued to burn. They lifted their weapons and aimed them at C4.

The woman raised her hands again, and another orange-and-yellow bolt licked out and touched the gas tank. The resulting explosion was even more pronounced and flattened all four gunners.

Sprinting for all he was worth, ignoring the bleeding hand, Refit closed the distance between himself and Gibney. Ahead of him, Scratchbuilt tore more concrete from the street when he yanked his feet free.

The second car was on Refit before he realized it because he'd been so focused on the woman and the van. Reacting at the last second, unable to completely clear the car, he leaped upward.

The car's windshield struck him in the side, breaking ribs and throwing him onto the roof. He rolled as it passed under him, then dropped to the street. Blocking the pain, he struggled to his feet, noticing for the first time that his left elbow was broken. It was just meat. He maintained his grip on the Detonics as he stumbled forward and tried to catch his breath. He heard the squeal of brakes and realized that the car was swinging around for another pass. Two bullets caught him in the back, one of them cutting through the Kevlar armor and letting him know someone was using Teflon-coated bullets. He looked down at his waist and saw the blood staining his shirt. But he didn't stop running.

Scratchbuilt caught up with the van, reached out with the three-fingered claws that were his hands, and fastened them around the bumper. Then he lifted. The van came up, but the momentum already gathered pulled the MAPS along for a dozen feet, leaving trenches cut into the street.

A hail of bullets caught Gibney just before Refit reached her. The woman went down at once, and the patchwork giant knew she was dead. He hit the Burris's transmit button. "The woman just bought it, Net."

"Dammit," Underhill said with thinly concealed anger, "you people were there to prevent that."

Refit didn't argue because he didn't have the breath. One

of his lungs was filling up with blood, and Gibney's family was still on the firing line. The van's driver was struggling to get out from behind the wheel when Refit arrived. Raising his pistol, the FREELancers agent fired the last of his magazine into the man. Unable to reload with his injured hand, he dropped the pistol and stepped up into the van.

Gibney's husband, son, and daughter were scattered across the floor of the van. Refit didn't see the other gunner in the rear of the vehicle until it was too late to move.

"Die, you son of a bitch," the man snarled, raising his pistol. The reports were deafening inside the van.

Both bullets penetrated Refit's Kevlar armor and smashed against his broken ribs. Just meat, he reminded himself as he locked his good hand around the man's throat. He yanked, exercising his great strength, and threw the man out the back doors of the van. The man slammed against Scratchbuilt and dropped, unconscious, to the street.

The little girl was still screaming, her gag loose around her neck.

"Shhh," Refit said, getting close. "I've got you, kid. You're okay now."

Her eyes were wide and she wouldn't stop screaming. She was looking at the blood, at all the burn scarring across his face and the mismatched arms and legs that had belonged to other people.

Refit wouldn't let her emotions touch him. He sorted her out of the wreckage of the van as gently as he could, held her in close to him to protect her as she kicked and hit at him.

"I've got her."

Turning, Refit looked through the van's open door and saw Tandem 2 standing there. He was medium height and lean as a rail, with a mop of brown hair that was always unruly. Beside him was Tandem 1, a green-eyed blonde with a teenager's firm curves under her tight-fitting jumpsuit. Refit passed the girl over to Tandem 1, then freed the father and son. It was getting harder to hang on to consciousness.

"Get 'em clear," Refit ordered.

"What about you?" Tandem 2 asked. Concern etched his freckled face.

"Get moving," Tandem 1 said as Scratchbuilt's shadow fell across them. "He wanted to talk, he'd be on *Barnaby*."

A barrage of auto-fire hammered the MAPS metal skin and sparked off like tiny lightnings. Servomotors whirred as Scratchbuilt brought the 40mm grenade launcher on-line. He fired an instant later and the grenades slagged the second car.

Vision fading as he struggled to stay on his feet, Refit watched as the people in the third car obviously reconsidered their tactical options and tried to turn tail. Before the driver could clear the firezone, Agent Prime rappelled down the side of the building in front of the car. He dropped the last eight feet, coming down in a crouch and drawing the CO_2-reload multishot crossbow from over his back.

Six feet tall with bleached blond hair, piercing blue eyes, and a diamond-shaped scar on the right side of his chin, Agent Prime was every inch the fighting man. His red-and-gray uniform was crisp, filled with extra pockets that ran deep, and a double bandolier crisscrossed his chest. He raised the crossbow and seemed to fire without aiming.

The red-fletched quarrel sped true and took the driver in the shoulder, pinning him to the seat and putting the car out of control. Spinning, the sedan slammed through the doors of a warehouse. C4 closed in, her hands already glowing in readiness. No one appeared ready to continue the fight.

Unable to stand anymore, Refit fell. He heard the sound of police sirens in the distance, closing fast. He struggled to make his voice heard. "You guys beat it. I'll fade the heat on this one."

Scratchbuilt knelt, hovering protectively. He started to reach out, but the MAPS's hand was as big as his fallen teammate, and he drew back. "I'm not leaving you, amigo."

"That's an order, kid."

"When you're well, kick my ass for not listening."

"I'll look forward to it." Refit settled into the comfortable distance as parts of his body died. The punctured lung made it hard to speak.

"I'm in, too," Agent Prime said. "Kid's never been to jail before. And that's definitely where we're headed since we didn't have an umbrella over this little caper."

"The Dragon Lady's going to enjoy the hell out of this," Refit gasped. The car C4 had exploded was still burning, throwing garish shadows over the buildings.

"Told her we shouldn't have bought into this one," Agent Prime said. "Wasn't enough time to do a proper recon."

Face almost covered by the helmet he wore, Download stopped in front of them and looked down at Gibney. Perspiration covered his pale face and shone on the metal chin and cheek pieces. He carried a pistol in each hand. "She's dead." His hazel eyes looked hollow and haunted.

"Yeah," Agent Prime said without feeling. "Tough. Woman was a damned traitor to the GLA anyway."

Download looked at them. "I'm dead, too. I think. She keeps telling me she is, so I must be."

"Take it home," Agent Prime advised. "The locals are ringing down the curtain on this little production. You don't want to end up in a steel cage for the next few hours."

"No." Download walked away, still holding the pistols.

"Who was he?" Scratchbuilt asked.

"That masked man?" Agent Prime said. "Kid, you don't want to give me a straight line like that."

Refit gazed at the dead woman, feeling bad for her, even worse for the kids. He knew what it was like to lose family. Then the whirling blue cherries of the Chicago PD invaded the war zone. Before he knew it, he went into full cardiac arrest.

2

Chicago, Illinois   **4:12 a.m. CST**
Great Lakes Authority (GLA)   1012 Greenwich Mean
87.7 degrees W Longitude   October 24, 2023
41.8 degrees N Latitude   Tuesday
FREELancers Base
Status: Code Green

"Who do the police have in custody?" Lee Won Underhill demanded. A com-link no bigger than a hearing aid connected her with the nerve center of the FREELancers command post on the thirteenth floor of the building. She stood in her office peering down at the city, her arms crossed over her breasts.

"We've confirmed only Refit, Scratchbuilt, and Agent Prime," Philip Kent answered.

The office was furnished with Pacific Rim history. Chinese vases hundreds of years old occupied niches built into the lacquered teak walls. A full set of samurai swords hung on the wall behind her desk, offset by streaming dragons in pale yellow and teal on white silk banners that ran from floor to ceiling. Another wall was filled with books on warfare, strategy, and philosophy, broken up by glass and ceramic and ivory figurines with delicate features. Green plants hung from the ceiling and sat on the ledges of the two bulletproof windows overlooking downtown Chicago and Lake Michigan. A bamboo tree grew in a large pot behind the two visitors chairs.

"What about the rest of the team?" Underhill asked. She was five feet tall, with glossy black hair trickling past her shoulders, volcanic blue eyes, and a burnished butter complexion. She wore a gray business skirt accented with red and a matching jacket over a white shirt and red scarf. A trio of silver bracelets adorned her right wrist.

"All of them have checked in but Download."

"What's his status?"

"He's alive."

"Where?"

"We don't know for sure. He's not with the others."

She reached for the remote control on her desk and switched on the television hidden behind a recessed wall. The picture cleared at once as the wall pulled back silently. The Chicago networks were already covering the story and were making it sound like the FREELancers agents had been responsible for a bloodbath. "Contact him."

"We're working on it."

"What about the Gibney woman?"

"DOA at Chicago General two minutes ago."

"Her family?"

"The Tandems are with them."

"Have them brought here," Underhill said.

"Right." There was a pause. "Something else: apparently Refit has suffered some major damage. He's being transported to Chicago General. He's not expected to live."

"That's because they don't know him. Get Dr. Llewellyn over there. And I want a full complement of organs and limbs available for whatever transplants Refit needs."

"I'll see to it myself. Hornsby's on line nine. Calling with

all the righteous hellfire accorded to a representative of the
GLA's Council of Governors."

"Hold the call. I'll take it in a minute." Underhill sat
behind the desk and composed herself. She had never liked
dealing with government heads, and things had become only
more difficult since Governor Jim Bob Culpepper of Texas
had rejected all of NAFTA's promises and got elected on a
promise to keep "Mexicans in Mexico," in 2011. On February
11 of that same year, he began building a wall twelve feet
high that ran the length of the Rio Grand, topping it with
barbed wire and adding land mines and guard towers manned
by Texas National Guardsmen.

The rest of the US had been shocked, and Justice Department officials pursued legal recourse to get the Texas governor to stop building. Besides military resistance, Culpepper
also leaned heavily on his political prowess. Texas's electoral
votes weighed in considerably in presidential elections, and
an election year was coming up with no clear leading candidate. Hoping to get reelected, President Humboldt chose to
do nothing. A Texas senatorial filibuster was already in
progress at the time the governor of Arizona began building
his wall. Not to be outdone, he built his wall fifteen feet tall.

California, which had immediately started getting swamped
with illegal aliens, chose to start building as well, followed
almost immediately by New Mexico. The walls had signaled
the breakdown of the federal government.

The economy, which had continued to fluctuate—dividing
the US more and more into camps of haves and have-nots,
became the final point of contention in the great nation. Different economic areas fragmented, and the federal government fell into virtual ruin.

With the state governments suddenly in control of providing the governmental services Washington, DC could no
longer offer, they realized that regional alliances would offer
more resources for making the effort work. The first alliance
was the Great Lakes Authority. In the beginning it consisted

of the traditional Rust Belt States: Minnesota, Wisconsin, Illinois, Indiana, Michigan, and Ohio. Iowa petitioned for membership later, followed by Missouri.

Once the GLA proved that it could happen and be beneficial, the other alliances followed: the Middle Atlantic Alliance, Ohio-Lower Mississippi Basin Cooperative, Mega state of Greater Massachusetts, South Atlantic States Directive, and Rocky Mountain Alliance. The Pacific Coast states, burdened by a nuclear disaster and environmental problems, had remained pretty much on their own. Texas had become an alliance unto itself.

With the once great country split and the differences between the states so pronounced, conflicts between the alliances sometimes escalated to military retaliation, as well as economic guerilla tactics. Through it all, however, corporate America continued to roll along.

During those early years, Mayor Dorothy Hubbard of Chicago had earned her hash marks. She was still one of the most influential politicians in America, as well as one of the initial supporters of FREELancers. And Underhill had somewhat double-crossed her during the night. It hadn't been wise, but it had been necessary.

Letting out one last full breath, Underhill scooped up the phone and tagged the flashing light for the call waiting for her. The vid-screen on the connection cleared, focused on a slim, well-built man in a dark suit and unruly white hair. "Underhill," she said, lacing her fingers in front of her.

"What the hell is going on with you people?" Monroe Hornsby yelled. The Council representative appeared to be nearly apoplectic. Underhill didn't blame him. Hornsby had been assigned to damage control on the Gibney/Carter affair, now it was within inches of splattering across every medium in the InfoNet. "This was supposed to be a quietly run operation. There wasn't supposed to be a damn war zone."

"The FREELancers agency was hired to find out whether Dr. Gibney was selling Carter's patents to the black market,"

Underhill said. She tapped keys on her computer deck, then faxed the message across the phone line. Half the vid-screen was taken up by highlighted sections of the contract Hornsby had signed on behalf of the GLA and Iowa State University. "We found your security leak for you. It was your decision to try to save her family as well."

"And you wouldn't have?"

"Not if you hadn't filed the supplemental contract hiring us to do that."

Hornsby ran a hand through his hair. "Dammit, Underhill, if we'd let those people kill her husband and kids, the publicity would have been just as bad for us. You were hired to keep this from happening."

"Wrong." Underhill kept her voice neutral. "We were hired to find your industrial spy, then subcontracted to take her family back from the blackmailers. We turned her, broke her, and got her family back. The way I see it, you owe us the balance of the fee. I want it posted in our bank no later than nine o'clock in the morning."

"You'll have your money."

"We earned every penny of it." Underhill moved to punch off the call.

"Wait," Hornsby said.

The FREELancers administrator did, already anticipating what was coming.

"Who were the people Gibney was working with?" Hornsby asked.

"Recovery of that information wasn't mentioned in our initial contracts," Underhill stated. "If you'd care to open negotiations regarding that, call my secretary and make an appointment." She broke the connection.

Feeling edgy, she pushed up out of the chair and walked to the window. Usually she enjoyed the view.

"Penny for your thoughts, daughter."

Turning, she found the holo image of her father, George Anthony Underhill, standing near her desk. He'd been a tall man in his physical life, with sandy hair worn swept back and a salt-and-pepper mustache neatly clipped beneath a patrician nose. His eyebrows grew thick over eyes so pale gray they were almost silver. As usual, he wore black slacks and a white shirt with the sleeves rolled up to midforearm and the collar open.

"You'd be overspending this morning," she told him.

"Would I? I've been monitoring the situations as they've developed. I'd say you have everything well in hand."

"I wouldn't." Even when her father had been flesh and blood, before the inoperable cancer was diagnosed in 2013 and he'd been frozen cryogenically, Underhill had experienced problems in dealing with him. He'd fathered her in French Indochina, then hadn't seen her for twenty-one years till he'd found her controlling a large percentage of the black market in Ho Chi Minh City. Even after almost two decades of working together and founding FREELancers from the ashes of the old Fast Reaction Experimental Espionage division, they had become close, but not too personally involved.

Even FREE hadn't been the true beginning of their company. George Anthony Underhill's career had begun with Oberon, an espionage arm of a highly skilled outfit called Orion that had come into being during World War II. Though the Ganymede Bureau and Titan Team concentrated on low-key espionage done within accepted parameters, Oberon tested those self-imposed limits.

In the 1990s, when Oberon was at the height of its influence, George Anthony Underhill had been moved to its head, and had begun following his own personal vision of what covert teams should consist of. He selected people who were by nature loners, who weren't afraid to take on any assignment and had superior skills. Also during this time, metables began to appear within society more frequently.

Metable became a catchword of the late 1990s. No one knew for sure where the powers seemed to come from, but they were there. Some scientists said they'd always been there but had just lain in wait for discovery, for the right tools to come along to expose those skills. Others suggested that metables were nature's hesitant steps toward propelling the human race into its next evolution.

The most common metability was savantism. A Savant was someone who suddenly developed a skill or skills higher than humanly possible. Looking back, metable researchers documented possible metables in music and mathematical fields: Einstein, Da Vinci, Mozart, and Hawkings. But the advent of computers and cybernetics systems seemed to increase those numbers exponentially. Dr. Andrew Rhand, himself a metable in the savant field, proposed that Savants had been around for generations, but lacked the proper tools to utilize their talents.

As the powers became stronger and more wild, so did the physical body's adaptation to them. Besides powers that were in some ways akin to psychic skills, there were more physical ones regarding invulnerabilities to fire, drowning, poison, and other deadly forces.

Where the regular Orion departments hesitated over the use of metables, George Anthony Underhill actively recruited them, working with them to build their confidence and their skills. In 1999, a botched rescue attempt by the Oberon branch and the resulting scandal relegated Underhill's group to political suicide. No one wanted to unleash metable forces again.

George Anthony Underhill, though, wasn't about to give up on his dream. He'd been reunited with his daughter for some years, and when the US started fragmenting into state alliances, he'd started work to leverage the Oberon branch from the Orion group. In 2002, he succeeded. Everyone connected with the old agency expected FREE to fall on its face and quietly die.

Instead, the Underhills parlayed the agency into a successful business venture. In 2002 they recruited Dr. Andrew J. Rhand. Under Rhand's direction, research in both high technology and metabilities skyrocketed, and brought with it enormous profits that were poured back into the fledgling agency's coffers.

Needing a home base, the Underhills had negotiated a deal with Mayor Hubbard to locate in Chicago. The name was changed from FREE to FREELancers, and the group became a for-hire team of meta-normal agents wielding odd powers and great technologies, for rent to the highest bidder—provided the Underhills deemed the cause or causes worthy.

"Maybe you're being too hard on yourself," her father suggested. His image wavered for a moment as the building experienced a power surge.

"Things got out of control tonight," she admitted.

"Through no fault of yours or the team's. There's more to this than you can see at the moment, Lee. Trust that and follow your instincts. After a while, you start to see these patterns develop even before they emerge." Her father's image walked to the window and peered out. The computer matrix that managed the holo image wouldn't operate outside the office walls. But that was just as well because George Anthony Underhill was legally dead, and cryogenics experiments were very much against the law.

"I've got to get going."

"If you decide you want to talk, I'll be here."

"I know." Underhill grabbed her purse and briefcase, and headed for the door. As she closed it behind her, she glanced back at her father's image in time to see the atoms fall apart, whirl madly, and disappear. Her mind raced as she walked toward her private elevator. On the surface, everything seemed in place—except Download.

Old memories snapped at her mind and brought a sharp bitterness with them. Jefferson Scott was a weakness she couldn't afford—not all those years ago, and certainly not now. She entered the elevator cage and pressed the button for the basement level. The cage dropped at such a sudden rate it felt like gravity had been canceled.

Refit blinked his eyes open, straining at first against the harsh light above him. The keening siren and the swaying motion told him he was in an ambulance. A tube ran down his nose and throat and worked to suction the blood out of the ripped lung. A glucose bag hung overhead and was connected to the IV deep in his good arm.

The EMT was a young Hispanic woman in hospital neon blues. Her dark hair was pulled back by tiger's-eye combs. A neat, white scar in the corner of her mouth twisted her lower lip slightly and gave her an amused look. She wore gloves, a stethoscope, and a name badge that read 'Risa.'

"Guy looks like a jigsaw puzzle that's been forced together," the police officer said.

"He's awake, too." Risa looked down at the FREELancers agent and touched his forehead with gloved fingers. "How're you doing?"

"Been better." Refit had to force his voice past the tube in his throat, which already felt dry.

"Well, you're in good hands here," the EMT said. She made an adjustment to the glucose bag. "Have you to the hospital in just a few minutes. Your doctor's on her way."

"What's your name, pal?" the man asked.

"Meet Detective Amos Haddonfield," Risa said. "One-man crime fighting team, and Chicago's answer to darkest evil." She glanced at the medical computers operating off the sens-dots attached to Refit's temple, chest, and femoral artery.

Haddonfield scowled. He was a big man with broad shoulders and short legs, dressed in a gray trench coat and a dark blue suit. Short, bristling red hair poked out from under his snap-brim hat and made his eyebrows look like commas. His broad face showed a lot of wear and tear gained over at least fifty hard years.

"I wouldn't be so quick to talk about anybody's looks if I were you," Refit said.

"You're under arrest, wise guy," Haddonfield said. "I need a name for the report."

Moving his arm in spite of the restraining strap, Refit checked his pockets. "You got my wallet and ID."

Haddonfield grinned and it was totally without mirth. "IDs can be forged."

"And you figured I might be whacked out enough to slip if you asked me?" Some of the tightness in Refit's chest was disappearing, but the area was going numb, too.

"Maybe. Give me a name."

"Charles Henry Magastowkawicz. Same as on the documents in that wallet. And I know how much money I had."

"Terrific. You're batting a thousand. Save you the cost of a CAT scan, Risa." Haddonfield handed the wallet back. "Says here you're thirty-eight, Charlie."

"Yeah."

"Rough years, I guess."

"Sure," Refit said. "But it's the good ones that really wear your ass out. Looking at you, I'd figure your life has been a regular riot."

Haddonfield ignored the jibe. His eyes were cool and distant. "We left a lot of dead people behind us. And one of them was on Sherman Carter's research staff, which means this thing could snarl up. Personally, I don't want to see that happen. So why don't you tell me what the hell is going on."

"Can't." Refit coughed, and Risa adjusted the tube.

"Or won't?" Haddonfield asked.

"You pick," Refit said. "I'll swear it was my idea."

"You've got a security clearance with the PD as one of the FREELancers agents," the detective said, "but that's not a blank check. You people are supposed to notify us about your activities. My captain says he didn't hear squat about this fiasco tonight."

"He wasn't supposed to."

"Lovely. I'll tell him." Haddonfield shifted, getting a new grip on the overhead railing. "I were you, I wouldn't count on the mayor pulling you out of this thing too much. Hubbard don't like getting crossed either."

"Did you identify any of those people back there?"

"My very next question," Haddonfield replied.

"I didn't. Things were hectic."

"They're still ciphers to us," the detective confided, "but we'll get it figured out."

"Hey," Risa said, peering through the window, "we're heading the wrong way."

Haddonfield looked over her shoulder, then back at Refit. "What the hell is going on? Did you have something to do with this?"

The FREELancers agent pushed himself up painfully, his mind overriding the rebellious response of his limbs. He glanced out the window and guessed they were somewhere along Lake Shore Drive in the North Avenue Beach area. "No."

The EMT reached for the com-link with the ambulance cab and pulled it to her ear. "Chris. Hey, Chris, what's up?" Then she noticed Refit coming to his feet and turned her attention to him, putting a hand to his bandaged chest. "Dammit, I spent twenty minutes getting you stabilized and I don't need a repeat performance right now."

"Something's wrong," Refit growled. They were nowhere near the hospital. His mind was operating at peak efficiency, but his body was sluggish. He pushed the woman's hand from his chest.

Risa hung up the handset, obviously frustrated.

Leaning against the cab wall, maintaining his balance with difficulty, Refit grabbed the sliding peep cover leading to the front of the ambulance. It wouldn't move. "Key?" he asked the EMT.

"No." She looked worried.

"Back door?" Refit asked Haddonfield.

The police detective reached behind him and tried the door, shaking his head an instant later. "Locked."

"Whoever it is," Refit said as he scanned the interior of the ambulance, "that call let them know we're aware everything's not kosher." He reached under the gurney he'd been on and found a strut an inch thick and almost three feet long. He yanked, but it didn't come loose. Searching through a medi-kit, he found a pair of pliers. Locking on to the nuts at either end of the support strut, he broke them off and extracted the metal rod. Whatever power let him be a universal recipient of other people's parts also allowed him to access everything those parts had to give. As a result his strength and endurance were incredible, and his speed was far above normal.

Thrusting the palm of his injured hand behind the peep door, he braced himself and pulled. The force ripped at the bound exit wound in his stomach, letting him know the injury was a serious one, maybe not even survivable without further medical aid. His body held amazing recuperative powers, but not without massive tissue and organ transplants.

The door held.

Cursing, he redoubled his efforts. The metal shrieked, then came free. He thrust his arm and head and the metal strut through the opening, taking the situation into account immediately.

An Asian man sat behind the wheel, dressed all in black and not hospital blues. The whirling light bar mounted on top of the ambulance cast eerie splashes of color across the bug-spattered windshield and the vehicle's nose.

Without hesitation, the Asian reached into a fold of his uniform blouse and pulled out a small pistol.

Refit slashed the metal strut down and knocked the pistol away. It bounced against the floorboard on the passenger side. The man screamed in pain, and the patchwork giant knew he'd broken bone. Out of control, the ambulance wandered across one lane of traffic and hit a produce truck broadside. The impact jarred everyone and made the driver focus on gaining control of the vehicle.

Working on the sudden rush of adrenaline surging through his system, Refit battered the panel with his chest and shoulders and ripped it loose. He grabbed it with his good hand and yanked it back to the gurney.

The black-clad Asian's hand flicked out in a rapid dual extension. Only a glitter of movement betrayed the spinning stars.

With nowhere to maneuver, Refit let the sharp-edged stars sink deep into his flesh as he reached for the driver. The ambulance was doing ninety now, the passing lines on the street looking like dots. A small Asp subcompact came into the ambulance's path and the emergency vehicle overtook it in seconds. The crash sounded like the wheels of hell coming off. The ambulance shivered but kept its bearing while the Asp turned turtle and skidded away, sparks from the tortured metal raining down over the approaching line of traffic.

Refit locked his fingers in the guy's neck and closed them. "Unless you can grow a new throat," he growled in warning, "stop this vehicle now."

The guy nodded, put his foot on the brake and slowed, then swerved hard.

Lashing out with his other hand, Refit bounced the guy's head off the window, spiderwebbing the reinforced glass and knocking him out. The ambulance wandered over both northbound lanes, heading for the median and the oncoming traffic.

Groaning with effort, he pulled the unconscious man from behind the wheel and slid into place himself. He gained control with difficulty, then pulled back across both lanes of traffic and parked at the edge of the street.

Winded from his efforts, he opened the door and got out. Moonlight played off Lake Michigan, then dappled again as headlights shone over the waves. Advertisements rattled in neon up the sides of massive buildings that had been constructed in Little Japan to house Japanese business interests.

"Problem?" a man asked as he got out of the luxury sedan that had pulled up behind the ambulance.

Refit shielded his eyes but the man appeared only as a silhouette against the glare of the headlights. Behind them, the wreckage left by the ambulance lay in flames and in pieces. "You got a cellular phone?"

"Yes."

"Borrow it?"

"Sure."

Refit opened the back of the ambulance and helped Risa out. Haddonfield managed under his own power. Spots swam in the patchwork giant's vision as he walked toward the car. He wished he had the Burris so he could contact Underhill directly, but that had been taken by the police.

A thrumming sounded overhead, coming closer.

Hackles rising, Refit glanced up and saw the wasp-shaped BirdSong JK91 heligyro approaching. The stubby, movable wings under the main rotor were canted up so it could descend. Heligyros were still considered exotic craft and not many businesses had them.

When he looked forward again, Refit saw that the luxury sedan's other doors had opened and men had gotten out. They all held machine pistols, trained on him. Traffic crept by, and the headlights washed over the scene, but no one appeared interested in getting involved.

"Haddonfield," Refit called out.

"Your call," the detective said.

"Don't," the man from the luxury car warned. With the green glow emanating from the instrument panel, Refit realized that man was Asian as well.

The FREELancers agent's mind worked furiously, trying to tie in the earlier action with what was going on now. There was nothing to work with. Marshaling his remaining strength, he yelled, "Now!" He turned quickly, moving toward the EMT and scooping her up over his shoulder. He was strong enough and fast enough that he got the jump on the men in the car.

He ran for the lake, hoping down there among the scrub brush and uneven terrain that they could make an escape. His legs trembled but he made them work. It was just meat, and he was stronger than meat. Out of the corner of his eye, he saw Haddonfield firing from a modified Weaver stance, then a bullet caught the big detective in the chest and knocked him backward.

Concentrating on his speed and balance, Refit knew two more strides would bring him within leaping distance of the dark water. He hoped the EMT could swim.

Then a cone of light surrounded him and bullets clawed at the broken ground around him. At least four rounds hit him in the back and knocked him off-balance. He fell, wondering why they hadn't gone through. When the warm lassitude crept through his extremities, he knew he'd been hit with Para-bullets.

He skidded on the ground, coming to a rest on his back only a few feet from the drop-off leading to the lake. Unable to move, he watched the heligyro descend, whipping dust and grit over everything. The men from the luxury car closed on him, moving fluidly and looking like wraiths amid the swirling debris.

Refit watched, unable to close his eyes as the poison wreaked havoc with his weakened system. Whoever they were, the enemy seemed to want him alive for now. But he didn't know if that was a blessing or the opening to something much worse.

3

Chicago, Illinois   *4:21 a.m. CST*
Great Lakes Authority (GLA)   *1021 Greenwich Mean*
87.7 degrees W Longitude   *October 24, 2023*
41.8 degrees N Latitude   *Tuesday*
Cook County Jail, Chicago
Status: Code Yellow

"You okay, kid?"

John-Michael DeChanza looked up at Agent Prime and nodded. "Sure. I was just wondering how to get this off." He held up his ink-stained fingers.

They were down in the booking department in the bowels of the jail. Track lighting hugged the stone ceiling and shone on the barren walls and floor. Three uniformed cops kept them under constant surveillance even though cuffs were around their wrists and ankles. Both of them wore orange jumpsuits with PROPERTY OF COOK COUNTY JAIL stenciled across the back.

Outside the Scratchbuilt armor, DeChanza was a gangly teenager. His black hair trailed down to his shoulders and accented the high cheekbones bequeathed by his Mesquite

Indian and Central American heritage.

"You'll get it off soon enough," Agent Prime said. He sat on one of the low wooden benches in the hallway, his legs up in front of him in lotus fashion in spite of the ankle chains. His pale blue eyes seemed cold and distant.

"I can't believe they're really arresting us." DeChanza let out a low, frustrated breath. In the MAPS armor, he could have blasted his way out of the building, even torn down the walls with his hands if he'd had to.

"That's what Refit was trying to tell you." Prime made a diamond shape between his forefingers and thumbs and stared steadily into it. "He didn't want you here."

"He might have been dying."

"He said no."

"After everything he's been through, would he know?"

"He'd know."

"It's not good for a man to die alone, without his friends or family." Memories stirred in DeChanza's mind. His homeland had been constantly wracked by war between the Contras, Sandinistas, Mesquite Indian revolutionaries, Cuban mercenaries, US advisors, and Israeli security teams.

"Kid, you get into this business, and I mean into every dirty little crook and cranny, and that's the kind of future you're carving out for yourself."

DeChanza didn't let the words touch him. Although he was an agent-in-training for the FREELancers, his primary motivation for staying with the organization was so he could provide for his mother and three younger sisters. His father had died in the war, and DeChanza had taken on a man's responsibilities before he was anywhere near a man himself. He shifted topics. "I wonder how he's doing?"

"Refit?" Prime shrugged. "As long as they keep up with that ugly head of his, they'll put him back together."

"But why arrest us? We've worked with the police."

"Sometimes," Prime agreed. "And sometimes in the past we've worked against them. You don't remember that because it was before your time, but the police do. They don't really consider us trustworthy."

"Because we do what we feel is necessary?"

Prime's lips thinned in a near-grin. "Because we can be bought. Don't paint such an altruistic picture of the 'Lancers, kid. They're an organization motivated by profit, and Lee Won Underhill is one ass-kicking businesswoman."

Footsteps spanged along the hall.

Looking over his shoulder, DeChanza saw a black cop escorting three Asian prisoners down the hall. The entourage stopped just short of the FREELancers and the cop waved them to another bench. A heavy-shouldered man with long hair and a Fu Manchu mustache gazed at the young agent from under hooded eyes.

DeChanza broke the eye contact. When he glanced at Prime, he saw the agent rubbing circulation back into his wrists. The empty cuffs were laid across his leg. "How did you do that?"

Prime opened his mouth and revealed the slim sliver of metal between his teeth.

"You can pick locks?" DeChanza said.

Prime snapped the cuffs back in place. "Jeez, kid, why don't you announce it to everyone."

"Sorry. If you can pick locks, why don't we escape?"

"Because picking locks and breaking out of jail are often two very separate things."

DeChanza looked down the hall and saw Detective Thornton coming from the room at the end of the corridor.

The homicide detective was thick and beefy, with short-cropped brown hair and a mustache that crawled over his lip. He stopped in front of the younger FREELancer and put his hands on his hips. "You can still save yourself some grief, John-Michael. You're a minor. If you play ball with us, I can get the DA to go easy on you. Otherwise, you're liable to be tried as an adult."

There was only a moment of hesitation. Ever since they'd

fled Somotillo, DeChanza had been responsible for his mother and sisters. He was gambling his family's future on Underhill's ability to get them out of trouble, too. But without the FREELancers, any future seemed dim.

"No," he said in a strong voice.

"I think you're making a mistake," Thornton said, "but it's your funeral. Let's go. They're ready for you."

DeChanza and Prime followed the homicide detective down the corridor and through the door. The room looked like a wire-head's dream come true, filled with cybernetic devices for sorting, filing, and searching for human beings through holo imaging, fingerprints, serology, and limited cloning. Pictures in tri-dee lined some of the walls, showing murder scenes with blood that looked like it had just been spilled. Then DeChanza realized Thornton was handing him a placard with a number on it.

Obeying the homicide detective's direction, the youth stepped in front of a white backdrop as the other man in the room took up a position behind a computer-augmented 35mm camera.

"Front and center," Thornton called out as the black cop led the three Asian prisoners into the room and made them sit. "Hold the sign up across your shoulders."

The light flashed, blinding DeChanza for a moment.

"Turn to your right," Thornton directed.

DeChanza made his voice hard and looked at Thornton. "When do I get my phone call? I'm supposed to get a phone call."

Thornton looked at him for a moment, then glanced over at Prime.

"Television," Prime said with a shrug. "It's the first time he's been arrested."

Chicago, Illinois   ***4:31 a.m. CST***
FREELancers Base
Status Upgrade: Code Red

Matrix watched the computer monitor as her fingers flew across the keyboard in front of her. No one else was in the small computer room.

Onscreen, the programming she was running zipped through numbers and bytes at a speed that would have red-lined most other cybernetics systems. While one hand continued to peck away at the keyboard, she booted in a phone line with the other. She fit her headset on, then adjusted the wire mike in front of her lips.

"Underhill," the administrator's voice answered on the second ring.

Noticing the strange sound to her boss's voice, Matrix tagged the mouse, opened another window on the monitor, and verified that Underhill had taken the call on a cellular phone in one of the organization's two Alfa Romeo CLS Quadrifoglio 169s.

"Matrix here," she said. "There's been some trouble." She went back to a two-handed assault on the keyboard, feeling the Savant personality stirring restlessly in the back of her mind. "Refit never made it to the hospital."

"Why?"

"I don't know. I was assisting in the search for Download when I got the Code Yellow on Refit. I'd already fed his location into the computer, since he's technically still on assignment, and it was tracking the homing device planted in the base of his skull when he veered off course. The last clear location I had on him was on Lake Shore Drive somewhere in the North Avenue Beach area. I tied in the computer search programs to the cellular phone towers to attempt to triangulate his position, but he's been airborne—" she checked the lower window on the screen, "—for two minutes, seventeen seconds now."

"Have you contacted the hospital?"

"Immediately. They tried to reach the ambulance but couldn't get through. Of course, that's not unheard of."

"I know. Have C4 and the Tandems arrived?"

"Yes. They're in debrief now."

"Put them on alert. If you can find Refit, we may have to send them after him."

"Okay." A scarlet blip popped on the monitor. Matrix accessed the new information, opening still another window for it. Her mind easily slipped through the changes. Once she'd been Irene Domino, a housewife and mother of two. Then her Savant abilities had surfaced, causing blackouts and finally creating an alternate personality that had reached out and done things she'd never dreamed about with computer systems. Only a limited number of people who developed latent Savant abilities formed another personality, and very few of those personalities would deny the moral programming of the core personality. At first that ability had manifested by allowing her to beat her eldest child at video games, then it had progressed into rewiring an automatic teller machine to provide cash when the family was undergoing financial hardship.

As a result, she'd served two years in a medium-security women's prison. Her husband had divorced her and taken custody of their children. She hadn't seen them since. During her prison term, Underhill had contacted her with the offer of a job and counseling till she came to terms with her Savant self. She'd accepted. The changes she'd undergone even in prison with very little access to computer systems had scared her. Almost six feet tall, she weighed only one hundred and ten pounds. She'd chopped off her hair to a short crew cut and adopted a pair of red-tinted goggles because normal light hurt her eyes. Before trying to see her children again, she wanted to know she could be normal. Even now, with years of counseling behind her, if her mind focused on a problem, there was a chance her Savant self would take over and black out her conscious mind, sometimes for days.

"Police have found the ambulance," Matrix said, reading the copy as the cursor printed it out.

"Stay with it," Underhill instructed. "Monitor the police investigation and the media reports that are filed."

"Okay."

"And the instant you find out about Download or Refit, let me know."

Matrix said she would. Relaxing in the chair, feeling the adjustment mechanisms kick into place to provide the most comfortable seating, she concentrated on the problem, keeping her Savant self at bay, and trying to ignore the fear that she wouldn't be able to beat it back much longer.

Chicago, Illinois   4:35 a.m. CST
En Route to Cook County Jail
Status: Code Yellow

Lee Won Underhill punched the buttons on her cellular phone with one hand and drove with the other. The Alfa Romeo CLS Quadrifoglio 169 ran smooth and sleek and expensive as she made the turn off Halsted Street and headed southwest on Ogden Avenue. The Italian sports car was leading-edge technology fleshed in steely speed. Most of the enhancements offered weren't going to be available to the public for another five years.

Philip Kent answered on the first ring.

"I'm still waiting on that call to Hubbard."

"She's not in," Kent replied. "One of her aides is tracking her down. I should know something in minutes."

"What about the people who attacked the Broken Goblin team?" Underhill glanced to her left and saw the untenanted hulk of the old Sears Tower standing against the lightening sky. She knew the other tall buildings created the shadow world within the inner city where night predators still worked. Organ jackals ripped their bloody wares from the homeless; wire-heads begged, borrowed, and stole for their next dollar to buy into the latest virtual reality existence that would take them away from their squalid lives. Hope was a thin commodity for some people, even in the GLA.

"It looks like WEBTWO activity, but I can't confirm that."

Underhill kept her foot on the accelerator even as she blew by a police cruiser at a hundred miles an hour. Pursuit started at once as the police car's lights came on and he sped up.

WEBTWO was one of the rival directorships that had split from the WEB just after the turn of the millennium. Already involved in the black market, trading secrets, and supplying illegal weapons, WEBTWO invested a lot of its resources in designer drugs, computer crimes, and exotic weaponry. It had also recruited a cadre of metables, making it an increasingly dangerous foe.

"Matrix is checking deeper into their identities," Kent went on. "Hold it. I think Hubbard's call just came on-line."

Glancing in the rearview mirror, Underhill saw the policeman's face behind the windshield of his car as he read the special plate on the Alfa. Mayor Hubbard had granted diplomatic immunity through the Council of Governors to certain FREELancers vehicles. The cop banged his fist down on his steering wheel and dropped away.

"I got her," Kent said.

"Patch her through." The exit for Western Avenue was coming up, and she took her foot off the accelerator.

"Lee," Mayor Dorothy Hubbard said, sounding spry despite the hour, "I understand you've had a busy night."

"Tonight's only the culmination of several busy days," Underhill said. "I need to ask you a favor."

"Ask," Hubbard said. She'd spent years helping form the state councils into the GLA and survived two elections during demanding times when the citizens expected miracles. Nothing from her office, whether through political channels or as a favor off the books, came for free.

"You've got two of my people in the Cook County Jail. I'd appreciate it if you could get them cut loose."

"I was intending to call you about that later this morning."

"It can't wait. Another of my operatives was abducted from an ambulance while in transit to the hospital."

"By whom?"

"I'm not certain." Over the years, Underhill had learned that the best way to deal with Hubbard was honestly. The woman had a sixth sense for falsehoods that was nothing short of uncanny. So when the FREELancers administrator had to lie to her, she tried to make it a first-rate presentation, and over the years, she'd never been caught—exactly.

"Who's the operative?"

"Refit."

"With him, it could be a personal vendetta. I don't think there's anyone I know who's done business with him and not gotten rubbed the wrong way."

"I'm not ruling that out, but I also realize that my people in Cook County Jail could be in danger as well."

"I want to know what was going down tonight for starters."

"I can't give you that."

"Then let me think of something else I might want," Hubbard said, "and I'll get back to you."

"Do that," Underhill responded, "and when I lose two people inside that jail, you'll understand when I seem reluctant to pull another behind-the-scenes assignment for you regarding the welfare of this city."

"Don't you dare play hardball with me," Hubbard said in a sharper voice. "I've been doing jumping jacks in this city with a knife at my throat for a long time now. You don't want to bite the hand that feeds you. If it hadn't been for me, your organization wouldn't have gotten started."

"But it has," Underhill said, "and relocation isn't out of the question. You gave FREELancers the chance to show that a mercenary metable force was a viable product. It has. There's a number of places that would have us now, and probably cut us a hell of a deal. We've proven ourselves."

"Who are you protecting?"

"My client, as always."

"Legally, you've no right to do that if asked by the proper authorities."

Underhill knew that. Legal protection over how the FREE-Lancers operated was still being ironed out. "Fiscally, there's no other way I can do business." The gray steel hulk of the jail was just ahead of her on the right. Less than two blocks down, a Japanese bar—unfettered by the restraints shown to domestic taverns—was in full swing, the neon sign outside advertising pachinko, opium-based liquor, and sex. A police car sat across the street from it, the two officers dressed in full riot gear, eyeballing the black-clad Japanese bouncers. Many of the other buildings were vacant, the owners having given up on the crime-ridden neighborhood and cut their losses.

"Let me make a phone call," Hubbard said, "but you owe me one."

With a smile, Underhill broke the connection and rolled the Alfa into the security-monitored parking area.

4

Rinji 8 *Space Station*   **7:41 p.m. *(Tokyo Main)***
Orbit Shoda   **1041 *Greenwich Mean***
29,352.13 *miles out*   **October 24, 2023**
Present position: Over the Balkans   **Tuesday**

Grant DiLuca rubbed at his eyes with the heels of both hands but his vision remained bleary. He'd pulled too many hours even in zero-g to function at peak efficiency.

Tall and thin, clad in the scarlet one-piece of Yukiko Corporation, DiLuca stood out from his coworkers. His short-cropped hair was dyed in startling red and white stripes. His bloodshot eyes were concealed by mirrorshades that his present supervisor positively despised, making him wear them even more. A seventy-eight-hour beard growth stubbled his chin.

He stood on the outer deck surrounding the heavy machines that looked incapable of the delicate work they would be required to do in the next few hours. Noise from the engineering crews working on the machines for the final fittings echoed throughout the heart of the space station. The vibrations trembled up DiLuca's legs.

"You doing okay?"

DiLuca spoke Japanese like a native. He'd been with Yukiko Corporation for three years, and four other Japanese conglomerates before that. "Fine."

Kentaro Higira stood near one of the station's support struts to DiLuca's right. Compact and neatly groomed, his one-piece crisp and pressed, he was Yukiko Corporation's ideal of a cybernetic programming specialist. Except for the fact that he didn't have DiLuca's insight and creativity, he would have been heading up the Fusuma Project on *Rinji 8*.

"You need sleep," Higira said.

Shaking his head, DiLuca said, "Not this close to completion."

"You're nervous."

DiLuca looked at the other man. In the beginning of their relationship, the American hadn't liked the other man. He'd guessed that Higira was there more to spy on him than anything else. But Higira was obviously well schooled in cybernetics and was willing to learn from the radical thinking DiLuca had put into the project. "We're about to put substance to dreams I've had for years. You're damn right I'm nervous."

"Yukiko Corporation saw your project as a good investment. Even if it isn't everything you hope for, it will be profitable to them."

DiLuca shoved his hands in his pockets, knowing it didn't do any good to cry over spilled milk. In order to get the project properly funded, he'd had to sign over rights to most of his design work. If the project failed, he knew he'd be out on his ear as fast as they could get him groundside. And his work would no longer be his. That hurt more than anything. His stomach growled apprehensively.

Excusing himself, he walked back to the small office that had been built on the other side of the Plexiglas-and-steel walls that maintained the integrity of the manufacturing center. The office was his and wasn't subject to the cleanliness standards of the rest of the space station. Two desks butted up against each other, taking up most of the available area, but giving him workspace that let him dump books, micro-CD chips with reams of research on them, and scratch paper. Two of the walls were polarized for one-way privacy, and the other two were covered with posters of sports stars from women's professional hockey teams, a movie poster of Harrison Ford in *Blade Runner*, and an advertisement for FREELancers.

Normally, Yukiko employees weren't allowed to have personal items in their workspaces, but DiLuca enjoyed fringe benefits no one else had—at least, as long as the CEO believed in the Fusuma Project.

He took a couple of antacid tablets from one of the desk drawers, chewed them up, then washed them down with a stim-spiked carton of orange juice. The drug whisked through his system at once. He dropped down in a swivel chair in front of his computer deck and blanked the walls because he couldn't stand watching the slow process anymore.

Glancing at the FREELancers advertising poster, he couldn't help grinning. The poster showed a picture of Captain Ares standing there with a wide grin on his boyish face as he held his red cape in one gloved hand. His silver bodysuit hugged his broad shoulders and narrow hips and tucked into calf-high red boots. A big red **A** covered his upper chest. Blond hair peeked out over his ram's-headed cowl, leaving a domino-mask effect that flared over his blue eyes.

NEED HELP? the poster asked in sharp-edged blurbs. CALL FREELANCERS.

Suddenly, the office door shushed open.

DiLuca turned, shocked. No one had access to his office. His fingers slid along the edge of his desk, seeking the security alert button. Before he could press it, the man at the door took a small pistol from the flat case he carried and shot DiLuca in the chest with three measured rounds.

The impacts threw the cybernetics programmer backward. He stumbled over the swivel chair and went down, managing to land on his side so he could watch his attacker. Motor control left him in seconds.

"Believe it or not, buddy," he heard the man say, "but I'm going to save your life. At least for a while."

Chicago, Illinois   4:43 a.m. CST

"Hey."

Coming out of the Savant near-trance he'd put himself into, John-Michael DeChanza looked up and saw a huge man standing in front of him.

The guy's hair was long and shaggy, and hung in greasy strands to his shoulders. A curling beard surrounded his moon-face; an indigo swastika was tattooed on his left cheek below his eye. Another tattoo, a flaming-skulled skeleton in biker's leathers, rode a big motorcycle in a wheelie on his right forearm, and his left bicep carried a tattooed version of the Harley-Davidson emblem. He'd been given one of the jail's orange jumpsuits to wear, but somewhere along the way he'd ripped off the sleeves and collar.

"What?" DeChanza asked.

"Going to have to give him a little time to catch up, Rattle," said a bald-headed, ebony-skinned man who was also wearing a ripped jumpsuit. A sapphire-colored diamond had been tattooed around his left eye, and someone a long time ago had bitten off the top of his ear on that same side.

"You think so, Mace?" Rattle asked, leaning closer.

"Yep," Mace answered.

Looking around them, the young FREELancer agent saw two more men who looked like they belonged with Rattle and Mace. They were in the main holding cell awaiting charges. The walls were stainless steel and obviously reinforced against whatever metabilities might slip through the DNA testing that usually showed the police who they were dealing with. Surveillance cameras hung from every corner, masked by bulletproof shielding but were only as vigilant as their human operators. Electrical batons hanging from the walls could be used by waldoes to subdue any type of rebellion or violence. And if that weren't enough, the force-field-augmented steel bars could be set up to contain an anesthetic gas that would render the cell's occupants unconscious.

"Figured a big-time hero like this would be a quick study," Rattle said.

DeChanza centered himself and kept quiet, intending to ride out the situation as calmly as possible.

"Maybe," Mace suggested, "they got some dumb ones, too."

"That what it is, kid?" Rattle grinned, leaning closer. "You one of the dumb ones?"

"No." DeChanza peered through the group to see if Prime was paying attention. To his dismay, the other agent was sound asleep on a top bunk.

"I don't remember seeing you in those television commercials," Rattle said. "Which one are you? I know Refit's the ugly one, and the one in the sexy bikini is C4."

"Volatile," DeChanza said, hoping to use the other FREE-Lancers' reputation for exotic metabilities to back the man down before things got out of hand.

"Volatile," Rattle repeated. He waved his arms. "So what can you do?"

Other prisoners started to draw closer as curiosity got the better of them.

"I can make internal organs rupture," DeChanza said, putting as much integrity into his words as he could manage. "Make a guy's eyeballs pop from his head if I want."

Rattle looked at Mace. "You ever hear of anything like that?"

"No way."

"How about any of you?" Rattle asked the crowd. The consensus seemed to be that DeChanza was lying. The biker turned back to face the young FREELancer. "You're going to have to show them." He leaned in, his face only inches from

DeChanza's. "Do me. My eyeballs pop out, they'll believe you."

DeChanza knew there was nothing he could say, so he waited to see what would happen.

"I killed a lot of people, kid," Rattle said as he took a can of lighter fluid from somewhere inside his jumpsuit, "even a few metables, but never a FREELancer. Think I'm gonna make my bones tonight." He uncapped the lighter fluid and soaked his arms and head.

The scent was so strong it burned DeChanza's nose and turned his throat dry. He shifted his weight, bracing his back against the wall and lifting himself on the balls of his feet, getting ready to spring up.

"Light me," Rattle said. The other biker produced a lighter, flicked it, and held the tall blue-and-yellow flame only inches from Rattle's hands. "I'm a metable too, punk, so you don't scare me one bit." He dipped his hands toward the lighter. As soon as contact was made, flames jumped up his arms. Running his fiery hands through his hair, he set his head on fire, then grinned through the flames. Without another word, he reached for the young agent.

DeChanza didn't have time to think about his actions. Instinctively, his mind turned to mechanical and structural awareness. He lashed out with his foot and caught the side of the biker's knee. It took only seventeen pounds of pressure to break a normal person's knee, and the adrenaline jumping through his system had bumped him up more than that.

Rattle's leg snapped with a loud crack, followed immediately by a yell of pain. Still on fire, he dropped to the cell floor, clearing a path through the onlookers.

Taking advantage of the confusion, DeChanza pushed himself up and ran over the downed biker, planting a foot in the middle of the man's belly and leaping toward the beds. "Prime!" he shouted, as he stopped at the nearest bunk.

Prime came awake at once and vaulted down from the bed. Mace had thrown himself at DeChanza, followed by the other

two bikers. Moving gracefully, Prime intercepted one of the
bikers with a forearm shiver that drove the breath from the
other man's lungs.

DeChanza's fingers found the bolts holding one of the
bunkbed's support struts. Normally, it would have taken
wrenches to get the bolts loose, but he turned them in his
fingers because of his metability. In a heartbeat, the strut
came free in his hands, dropping the top bed onto the bottom bed with a crash and protesting yells from men who'd
been on both of them. He turned to join Prime.

After deflecting Mace, Prime had established his distance
and gone into a martial arts stance. One of the bikers came
within reach, and Prime caught the blow that was aimed at
his head, elbowed the man in the stomach, then hit him
three times in the face.

"I see you're not getting on with the local riffraff," the
FREELancers combat ops leader said.

"No."

The last biker to enter the fray came in a rush. Prime
feinted, then came around in a whirling kick that sent the
man flying back the way he'd come.

DeChanza stood his ground and held his captured strut
with sweat-damp palms. A man nearby grabbed the end of it
in both hands and started pulling.

"Damn freaks!" the man yelled as he yanked on the strut.
"You're not going to come in here and start pushing us
around!"

Instead of fighting for the metal strut, DeChanza shoved it
at the man, catching him in the neck and sending him away
retching. The young FREELancer agent recognized the mob
fury building up in the inmates.

"What the hell is going on?" a voice roared.

For a moment, the violence in the cell terminated. Three
uniformed police officers stood at the door with three prisoners. DeChanza recognized them as the three Asians he'd seen
earlier in the booking room.

A man wearing sergeant's stripes stepped forward and unlocked the door, reaching for his handi-talker. Before he could get it, the three Asians launched into action. They attacked the cops and put them down with an assortment of lethal moves, seizing their weapons at the same time. Then they turned those captured guns toward the FREELancer agents and opened fire.

DeChanza dove behind the nearest bed, and bullets ripped into the mattress searching for him. Glancing under the bed, he saw the center Asian step from between his companions. The man was a head taller than the others, and carried considerable girth, like a sumo wrestler dressed in an ill-fitting suit.

The gunshots echoed inside the corridors as the two men reloaded. Then the sumo wrestler shouted and slammed his palms together in front of him.

DeChanza felt the terrible vibrations of the sonic boom tremble through him. The concussive force shoved the beds and the prisoners back against the far wall. Taking the brunt of the sonic boom, the cell bars collapsed like matchsticks and the force-field generators fizzled.

"John-Michael."

Turning, DeChanza saw Prime, crouched behind one of the beds, looking at him.

"Give me that pole, mate."

DeChanza tossed the strut over.

Prime caught the strut in midair, moving as fluidly as a ballet dancer. He came to his feet, cocked back his arm holding the strut, and whipped it forward like a human bowstring just as the Asian metable started to clap again.

The strut covered the intervening distance in a blur, and seemed to materialize in the center of the sumo wrestler's chest. For a moment, the man stared at it dumbly, then he grabbed it in both hands and fell forward.

"Move out, kid!" Prime ordered, rushing forward. The remaining Asians spun toward him, bringing their guns up.

Pushing himself up, DeChanza ran, knowing they were going to rush into a hail of bullets.

Then Prime went airborne in a flying kick that took one of the men down with a sickening crack. As the other man tried to twist around to track him, the pistol already belching out muzzle-flashes, Prime got his feet under him, ducked under the sweep of the pistol, and delivered a bone-cracking palm thrust to the man's chest.

By the time DeChanza reached the collapsed wall, the fight was over. Security Klaxons screamed throughout the floor.

"Going to be a bloody free-for-all here in just a minute," Prime said as he patted down the bodies of the three men. "We stay here, we'll be damned sitting ducks." He turned up magazines for the pistols and a small radio transceiver. "Whoever these johnnies are working for, they aren't alone." He reloaded the weapons. "You think you can find that tin-can suit of yours?"

"Sure."

"Get it done, and let's try to avoid the rest of the local constabulary while we're about it." Prime raised one of the pistols as the other prisoners in the bullpen started to rush out. He fired three shots into the roof, scaring them back.

DeChanza massaged his left wrist as he jogged for the end of the hallway, away from the main reception area of the jail. At his mental command, a band that had been the same color as his skin turned cobalt blue and revealed itself as a four-inch-wide bracelet. Constructed of electronics and polymers that were invisible to almost all metal and electronics detectors, the device shouldn't work, according to Dr. Rhand, the FREELancers Research Ops department head. But it did because, like the Scratchbuilt armor, DeChanza's Savant metability was the driving force behind the device.

"I've got it," the young agent said as a lemon-colored blip appeared on the bracelet's surface. Under it, a small window opened and began a brief readout. "The weapons systems are off-line."

"As long at it'll move."

"It will." Looking up, DeChanza saw the metal wall blocking the corridor. "Trouble."

"And me without explosives," Prime said. They came to a halt in front of the electronically locked door. Noise from behind let them know a crowd was on their heels. "Take a look about, mate, and let's see if there's some way we can shut down the power."

"They won't have it on this side." DeChanza knelt in front of the locking mechanism, placed his palm on it, and tried to feel his way into it.

On the walls, tracking monitors, placed so the jail security personnel could search the building quickly in the event of an escaped prisoner, flared to life, and the images flickered through the different corridors and levels.

"Sometimes," Prime said, "they'll leave a way for a mate to short across and muck up the rest of the system." He was holding on to a main ceiling support beam and shoving tiles out of the way, peering up into the dark crawl space.

A tumbler clicked in DeChanza's mind as he made contact with the locking mechanism. He felt the Savant-state pull at him magnetically. He stuck out his forefinger and pressed it against the key slot, barely getting a fingernail inside. He twisted.

With an audible click, the lock opened.

"Got it," he said to Prime.

"Good. I've got something up here too." Prime leveled one of the pistols. "Main power-supply juncture. Maybe it'll tilt the odds in our favor somewhat." He fired four rounds.

With a liquid sputter and a firefall of sparks, the lights on the floor went out. Emergency spots mounted on the walls came on, but left pools of swirling shadows for the FREE-Lancers agents to maneuver in. The monitor system died.

"Go," Prime said as he dropped from the ceiling.

DeChanza bolted through the unlocked door and ran for his life, following the lemon-colored blip toward the Scratchbuilt suit.

5

NASA Space Shuttle Lemuria   **4:59 a.m. CST**
Free Space   **1059 Greenwich Mean**
24,567.19 miles out   **October 24, 2023**
Present position: Over Hawaii   **Tuesday**

"Acknowledged, *Lemuria*, your assistance is appreciated." Surprisingly, the voice on the intership frequency didn't sound edgy or tense.

"Roger," a West Texas accent answered back. "You people just hang on. We'll have an embarking crew there in minutes." The radio operator smiled, then turned around and gave Aramis Tadashi a thumbs-up. "They don't suspect us."

Tadashi nodded and kept watching the monitor in the shuttle's helm. Onscreen, the Japanese shuttle, *Kimiko*, floated dead in space, no lights on at all. She'd been without her life-support systems for thirty minutes, enough to spook even the most hardened space crew.

Working the magnetic soles of his boots, Tadashi headed for the payload area of the *Lemuria*. He was a tall man, with Oriental features that might have been mistaken for Japanese, except that he knew he came from the back-alley loins of

Singapore.

The streets had raised him, first as a beggar, then a thief, then an indentured servant to the Japanese Space Service. He preferred to think of those periods as previous lives. He stepped through the airlock and nodded to Cydney, his second-in-command. "Ten minutes."

His feet together, Cydney gave a brief bow. "It will be done."

Smooth-faced and unblemished, Tadashi was a handsome man. His hair was cut short in military fashion, and his mismatched eyes, one brown and one green, immediately captured the attention of onlookers. He was thirty-two years old and had just taken his most aggressive step on the road to carving out a kingdom for himself. The NASA space suit he wore was pale blue from the boots to the gloves, and matched the bubble-faced helmet under his arm.

A Yakuza gangster warlord had rescued him from almost certain death. While on R & R in Hong Kong, Tadashi had killed two men with a fisherman's knife after they'd cheated him at cards, thinking he'd been too drunk to notice. He'd surprised the first man, taking him from behind out in the alley, and faced the other man fairly. The gambler had still died. And the Yakuza warlord had managed to get Tadashi released from both the Hong Kong police and the JSS and into the Yakuza's custody.

Now Tadashi had a chance to build his own empire from the ashes of another—if someone didn't hand him his head first.

Eight men waited for him in the payload area of the shuttle. All of them were loyal to him and had martial training in some capacity. They all carried the special CO_2-powered fléchette pistols he'd ordered for the raid.

"Ready?" Tadashi asked Cydney.

The man nodded, then kicked free of the floor and hung suspended in the center of the payload area. A manned maneuvering unit was tethered near the double doors opening outward from the *Lemuria*, looking like a **U**-shaped child's flotation device for a pool.

In quick order, the boarding team pushed up from the deck and lashed on to the MMU. Tadashi was the last. He put his helmet on, making sure the seal was airtight, then opened the air-mix ports. He flipped the radio toggle on with his chin and opened up the channel. "Grimes."

"Here."

"We are ready." Tadashi put his gloved hands up to keep him from bumping into the closed hatch doors.

"Docking coming up in twenty seconds. We'll be on their blind side, so they won't see you coming until you're there. Fourteen seconds, thirteen . . ."

Tadashi listened to the countdown and saw the double hatch doors open at zero. The atmosphere inside the NASA shuttle boiled out. Cydney used the compressed-air jets to drag the boarding team out into space.

As always, the sheer openness of the wild black thrilled Tadashi. The earth was a huge blue globe above them with white masses that were clouds. He knew, but couldn't verify visually, that they were somewhere over the Pacific Ocean. For a moment his mind played with the possibility of the long fall involved. Then he forced his imagination back to the job at hand.

Cydney jockeyed the MMU expertly, trailing all of them over the open doors of the *Kimiko* like some fantastical kite tail. The payload well of the Japanese shuttlecraft was deep and dark.

Tadashi freed the fléchette pistol from the chest holster, slid his gloved finger through the specially sized trigger guard, and waited. Three men stood below, wearing crimson space suits with the Yukiko Corporation logo.

At first they appeared uncertain, then two of them started for the door, moving with the interminable slowness afforded in zero-g.

"Kill them," Tadashi ordered. He opened fire at once.

Powered by compressed gas, the six-bladed fléchettes sped straight and true, opening the space suits and sinking into the vital organs underneath. In seconds the three men were down, and long crimson ribbons made up of perfectly round globules of blood roped out toward space.

Cydney brought the MMU down, then tied on to one of the docking poles in the cargo hold. Moving carefully, Tadashi led his team deeper into the bowels of the shuttle. With all their electronics out, the people inside the shuttle wouldn't know about the ambush until it was too late.

The airlock was open. They filed inside, then manually closed and locked the door. Once everyone was in place, Cydney took a wrench from his equipment belt and rapped sharply on the hull.

A moment later, the hatch began to turn. A hiss of air, audible even through Tadashi's helmet, signaled the flooding of the chamber with atmosphere. He took off the helmet, knowing the *Kimiko* crew would be expecting him to come in bareheaded.

"We are glad to see you," the young man on the other side of the doorway said as he stepped back to allow entry.

Tadashi raised the fléchette pistol and fired two rounds. Bone crunched, and blood spilled. Reaching up, Tadashi slapped a filter over his mouth and nose. Because they were still operating in zero-g, the blood would float loosely in the air, able to be breathed in and flood the lungs until the filters sucked it out.

The command post center was small, and the three men seated in the chairs weren't expecting anything to go wrong. They all died in various poses of ineffective retaliation.

"Kerrick," Tadashi said, addressing the sysops.

The woman went forward and sat in front of the on-board computer. Her copper-colored hair was piled up on her head, and her face was only a few shades darker than the sterile mask she wore. Blood, held out by the filter, had misted the area between her lips and nostrils.

Using his radio, Tadashi keyed up and said, "*Lemuria.*
We're in control here. Have the power restored."

"Coming."

An instant later, the various navigational computers and
life-support components came back on-line. Rows of indica-
tor lights flared in reds, blues, greens, and yellows. The
Kimiko shuddered as her heart started to beat again. Four of
Tadashi's boarding crew fell to tasks already assigned to
them, going over the checklists Cydney had prepared. The
second-in-command barked orders to his people and drove
them unmercifully.

Tadashi checked his watch and found that they were still
comfortably inside the eighteen-minute window they'd
worked out for the seizure. He walked to the command seat
and sat down. "Open the screens," he instructed Kerrick.

"Done," she said.

The three screens opened, showing views fore, port, and
starboard. The *Lemuria* was a finned triangle in the starboard
view.

"Where's the *Rinji 8?*" Tadashi asked. A bright bubble of
blood coasted by his head, coming into orbit around his
larger mass. Irritably, he waved at it, only to see it implode
and stick to his glove.

"We're tracking now," Cydney answered, approaching
with a workdeck in his hands. The small monitor screen was
crystal clear and in color. "There. We have the space station
now." He touched a small device in his left ear. "We're monitoring their communications bands. They suspect nothing."

"How soon before we have thrust capability?"

"Two minutes," Kerrick answered.

"The interception with the space station?" Tadashi asked
Cydney.

"Piece of cake."

Tadashi nodded. Even when he'd been with the Japanese
Space Service, he hadn't understood everything about the
hardware, and even less about the various orbiting tech-

niques and laws of gravitational wells. His skills had led him into violence, and he was acknowledged as a master by Sun Andoc, head of the Andoc crime family. The time spent with Andoc had taught him a lot. Learning how to pick people necessary to complete an operation was second nature.

"We're being hailed by the *Lemuria*," Kerrick said, putting a hand to the earpiece she wore.

"Put it on."

The fore screen altered, fuzzing over with dirty gray ice for a moment, then clearing back off to reveal Grimes at the NASA shuttle's helm. "Got a patch-through for you from Starstrider."

Tadashi nodded, straightening in the command console as the monitor blurred again.

"Hello, Aramis," a soft southern voice said. "How are the accommodations?"

"Fine," Tadashi said. As always when facing the other man, Tadashi felt the feral tightness along the back of his neck of one predator recognizing another.

Louis Lassiter owned NASA these days, after selling out US Tobacco and Snuff just ahead of the ban imposed by the regional alliances of North America against smoking. Most of the fortune he'd made from the sale had gone into the acquisition of NASA from the bankrupt federal government.

Lassiter was a thin, nondescript man in his early sixties. His brown hair was cut short and lay neatly along the planes of his head. Tadashi knew from information the Andoc family had on the man that Lassiter had at one time intended to become a minister. He still maintained religious overtones in his business and private lives. Dressed in a conservative brown suit that hadn't been custom-tailored, though it was of good quality, he looked mild—except for his eyes. Lassiter had the deadest brown eyes Tadashi had ever seen.

"Our contact in Chicago has taken one of the deliveries you promised," Lassiter said. "There seems to be a problem with two of the others."

"They'll be made," Tadashi said. In order to get use of the shuttle and a later pickup at *Rinji 8*, he'd had to bargain with another party to put up the cash for Lassiter.

"I'm sure they will," Lassiter said, with a cold, thin-lipped smile. "I've not the slightest doubt in you."

"What about the spoofing programs?" Tadashi asked. It was enough of a nudge to remind the other man who was employing whom for this operation.

Lassiter leaned back in his chair and put three fresh sticks of gum into his mouth. "They're in place, my friend. Do you think I'd talk to you on an unsecured channel?"

Leaning back in his own chair, Tadashi looked at the man. "No, but I don't want to misplace my confidence."

"Hardly." The comment brought an honest chuckle from Lassiter. "Whatever goes on in space, I own it, know about it, or have it under surveillance. You can bank on that."

"I just want your organization to take me to the *Rinji 8* and back again. Without setting off any alarms."

"You toe the line on those specs we gave you," Lassiter said, "and I can guarantee it. As far as the space station or any other satellite or ground control systems know, the *Kimiko* has been under way this whole time. You can make up the difference easily if your pilot is worth his salt."

"Her salt," Kerrick said quietly enough that Tadashi heard it but the microphone didn't pick it up.

"You know," Lassiter went on, "you never did say what you wanted from that space station."

"No," Tadashi said, "I didn't."

A tense silence followed, underscored by the hiss of the airlock as the corpses of the *Kimiko's* original crew were flushed out through the loading bay into space.

"If there's anything else—" Lassiter said.

"I'll let you know." Tadashi glanced at his watch. The second hand was sweeping on. "Tell my client that she can expect further deliveries. Everyone concerned knew this wasn't going to be easy." He snapped off the com-link.

"Stand by for thrust," Kerrick called out.

The boarding party belted into the acceleration seats. When the thrusters kicked in, the last bubbles of blood that hadn't been suctioned off by the shuttle's air reclamation cycle splashed wetly onto the floor.

Tadashi's mind raced as satisfaction filled him. He'd been born in the gutter, raised himself up by his willingness to risk his own life and take the lives of others. Now he stood on the threshold of an empire. Only a handful of people placed high in the Japanese government knew what the research teams aboard the *Rinji 8* were working on. Not all of them knew Grant DiLuca was going to be successful.

Tadashi did, and that knowledge was going to turn him into one of the most powerful people on the planet. He smiled as the shuttle sped through space, warping into the orbit needed to overtake the *Rinji 8* and his new destiny.

Chicago, Illinois   *5:03 a.m. CST*

Breath rasping in his lungs and burning his throat, John-Michael DeChanza slid down the cables in the darkened elevator shaft toward the basement level in the county jail. His hands ached from holding the wad of curtains Agent Prime had liberated from an office along the way. Even through the fire-retarding material he felt the heat caused by the sliding friction. His shoes felt hot too.

The roof of the stalled elevator cage came up quicker than he'd anticipated. His feet struck hard enough to go slightly numb, and his thigh muscles quaked from compensating for the impact. He grunted as his breath left his lungs.

Agent Prime was on his heels. Kicking free of the cable, the warrior dropped the final ten feet and, with little noise, landed standing. "Ready?"

"Yes." DeChanza got to his knees and pried at the escape hatch in the top of the elevator cage. The lemon-colored blip on his bracelet was stronger now. He locked his fingers under the edge of the hatch and pulled it open. The cage's interior was totally black.

"You're really making a night of it, kid," Prime said with a light note in his voice. "You're getting your first arrest and your first jailbreak all in one easy lesson."

DeChanza slipped his hands in the gap and leveraged the doors open. Beyond the doorway, illuminated by emergency lights mounted on the walls, the impound garage held a maze of cars, motorcycles, a GEV, and four MAPS armored suits. The Scratchbuilt unit looked like a mechanical ape because it was too tall to stand erect in the garage. The armored suit rested on the knuckles of its three-fingered hands. A half dozen sheriff's deputies with flashlights and crackling radios were cycling through the confiscated property.

"Can you get inside the armor?" Prime asked in a whisper.

"That suit is a part of me," DeChanza said. "I built every piece of it with my own two hands. No one can keep me out of it." He'd surrendered his smart-card upon arrest. Without it, the armor generally wouldn't power up.

"Then let's be about it before we're found out. Remember, those lads upstairs didn't come alone."

"Whenever you say." DeChanza got himself up and ready to run, wishing his hands weren't so cramped from the elevator cable.

"Do you see the exit?"

Peering through the gloom, his vision slightly disturbed by the flashlight beams raking the garage walls, the young FREELancers agent spotted the rolling steel doors at the apex of a long ramp leading up to street level. "Yes."

"Capital. Then let's get it done."

Waiting till the deputies were away from the Scratchbuilt armor, DeChanza raced through the dark aisles. Pausing behind a Harley-Davidson motorcycle, crouched down on his hands and knees, he judged the distance separating him from the armored suit. Just as he was about to run the last twenty feet, a new group of deputies came down the stairs and started shouting orders, spreading everyone out.

"Evidently they missed us upstairs," Prime said. "Figured we'd head down here. We need a diversion."

DeChanza spotted a two-gallon gas can and a hundred feet of extension cord near a live surge protector at the bottom of a nearby rack of shelves. Glancing up, he found the exposed metal pipe that held part of the garage's power lines running along the nearby wall. A workman's leather tool belt lay coiled in a nearby toolbox. "I've got one."

"Go to it."

Reaching into the tool belt, DeChanza removed a box knife and a roll of electrical tape. He used the knife to cut off the end of the extension cord, then flaked the copper wires bare with neat slices, twisted them together, and tossed it over the power cable. The gas can was almost full. Opening the lid, he adjusted it so the funnel would work, ran the extension cord down the funnel's mouth to just above the level of the liquid, then fixed it in place with the electrical tape.

"Have you always been this destructive?" Prime asked.

"Grew up in a rough neighborhood," the young agent responded. He found a hose clamp in the tool chest, totally unloosened it, then stood up in the shadows as he affixed the extension cord to itself so it would hold the gas can about three feet from the ground. He tested the friction of the pipe and found that the cord slid easily. As he ducked down again, a flashlight beam licked across the cinder-block wall.

The deputies closed in, searching the impound garage systematically.

"This will buy some time," DeChanza whispered, "and maybe make them night-blind for a few minutes." He switched the surge protector off, then plugged the extension cord in. His finger rested against the "on" button. "When you get ready, give that gas can a shove."

"No time like the present." Prime stood and hurled the gas can like a shot put, with plenty of shoulder.

Shouts rang out at once as the extension cord sang along the length of the power cable. A support strut caught the cord a little over twenty feet away, and the gas can swung wildly. Someone started shooting, then a fusillade of bullets chipped into the cinder-block wall near the FREELancers' position.

"Ready?" DeChanza asked.

"Do it."

Closing the switch, DeChanza turned his head away and shut his eyes. Still, the resulting explosion painted livid shadows against his eyelids in fiery reds. The heat of the blast washed over him. The hollow boom rolled through the cavernous garage.

"Go!" Prime ordered.

DeChanza ran, staying low, bouncing off his palms twice to push himself back into a running position. He collided with the Scratchbuilt armor with bruising force, then shoved himself around the side, heading for the access panel in the back. The high sheen of the armor reflected the spreading fire dripping from the wall. Manlike in shape, the arms of the MAPS were longer than the legs, giving it an arthropod appearance. The face held no features, only a dim sensor-visor. The powersuits had been designed to replace tanks while keeping the maneuverability of an infantry unit.

Using the handholds built into the MAPS, he climbed up the armor's back. Bullets whined from the suit as someone spotted him and opened fire, yelling for the other deputies. He slammed the bracelet against the access panel and heard the whine of servos inside the armor. The hatch hissed as it swung open.

He dropped inside and scrambled for the control console. Where other MAPS half the Scratchbuilt armor's size could comfortably hold a three-man ops team, DeChanza's creation had enough room for only him. A fully contoured chair sat in a horseshoe-shaped command center. Dials, readouts, monitors, keyboards, and feedback systems covered all the available space.

He rubbed the bracelet against the smart-card slot. Sparks jumped, running down into the slot. "C'mon, big guy, we've got work to do."

Abruptly, the access hatch slammed shut and the monitors lit up, giving him a 360-degree view of the impound garage. Then they went dead as he tried to key up the infrared function. The cursor on the computer monitor flitted in and out of existence like a rapid heartbeat.

<Possible ID: DeChanza, John-Michael. Confirm?>

After belting himself in, the young FREELancer agent tapped the keyboard. <Confirm DeChanza. Password Esmerelda.> It was his mother's name.

<Password accepted. Stand by for visual check.>

DeChanza heard someone banging against the access panel. Even with the smart-card, the armor wouldn't let anyone else in as long as someone was in the seat unless they had his override password. But some of the hydraulics systems were vulnerable to knives and crowbars.

A robot arm extended down from the hull above his head and held out what looked like a periscope. He pressed his face to it, holding his left eye to the lens.

<ID confirmed. Welcome, John-Michael.>

"Yeah, yeah. Let's get this show on the road." Sensor-cuffs shot out of the seat and attached themselves to his feet and hands, and a cybernetic veil dropped over his face. In seconds the MAPS unit had powered up and his movements were Scratchbuilt's. The cyberveil responded to his thoughts, and flipped through the ops menus open to him. He electrified the outer shell of the armor and caused two men to jump away.

The infrareds came on, the illumination thrown out from recessed lamps located around the armor. He picked up Prime almost at once. The other agent had hot-wired a 125cc trail bike and was pinning down his pursuers with selective fire from his captured pistols.

"Let's go, kid!" Prime yelled. "I'm not armored."

DeChanza couldn't stand up in the room. The Scratchbuilt armor was easily ten feet too tall. He crouched down and used his arms to balance himself as he headed for the ramp leading to the street door. The weapons pods were still inactive. Without looking, he reached up and activated the chip player. The armor's console filled with the thundering beat of Bob Seger's "Old-Time Rock and Roll."

The doors were solid steel. DeChanza figured if he had the time, the armor could have torn through them. But he was running against the clock. Gathering speed, he hurled himself at the wall beside the door.

The harsh splintering of brick and mortar and the wrenching of steel beams overloaded the armor's auditory pickups for a few seconds. Locked into the input of the cyberveil, he felt the resistance of the wall go. The illumination of the emergency lights gave way to the night-darkened streets as the wall ruptured. Wailing like banshees, sirens screamed through the din.

Shaken by the collision, the seat harness tight around his body, DeChanza fought for control, managing to push the Maps to its feet and swing back around to look into the impound garage.

Agent Prime streaked for the ramp, but there was no way out. Bullets sparked cars and shelving around him. By the time he could ditch the cycle and climb the fifteen-foot gap, someone would pick him off.

Thinking quickly, DeChanza extended Scratchbuilt's right arm through the opening and planted the fingertips against the concrete floor. His hand was four feet wide.

Gunning the motorcycle's engine, Prime drove up Scratchbuilt's arm to the shoulder joint and flew out toward the street.

Grinning under the cyberveil, DeChanza withdrew the arm as the sheriff's deputies closed in. As an afterthought, he slammed the back of his hand against the steel doors and hoped he jammed the locking mechanism. Both of them dented.

He turned around, standing now. Prime was in the street, waving wildly, pointing upward. DeChanza looked—and caught a sizzling rocket right in the face.

6

Chicago, Illinois   ***5:09 a.m. CST***
Great Lakes Authority (GLA)   ***1109 Greenwich Mean***
87.7 degrees W Longitude   ***October 24, 2023***
41.8 degrees N Latitude   ***Tuesday***
               Cook County Jail
               Status: Code Red

The unexpected impact of the explosive knocked John-Michael on his tin butt. He flailed out with his arms to recover. "Oh, man," he yelled, "what the hell hit us?"

< Warning! Damage has been taken. Outer hull efficiency has been reduced to seventy-two percent. Suggest evasive maneuvers. >

"So do I," DeChanza said. "But from what?" He scanned the area as he got to his feet. Prime was racing down the sidewalk on the other side of the street, the trail bike leaping curbs.

Then movement caught his attention and he locked onto the BirdSong JK91 heligyro less than a hundred yards overhead. It was armed with a 20mm chain gun and 30mm rocket pods on either side of the landing gear. Dark blue and cream, it stood out against the early morning.

Before DeChanza could move, the rocket pods belched flames again. Both warheads scored on his chest area. The impacts drove DeChanza backward but he managed to stay on his feet. Fiery debris clung to the armor in two scorched areas.

<Warning. Further damage has been accrued. Outer hull efficiency down to fifty-three percent.>

The heligyro flashed by, then heeled around for another approach. Working the cyberveil, DeChanza monitored the impulse from the weapons-control systems to the rocket pods, sensing the moment of ignition. He ducked to one side, fast enough that the restraining straps on the seat cut into his flesh despite the padding.

One of the rockets missed him, gouging a crater in the street, and the other struck him in the leg. Tremors rattled up inside the Scratchbuilt unit's massive frame. Six thousand pounds of ceramics and steel could withstand a lot of damage, but the heligyro's firepower was adding up.

"John-Michael."

Recognizing Lee Won Underhill's voice over the radio frequency, DeChanza responded, squaring off with the BirdSong JK91 again. "Here."

"That's not a police heligyro."

"My weapons systems are off-line," the young agent responded. Accessing one of the port-side cameras, he spotted Underhill standing behind the glass doors at the front of the county jail. She held a cellular phone to her face.

"Then get the hell out of there," Underhill said.

Breaking off the attack, the BirdSong JK91 dropped altitude and streaked for the front of the county jail. Flying with amazing skill between the buildings, the heligyro opened fire with the chain gun and rocket pods.

DeChanza guessed that the crew was able to break into the frequency and had recognized Underhill's voice.

The blazing display of massed firepower collapsed the front of the jail. DeChanza had a momentary impression of Prime throwing himself over the FREELancers administrator, then smoke and debris took away the scene.

"Scratchbuilt!" Underhill yelled. "Clear the area! Now! That's an order. We're okay in here."

Anger burned in DeChanza as he watched the heligyro climbing again at the other end of California Boulevard. He turned and ran, his mind already working out the fine details of his plan. Back the other way was a clutch of buildings that had been condemned and were waiting to be torn down. He was counting on the pilot thinking he was going to try to hide among the multistoried buildings.

Accessing other equipment aboard the Scratchbuilt, DeChanza jammed the heligyro's computer-assisted firing systems with the armor's multiband broadcaster. He had the MAPS up to its max of 65mph by the time the gunner figured out what had happened and made it clear to the pilot.

Using the 360-degree view afforded through the on-board systems, DeChanza saw the heligyro follow him. The aircraft dropped altitude again, accelerating in his wake, catching up to him. Prime and Underhill tried to get his attention over the radio, yelling warnings to him. He ignored them, concentrating on the sequence of events he needed to pull off in the next few seconds.

The buildings were tall around him, running twenty and thirty stories high. He was three stories tall himself. The JK91 closed to within two hundred yards, gaining dramatically now.

His mind clear, engaged in the Savant state, DeChanza, wearing the Scratchbuilt armor like a second skin, waited for his opportunity. He knew he'd have to take at least two more rockets, and they dropped from the pods streaming gray smoke. Both of them hit him in the lower back. He ignored the warning about the damage, struggling with the hydraulics and gyro systems to maintain his balance.

The BirdSong JK91 was fifty yards back and fifteen yards out of reach above him when he made his move. The pilot was obviously trying to gain the higher deck for a moment and return to attack again. DeChanza knew the suit wouldn't handle another successful rocket attack without a major malfunction.

Working the powersuit as if it were his own body, DeChanza leapt for the building on his right. The structure shivered when he hit it with the force of a wrecking ball. The hands and feet dug into the sides of the building, punching their own holds as he climbed forty feet as quick as a monkey. A billboard advertising the lucrative careers offered by the Japanese Space Service crashed into the street.

The heligyro pilot tried to evade the Scratchbuilt unit when it came up within viewing range. But it was too late. Little compassion touched DeChanza's heart as he doubled up his three-fingered hand and made a fist the size of a fifty-five-gallon drum. He swept the fist backward, the trajectory dead-solid perfect.

When the big fist connected with the BirdSong JK91, the heligyro came apart in a giant orange-and-black fireball. The explosion shook the Scratchbuilt armor free of the building. Feeling the sickening twirl of the inner gyro stabilizers, DeChanza kept the suit upright with difficulty. The boot-shaped feet sank deep into the street as the broken heligyro rained down in pieces around him.

"John-Michael," Underhill called.

"I'm okay," DeChanza responded. A phalanx of sheriff's cars and Chicago PD prowlers swirled around his legs and closed in, their blue cherries on the light bars spinning like possessed tops. "But it looks like I blew my escape."

Uniformed officers vaulted out of their cars and took up positions with their weapons pointed at him. The small arms stuff he didn't worry about, but some of them had IR-guided rocket launchers. With the damage done to the armor, he didn't think he could break the cordon without a fight.

Thinking of going back to jail depressed him. Even though he was used to the cramped, confined space inside the Scratchbuilt armor, being imprisoned was something else entirely.

"Don't worry about the escape, kid," Prime said. "The boss lady arrived here with our '*Get Out of Jail Free*' card in hand."

Already leaders moved among the combined sheriff's deputies and policemen, and weapons were put away. DeChanza smiled as he stepped over the line of police cars.

7

"You're sure about this?" Seated in one of the chairs in front of the desk, John Gibney looked up at Lee Won Underhill. They were alone in her office. He was referring to the fact that his dead wife had been selling Dr. Sherman Carter's research to an undisclosed source.

"Yes." Underhill's answer was purposefully unrelenting. She stood at the window overlooking Lake Michigan, light from the rising sun spilling into the room over her shoulder.

John Gibney was a rawboned man, an unemployed construction worker whose skin had been permanently darkened by long days and harsh climates. Dark circles looped under his eyes. The whites were still bloodshot from crying. His wife's body was on the medical floor of the FREELancers building, and he'd been there a few minutes ago. His children were still downstairs being cared for by sympathetic office staff. He wore overalls and a Chicago Cubs tee shirt.

"We need to talk about how you're going to handle the media on this," Underhill said. "I can't protect you and your family here much longer."

"Oh, God, this'll kill Clarice's momma."

Underhill remained quiet, letting the man's own fears sink into his mind.

"How much," Gibney asked in a hoarse voice, "how much was she getting from those people?"

"We don't know." Actually, Underhill did. Most of the money had been hidden in accounts down in the Cayman Islands. She'd already recovered it.

"I can't tell people that she was—" He looked at her desperately. "Do we have to tell anyone?"

"I'm going to be drawing some heat on this too," Underhill said. "You've seen how the media can treat this organization. They'll blow this operation up as though it were worse than the sinking of the *Titanic*."

"But your people did everything they could to save my family," Gibney said.

"The media people will attempt to get you to change your mind about that. They'll sway you if they can, because it'll make a better story. More controversy."

Gibney shook his head. "I won't let them."

She paused, letting time hang between them so he would know it was working against him. Then she said, "If you can take that tack with the reporters and stick to it, I'll do what I can at this end to cover up your wife's involvement. But we're going to have to give the media the same story." Underhill sat behind her desk, getting them back on the same level so they were just co-conspirators instead of corporate executive and unemployed construction worker. "We'll say that you and your children were kidnapped, then your wife came to us for help. No one has to know she was involved in anything criminal. The way we'll tell it, this was her first contact with these people. After a few days, this story will fade away."

She buzzed for her secretary. The woman entered, took Gibney by the arm, and led him from the room.

Underhill punched the intercom button. "Kent. Get Monroe Hornsby on the phone for me."

"Coming up."

Underhill reached into her desk and took out a flat metal case. Flipping it open, she took out one of the prepped syringes inside, then quickly injected herself in the leg. Deathly allergic to many of the airborne pollutants carried across North America, she had to have four shots a day to remain healthy. She reached behind the desk for the coffeepot, poured hot water in a cup, and swirled green tea in with a spoon. It tasted spicy and hot.

"Boss," Kent called.

"Yes."

"I've got Hornsby."

"Put him on." Underhill turned to face the phone's vidscreen. The monitor cleared, revealing Hornsby in a fresh suit and a smile. "Good morning, Monroe."

"Good morning, Lee. I don't have much time. If you're calling about my reaction earlier this morning, I was out of line. The department heads at Iowa State seemed completely happy that we've solved the problem."

"I'm glad to hear that. I've got a favor to ask. When you talk to the media, I need you to leave out any mention of Clarice Gibney's guilt."

"What?" Hornsby looked stunned. "Lee, if this is some kind of joke—"

"No joke," Underhill said. "I just cut a deal with her husband. In exchange for his glowing recap of how FREELancer agents tried valiantly to save his wife and family, I agreed to leave out any mention of her stealing Carter's research."

"Why? So you can take care of that precious image you want for the FREELancers instead?"

Underhill ignored the sarcasm and anger. She was negotiating, and she couldn't allow emotion to touch her because it was too expensive. "We're all exposed here. If Gibney wanted to, he could get a phalanx of lawyers and keep FREELancers and Iowa State University tied up in court for years regarding possible civil damages. His wife was killed, and we were all involved."

Hornsby was silent.

Underhill leaned back in her chair, her voice like ice when she spoke. "There's a case that can be made against the security section over Carter's research. Maybe a jury will feel you should have made it more difficult for Clarice Gibney to gain access to those developments, making the temptation harder to act on."

"Lee, c'mon—"

"And it won't take a really smart lawyer to realize he could blackmail your group by threatening to reveal that this morning wasn't the first time Clarice Gibney met with the people she'd been working for. How do you think your investors will feel about that? They'll be asking themselves how much Gibney gave to these people before she was caught. I can imagine a few civil suits within short order as some of the really heavy hitters try to leverage their investments back out of Iowa State thinking that the research Carter is working on now is about to be duplicated somewhere else, realizing little or no profit for them. If I have to, I'll point Gibney at the right firm. And I'll mention to him that I have tapes they can subpoena where Clarice Gibney mentions that she's had other meetings with these people."

Hornsby cut loose with a string of obscenities.

Underhill sipped her tea and let the man wind down. "Look at it this way," she said when he'd finished, "you may lose a moment of glory with the media, but you don't have to worry about it coming back and biting you on the ass either. And there's a silver lining to this particular cloud. We recovered most of the money Gibney had been paid for her spying."

There was a pause. "How much?"

"Seven million and change." Before the man could say anything else, Underhill went on. "We were also able to recover documents showing the deposits. You'll be able to go back and figure out what Carter was working on during the period covered by the deposits, maybe help out in the damage control for lost research." And Hornsby would see that she hadn't touched a dime of the money.

"That's good," Hornsby said, sounding slightly mollified. If he couldn't have the privilege of roasting an industrial spy, money in the bank was still money in the bank.

"According to the contract you signed, there's a fifteen percent finder's fee on recovered cash," Underhill went on smoothly.

"Yes." The man didn't sound as happy.

"I want a cashier's check made out for that amount in John Gibney's name," the FREELancers administrator said, "and presented to him within an hour after I surrender the money to you. Tell him it's part of an insurance package that his wife had." She glanced at the clock. "And I'm still expecting that deposit on the balance of our fee in this morning's business."

"It'll be there. Why are you giving the money to Gibney?"

"The man lost his wife, and his children lost their mother. He's going to need help."

"You could give it to him."

"It'll mean more coming from Iowa State University."

"And the media won't be able to use the donation against FREELancers. It won't look like you're buying him off."

Underhill said, "I've got a busy day ahead of me. Is there anything else we need to discuss?"

"No."

The administrator broke the connection and leaned back in her chair. Her neck was stiff and a tension headache pounded at her temples. Glancing at the legal pad on the desktop, she quickly added a couple of items to the list she needed to act on.

Light swirled in the center of the room and the holo of George Anthony Underhill took shape. He smoothed his mustache, a habit held over from his corporeal days, and looked at her. "Trouble?"

"I just blackmailed a man who's lost his wife, and possibly alienated a very powerful and profitable client."

"And why did you do those terrible things?" her father asked in mock disapproval.

"To put a lid on the situation," Underhill replied. "The wheels came off the operation this morning, and there's no telling how FREELancers will be treated by the media."

"Oh, I think there are plenty of indicators. When this unit was first started up, I met dissension at every turn because I was employing freaks, metables, people who didn't meet with popular approval. You've managed to change a lot of that. Mayor Hubbard has felt comfortable enough to endorse the FREELancers, and so have some of the other government agencies."

"But they don't trust us," Underhill said, "unless they have us under contract. There isn't a government agency out there that we haven't worked both for and against at one time or another."

"That's what being a FREELancer is all about," her father said. "We walk the thin edge of life, Lee, and one slip could be disastrous, but we get to make our own decisions. That is worth anything."

"Some days that doesn't seem so clear-cut."

"No. But your arguments to Hornsby were valid. And you've seen to it that Gibney will have a foothold on being able to care for his family. All in all, I'd say you've put in a good day's work."

Underhill studied her father. "You think so?"

"Yes." He crossed the room and placed his hand on top of hers. Even though she could feel nothing, the gesture meant a lot. "Lee, there's not anyone I'd rather have heading this organization in my absence. You bring much to FREELancers, maybe even some things I never could have. I'm learning from you."

She wished she felt as confident, then got angry at herself for ever doubting. She was capable of harsh decisions. She'd made them in the past, and there were more to make in the future. "Thanks, Dad," she said as she gathered her papers.

8

Dry Bones Mesa, New Mexico   **6:11 a.m. MST**
Rocky Mountain Alliance (RMA)   **1311 Greenwich**
                                     Mean
106.1 degrees W Longitude   **October 24, 2023**
35.3 degrees N Latitude   **Tuesday**

Gitano Proudelk struggled against the giant spiderweb that held him. The web strands were as thick as his wrists and coated with a shiny adhesive that held him fast. He was in the place of the thunderers, the spirits of his people.

Vibrations, slight but sure, trembled along the length of the web strands, and he knew something was coming.

Proudelk concentrated on his breathing, pulling it into the center of his being, then pushing it all back out. His grandfather, called Virgil Foxfoot because no one could hear him coming when he wished them not to, had taught him breathing and the skills of a warrior and shaman. All of those he was still learning.

But his problem now stemmed from the metability he had discovered in himself. On the res it was considered a white man's disease, something to be spurned. For three years he

had felt the pull of it deep within him and had fought it.
Dreams had haunted him at those times, and he kept what he
could of the metability, the part that did not seem alien to the
Old Ways his grandfather had taught him.

The ability to work with animals had always been his.
Since he'd been a boy, he'd been valued as a trainer for the
horses and dogs that helped work the cattle kept on the res.
Now, people who had bartered with him for his services
wouldn't ask him to perform even the simplest task.

The other parts—like the great strength and quickness and
the ability to know where other people were by touching
objects they'd touched—he'd worked to conceal at his grandfather's insistence. Not because his grandfather was ashamed
of him, but because the old man had known the People
wouldn't understand.

The spider, when it came, was a fiddleback, light brown,
deceptively spindly, and over ten feet tall. The darker brown
violin-shaped marking on the top of its body wasn't visible,
but Proudelk knew it was there.

Suddenly the spider reared up on its hind legs and came at
Proudelk with supernatural speed. He set himself, knowing
there was no way to run. Only feet away, the fiddleback
stopped.

"Have you come to die, then, Gitano Proudelk?" the
fiddleback asked in a voice that pealed like thunder.

"I am here to learn how to live," Proudelk responded.

"The secret of learning to live is in learning how to die. Do
you fear death?"

"Yes."

"You have learned that, and that is what you must unlearn
if you are to live your destiny." The spider extended two of its
legs. "Come to me. I will show you death, let you experience
and taste of it. You will learn that fear is useless."

"No." Proudelk stepped to the side, not wanting to step
back. The sticky web tried to hold his feet. "Fear, if properly
honed, drives a warrior to more greatness than he could know

in a calm mind. Take that, and you take one of my weapons."

"But you know a sick fear, too," the fiddleback said. "That leaves you unfinished. The sick fear will devour you."

"I am everything I have learned to be."

"Yet you remain afraid of what you could be."

Proudelk had no answer.

"Your destiny is greater than you ever imagined."

"I want only to live in peace with my people."

The spider laughed. "Life has a way of being both more and less than what a man wants, Gitano Proudelk." It paused, as if considering. "If I wanted to kill you, would you be able to stop me?"

"I would fight you."

"Why?"

"Because if you won, there would be things left undone in my life." Proudelk shifted again, watching for any sign of movement from the fearsome creature.

"Would you be afraid for your spirit?"

"No. It is whole, strong; you could not hurt that."

"So you would fear only for things you left undone?"

"No. Not entirely. I want to live."

"Then let that be your answer, Gitano Proudelk, and go live." The fiddleback cast out a shimmering net of spider silk that floated over the young Navajo.

Proudelk experienced a moment of peace, then he blinked open his eyes and knew he was back inside the sweat lodge. The air was hot and thin, barely servicing the needs of his body. He wore a loincloth and was covered with perspiration.

The sweat lodge was a dome made up of rocks he and his grandfather had gathered. He couldn't see through it so he didn't know if it was night or day. It was too low to stand, and there was no real room to move around. Bracing himself, he put a hand out and started pushing rock away. The stones pounded down the sides of the dome in loud clatters. He had to stop and rest three times before he had a hole big enough to crawl out through.

He smiled at the rising morning sun out over the arroyo only a few feet away. His grandfather squatted at the steep edge overlooking the stream nearly three hundred feet down. Beside him, a rabbit was slowly roasting on a spit over a low fire and looked almost done. Smoke from the fire drifted over the broken mesas around them.

"Good morning, grandson," Virgil Foxfoot said. "The rabbit is waiting on you." He was a short wiry man, his face a road map of past struggles. Lean and worked as a piece of rawhide, Foxfoot didn't look like a man who'd seen nearly eighty winters. He wore a blue bandanna to hold his shoulder-length gray hair back, and a short-sleeved Western shirt, jeans, Nocona boots, and a belt buckle the size of a Buick hubcap. Dark Foster Grants covered his eyes.

Out in the strong wind floating through the arroyo, Proudelk felt much cooler but still parched. He took up the waterskin they'd brought and drank slowly.

"Not too much," his grandfather said. "You've been dreaming for three days. You get too much water too soon, you'll be sick."

Proudelk nodded and stopped drinking. He cupped his hand, poured, then splashed some water across his face. Already he was feeling more refreshed, and his stomach rumbled at the smell of the roasting rabbit and the pot of chicory coffee on heated stones beside it. "I dreamed, Grandfather."

"Good. We must talk of it. Eat and gather your strength. You'll need it soon."

"You got lucky with the rabbit," Proudelk said as he slipped into his jeans, sleeveless denim shirt, and moccasins.

"I already had my breakfast this morning. This was for you."

"How'd you know I'd have my dream by now?"

The old man smiled. "My medicine is strong, boy, and yours has a power that makes it easy to read." He pointed to the northeast.

Proudelk looked and saw a line of dust coming toward

them from Santa Fe. "Who?"

"The people from FREELancers," Foxfoot said.

"I can't see that far."

"Neither can I. But I know what time I told them to be here."

"You sent for them?"

"Yes." His grandfather looked at him, his expression implacable behind the dark-lensed sunglasses.

"Why?" Proudelk was angry. The outsiders had tried to contact him for weeks, but he'd avoided them.

"The moment you saved Edward Sharpnose, your life was changed. You need more than I can offer you. This lady, Summer Davison, I think maybe she could have some answers."

Reluctantly, Proudelk sat on crossed legs and watched the approaching line of dust. He didn't feel hungry anymore, but he took up the spitted rabbit and began pinching bites off with his fingers. Surprisingly, his appetite returned, and he savored the taste of the rabbit grease.

Foxfoot sat beside Proudelk. "Now tell me of your dream before they get here. We must talk of it because it will shed some light on what we're supposed to do. Dreams are very strong things and must not be ignored."

Chicago, Illinois   ***7:23 a.m. CST***
Great Lakes Authority (GLA)   ***1323 Greenwich Mean***
87.7 degrees W Longitude   ***October 24, 2023***
41.8 degrees N Latitude   ***Tuesday***

She was a nightmare, and Download couldn't get her out of his mind.

"So I'm dead," she said calmly.

"Afraid so," he told her truthfully.

"How long?"

"A few months. Maybe a year."

"You could be wrong," she suggested.

"We could check."

She was quiet for a moment, thinking. "Not yet."

"Scared?" he asked.

"Yes." She wouldn't look at him when she answered.

Download, dressed in a hooded, olive-drab raincoat that effectively hid the Octopus from the truckers, sat at a semi-clean booth in a truck stop called the I-94 Breakdown near Skokie.

The woman's name was Eden Frisco, and she occupied Download's mind so solidly that he could see her sitting across from him in the booth. He knew it was probably a hallucination brought about by his own fatigued mind so he could better deal with what was going on inside his head. However, it had never happened before, so he wasn't really sure. What he was sure of, though, was that if he'd gone back to headquarters and told Dr. Rhand or Underhill about the dead woman in his mind, they'd have put him on tranquilizers and in a straitjacket till they were sure he wasn't going to lose it.

"How did I die?" Frisco asked.

"Work," Download answered simply. The woman had been a Chicago PD cop until a few months or a year ago. The skills that had been lifted from her had been in regards to handgunning. She'd been a champion in police circuits, and had been a member of a SWAT team.

"How?"

"Maybe you should let it go till we figure out what we're doing here." From what he could see, Eden Frisco had been a pretty woman. In her early thirties, she had a good figure, dishwater-blond hair that was cut short and spiky, and a crooked-toothed smile that endeared her to Jefferson Scott. Seated across from him, she wore the dark ballistic outfit of the SWAT team, the matte black armor covering vital areas but leaving her with plenty of motion. He wondered how she pictured herself.

"Don't blow smoke at me." Her anger was real.

"You and your partner were brought down at a DEA drug

bust," Download said. "The DEA had turned up a large-scale Canadian supplier and needed help shutting the pipeline down. They asked Chicago PD, and your unit was volunteered. Trouble was, the drug runners had a deep throat in the department who set you guys up. You and your partner died, but the bent badge in the department was brought out into the open." As deep as he was into her mind, the police lingo came easily to him. Or possibly it was the other way around. He was never sure.

"Who was my partner?"

She was testing him, and he knew it. "Guy named Dwayne Cook." Scott sipped his coffee. It had grown cold while he was sitting there, but he didn't care.

"How did I get inside your mind?" Frisco asked.

Earlier, while walking through the alleys and back streets of the city, Scott had explained about the Download device. She knew about the technology behind the skill-lift even if she didn't understand how it was done.

"You were on a respirator when you arrived at the hospital. The doctors knew they were going to lose you. Remember the contract you signed with FREELancers?"

She wrinkled her brow in thought. Scott glanced in the window beside them and saw his reflection but not hers. "Yes," she answered. "Something about experiments regarding cybernetics and my experience with handguns."

"That's it. The doctors contacted Dr. Rhand, our research ops, and he sent over a team with the Download device. As they were copying your brain waves, you died. Somehow *you* ended up on the disk as well."

She didn't flinch from his words. "So I'm a ghost."

He returned her frank gaze full measure, not knowing how to answer. In the past, skill transfers had left residual personality imprints, but most of the time it had been as if they were people in another room: he could hear them, but not talk directly to them like he could with Frisco. But those imprints had crowded his mind at times till he felt lost within himself and had blackouts where he didn't know what he'd done. A few times he'd woken up in the psychiatric ward at headquarters, or in ICU.

"To me you are," he replied.

"What do we do?" she asked.

"I don't know. But I do know I can't have you bumping around inside my head like this. To say the least, it's distracting."

Her laugh was weak and bitter. "So who you gonna call?"

"I don't know," he replied. He wanted a drink really bad. Before joining up with FREELancers as a guinea pig for the Download device, he'd been treated for substance abuse and clinical depression. If he fell off the wagon, that first drink could last for months, and might free up even more of the personalities that occasionally surfaced inside his mind.

"Is there anyone you could talk to about this?"

"No. I try, and they'll lock us both up."

"So what happens when you get me out of your head?"

"I don't know."

"Do I die?" Frisco asked.

"Technically," Scott said, "that's already happened."

"I don't buy that. If I was dead, I wouldn't be here like this."

"In a little while," Download said, "you're going to start fading anyway."

"What do you mean?"

"Those disks," he answered, "are meant for short-term memory retention at best. A few hours, and whatever skills were transferred wipe themselves out."

Frisco's face hardened. "You brought me here to wait it out, hoping I'd fade."

"Eden," he said gently, "you're not real. Evidently the disk captured some of your will to survive, and that's caused this confusion."

"If anyone here is confused," the woman said, "it's you. When we were out walking earlier, I could feel the rain on my face. And I've got a headache that you wouldn't believe."

Download glanced at the windows. The spitting rain that had started less than an hour before continued, giving the streets a hard sheen and dappling the restaurant's glass. "Those are my feelings. My headache."

"Then how can I tell the coffee is so bad?"

"We have similar tastes."

"I have my own cup." Frisco held it up to show him. Steam wafted from the dark liquid.

A grin twisted Download's thin lips. "Nice trick, but I happen to recall the waitress served me, not you."

Her features turned angry, and she threw the cup of coffee at him. He braced himself, reminding himself, as the coffee fanned out toward him, that she wasn't physically real. Inches from his face, the scalding liquid vanished, taking the cup with it.

"Are you okay?"

It took Download a moment to realize the female voice wasn't coming from Frisco. He looked up and saw the young waitress looking down at him with concern.

"Sure," he said.

"Look, don't take this personal or anything. I understand that it's kind of wet outside, but you've been sitting there talking to yourself for the last hour, and you're making my boss nervous."

Download looked at Frisco. "See, you're not real."

Frisco leaned back in the booth and crossed her arms over her breasts.

"Hey."

Looking back at the waitress, Download said, "Who told you I'd been talking to myself? I've had to get my own coffee refill twice."

"My boss." The waitress hooked a thumb over one thin shoulder. "He says you should go now. The coffee's on the house."

A number of the truckers were staring at Download. He'd taken the helmet off after the firefight and stored it in sections in the pockets of the jacket. The hood made it hard if not impossible to see the brain taps wired into his head. Spotting the truck-stop boss was easy. The man wore a white apron and chef's hat and looked like a pit bull with a Special Forces tattoo on his left forearm.

"No prob," the FREELancers agent said. He reached inside his jacket, took out money, and dropped it on the tabletop. "But I'm not a charity case." He glanced at Frisco. "Let's drift."

He left by the rear entrance, standing under the small purple canopy for a minute while he adjusted his hood before trudging out into the light rain. The brain taps allowed infections to build up at times if he didn't take precautions. He didn't know where to go, so he picked a street and followed it. The linear path was comforting.

"There are other people in here with us," Frisco said.

Download had to grin at the irony of it. "At last, someone else believes me, but it has to be someone no one else can see or hear either."

"No one else knows?"

"No."

"But you've told them?"

"Countless times."

"There's no way of detecting them?"

"No."

The ensuing pause made him uncomfortable. It made him uneasy knowing that someone else might be thinking with his brain, because he knew he was capable of deep and devastating intrigues. His moral conduct before joining the FREELancers had sometimes been far outside society's norms, and he still skated the line at times.

Skokie was coming alive around him. Traffic whisked along through the wet streets, and twice cars splashed water up onto the curb and soaked his pants.

"How do you stand them?" Frisco asked.

"Maybe I don't. Lady, ever since I got this device wired into my head I've been doubting my sanity. And I wasn't any too sure of it before."

"Then why do you do it?"

He crossed the street because a marketplace on the other side of the block had an awning that kept the rain off him. Two wire-heads begged for change with cardboard cups swiped from a mental health funding drive that had ended months ago. They shivered inside their torn concert tee shirts and holey jeans. Download hated this part of the city. Wounded dreams limped on, powered by quarters, dimes, and nickels. He dropped a handful of change into the cups.

Down the block, a computer-operated street cleaner shushed down the gutter, spraying water and coming toward them. As it passed Download, it scanned his ID as a citizen and veered away from him. The wire-heads pulled back immediately, cursing vehemently, letting Download know their citizenship had been revoked at some point. The street cleaner wouldn't recognize them other than as a potential hazard, and would have drenched them.

He shoved his hands inside his jacket pockets. "Starting out, I told myself it was because I loved the lady who asked me."

"Did you?"

"Once, maybe. But things change."

"She didn't love you?"

"Once, maybe."

"But now she doesn't?"

"If she does, she has a peculiar way of showing it."

Frisco fell silent and seemed to be thinking. The marketplace was closed, and Download glanced in at the rows of goods waiting to attract customers later.

"Sometimes it's hard to tell someone you love them," Frisco said.

Download waited for the light to change at the corner, then walked across the street. He knew Underhill was going to be pissed at him for not checking in, but he didn't care. FREE-

Lancers had brought him new problems, given him no training to handle them, then denied they existed. "I'll buy that,"
he said.

"So, if you're sure she doesn't love you, why do you stay?"
Frisco asked.

"I'm not an altruist."

"That I had figured out. Is it the money? The need to play
hero?"

"No," Scott replied, feeling his voice tighten. The dead cop
was making him face more truths about himself than he ever
wanted to at one time. "I just haven't figured out my next
move."

"How long have you been with the FREELancers?"

"Three years." A wave of nausea almost overwhelmed
Download. His knees buckled, and he had to lean against a
wall until the sudden dizziness passed. "What are you
doing?"

"Nothing. Are you all right?"

As quickly as it came, the nausea passed. Download stood
and glanced around, waiting for it to come back, but nothing
happened. "I'm fine." He spotted a telephone and headed for
it. There wasn't a doubt in his mind that Frisco had something to do with the attack, whether overtly or blamelessly.
He had to talk to Dr. Rhand.

"Do you talk with the other people inside here?" Frisco
asked.

"No." Scott dug money out of his pants and started to work
the phone. He glanced in the window of the convenience
store he stood beside and peered at his reflection. Other than
looking pale, nothing seemed to be the matter.

"I can't either."

After he had the money in the slot, Download punched in
one of the special numbers he had for Dr. Rhand's lab. There
were cut-outs along the way that wouldn't allow the call to be
traced to the FREELancers building.

"Jefferson," Frisco said in a quieter voice, "I've got a

daughter. Emily. I guess she's twelve now."

The phone started to ring at the other end, and Download hoped that Rhand was up. The research ops kept irregular hours, but generally if he was asleep, no one would disturb him.

Frisco went on. "I never got to tell her good-bye."

One of the lab staff came on the line, and Download asked for Rhand. He was told to wait.

"I want to talk to her," Frisco said.

"No way," the FREELancer agent replied.

"Just for a few minutes."

"Look, think this through. What would you tell her? 'Sorry Mommy came back as a skid-row bum, but I just wanted to tell you good-bye.' Your husband would have me arrested, locked up in a sanitarium, and have the key thrown away. I'm not about to open myself up for that kind of grief."

"Rhand," a deep basso voice said over the phone.

"It's Scott." Download's head started to throb even harder and the nausea returned with a vengeance. "I think I'm in some deep guano here, Doc."

"Where are you?" Rhand asked.

Download had to look around to figure it out because he hadn't been paying much attention. A pawn shop specializing in bionic limbs and war mementos was only a short distance away. As he watched, a wire-head lurched from the pawn shop and slipped a chip into a socket behind her left jaw. Overcome by the programming, the wire-head stumbled into the alley and sat down, lost in her latest daydream. "Somewhere in Skokie." Before he could focus on the street signs, incredible pain ripped through his head. He dropped to his knees and retched, bringing up only coffee.

"Scott," Rhand bellowed over the phone. "What's going on?"

Putting a hand on each side of his head, Download fought to push the pain away. The phone receiver dangled only inches from his hand but he couldn't make himself reach for it. He stared down at the pool of rainwater he was kneeling in. His face seemed to come apart, dropping out in sections to reveal the softer features underneath.

In seconds his image had disappeared, leaving Eden Frisco in its wake. "I'm sorry," she said. "If there were another way, I'd do it."

Download's arm reached for the receiver as the pain faded. At first he thought he'd moved the arm, then he watched as the arm hung up the phone.

"There's not much time," the dead woman said. "I've got to hurry."

Download's body got to its feet and walked toward the curb. His fingers slipped inside his mouth, and he gave a shrill whistle that stopped a taxi. He'd never been able to do that before.

"Sit back," Frisco said as she opened the taxi's rear door. "If you're right about me fading, you'll have this body back soon." She slid into the backseat and gave the address.

Trapped inside his own mind, Download had no choice but to go along.

9

Rinji 8 *Space Station*   **10:47 p.m. (Tokyo Main)**
Orbit Shoda   **1347 Greenwich Mean**
29,119.04 miles out   **October 24, 2023**
Present position: Over Antarctica   **Tuesday**

Aramis Tadashi sat hunched forward in the control console on the Japanese space shuttle *Kimiko* and watched the digital numbers in the upper left corner of the forward screen count down as they neared the space station. It hung against the black velvet of space, looking like a barbell with five weight disks of different sizes spaced along its length. Feeler-probes dashed around it in close orbits, tracking and monitoring everything for miles in every direction.

"We're going to make the docking ring in three minutes," Kerrick said calmly. She piloted the shuttle with a sure hand.

Tadashi knew the rest of his team was paying attention. *Rinji 8* was home to a rotating crew of one hundred twelve. Of those, he owned eight people outright. That left one hundred four people for his crew of seventeen to handle.

"Increase magnification," Tadashi ordered.

"Coming," Kerrick said. Her hands drifted over the controls

and in quick response the monitor changed, showing a larger image of the space station.

"Where's the beacon?" Tadashi asked.

Kerrick was quiet for a moment, searching. Then, "There." The monitor shifted views and magnification again, focusing on a small rectangle on the steel skin of the space station. In reality, the beacon was the size of a matchbook and sent out a signal on burst transmission, carefully set so it wouldn't be picked up by the communications equipment on the *Rinji 8*. If the arrangements inside hadn't been set up, it wouldn't have given off a signal.

"Has our approach been confirmed?" Tadashi asked.

"Yes."

Tadashi stroked the butt of his fléchette pistol. Today would mark the official beginning of Family Kaemon, with himself as its leader and founder and visionary. "They suspect nothing?"

"No. I put that program together myself," Kerrick said. "As far as they know, we're the relief crew for some of their people."

Tadashi felt the shuttle shudder slightly as its course was altered by the retro-rockets. Gravity vanished as its rotation halted as well.

The monitor filled with the image of the docking ring closing on the nose of the shuttle. On the left monitor, the white length of the shuttle's orbiter access arm snaked out five feet and stopped.

The radio crackled and a male voice came over the frequency, speaking in Japanese. "*Kimiko*, you are good on final approach. See you soon. *Rinji 8* out."

"Acknowledged, *Rinji 8*. *Kimiko* out."

The shuttle bumped gently into the space station and two of Tadashi's crew hustled to secure the orbiter arm against the airlock. Kerrick finished the docking procedures, locking them into the *Rinji 8*. Slowly, they started to turn but it didn't affect the weightless condition. Only the fields of refer-

ence through the port and starboard monitors let Tadashi
know they were in motion.

He unbuckled the seatbelts and pushed himself out of the
chair, slowly floating toward the floor. His magnetic boots
adhered to the floor with hollow clicks. "Let's go," he said,
slipping the fléchette pistol from its holster.

Taking the lead, he floated through the floor deployment
tunnel, then shoved himself along the orbiter arm. At the
door, he paused and slipped his helmet back on.

The airlock opened slowly because the operators on the
other side had trouble bracing themselves. When the first
man stepped into view, Tadashi sent three fléchettes spinning
into his throat. The air was instantly colored by a crimson
mist.

Without hesitation, he waded through it and stepped into
the space station. Seven people were in the receiving dock. A
woman in a blue security jumpsuit twisted toward Tadashi,
working with the lack of gravity rather than fighting against
it. Strapped to her lower right arm, the British Malamuke
taser came around in a threatening arc. The first dart leaped
at him, stringing the thin wire after it.

As he targeted the woman, the dart struck him in the
chest. For a moment his suit's inner visor readouts went off
the scale as the electrical charge surged through the wire and
ran through the suit. Shielded by the suit's inner layers,
Tadashi felt only a tingle of the voltage. He squeezed the trigger twice as the woman's remaining dart leaped at him,
struck his face shield and skidded off, leaving a scratch that
caught the glare of the overhead lights.

Both the fléchettes caught the woman in the forehead. Her
body jerked for a moment, then floated like a puppet with its
strings cut.

"What the hell is going on?" one of the men demanded.

Tadashi shot him too, then turned his attention to the two
men fleeing up the ladder leading to the transport tunnel
connecting the five decks of the space station. The reception

area was part clearinghouse and part storage area. Wire-mesh cages held crates and bins of goods that could handle exposure to the unforgiving cold of space if necessary. Space suits hung on racks outside a survival blister less than ten feet away.

Still holding the fléchette pistol in his fist, Tadashi took two steps to a wall covered with controls and computer equipment. He grabbed the corner of a covering under an atmosphere gauge to his left, then yanked it open.

"No!" one of the men yelled, diving at him.

Tadashi battered him back with the pistol and accessed the scrambled frequency in his suit. "Lock down!" He raked the fingers of his gun hand across the belt controls for the magnetic shoes, bumping them up to their maximum efficiency. Then he stabbed his fingers into the open electrical box, hitting the red plunger.

In response, vents opened across the warehouse floor, releasing the atmosphere into space. Unsecured, the dead bodies and two of the men were sucked through the massive apertures. The openings were part of the space station's fire-suppression systems in the event there was a fire in the warehouse from stored chemicals. Activating them also caused a lockdown of the hatches. The man at the top of the ladder couldn't get out, trapping him with the other two men. It took them only minutes to die from cold and suffocation.

During that time Kerrick had taken her place at the computer satellite working off the space station's primary support systems computer and jacked into the network with the small notebook computer she wore attached to the front of her space suit. Seconds later, it had merged with and overridden the lockdown systems.

"Blow the rest of the charges," Tadashi ordered, maintaining his magnetic boots at their peak. As extra insurance, he grabbed a post ring mounted on the wall.

"They're going now!" Cydney responded. The charges had been placed by the on-board team over the last few weeks.

Rinji 8 shuddered. Inside the space station, Tadashi knew

alarm systems were going insane. Lights flicked out and night drenched the warehouse. His space suit's helmet light came on automatically. Less than a minute later, the space station's emergency systems kicked on, managing a weaker glow. He rode out the shivers that arced through the structure. "Kerrick, give me a damage report."

"Coming." The woman keyed in the preset sequence. An analog schematic bloomed into display on the monitor embedded in the warehouse wall. She quickly shifted through the successive frames, searching. "Dammit."

"What is it?" Tadashi released his hold, switched off his boots, and kicked over to her position, thudding gently into the wall.

"Lab section was more protected than I'd thought it would be," she said. "Had its own backup. Their security systems tagged the chameleon foolie I introduced into the safeguard setups. We blew the access hatches like on the other decks, but the security backups maintained the atmosphere."

"How many are alive?" Tadashi asked.

Kerrick consulted the schematics, then worked on the keyboard. "Internal scans show nineteen people."

"What about the emergency beacon to Tokyo?"

"No way around that one," Kerrick said. "It went on burst transmission. They know by now that there's been a major security and hull breach."

"Still gives us forty-three minutes before they can get a satellite close enough to do a recon."

"What about the lab hull?"

"I'll take care of that." Tadashi kicked off the wall in a practiced move. All the grace he'd once had in zero-g had come back while in practice sessions at the NASA facilities in Florida.

He caught one of the middle rungs of the ladder leading up to the transport tunnel, worked the latches, and pushed his way through the airlock. The tunnel was eight feet across, housing emergency lights and handholds in three lines.

Thirty feet farther on, the tunnel was blocked by a massive steel door. His helmet light played over it while he read the inscription on it and got his bearings.

Switching from the first set of handholds, he went left, then up to the middle of the tunnel till he found the repair and maintenance hatch. "Lester."

"I'm on my way."

Glancing back, Tadashi saw the man peel loose from the group gathered around the deck hatch and float toward him. Lester carried a long electrical wrench with an adjustable torque. Settling over the repair and maintenance hatch, he worked on the bolts holding the hatch in place. In quick succession, they turned loose and floated away.

Tadashi grabbed the lip of the opening and hauled himself through. The repair and maintenance tunnel ran the length of the *Rinji 8*, providing access to all decks.

He fed a fresh clip into the fléchette pistol, then flipped on his left forearm light as the rest of his team came through the opening. Kerrick remained in the warehouse section, tied in to the computer systems.

"You've got two people in the tunnels with you," Kerrick said. "I picked them up on the space station's internal infrareds."

"How far?" Tadashi moved forward easily.

"A hundred and ten yards. They're closing on your position."

"Who are they?"

"Computer reads their ID chips as maintenance staff."

"Shouldn't be a problem," Tadashi said. "They probably got caught outside when the space station blew."

"Maybe. But this is one of Japan's highest security projects. Chances are, they'll be armed."

Tadashi closed the com-link and motioned one of his men ahead of him. Tense seconds later, they made visual contact with the two *Rinji 8* maintenance men. Ignoring the calls for identification over the space station com-link, Tadashi waved to his lead man.

Rays of light spewed out and tagged both maintenance men. The Orion pulsers with which most of the members of the boarding team were armed were low-grade lasers, but extremely deadly in the right environment. Tadashi killed both men, leaving only charred space suits behind, without harming the space station walls.

At Deck Three, the center deck where the zero-g lab was, Tadashi waved his airlock team into place outside the access hatch. They worked quickly and efficiently to set up a temporary airlock. The yellow dome was framed by aluminum alloy support struts.

"Set," Cydney called out, holding a high-grade construction laser against the inner hull.

"Do it." Tadashi looked away.

The intense flash of power reflected from the outer hull, acting like captured lightning. It would have blinded anyone looking at it.

The atmosphere leaked through the five-inch hole rendered by the industrial laser. Working quickly, Cydney dumped three spherical objects through the opening. When he moved out of the way, a man standing nearby slammed a Qwikseal over the hole as light erupted inside the deck.

"Airlock's up," another man called out. "Standing by to pressurize."

Tadashi floated into the temporary airlock. It barely held his whole crew. "Pressurize," he ordered, "and rip that hatch out of the way."

"Pressurizing." Air hissed into the airlock from the bleed lines the crew had tapped into for Deck Three. The atmosphere mix was colored with red swirls, letting Tadashi know the riot gas that had been dumped into the inner hull had spread. "We're equalized."

A heartbeat later, the access hatch swung away.

Tadashi took a Thunderflash grenade from his belt, pulled the pin, and shoved it through the hatch. Taser darts jumped through immediately after, then the intense flare created by the grenade made the polarized shields of the space suit helmets go dark.

"Go!" Tadashi shoved himself through and toward the top of Deck Three. A man, racked by spasms caused by the riot gas, came at him out of the roiling red fogs. Tadashi shot him twice in the heart. As the man died, his magnetic shoes locked to the steel deck plate and held him standing in place even though his muscle coordination was gone.

A security man with a .308 Netmaster brought the rifle to his shoulder and fired. The nylon weave spread out like a parachute.

Tadashi moved immediately and shouted a warning. The net narrowly missed him, but wrapped up the man trailing him, leaving him floating loose in zero-g. Sweeping his arm, Tadashi picked off the net-gunner before he could ready another round. Tasers weren't a problem, but the net guns were.

The red-dyed riot gas swarmed in the lab area as the vents struggled to expel the invasive chemicals through the make-up air vents. Bumping into one of the manufacturing presses, Tadashi found a handhold and propelled himself farther up, managing to grab the circular catwalk's guardrail.

Two men rushed toward him. Both wore air filters that covered their lower faces. One of them carried a buzzbuster with a handle glowing ruby showing a charge was ready. Still in motion, Tadashi fired and put both of them down. The impact knocked them back and they landed with a solid *clank* against the metal platform.

"This way," Cydney directed, floating down beside him and pushing the dead men out of the way.

Tadashi put a fresh clip in his weapon and followed closely behind. A quick glance around the manufacturing plant showed him that his people were in full control.

"Kerrick," Cydney called over the radio.

"Yes."

The man shook the door lever he held. "The locks on Deck Three are still operational."

"Give me a second."

A moment later, the locks disengaged with loud *snicks* that echoed through Tadashi's suit audio. He trailed Cydney inside and saw the long, lean man lying unconscious on the floor, his mouth and nose covered by a rebreather mask connected to the oxygen filter beside him.

"DiLuca?" Tadashi asked.

Cydney pulled the rebreather mask away and looked at the man's face, grabbing his chin and studying both profiles. He slipped the mask back on. The man was already starting to cough from the riot gas. "Yes."

"Get the computer files," Tadashi ordered. He holstered his fléchette pistol, then reached down and tucked the oxygen filter inside DiLuca's one-piece. Grabbing the unconscious man by one foot, he lifted him easily and shoved him outside into the arms of two men who were waiting. They wasted no time in binding their charge with ordnance tape and pulling him back toward the temporary airlock.

Turning back to Cydney, Tadashi watched the man operate. Where Kerrick was deadly with systems, specializing in crash-and-burn techniques, Cydney understood theoretical technologies. He'd taken his outer gloves off and worked with thin black ones. The riot gas was totally based on absorption through the lungs and wouldn't soak into skin.

"Kerrick," Cydney said, his voice hollow and emotionless, letting Tadashi know he was in full Savant-state, "ready to start downloading."

"Go."

"Transmitting."

"Receiving."

"They're coming batched," Cydney said. "The program is divided up and saved in hidden files. I'm searching the archives. You'll get them in no particular order."

"Understood. Aramis, you're down to seventeen minutes on this mission's window."

"I know," Tadashi said. He was perspiring heavily inside

the space suit.

"It's not all here," Cydney said in a panicked voice. "Something's missing. I can feel it."

Tadashi leaned in closer, trying to make sense of the data flowing across the monitor screen. "What do you mean?"

"Part of the program is missing."

Tadashi didn't doubt his second-in-command. Cydney was a metable with Savant abilities that were incredible. Although he was unable to create computer programs, the man could understand them well enough to work them after being exposed to them once. When he'd worked in the civilian world, Japanese corporations had used him to field-check programs and technology they built. Then one day he'd decided to cross the line and become an industrial spy. Once he'd been found out by an employer, he'd gone to work for the Andoc Family on raiding teams boosting techware from various corporations around the world. Tadashi had won him over to his side, bargaining with Cydney's greed.

Tadashi flashed his forearm light inside Cydney's helmet. The man's eyes were glassed over.

"Can you rebuild the missing program?" Tadashi asked calmly.

"No. The missing program is very integral, unique."

"It's no problem," Tadashi said as much for himself as for the other man. "We'll talk to DiLuca. After a while, he'll be more than happy to help us."

Cydney kept working at the keyboard.

"Five minutes," Kerrick said.

Knowing the man was totally locked-in by the Savant-state, Tadashi reached into the pocket of his suit and took out a readied tranquilizer. He plunged the needle through Cydney's glove into the meat between his thumb and forefinger and pressed. Within seconds, Cydney was out.

Tadashi grabbed the man and pulled him along, knowing they were going to be past the ops window. He paused at the airlock and passed Cydney off to another man, sending them both on. Anchoring himself to the wall with the magnetic shoes, he extended his hands before him. He'd kept his own metability secret for years, and only a few of the upper echelon of Family Andoc knew it.

At first his power had manifested itself as a type of telekinesis—he'd thought. He'd been able to lift metal objects and move them. It was hardly anything to command respect. Then, eight months ago, while representing Family Andoc's interests in a negotiation with heads of Family Nuygen in South Chicago, a FREELancers operation into Nuygen business resulted in a phased-wave explosion that leveled three warehouses.

After making his way free of the wreckage thirteen hours later, he found his power had changed. On the way to the airport for his return flight to Japan, while Chicago police officers searched for him, he'd almost been run down by a car. Unable to move out of the way, he'd instinctively used his metability, lashing out with enough force to lift the car from the street and send it tumbling to the side. Since then, his power had been growing exponentially, and he'd discovered that it was based on magnokinesis.

The lab equipment below represented a threat. He knew for certain that no copies of the program existed in the files. DiLuca had been unrelenting about that. But there was a chance that the Japanese researchers could build on DiLuca's work, undermining the importance of his theft.

Concentrating, he felt the power grow within him, then he lashed out. Green-tinged yellow beams jumped from his hands and smashed into the deck wall opposite him. The wall bulged outward, then for a moment it seemed it might hold. He added more effort. When the wall collapsed, the space station gave another dying shudder, and loose debris was sucked from the massive hole. With a few more calculated bursts, he cleared the manufacturing equipment in twisted and torn lumps that floated through the hole as well.

Finished, he felt weak and giddy. He'd never used that

kind of power before. But he reveled in the fact that he'd done it. The gaping hole that let space into Deck Three was proof that no one could stand against him.

Within seconds, equilibrium had returned to the deck. He pulled his magnetic shoes free and pushed himself into the repair and maintenance tunnel. They were on a very tight schedule, and Grant DiLuca had yet to be questioned.

10

"Are you still alive, monster?"

Still groggy, Refit kept his eyes closed and listened, trying to figure out where he was and what was going on. The feminine voice was taunting and familiar.

"You don't have to play games with me. My medical experts assure me that not only are you alive, but you're awake as well."

Refit opened his eyes, having placed the voice in his memory. "Deadline."

"Mind's like a steel trap," the young woman said sarcastically, "but you've got a face like acid rain."

Saving his breath, Refit checked his surroundings. He was in a medical facility, though he doubted it was a hospital. Machines filled one wall, all festooned with readouts in the forms of gauges, LEDs, and printouts. Tubes and hoses connected him with most of them. The smell of antiseptic and pine filled his nostrils when he breathed in.

In front of him was a bank of windows that he figured for one-way glass. The illumination in the room came from overhead and was kept low.

"Where are you?" he asked.

"Here."

Refit tracked the voice to his right and saw Deadline standing beside his bed arranging cut flowers in an expensive vase that looked antique.

Her real name was Crystal Young, but he knew she preferred to be called Deadline. Dressed in a light blue evening gown with a silver swoosh running from right shoulder to left hip, Young was a beautiful woman. Her skin was light chocolate, the color of café au lait, and her black hair rounded down to the tops of her shoulders. Her red lipstick made her look predatory. Her left eye was covered by a soft blue housing with a microscope extension. The housing extended past her eye and covered her ear as well. A small box at the base of her neck contained the battery pack.

"You got some nerve, lady," Refit said, "calling me a monster when you're Doc Random's own little pet Frankenstein. What rock did you ooze out from under?"

"One big enough to bury you," Young assured him sweetly. "Could have done it already, but I decided not to. I even had my medical staff replace your ruined lung and heart—at considerable cost. Of course, there was no reason to replace the ruined limbs."

"Couldn't resist toying with the food a little longer, huh?" Refit took stock of himself, realizing he had an easier time breathing. But the rest of his body seemed to be in the same shape as before.

Young smiled sweetly and approached him slowly. She laid a palm on his injured hand, then applied pressure.

Refit tried to burst through his bonds, but couldn't. Tight-lipped, he didn't scream out in pain, refusing to give her the satisfaction. It was only meat, and borrowed meat at best.

She leaned toward him, close enough to whisper in his ear. "Sometimes, it's necessary to have live bait in a trap."

Dry Bones Mesa, New Mexico   **_6:53 a.m. MST_**
Rocky Mountain Alliance (RMA) **_1353 Greenwich_**
                                                                   Mean
106.1 degrees W Longitude   **_October 24, 2023_**
35.3 degrees N Latitude   **_Tuesday_**
                Assignment: Project Nighthawk
        Tactical Ops: Public Relations, Recruitment
                 Status Upgrade: Code Yellow

"Tell me about this boy we're going to see," Agatha Greywood said as she drove the lumbering Jeep Cherokee in four-wheel-drive mode over the broken desert floor.

"Didn't you read the file?" Summer Davison asked, shifting in her seat but failing to find a comfortable position.

"Of course." Greywood took time from her driving to give her a suspicious glance. "I am very thorough in my assignments. But hearing it from you might offer some further enlightenment." She was a slim lady in her early sixties with piercing blue eyes. Her prematurely gray hair was done up in a French braid, and despite the heat she wore a long, sweeping dove-gray dress with red piping. Her code name was Golem, and she had a poltergeist metability that allowed her to go into a trance and manipulate objects over a far distance. She was also an artist and found it easier to go "enside" objects she herself had carved, usually stone, clay, or wood creatures that were only vaguely manlike in appearance. While she was "enside" she could only make the possessed objects act in a typical manner: a ball would roll and a legged creature could walk, but a winged creature could not fly, although she'd been able to get some to glide upon occasion. Upon discovering her and learning where her artistic abilities came from, Underhill had blackmailed her into joining the team. When not on assignment for the FREELancers, she had a successful career as a sculptor.

She glanced through the dust-encrusted back window and made certain the other Jeep was still following. About fifty yards back, it surged over a hill and wound after them.

Tall and curvy, with long hair that looked bleached bone-white pulled atop her head, Davison wore a stylish gray-and-red business suit with the skirt cut short enough to take advantage of her long legs. She referred to the FREELancers company colors as "blood and concrete," and preferred a variety when on her own time. As director of public relations for the FREELancers organization, it was her job to make sure whatever bad press that came their way was deflected, deflated, or defeated. To her, metables were hard to control. People like Download, Refit, and some of the others had disabilities that caused them not to want to fit in with the rest of society or would not allow it because of physical deformity. She and Underhill disagreed about that, and so did Refit and Centaur.

"I was at a Native American Association demonstration in Albuquerque seven weeks ago," Davison said. "Daniel Moonstone was arranging a labor strike in response to the hangings of six AmerInd youths on reservation lands. Apparently he had someone inside the inner workings of United Western States Beef Growers Association and knew about a purge UWSBGA was planning against lands the NAA hoped to purchase for res expansion. The boys were hung by Colonel Darrel Barkley of the UWSBGA's Regulator force, and were supposed to be rustlers."

"As I recall, that was never proven."

"No."

"But then," Greywood said as she neatly avoided an armadillo moving across the trail they were following, "enforcing vigilante justice rarely involves anything resembling a court of law."

"There were a number of the NAA who wanted a more direct response to the murders than a labor strike," Davison continued, reaching up for the support bar mounted on the ceiling. The steep incline that would take them near the top of the mesa was rough. "But Moonstone talked them out of it. With the cheap labor pool available on the res, several manufacturers have located, with generous leases, either on Indian lands or near them. Moonstone intended to have the business section of the RMA police itself."

"And that was when his daughter-in-law and grandson were kidnapped."

"Yes. His son died a few years back, and they are the only family Moonstone has. Chasta Sharpnose and her son, Edward, were taken by force from their hotel in Albuquerque. She escaped a few hours later and was found by one of the search parties Moonstone organized. However, her son was still in enemy hands."

"Enter Gitano Proudelk." Greywood managed the bucking 4WD with grace and almost a touch of elegance.

"Yes. He stepped forward with his grandfather and asked Moonstone for one of the boy's personal possessions and two warriors. Then he vanished into the desert and Moonstone would let no one follow. Seven hours later, bloody and battered, Proudelk returned with the boy. Of course, national news coverage got hold of the story and spread it across the nation."

"And the kidnappers?"

"All Regulators that had been released from duty for excessive behavior a few days prior to the NAA protest. They were also the ones who pointed the young Indians out as rustlers to Barkley."

"Convenient."

"Very. The UWSBGA went on to say the Regulators may have made an error and were willing to discuss damages to the families."

"What is Proudelk's metability?"

"His grandfather, Virgil Foxfoot, confirmed the telelocation ability, but nothing else. He's set himself up as Proudelk's agent, more or less, and he's playing his cards close to the vest."

"How does Proudelk feel about the possibility of becoming a FREELancer?"

"I've never really talked with him."

Greywood took her foot from the accelerator and gently tapped the brake. "It seems as if you're about to get your chance."

Ahead of them, on a flat spot on the side of the mesa two hundred feet above the desert floor, an old pickup, faded to an orange-red that almost matched the mesa walls, waited. Two figures squatted in the shade of the wooden racks as the sun spilled over the broken skyline behind them.

"That's them," Davison said. She recognized them both from the Polaroids Foxfoot had FedExed to FREELancer headquarters. She lifted the CB radio's handset. "Charm."

"Yeah," Drake responded. Simon Drake, code-named Charm, was of medium height and well built, with a presence that had won him critical acclaim, under a different name, on the stage in London. His chestnut hair fell into place perfectly, and even though Davison knew part of Drake's effect on her was due to his metability regarding control over the emotions of others, she often caught herself wanting to run her fingers through it. He kept his gray-and-crimson uniform with the FREELancers logo over the heart neatly pressed. His smile was infectious, but often didn't touch his smoky gray eyes.

"We've reached our subject. Stay back and give me room to talk."

"Right."

Davison glanced back over her shoulder and watched as Drake pulled the Jeep over to the side of the narrow road and parked. If Proudelk decided to join the FREELancers, she wanted it to be because of the things the organization had to offer, not because of Drake's empathic meta-nature.

A woman got out on the passenger side of the other Jeep and stood beside Drake. Her code name was Dervish, and she was the only female practitioner of the Islamic combat form known as the Blade of Sirocco. Christened at birth as Karolyn Winters, she never answered to the name. Petite and olive-skinned, possessing features that had never known cosmetics and would never need them, she was in her midtwenties and looked somber but not dangerous. She wore a modified red-and-gray uniform that cloaked her figure to a degree and soft-soled, calf-high leather boots. A wickedly curved scimitar hung down her back, the haft sticking up over her shoulder. A wavy knife fully ten inches long was thrust through a sash at her waist.

The two AmerInd men stood as Davison and Greywood stepped out of the Jeep. The young man was truly handsome, and Davison was already setting up a photo-shoot in her mind as she took in the long hair held back by the yellow bandanna and the taut lines of his broad body.

They exchanged introductions, and Davison was aware of the probing way Proudelk gazed at her. She had to wonder if he was telepathic too.

"My grandson did not know you were coming," Foxfoot said, "so he may not be as prepared to speak of this as you would wish. But I felt if I had given him a choice, we would not be here now."

"I understand," Davison said.

"If I had been given a choice," Proudelk said, "we would not be talking. My home is here. My family. My place is with my people."

"You could be in danger here," Davison said. "And anyone around you. Ever since you rescued Edward Sharpnose, the world has known about you. I'm aware that you've gotten offers from different agencies regarding possible employment. I've confirmed agents from WEBONE and WEBTWO, the CIA, FBI, the Orion Foundation in Mexico City, even the IRS."

The look on Proudelk's face told her he knew nothing of those offers. Davison glanced at Foxfoot.

The old man put his hands in the back pockets of his jeans. "I saw those contracts they were offering, but none of them looked good."

"And you think working with these people will be?" Proudelk demanded.

Foxfoot didn't flinch, met his grandson's gaze evenly. "Yes."

"Why?"

"Because they help people. Maybe they can help you."

"I don't need help."

"Gitano," Davison said.

His head snapped back around to look at her.

"In my opinion, every metable needs help in understanding his or her abilities. Usually these powers come on at strange times, times that are already difficult. Puberty, times of crisis, stress, danger. There're a lot of triggers. FREELancers can help."

"Like your people helped that woman and her family this morning?" Proudelk asked. "She's dead."

"Her family was saved."

"I'm sure she's really glad to know that." Proudelk held up a hand and walked away. "Look, my grandfather made a mistake."

"Grandson!" Foxfoot's voice was rolling thunder against the flat surfaces of the mesa towering above them.

Proudelk turned to face him.

"Since you saved Edward Sharpnose, you knew you could no longer hide. You are different. Your path is going to take you far from everything you've ever known. That's what your vision was trying to show you." Foxfoot paused, then clenched a fist in front of him. "You must not be afraid to journey. Only then will you fulfill your destiny."

Davison didn't know what they were talking about, but it seemed to make an impression on the younger man.

Proudelk looked at her again. "I don't need help understanding these powers. I can figure it out for myself."

"You can make a difference," she said in a soft voice.

"That's the greatest curse a metable has."

"Evidently not everyone feels that way," Proudelk said. "Even down here I listen to stories on the radio talking about how someone with metable powers has robbed a bank, killed someone, or committed any of a dozen other felonies. Texas has a band of metable mercenaries working out of their Independent Operators International. They're more or less legalized assassins."

"FREELancers isn't like that," Davison said.

"It's easy to say that."

"Then come see for yourself. Take a look at the employment contract and benefits we offer, then decide for yourself. If you don't want to work with us, we'll bring you back home."

Proudelk shook his head. "I don't know."

"Look," Davison said, "the number of metables seems to be growing every day, but there are still so few of you that having you working for someone is worth a lot to the right people. Some will try to employ you legally, but others may use whatever means are necessary."

"Grandfather, I want to live my life here. With you."

"I'm an old man, grandson," Foxfoot said. "My days here will not last much longer, then you will have no family. Already some of the people in the town have shunned us because of your powers. Some of them are afraid you can know their minds, and thus whatever secrets they choose to hide."

"That's not true."

"But they do not know this." Foxfoot laid a hand on Proudelk's shoulder. "You have been a good grandson to me, and now I must be a true father to you by letting you go."

"No. There's still much to learn about the Old Ways if I am to be a medicine man like you."

"And you will learn. I am not going away so soon, but I know in my heart there are other things you must learn as well." Foxfoot gently touched Proudelk's brow with his forefinger. "You have had your first vision, but I have had many.

Calling Summer Davison here today was the result of one of
them."

"Then . . . I have no choice," Proudelk said.

The old man shook his head. "No. But you will not go
alone, grandson. Though I've never left this place, the home
of our people, I will go with you now."

Davison worked valiantly not to let her surprise show, but she
wondered what Underhill would think about the arrangement.

Chicago, Illinois   **8:01 a.m. CST**
Great Lakes Authority (GLA) **1401 Greenwich Mean**
87.7 degrees W Longitude   **October 24, 2023**
41.8 degrees N Latitude   **Tuesday**
                    FREELancers Base

"Matrix is on line five," Kent said.

"I'll take it," Lee Won Underhill replied as she poured
boiling water and made more tea. Agent Prime sat on the
other side of her desk, cleaned up and in a new uniform. C4
and Marsha Martini occupied the couch. Jimmy Conrad
leaned against the closed door with his hands in his pockets.
A tattered copy of Robert A. Heinlein's *Red Planet* poked out
of the pocket of his uniform blouse. "What about the media
blitz?"

"The reporters are lined up and waiting downstairs.
They've been told ten minutes."

Underhill glanced at her watch. "If I'm not there, have
Matousak do a general debrief until I arrive. And keep Gibney away from those people until I'm there to referee."

"Right."

Underhill punched up line five as she sat at the desk. The
vid-screen cleared and Matrix's lean features came on. The
woman's eyes still held a distant glaze to them, and the
FREELancers administrator knew she hadn't been long
returned from full Savant-state.

"I've ID'd three of the people who were in the attack on

Broken Goblin," Matrix said without preamble. "Two of them were WEBTWO agents from Seattle who'd been released from the agency."

"They were released?"

"For insubordination or repeat failures. I found them on the intel cybernetic tap we have on WEBTWO's activities. I have a feeling that the third man had been released also."

"What makes you think that?"

"The way his paperwork's being handled at WEBTWO."

Underhill sat back in her chair and sipped tea and thought, working to put the pieces together. "Who was employing them?"

"I checked around the usual places," Matrix replied. "They were listed with IOI in Texas. So were some of the others once I started searching there."

"They were all mercenaries?" Prime asked. His blue eyes hardened.

"That's not confirmed," Matrix responded, "but sixty-three percent of the known participants in this morning's attack have at some time belonged to mercenary groups."

"Where did they get the money to pay Clarice Gibney?" Underhill asked.

"I don't know."

Alarms jangled inside Underhill. "Go back to the Cayman Island accounts and recheck them. Something's not right here. I could see WEBTWO or one of the crime families coming up with eight million dollars to pay Gibney, knowing they would find a buyer for Carter's research later, but not a loose group of independent operators. No way would they have a cash flow like that."

"I'll see what I can turn up," Matrix agreed.

"If you can, follow the money back," Underhill said. "Gibney deposited the cash herself. She had to have gotten it from somewhere inside the United States. There has to be a trail. Update me as soon as you know something." Underhill broke the connection. She looked at Agent Prime. "You know some of the local brokers for street talent."

Prime nodded.

"Take C4 and see what you can turn up."

"Bribery?" Prime asked.

"Within reason," Underhill replied. "Make a draw of whatever you need from petty cash."

"Something more physical?" C4 asked hopefully.

"As needed. Nothing lethal. We're still treading thin ice here as far as the Chicago PD is concerned."

"What about Jimmy and me?" Marsha Martini asked.

"I want the two of you to keep checking the hospitals for Download. He's got to be somewhere."

Martini sat back in the couch and looked dismayed.

"It's important," Underhill said. "As far as we know, he wasn't wounded this morning, but that still doesn't mean he wasn't taken like Refit was." Out of the corner of her eye, she saw Conrad draw a circle in the air with his forefinger. She ignored it. The Tandems might be openly rebellious at times, but they did their work.

She dismissed them, assembled her notes for the press meeting, and got ready to leave. The phone rang. Knowing Kent wouldn't have bothered her unless it was important, she lifted the handset. "Underhill."

"Got a hot one here," Kent said. "Crystal Young. She said you'd want to talk to her."

"Put her on." Underhill took a seat while Kent made the transfer. Crystal Young, Deadline as she preferred to be called these days, had been a member of FREELancers at one time.

President of her own corporation, YoungLife, Inc., she'd been a millionaire by the age of twenty-one. She'd worked on establishing a political affiliation with Mayor Hubbard and on Dr. Rhand's ego to join FREELancers. After enlisting, she'd been outfitted with the Deadliner, a second-generation apparatus created on the understandable principles of the Download device. Where Download's skills came from a disk containing an individual's abilities, the Deadliner used homogenized mock-ups made up through computer programming. The borrowed disk skills weren't as good as those gleaned by Download, and lasted only one hour. Another unforeseen drawback to the Deadliner was Young's addiction to it, though it was never confirmed whether that was a failing of the device or the person.

Upon the threat of forcible reacquisition of the Deadliner, Young had fought then ran away, taking refuge in the security offered by her own companies. A lawsuit had been filed on behalf of FREELancers and Dr. Rhand to get the device back, but Young had managed to mire the hearings down till almost nothing was happening. Underhill had also learned that Young had started getting involved in criminal activities, though nothing had been proven yet.

The vid-screen shifted, sorting out into colored pixels that made up Deadline's face and shoulders. As always, she was strikingly beautiful, working her outfit around the soft blue of the device wrapped around half her head. The background was rich, but not unique enough to stand out in a later search.

"What do you want?" Underhill demanded.

"My, my," Deadline said, "you do seem edgy today."

Underhill made a point of looking at her watch. "I've got fifteen seconds."

"You're not going to try to trace this call?"

Underhill didn't respond. All previous efforts to trace or even record Deadline's calls or threats had resulted in wasted effort.

"Okay, darling, I'll make it short and sweet. I've got your missing Mr. Potato Head, and it's going to cost you to get him back." Deadline leaned forward, put her elbows on the cleared desktop, and smiled. "It's up to you whether you get him back in one piece."

"How do I know you have him?"

Deadline opened her palm. A spark of light jumped from her hand and became a spinning triangle that in turn became a still picture of Refit lying in a hospital bed.

"What do you want?"

"That nasty lawsuit your people have against me in court," Deadline said. "It's coming up on the docket next year. I'd like to see it dropped."

"How do I know he's still alive?"

"You don't have any choice but to trust me."

"I need time."

Deadline leaned back and wrapped her arms around herself. She smiled easily. "Sure. I expect my lawyer to be notified by your lawyer no later than five o'clock today that the motion has been filed to dismiss the lawsuit. Otherwise, I'll mail your jigsaw man back to you over the next few days. *Ciao*."

The vid-screen blanked.

Underhill punched in Kent's number with no real hope. "Tell me you traced that call."

"I'd be lying."

"Dammit." Underhill hung up her phone and headed for the elevator and the media conference she was already late for.

11

Pausing at the back entrance to the stage area of the media reception room, Underhill focused her concentration, then stepped up to the podium. The platform was festooned with microphones. Cameras began flashing at once, gathering speed and intensity. Instinct and experience guided her as she hit her marks. She was dimly aware of Matousak introducing her and stepping out of the limelight.

Between seventy and eighty newspaper, TV, and radio reporters filled the large room, many accompanied by cameramen. They sat in folding metal chairs because those were the rules as handed down by Underhill. Eight guards, uniformed in FREELancer crimson and silver, stood in front of the raised stage area. Wrist-mounted tasers were nearly hidden in the loose folds of the shirt sleeves, and stun batons were tucked out of sight in the specially fitted knee-high boots.

The ceiling was fifteen feet high. There were no windows in the room because Underhill had learned firsthand the dangers of snipers. Instead, portraits of current and past FREE-Lancer agents hung on the walls.

The FREELancers administrator kept her business professional and her words clear so the audio people would have no problem picking her up. Her sentences were short so sound bytes for the various telecasts could be rendered easily. She never spoke at length on anything because that would leave more room for error and misinterpretation—and because her time was worth more spent on operations. Even if one assignment was wrapping up, there were usually a half dozen others in various stages of development.

"I trust Mr. Matousak has brought you up to speed regarding this morning's activities," Underhill said, "so I'll take questions now."

Hands raised in the audience and she selected one. A short, slender woman stood up. "Haley Piper of the *Sun-Times*, Ms. Underhill. I'd like to know why, if FREELancers has a good working relationship with the Chicago Police Department, that no one in that department was contacted regarding the kidnapping of the Gibney family."

"Time was of the essence," Underhill said. "When we were notified of the kidnapping and asked to take part in retrieving the family, I felt calling in the police department would only complicate matters." She pointed to another reporter, a tall bearded man who hadn't seen thirty yet.

"Mark Hardaway," the reporter said, "of Channel 28 Instant News. There were a lot of dead people at that scene this morning. I was there. It sounds pretty complicated to me. How can you be sure the police department wouldn't have been of help?"

"I like your question, Mr. Hardaway. You get a news story either way. If I say that things weren't complicated, you can list the number of people who were killed and make me look like an idiot. However, on the other hand, if I say I am sure the police department would have been no help, you could use that to work in a story about FREELancer-police department rivalry."

The reporter shrugged.

"Let me say this," Underhill suggested, "and you can quote me." She paused, staring straight at him. "This organization has a responsibility to its clients, and to the governments around it. In that order. When I make a decision to act or react in a certain way on a client's behalf, it's because I believe the client will be best served in that way."

"What if you're wrong?" Hardaway persisted.

"FREELancers sells a service, Mr. Hardaway, the same way a lawyer does. A prospective customer will look at a lawyer's record, not expecting him or her to have won every case, but to have won a large percent of them. I stand by this agency's records. If you can find someone providing the same services we do more efficiently, let me know."

A woman in jeans and a white blouse stood. "Martha Trimble, *21st Century Rolling Stone*. Who hired you to rescue the Gibney family?"

"I can't answer that. Next question."

The interview continued for another ten minutes, then Underhill brought John Gibney on stage, deflecting attention from herself while the reporters went for the actual testimony of events that they knew she wouldn't give. For the first few questions, everything went well. Gibney was understandably emotional about the situation. Underhill selected reporters for him, staying away from the ones she knew to be more sensational in their work.

"James Waters, *Time Tele-Magazine*. Do you feel you and your family were adequately protected by the FREELancers agency, Mr. Gibney?"

"Yes," Gibney replied in a broken voice. "They did everything they could to protect us. My wife—Clarice—just wasn't so lucky." He glanced at Underhill for confirmation.

The FREELancers administrator knew that not one reporter

in the room missed the exchange. She stepped up to the podium again, replacing Gibney. "That's all the time we have for questions now."

"Excuse me, Ms. Underhill."

She looked toward the voice and spotted a lithe man in his late thirties getting to his feet in the middle of the crowd. "I don't know you," she said.

He was tall and tan and good-looking. A mop of sandy hair had been bleached by the sun, and a thin stream of freckles tracked across his sunburned nose. He wore an off-white sport jacket over a black turtleneck and black slacks. "Allow me to introduce myself. Skyler Deshane, the new anchor on NTEL-TV News."

"I'm afraid we're out of time, Mr. Deshane."

"I've been holding my hand up since the beginning, Ms. Underhill," the lanky reporter said. "Most of these people you called on, you seem to be on a first-name basis with. I'm the new kid on the block, so you didn't call on me. But tonight's my big night with the station. How's it going to look if all I have to offer our viewers is footage of every other reporter in town working this story but me?"

Beside Underhill's palm, the small monitor read out information on Skyler Deshane. He'd worked for nineteen other television news stations from coast-to-coast, with one assignment in Japan, over the last fourteen years. His experience meant that he could be trouble if he chose.

"Just one question I'd like to ask Mr. Gibney," Deshane said.

Underhill said, "Okay," and stepped back from the podium, letting Gibney move forward again.

"It's pretty simple actually," Deshane said. "I'd like to know what you're planning to do with the million dollars the FREELancers agency had deposited into your account this morning."

Gibney batted his eyes. "I don't understand."

Deshane's eyes widened theatrically. "I thought you knew

about the money Ms. Underhill authorized to be deposited
into your accounts."

Taking Gibney by the arm, Underhill tried to seize control
of the chaos that was sweeping the press room. "This interview is over." She headed for the door.

Reporters surged up at once, yelling questions, only to be
held back by the uniformed guards.

"There's more," Deshane yelled across the noise. The
reporters quieted, turning to him because he might offer
more of the story than Underhill was willing to give.

The FREELancer administrator froze at the door. The first
step in damage control was in knowing how badly an operation was hurt.

"That money came from Iowa State University accounts
that handle Dr. Sherman Carter's research," Deshane said.
"According to my informant, Ms. Underhill paid the university over seven million dollars this morning from a bank in
Miami, Florida. A little over a million dollars of that went in
John Gibney's account. The banks started clearing the monies
at eight o'clock because the Miami bank had worked the
transfer an hour ahead due to the time zones." He glanced at
his watch. "Twenty-two minutes ago. I've already got an
interview scheduled with the vice president who's overseeing
the accounts. Would you care to comment, Ms. Underhill?"

Without another word, Underhill started Gibney through
the exit. Ignoring the reporters who clamored for her attention, the FREELancer administrator closed the door behind
her and faced Gibney in the empty hallway. "We need to
talk."

"The money?" the man asked.

"It's there."

Gibney turned away, pacing a few steps, his hand massag-
ing the back of his neck. He looked at her. "That reporter
back there was right, you know. This sounds like you people
are trying to cover up something."

"The only thing I was trying to hide was Clarice's guilt,"

Underhill said.

"No." Gibney's face reddened. "You told me that this morning, and I believed you. But that was before all this money was involved. If Clarice'd had money, she'd have let me know."

"She didn't." Underhill let the statement hang, frozen between them.

"You're talking like I didn't know my wife at all," Gibney said in a soft voice.

"I don't mean to be hurtful," the FREELancers administrator said, "but maybe you didn't. At least, not who she was at the end."

"How do I know that she wasn't set up? Maybe she was working for you or the university all along and she got caught in the middle."

"You saw the tapes of the interview in my office," Underhill replied.

"Those could have been faked. You were the one who offered to say Clarice wasn't doing anything wrong. You told all those reporters out there that she was helping them out only to save us. But now there's all this money involved. A million dollars. That's too much money."

"Only a fraction of what Clarice got for her spying." Underhill waited, feeling him slip away. He was hurt and confused. He'd trusted his wife, and that trust had nearly cost him and his children their lives. Earlier that morning he'd trusted Underhill, but she'd lied to him, too. "I was going to let you know you about the money later. The university was going to tell you it was part of the insurance benefits your wife had."

"Why would they have done that?"

"I didn't give them a choice," Underhill replied. "If we work together on this, it can still be fixed."

"I don't think so," Gibney said. "Before I do another thing with you people, I'm talking to my lawyer."

"That may complicate things."

"Maybe so," Gibney told her, "but I know for sure that I and my kids haven't done one damn thing wrong in this whole deal. Now the rest of you, I can't say that about." He turned and walked away.

Underhill walked to the small office off the press room. Usually she took a little time to herself to assess how an interview had gone, and to make follow-up plans. Today there was no doubt. Deshane's questions had opened up a carotid artery.

12

Detroit, Michigan   *9:47 a.m. EST*
Japanese Embassy   *1447 Greenwich Mean*
83.1 degrees W Longitude   *October 24, 2023*
42.3 degrees N Latitude   *Tuesday*
Engawa Towers

Masohiro Kinoshita, chief ambassador at the Japanese Embassy in Detroit, sat at a small table on the balcony overlooking the Detroit River. Tall and dark-haired, though some of the hair was beginning to gray, he sat quietly, listening to the British voice on the CD. It was the latest edition of the *Hagakure* made in English, and it was the first he was satisfied with. As customary, he wore a black suit and tie, and his feet were covered by black socks that reached up to his knees. His shoes occupied a corner of the balcony by a miniature Japanese garden.

Ever vigilant about security measures, Kinoshita had ordered the balcony covered with bomb-proof glass when the Japanese had taken legal possession of the Renaissance Center and renamed it nineteen years ago. That way he could enjoy the placid calm offered by the river without risking his life and the Japanese Diet's investment in the embassy.

The door buzzer chirped.

Reaching for the intercom toggle, Kinoshita flipped it and said, "Hai."

"Begging your pardon, Kinoshita-san," a woman's voice said, "but I have something most urgent for you to look at."

"A moment, please." Lithely, despite his forty-five years, Kinoshita rose to his feet and slipped on his shoes. He took the disk from the player and walked into his office.

Where offices in Tokyo remained small and functional, the Diet heads had decided to adopt an air of Western decadence in their embassy. Paneled in dark cherrywood, illuminated through recessed lighting, the office was large and airy. An interior landscape designer came in three times a week to take care of the plants and trees in pots and holders, and along one wall where a person could actually walk beneath trees and on a grassy lawn for ten feet. Birds stayed within the perimeters of the mock-forest, kept there by a wall of subsonics mounted in the floor and ceiling.

The desk was chrome and sandalwood, deep and elaborate. Recessed niches inside the desk held a computer, telephone, monitors that picked up the various security channels, and a host of other spying and defensive devices.

Kinoshita pressed a button that closed off the balcony, polarizing the glass so that no one could see in but he could still see out if he wished. It also cut off the natural sunlight, which was why he'd left it open earlier. Then he hit another button. A security monitor popped up out of the desktop and showed him the hallway in front of his door.

Young and vibrant, clothed in a white kimono with a monarch butterfly design woven into it, Tomiko Ikawa stood at the door.

"Enter," Kinoshita said, punching another button.

At the other end of the room, the door slid sideways and Ikawa walked in. "I hated to disturb you, Kinoshita-san, but this could not wait."

The ambassador waved the comment away. Ikawa had been his personal assistant since he'd accepted the post in Detroit. He knew she would never interrupt him needlessly. "What is it?"

"A message from Yoshio Nishida. He ordered me to relay it at once."

"Do you know what this is about?"

"No," Ikawa said, her face calm and serene, "but I know the JSS was concerned about security measures being breached this morning."

"Where?" Kinoshita knew that Ikawa routinely broke into other operations being conducted by the Japanese intelligence community, as well as ones in the US, Canada, and Mexico. Cut off so far from Tokyo, though living with his homeland's economic pulse under his thumb, the ambassador had learned the value of such illegal activities. Especially since Ikawa showed such adeptness.

"Shoda Orbit."

Lacing his hands behind his back, Kinoshita considered the information. "The space station?"

"*Rinji 8*. Hai."

"What have you learned?"

"Nothing." Ikawa paused. "Or perhaps something after all. Since picking up on this, I have noticed that all communications between the upper management of the JSS have been shut down."

"An accident?"

She shook her head. "I don't think so."

Kinoshita didn't like returning a call to someone like Nishida without at least having something to work with. "Very well. Have a scrambled phone line set up to my office."

"It's ready now."

He handed her the newest CD version of the *Hagakure*. It had been readied on audio for the American workers they used in the outer perimeters of embassy business. Even though Japan had officially purchased Detroit many years ago, it was still wise not to grind that fact into the local populace of

Americans that had chosen to remain within the city limits. Moving them would have been expensive, and they had proved to be a fairly cheap labor pool for the most part, if not overly efficient. "Please forward that to production and get them started on it. I have found it most enjoyable, and it gets across our message to our new employees very effectively."

Ikawa bowed, then left the office.

Taking his seat at the desk, Kinoshita put his call through to Tokyo. He glanced at the clock on the wall above his grandfather's World War II rifle mounted above a Rising Sun flag. In nine more minutes, it would be Wednesday in Japan.

Nishida lifted the phone on the second ring, bringing up the vid at the same time. "Something has come up. We are on a secured line?"

"Of course." Kinoshita was intrigued. Never before had he seen his superior so nervous. Usually Nishida was the epitome of calm-and-collected thinking.

"You know of the *Rinji 8*?"

"Hai."

"It was raided today."

"When?"

Nishida's face was round and heavy, but the hooded eyes were filled with bright intelligence. "One hour ago, as near as we can figure it."

"When did you learn of this?"

"Perhaps twenty minutes ago. Whoever these people were, they managed to knock out our satellite systems for a time. My research people still aren't sure how long we were off-line."

"You're talking about a physical raid, then?" Kinoshita asked. The immensity of such a project was staggering to him. "Not merely through the computers?"

"Hai. Look." The picture of Nishida resolved itself to the lower right corner of the vid-screen. The area left over blinked quickly, then became the familiar shape of the space station.

Only it wasn't the same. Debris floated around it in differing orbits. All five decks spun slowly, great holes ripped in the sides.

"Who did this?" Kinoshita asked.

"We are not certain."

"Was it an inside job?"

"No." The Diet politician acted embarrassed. "At least, not entirely. We believe they might have had one or two people inside the space station aiding them when the strike came."

Kinoshita's mind worked quickly though he let none of that show on his face. If Nishida knew that the space station might have housed traitors, then the man would probably have a good guess as to who had attacked the *Rinji 8*. Now he just needed to know why the man would try to hide those facts from him. "If these people got into space," he said, "they needed a way. Have you talked with Louis Lassiter?"

"A discreet inquiry was made but a few moments ago. He assures us he knows nothing of the attack."

"He's lying. The only other company able to launch a shuttle is Lone Star Space on Matagorda Island in Texas. And they wouldn't get involved with something like this."

"My intelligence people agree with your assessment, but finding the guilty party who provided transportation is something we can worry about at a later date. We need to find the raiding party. Something very important was taken from the space station."

"What?" Kinoshita asked. For all her investigating, Ikawa had never discovered exactly what was being worked on in the space station these past few months.

"I cannot say." The vid-screen blinked, restoring Nishida's picture.

"Then what would you have me do?" the ambassador asked.

"We want you to retain the services of the FREELancers."

Kinoshita sat forward in his chair, totally stunned. The embassy was located within GLA territory, and he'd had dealings with the mercenary group before, but had never hired them. "Surely you can't mean that."

"I do. This isn't just coming from me, Masohiro. These

orders come down from the Diet."

"But how can you maintain security on this operation with the FREELancers involved? Lee Won Underhill is no one's fool."

"All of this has been taken into consideration," Nishida said. "This is what has been decided. There appears to have been some metable abilities used aboard the space station."

"We have our own people who can face such problems. We don't need the FREELancers."

"They have the freedom to move within the American state alliances. Our people do not."

"So you believe these people who attacked the space station will ultimately return to the United States?"

"Masohiro, my friend, as usual you are entirely too perceptive. These things you're asking, I can't go into. As your superior, I'm ordering you to retain the services of the FREELancers—this morning."

"Hai." Kinoshita quelled the rebellious feeling within him. "What will I tell them?"

"You will be briefed on your flight to Chicago."

"When do I leave?"

"One hour." Nishida paused. "Sorry to be so mysterious and bureaucratic with you, old friend, but much is at stake here. When I can, I will tell you all that I know."

Kinoshita bowed his head as the other man switched off the connection. He stood and walked to the polarized balcony windows, thinking hard. If Nishida was sure Underhill and her people would be needed because the perpetrators of the hijacking were bound for America, it was almost certain he knew the identity of the people who had committed the crime.

His first call was to Ikawa, to let her know she, too, would be going to Chicago. She accepted the news stoically, as he knew she would.

His second call was to Boston, to a private number he'd had for years but had never used. The phone light flashed, letting him know the line had been answered.

"Who?" a mechanical voice asked in English.

"Masohiro Kinoshita."

"Wait."

A moment passed. The ambassador's hand grew slick on the phone. He was trapped between the elements and a merciless sea, and he was about to prostrate himself before someone he thought he could trust only because her greed could be measured.

Abruptly, the vid-screen cleared. The woman was breathtakingly beautiful, her hair a deep, burnished bronze that accented her dark skin and Oriental features. Arched brows poised over predatory hazel eyes. Her mouth looked perfect, sculptured by an artist of the erotic. A beauty mark just above the right corner of her upper lip flawed her looks just enough to make them unforgettable. She wore a deep crimson blouse that accentuated her cleavage.

"You've never called me at home before," the woman said.

"No," the ambassador replied. "That should give you some clue as to the gravity of the situation." Behind her, the white wall was absolutely featureless. He didn't know if the phone had been answered in her home office or in her bedroom. The latter summoned up too many images, garnered from all the half-truths he'd heard for years.

Her name was Ruriko Nakeshita. Officially, she was the special assistant to the Japanese consul in Boston. Unofficially, she would be there no matter who held the office. Located in the major developing area of high-tech in Massachusetts, Nakeshita's main source of income was the theft of technology. There was no one she wouldn't bribe, blackmail, steal from, or kill to get what she needed.

Kinoshita usually kept his dealings with her brief, to the point, and at arm's length, never muddying himself with the undercurrent of her business.

"And what can I do for you?" Nakeshita asked.

"What do you know about the *Rinji 8*?"

"It was hijacked this morning, and something of incredible value was taken from it." Interest sparked deep in her eyes. "I felt the shock waves going through Tokyo's intelligence circles and the Yakuza even from here."

"Are the Yakuza involved?"

"I'm not certain. But I do know that Sun Andoc himself is taking an interest in what is happening."

"How did he learn of the attack on the space station?"

"Nishida."

Stone-faced, Kinoshita digested the information. If Andoc knew through Nishida, it meant the Diet official had called the Yakuza warlord first. Anger burned within the ambassador. It was no secret that Yakuza interests sometimes paralleled corporate interests in Tokyo. The Japanese Mafia had found a number of ways to funnel their illicit monies into even more money-making legal investments. Corporate business was only one of the avenues. Evidently they were also now working heavily with at least part of the Japanese government.

Kinoshita was disgusted. Even having Nakeshita on the payroll of the Liberal Democratic Party in Japan went against his code of Bushido.

"Were you just checking to see if I was up on current events," Nakeshita asked, "or is this conversation going somewhere? Time is money."

"I want you to look into this," Kinoshita said. "For me. I'll pay you for whatever information you turn up."

"They've got you working in the blind." Nakeshita smiled, and it wasn't a pleasant sight. "Ambassador, I intend to try to make this situation pay off for me in any way that I can. If I can make some money from you while doing that, I'll be glad to."

Kinoshita nodded and she switched off, leaving him with a dial tone and many dark thoughts.

13

Japanese Space Shuttle Kimiko   *9:18 a.m. CST*
Free Space   *1518 Greenwich Mean*
21,119.61 miles out   *October 24, 2023*
Present position: Over Australia   *Tuesday*

"Give me a minute and maybe I can figure out where he sent the missing programming."

Aramis Tadashi watched Kerrick sort through the files they'd recovered on her notebook deck. Screen after screen of unintelligible code strings flashed by without him understanding any of it.

"Maybe," Saito said in a thick voice that was accented from his long stay in the Philippines, "we could cut off a few of this guy's fingers. Let him know we're serious about getting the stuff we're after." He brandished a thick-bladed hunting knife. Of the special group Tadashi had gathered for the mission, Saito was the most bloodthirsty. "How many fingers is he going to need to do what we want him to do?"

"One," Tadashi answered. He glanced at their prisoner.

Grant DiLuca swallowed hard and tried to curl into a fetal position in the chair they'd tied him to. He was still slightly sluggish from the Para-bullets and the stimulants they'd used to bring him around. Still, he'd managed to hang on to the secret location of the missing programming.

"Want me to get started?" Saito asked, examining his blade.

Tadashi let the threat hang in the air for a time, then shook his head. "Not yet. I don't want him going into shock and dying. We may need him."

Turning away from the man, Tadashi watched space roll by in the three monitors. He fully understood DiLuca's reluctance to speak. The man knew that if he said too much, gave away all his knowledge easily—even if it cost a few fingers—his captors would shove him through the airlock. It was also possible that DiLuca was holding out in the hopes the Japanese corporation he worked for would come looking for him.

Tadashi figured he would have let someone cut every one of his fingers off as long as he had the hope of being rescued. Bionic hands didn't quite compare with the real thing yet, but it beat the hell out of being dead.

"You did well," Tadashi said, taking the knife from Saito and slashing through the ropes that bound DiLuca.

The man looked at him suspiciously.

"By hiding your research," Tadashi went on, "you made this a more profitable venture than I'd at first presumed."

"Who are you?" DiLuca asked.

"Aramis Tadashi." He chuckled with honest mirth at the frightened look that flitted through the research scientist's eyes. "You've been reading too many cop stories. Just because you know who your kidnapper is doesn't mean you're going to be killed. Other people who will know who I am after today will be much more dangerous than the authorities."

"Do you even know what you've got?" DiLuca asked.

Tadashi crossed one knee over the other. "In my background check on you and your program, I was told this could be the single most important discovery of this century." He turned a hand palm up. "As we've only just started this century, I thought that was most impressive."

"You haven't got a clue," DiLuca said in a quiet, amazed voice.

Reacting automatically, Tadashi reached inside himself for the growing metability. Yellow rays darted from his right hand and touched DiLuca's space suit. Tadashi felt the metal of the suit give only slight resistance as he flexed his power.

Without the benefit of gravity, DiLuca moved easily, tossed like a leaf in a whirlwind across the small expanse of the cabin. The scientist slammed up against the bulkhead opposite Tadashi, held by the metal fittings and reinforcements of his suit.

"Don't annoy me, insect," Tadashi threatened, "or I'll crush you." He clenched his fist, unleashing more of the power that coursed within him. After destroying the space station, he'd guessed that he would have been exhausted for hours. But the metability was growing, strengthening like a muscle each time he used it. The rays turned greenish, and the metal collar of DiLuca's space suit suddenly started closing like a noose.

The scientist hooked his hands inside the collar but couldn't stop the inexorable crush of metal. "Don't, please. I beg you."

Tadashi cut off the flow of power.

DiLuca crumpled into a ball, hanging in midair because there was no gravity.

"Make no mistake," Tadashi promised. "When the time comes and I get irritated with your behavior, you're going to die very painfully. If my people can't find that programming within the next hour, we're going to find out how tough you really are." He turned away from the man.

Cydney glanced up from the communications board. "The JSS knows about the *Rinji 8*."

Glancing at the clock mounted above the control boards, Tadashi said, "And us?"

"They can't find us. Lassiter's holding up his end of the bargain."

"Nishida?"

"He's contacted Kinoshita as we expected."

"Good." Tadashi leaned back in his chair. The pieces were all falling into place. All he needed was the missing programming.

"I know where it is," Kerrick announced. "He's been storing it in an earthside deck using burst transmissions." She looked up at him, her hands still flying across the keyboard.

Tadashi considered that. "Why wouldn't Yukiko Corporation catch it?"

"The transmissions were a carefully disguised WalterBee reversed foolie virus," Kerrick said. "Very hard to create and sustain. With all the code strands involved in the transmissions, I can see how a normal security-sysops would have missed it. On the surface, DiLuca was playing a multilevel role-playing game with an earthside player. But underneath, he was using the other player's deck as a storage space for his programming."

"How did you catch it?"

She smiled at him. "Because you pay me to be more than a normal security-sysops. And I've had some practice hiding things myself."

"Where is the programming?"

"In the deck of Matthew DiLuca."

"Who's he?"

"Our guy's twelve-year old nephew."

"And he has the heart and soul of the Fusuma Project and doesn't know it?" Tadashi asked.

Kerrick nodded.

"Don't hurt him," DiLuca cried out. "Hey, he's just a kid. He has no idea what's going on."

Tadashi exerted just enough power to make the space suit's metal collar quiver. DiLuca shut up. "Where is the boy?"

DiLuca shook his head. "Kill me if you want to."

"Kerrick?" Tadashi asked.

The sysop's fingers flashed across her keyboard. "According to the Social Security Administration, the number I found on the burst transmissions belongs to a Matthew Voight DiLuca. I also ran the number through Internal Revenue records and it turned up on the returns for Spencer Ford DiLuca. Accessing the Federal Census Bureau records, I found out that the two names belong to father and son. The last seven years the IRS returns were all mailed from the same address in Chicago, Illinois. Before that, they were from East St. Louis, Cape Girardeau, Taylorville, and Mount Vernon, all within the state of Illinois."

"What's the address?" Tadashi asked, turning to look at the scientist.

When Kerrick gave it, DiLuca paled.

A glow of triumph swelled within Tadashi as he switched his attention to Cydney. "We have people in Chicago. Have them find the boy."

Cydney nodded.

"How soon before reentry is possible?"

Consulting her computer, Kerrick said, "The soonest opening in Lassiter's network is in four hours. If we miss that window, it'll be another eleven hours."

"See that we don't miss it."

Kerrick moved the computer out of the way and took over the shuttle's manual controls. "There's something else you might be interested in." She flipped a switch, and the forward monitor flashed to a special bulletin on NTEL-TV with Skyler Deshane.

The reporter pulled no punches, and accusation against FREELancers in the matter of Clarice Gibney and Dr. Sherman Carter and Iowa State University dripped from every word. The story was as damning as Tadashi had arranged and paid for it to be.

Chicago, Illinois   **9:58 a.m. CST**
Assignment: Styxman
Tactical Ops: Soft Probe, Intel Recon
Status: Code Yellow

"His name's Addison Bysse," Agent Prime said as he got out of the dark blue armored sedan in front of the Chicago

Board of Trade Towers, locked the doors, and set the alarm. "When we find him, let me do the talking."

C4 gave him a glare. "Maybe I should stay in the car."

Prime shrugged. "Your choice, sheila. I'd prefer to solo on this anyway." He was dressed in black Dockers, a maroon chambray work shirt with a skinny black tie, British Knights, and an Australian outback jacket.

C4's smile was edged ice. She got out of the car and closed the door firmly. "In that case, I have to go. I want to see how a big-time professional like you works." Dressed in a white mini-dress and wearing white knee-high boots that contrasted sharply with her dark skin, she was already turning heads along West Jackson Boulevard. Blue-lensed sunglasses covered her eyes. She adjusted the small purse at her side.

"Bysse knows me," Prime said. "He'll be suspicious of you."

She gave a brief wiggle. "Think he'll have his bodyguards frisk me? That could be interesting."

"Don't cross me, sheila," Prime said in a cold voice. He turned away before she could say anything. Privy to all the members' background checks before admittance to FREE-Lancers, he was aware that C4 had once been street talent herself, the same kind of product that Addison Bysse manipulated all over the globe.

Her name had been Giselle Kesselring in those pre-agency days. Even then she'd never been much of a joiner, working for German counterterrorist response groups only by clearly defined contract. Much of her past was murky, but she'd never been tied to anything that didn't pass Underhill's scrutiny.

Prime's own beginnings had held another name as well. His official ID still listed him as Thadeus Johnson, but he never used it. Even his work at FREELancers was strictly cash-and-carry. He left no paper trails where he could help it. There were too many people, even from his CIA days and the international bounty hunter days after, who would kill him if they got the chance. His strength and his curse was that he was a believer in political ideals and dreams. And as he saw it, the United States was still the last bastion of those—even in its weakened condition.

Someone like C4 flew in the face of that.

"What is it exactly that you don't like about me?" C4 asked as they ascended the steps leading into the Chicago Board of Trade.

Prime gazed up at the statue of Ceres, goddess of grain, that looked down from the forty-fifth floor. "You can be bought and sold."

"Look who's calling the kettle black," the young woman said. "As I remember, you had your share of mercenary action back in your salad days."

Ignoring the jibe about his age, Prime opened the glass doors and passed through, heading for the fire stairs. "Check up on your history, sheila. You'll find that the operations that are listed as *maybe* being my work were always in the name of freedom. I took down war criminals, deposed tyrants living on the money they raped from their countries before fleeing, and international terrorists responsible for the deaths of innocent people."

"Kind of hard to miss the guys you took out with those red-fletched crossbow bolts." She followed him up the narrow steps in the dimly lighted shaft.

Prime didn't answer.

"Underhill sells FREELancers talents," C4 said.

"With judicious prejudice."

"Some of the folks at Langley and the Pentagon might not agree with your assessment. She's tangled with the CIA and military intelligence, and gone against what the American government has viewed as its best interests at times."

"Underhill has always contracted out for what's right."

"That's either the voice of a dyed-in-the-wool fanatic, or you and the Dragon Lady have something going on the side."

Pausing at the top of the stairs, Prime wheeled on the young woman. He controlled his anger because he refused to be anything less than professional on an assignment. But he fully intended to draw the parameters on the relationship and the open speculation. "I'm about to face down a guy who may have some information about the Broken Goblin fiasco. Now, either we stick to business or you get the hell out. Which is it going to be?"

"That holier-than-thou attitude really sucks." C4 was totally cool.

"Deal with it, or deal yourself out."

"I'm in." Her dark eyes glowed with anger.

Prime moved up the steps to the fifth-floor landing, then through the double doors opening on to the trading floor. Below, traders in ten different pit areas were shouting and gesturing, waving slips of paper as crowds of men and women in business suits yelled out orders to buy or sell stocks and futures.

Thirty feet away, at a private table, Prime found his man. Bysse sat between a pair of bodyguards who looked bored by the proceedings but alert just the same. As he approached Bysse, Prime knew the two men were carrying concealed weapons just by the way they held themselves. The tailoring of their suits was flawless.

Suave and debonair, Bysse would have given Simon Drake's clotheshorse tendencies a run for their money. He wore a dark charcoal suit and a peach ascot at his throat. His blond hair was pulled back in a severe ponytail. His freshly shaven jaws gleamed but held a blue sheen, joining with the dimpled cheeks to give him a predatory look. A thin blade of a nose dripped down from the dark brows that joined between his eyes. A notebook computer was open on the table in front of him beside a scratch pad and pencil.

At Prime's direct approach, the two bodyguards got up. The crowd around them barely noticed, most of them gazing hungrily at the big board running in front of them carrying the present stock and future quotes.

"We need to talk," Prime said.

Bysse gave him a passing glance. "My dear friend, the Major, how nice to see you. This is absolutely the worst time to chat."

Prime didn't break his stride. "Not the worst. Not yet."

One of the bodyguards reached for the FREELancer agent, his lead hand palm-forward while he reached beneath his jacket with the other.

With seductive ease, Prime grabbed the lead hand, bent it backward till something snapped, and fisted the man's jacket and shirt tightly together so he couldn't pull his weapon. He stepped to the side, taking the man with him to use as a shield from the other guard.

"Call them off, Addison," Prime ordered. "Or else you're going to be paying out some enormous bennies over the next few months while these guys heal up."

An irritated look crossed Bysse's face. He snapped his fingers at the guards. Instantly they separated and pulled away.

"Next time we meet," said the one whose hand Prime had broken, "I'll know you."

"You're a real buttercup, mate." Prime moved past the bodyguard without another thought. He knew what kind of men Bysse employed, and they were always ones the man could get total obedience from. The FREELancer agent dropped into a chair near Bysse so he could look at the notebook computer's screen. "Shilling for the insider traders?"

"Paying the bills," Bysse said without rancor.

"Really? For what year?"

Bysse laced his hands over the coffee cup before him and turned his attention to Prime. "Surely you didn't come here to denigrate how I make my income."

"No." Prime leaned forward. "I came here to talk about some ex-WEBTWO agents who turned up dead and in police custody this morning."

"I'm afraid I don't know what you're talking about." A phone rang, and Bysse reached under his jacket and pulled out a handset. "Do you mind?"

Prime turned over a hand.

Twisting away slightly, Bysse talked rapidly, then ended the conversation. "Sorry. That fellow's very nervous at the moment. Though not without cause."

His voice flat, Prime said, "The Gibney snatch."

"I know only what I see on the news." Bysse sipped his coffee, and went back to watching the big board as the stocks and quotes flowed by in neon colors.

"That's not what I was told."

Bysse's gaze was cold. "Then you were told wrong." He pointed at C4. "Who's your date?"

Kesselring came over, offering her hand. Her smile was bright and cheerful, and Prime thought it belonged on an alligator's snout an instant before biting off a man's arm.

"Giselle," she said as Bysse rose and took her hand.

His heels clicked together in European fashion. His eyes never left hers. "Enchanted," he said.

"You should be." She sat in the proffered chair, crossing her legs with enough care to draw attention to the action.

"And what is your relationship to our friend?" Bysse asked, sitting down.

"I'm his partner."

A magnanimous smile lit Bysse's face. "Surely you jest. You seem much too delicate."

She leaned forward conspiratorially. "I'm not."

Bysse laughed.

"Tell me about the ex-agents for WEBTWO," Prime suggested.

"Sworn to secrecy, I'm afraid." Bysse checked the board, obviously enjoying himself. "And don't think your Neanderthal behavior is going to work in here. Their security these days is tighter than a spinster's sphincter." He glanced at C4. "Excuse my language."

"You'll leave here soon," Prime said. "The Board of Trade closes at one."

"I'll be picked up by enough men to make you think twice

about coming after me," Bysse promised.

"I think I could manage to kill you."

"And ruin your agency's reputation?" Bysse shook his head. "No, I'm too small a fish for you to run that risk. FREE-Lancers already has enough trouble on its plate."

"My partner asked you a question," C4 said. "I suggest you answer him."

"Sorry, darling, I didn't figure you for the crude mentality too." Bysse appeared unmoved, leaning back in his chair and lacing his hands together over a knee.

"I want to show you something." C4 reached for his drink. Taking it in one hand, she dipped the forefinger of her other hand into it, then drew a streak on the tablecloth.

Bysse looked at the wet stripe with mock interest. "You read tea leaves as well?"

"Much better than that." C4 snapped her fingers and an orange-and-yellow bolt spit from her finger and touched the wet streak. A small explosion erupted in the tablecloth fabric, scattering flames in a foot-wide diameter.

Reacting quickly, cursing with flair and fluency, Bysse recoiled in his chair.

Flipping her wrist, C4 dumped the rest of the drink over Bysse. The man mopped at it frantically, but the liquid only soaked more steadily into his clothes. Hands beneath their jackets, the bodyguards glared at Prime.

The FREELancer agent had the butt of his own Sig-Sauer P-226 9mm in his palm, out of sight under the jacket.

"That was just a drop," C4 said with a malicious grin. "Care to imagine what I can do with a whole drink?"

Bysse waved the bodyguards away with a shaking hand. His eyes were black holes of fear. "What do you want to know?"

Prime leaned forward, never releasing the pistol, grateful for the Kevlar lining of the jacket. "You worked the delivery on the WEBTWO agents. I turned that up from Redfield less than an hour ago. You tagged him for the vehicle registration and the false IDs here in Chicago for the kidnap team."

"Redfield sold me out?" Bysse asked, unbelieving.

"Man was born with a price tag," Prime replied. "Tell me your part of it."

Unable to help himself, Bysse continued watching the action on the big board. "Simple handler action. I got the team entrenched, acted as go-between, doled out the money, and took my cut."

"Who hired you?"

"I don't know."

Prime let his features grow harder.

"Hey," Bysse said, "it's the truth. The operation was jobbed through a blank wall. Picked up e-mail on my private drop on a computer service I use on the information highway."

"You worked this blind? That's not something you'd usually be interested in."

"Didn't have a choice," Bysse replied. "Some investments I had in Tokyo went sour. I had a cash-flow problem, a damn arterial leak. This job came along at the right time, and the people behind it seemed to know me inside and out. The pieces were all there. All I had to do was put it together. Seemed like an easy piece of change. But I wasn't told the FREELancers would be involved."

"Give me something."

"I can't." Bysse held his hands helplessly away from his body.

"You always walk away with something sweet," Prime said. "In case a bit of blackmail will come in handy later."

Bysse started to shake his head, then saw C4 hold her fingertips only a few inches apart and send flirting bursts of orange-and-yellow energy sliding back and forth. "Maybe I have something." He cleared his throat. "I talked to some of the WEBTWO guys and found out they were recruited by someone still with that organization."

"An inside recruitment job?"

"Yeah. But the contract on the Gibney woman came from

outside and not within WEBTWO. I managed to find that out too."

"Who put out the contract?"

"Never found out."

"How come?"

"Man I was using to shadow the WEBTWO guy turned up in an alley a couple days later. Icepick through his brain. I left the situation the hell alone. By that time I had some of my money and knew I wasn't going to be touched by the operation." Bysse paused. "Until Redfield gave me up."

"Who's the WEBTWO guy?" Prime asked.

"That's mine," Bysse said.

"Not now," Prime replied. "Now it's mine."

Abruptly Bysse's attention riveted on the big board. His eyes tracked a stock. Without looking he took his phone from under his jacket and punched in a number.

Prime closed a fist over the phone and kept the man from dialing.

"Don't queer this," Bysse pleaded. "I need the money."

"The name," Prime prompted, keeping his fist tightly closed.

"Damn you!" Bysse swore with feeling. "You don't bring this guy down, he's going to want my ass. He'll know I gave him up."

"Tough."

Trading in the pits had reached a frenzy. Bysse's eyes burned. "Nix. Greg Nix."

"With WEBTWO in Seattle?" Prime asked.

"Yes. He's in a command position there. Interpol and the CIA have jackets on him."

Prime released the phone and Bysse made his call, talking hurriedly. When the man finished, the FREELancers agent said, "I don't want to have this chat with you again. If you haven't given me the straight skinny on this deal, I'll come back and bury you."

Gathering his personal effects, Bysse said, "After today, I'm taking my shadow off the ground. You muck up the deal with the WEBTWO double agent, I'm a dead man. I'll wait and see how the gunfight goes. From a distance."

Prime got up slowly, his hand on his pistol, and made eye contact with the bodyguards as he threaded his way through the crowd and walked toward the door to the stairwell. C4 was at his heels.

"He talked because of me," she said, excitement in her voice. "He talked because he knew I'd light him up like a match."

"I know," Prime said.

She drew even with him, matching him stride for stride as they went down the stairs. "You might want to keep that in mind the next time you feel like unloading on me."

"A threat like that," Prime said with a cruel smile, "makes me itchy. But if I had to, I'd take you out before you had time to fizzle. Bank on it."

14

Clad only in her bra and panties, Ruriko Nakeshita admired her lithe body in the full-length mirror that filled one wall of one of the walk-in closets of her penthouse manor. Olive skin glowed richly, showing its suppleness and some muscle definition without losing the feminine charms. At five foot even, she'd never let her weight get into triple figures. She had her long bronze hair piled atop her head and bound with a metallic gold scarf embossed with pearls.

She rummaged through the dresses, choosing a white one with puffy shoulders that hung to a sexy distance just above her knees, and a metallic gold one that would hug her curvaceous figure like a second skin, reveal an ample amount of her prosthetically enhanced cleavage, and end an erotic distance just below her crotch. A business suit, though she had plenty of those as well, was out of the question.

Lunch today was with an up-and-coming young vice president for Digital Magick, Inc. who was privy to the inner workings of proto-software being designed for virtual reality surgeries. It was supposed to revolutionize the medical industry, turning a doctor and his team into a hive mind while an operation was going on.

If she could get her hands on copies of the proto-software still in development and testing, four medical research groups were standing in line to pay her for them. Each one, of course, thought they were the only black market resource Nakeshita was dealing with. She intended to sell to all of them. Techware only had a resale value if the person buying it thought they were the only ones getting it. Once it was out in the public domain, it lost a lot of worth.

It was going to be a very profitable score on her part. Of course, the Japanese companies she was responsible to would get the information as well, though at least a week or two behind the others. It would be enough to keep them on the cutting edge of medical technology. She smiled at her joke.

The phone rang while she was holding the two dresses up against her and looking into the mirror. She settled the headset in place, kicking on the scrambler automatically. "Nakeshita."

"I have something that might interest you regarding the *Rinji 8*," a woman's voice said.

Nakeshita's mind raced. She had more than a dozen capers going on at the moment. She locked in on the space station and Kinoshita's call earlier. "Yes."

"A JSS emergency shuttle team has docked with the wreckage of the space station."

"What have they found?"

"Eight of the crewmen are missing, as well as the research scientist, Dr. Grant DiLuca."

"Interesting," Nakeshita said, considering the two dresses further. "See what you can find out about the crewmen."

"I'm working on that. I figure they were bought off by

whoever planned the strike on the *Rinji 8.*"

"Good girl. I see I've taught you well. What about DiLuca?"

"I've got a file on him."

"His parents?"

"Both living in Alton, Illinois. Retired."

"His contact with them?"

"Minimal. Apparently he didn't get along well with his father."

"Keep them on the active file. Is he married?"

"No."

Nakeshita knew from experience that men tended to tell women more about things if they didn't expect the woman to understand what they were talking about. Being the wife of a research scientist would have made Mrs. Grant DiLuca a prime candidate for a sympathetic but skilled interrogation. Nakeshita had a number of reporters on her payroll that could have done the job. "Girlfriends?"

"No. He was stationed in Tokyo before going to the space station. There were a number of women in various escort services."

"Anyone special?" Nakeshita also knew that no one, especially a man, was an island. Men liked to brag of their conquests at some point.

"No."

"Friends?"

"His communications from Yukiko Corporation were monitored."

"He would have known that," Nakeshita said.

"He did. And his communications from public phone booths and over computer BBSs were monitored as well. From what I have seen in the files, there's no one he was particularly close to. Except for his brother's son."

"Tell me about that."

The informant did, mentioning that DiLuca had gotten a special provision to talk to the boy even from the space station at Yukiko Corporation's expense.

"Obviously, he is quite fond of this boy," Nakeshita said when the other woman had finished. "Do you know where he is?"

"Springfield, Illinois. I took the liberty of having an agent talk to the DiLuca family's neighbors in Chicago. Apparently the boy is a fan of the FREELancers and has gone to a telethon featuring three of them."

"Get someone down there," Nakeshita said, "and find this boy. When DiLuca turns up, and I feel that he will, his nephew will make a good bargaining chip."

"It's done."

"Good."

"However, there's something else you need to know."

"What?" Nakeshita asked.

"The Yakuza are scrambling around this situation as well. Sun Andoc continues to show a personal interest. The Yakuza invested heavily with Yukiko Corporation to develop DiLuca's research."

Nakeshita thought about that. It wasn't unusual for the Japanese Mafia to take part in Japanese business. Crime paid handsomely and steadily, but didn't always allow for power in the political arenas for someone who loved the limelight. "I'll look into it. In the meantime, find this boy."

"What do you want us to do with him?"

"Take him into custody with as little fuss as possible." Nakeshita broke the connection, feeling the adrenaline kick in as she contemplated the intrigue presented by the *Rinji 8*. She loved secrets, not so much having ones of her own, but stealing away the ones of others.

She took a last look at the dresses, then chose the gold one. The Digital Magick, Inc. vice president was young. His glands would eventually rule his ability to think linearly, and his youthful confidence about his own prowess would become a challenge he wouldn't be able to resist. With this dress on, she thought today might be the day.

Chicago, Illinois 10:13 a.m. CST

"Aren't you going to call in and tell Underhill what you found out?"

Agent Prime steered the sedan to the side of the road by a chicken take-out place, then turned his attention to C4. "Sure. But I have to make a phone call first. Wait here." He got out of the car before she could reply.

The city had turned muggy again, warming up and turning the early morning rain into a heavy humidity. Prime stepped through the crowded street as office workers with staggered shifts went about their day's work. A bike messenger, his breathing labored, narrowly avoided him, the rubber tires whickering through the pooled water on the sidewalk.

He knew Underhill would give him hell for what he was about to do. But whether the lady admitted it or not, the agency was at war with someone. He'd listened to the news in the car, heard about the money lifted from the Caymans, and learned how bad it looked for Underhill.

A pay phone was hooked into a graffiti-covered wall. He dropped money into it, checked a Rolodex built into his watch, and punched in a number. He didn't worry about losing the watch and the confidential data it contained. It was built with a special computer link that identified his DNA. Once the watch was removed, it would explode within three minutes. If necessary, it could also be used as a grenade.

Out on the street, a trio of MAPS units moved like stiff-legged giants as they set up a cordon around an apartment building. Before they could get the crowd back, a half dozen laser bursts lanced out from the structure, scoring on the bystanders and dropping them in their tracks. One of the MAPS had an illegal camcorder fastened to its head, and Prime knew one of the news stations had paid big bucks for the service. In the minute it took him to make the call, two of the MAPS units invaded the lobby of the apartment building and came out with at least ten white-sheeted KKK members held at gunpoint.

"Riley Airlines," a smooth voice answered.

"I need to speak to Jean-Paul D'Arnot," Prime said, giving the French name the correct pronunciation.

"Who should I say is calling?"

"Reaper."

"Wait one moment."

Prime listened to the old-time canned music, grimacing as he recognized the twentieth-century schmaltz of Barry Manilow. A moment later, the switchboard operator came back on.

"Mr. D'Arnot would like to know if he can call you back."

"Sure." Prime read off the number of the pay phone, knowing the WEBTWO section chief would want to talk over a scrambled line. "How long before I hear from him?"

"Perhaps as much as three minutes."

Prime thanked him and hung up. He watched C4 get out of the car, walk to the chicken take-out place, order, then sit at one of the outside picnic tables. With the action going on across the street, the take-out place's business was standing-room-only. By the time the phone rang again, C4 had already been propositioned by street youths who looked as if they had just crawled off morgue tables and been dressed by a voodoo priestess. C4 seemed to enjoy teasing them.

Lifting the handset on the first ring, Prime said, "Reaper."

"I haven't talked to you in a long time," Maxwell Robeson said. His voice was low and full.

"Different sides of the fence," Prime replied.

"Same work."

"Maybe to you."

Robeson chuckled. "Always the idealist. Haven't you noticed how that's always gotten you in trouble over the years?"

"It's what's kept me going when nothing else has made sense."

"There's more money and bennies in taking things away from people than in hiring on to make sure they keep what's theirs," Robeson said. "Ask me how I know."

"You've got a guy in your organization who's moonlight-ing," Prime said.

"You think so?"

"Yeah. The Gibney situation here in Chicago?"

"I'm familiar with it." Robeson sounded cautious.

"Three guys who were once WEBTWO agents turned up dead this morning."

"That didn't make the news."

"Underhill chose to sit on it as far as the media is con-cerned. She saw no reason to start slinging mud."

"Mighty white of her," Robeson said. "But it appears she's about to get burned on the deal anyway."

"Remains to be seen. In the meantime, your organization has a hole."

"This is where I'm supposed to ask you what you want in exchange for the names?"

Prime shifted, cupping the phone on his shoulder. "I'm going to check with Underhill and see if we can work a deal."

"I'm supposed to wait after you drop a bombshell like that on me?"

"No. What I'm going to propose to her is that we give you the names and faces we have from the operation this morning, and you give us the files on those people."

"No way are you getting everything in those files."

"Don't want it," Prime said. "If this was a WEBTWO operation, we'd know it by now."

Robeson didn't say anything.

"Your organization had tabs kept on them after they went their own way."

"To an extent. If they really went to work for someone else, we may have missed it."

"I'll call you this afternoon. Underhill may not want to deal. The last thing she needs is to be caught getting into bed with WEBTWO on anything. Then it'll look like she set everyone up."

"True."

"In the meantime, let me give you what I have."

"Why?"

"I can't do anything with it, and if these people are going to be this messy, someone needs to get them off the street. And because I'll know that you know you owe me one."

"Okay."

"The ex-WEBTWO agents here in Chicago were handled by Addison Bysse. I believe you know him."

"Yeah. You're sure about this?"

"Take it to the bank."

"I'll do that. Call me this afternoon."

"Done," Prime said and broke the connection. The pieces were still moving around out there on the unseen battlefield. But now he was moving some of them as well. It would be interesting to see what took shape.

Chicago, Illinois   10:31 a.m. CST

"Where are we?" Download asked, peering down the building corridor in both directions.

"My apartment," Eden Frisco answered inside his head. She used his hands, taking a credit card out of his pocket and slipping it between the door lock and the jamb.

Download watched his hands with interest. He'd almost gotten used to someone else using them. In a way, it felt nice not to have to take responsibility for his actions. He felt as if he were cocooned inside his own brain.

"Place went condo nine months after we moved in." Frisco said. "Only way we could stay was to sign a purchase agreement. We weren't in any shape to go apartment hunting, and at the time it seemed the right thing to do."

"Your husband might have sold it after you were killed." Download felt the woman's thoughts touch his, cold and alien.

"You ever try to sell an apartment in this part of town?"

"No."

"Well, it's damn near impossible."

Out of the corner of his eye, Download saw an elderly woman going into an apartment four doors down. The woman froze, studying him. "We've got company."

"It's Mrs. Palumbo." Frisco used his hand to wave at her, and his lips twisted into a smile.

"She could be a problem," Download said.

"No way. I've known her for ten years."

"You don't exactly look like yourself today."

"Oh, yeah."

During the last hour, Download had really started getting worried. No matter how hard he tried, he couldn't take back control of his body. That had never happened before. And he'd started to feel the Eden personality fade. If the personality slipped away while he was out of control of his body, he had to wonder if the experience would leave him paralyzed.

The lock clicked in Frisco's hands. "Got it," she said triumphantly. She pushed open the door and went inside.

The living room was tastefully decorated in pastels. Green plants occupied every available space. Download followed Frisco inside his brain as she walked his body around the room. He felt her confusion.

"Are you okay?" he asked.

"It's different," she whispered in his voice. "The same, but it's different."

"Maybe your husband did sell it," Download suggested. They walked into the kitchen where the main motif seemed to be mushrooms as canisters, on hand towels, and preserved in crystals that hung from the ceiling as a mobile.

"No. That's my husband." She pointed to a picture on the living room wall.

A slim, mustached man in a three-piece suit sat in front of a fountain talking to a group of other men similarly dressed.

"That's one of his favorite pictures," Frisco said. "I took it after he won his first big case. He didn't even know I was there."

"He's a lawyer?" Download asked.

"Assistant district attorney," she answered. "That's how we met. I was in court, testifying on a case he'd put together."

"Who else lives here?"

"My daughter, Emily."

"Maybe she redecorated."

"No. She's only twelve . . . or thirteen now, I guess. She hates—hated me."

Download felt the maelstrom of confusion and hurt open up inside his mind and threaten to sweep him away. With difficulty, he took himself above it.

Their stay in the daughter's bedroom was brief, and Frisco seemed satisfied that little had changed in that area. Posters of TV stars and musicians seemed to be the major statement, reminding Download of his own younger sister. For a moment, though, he felt confused, wondering if the memory of a young sister was only a facet of still another personality overlay in his brain. He pushed the question aside. Enough soul-searching was taking place without it.

The main bedroom sent Frisco into a state of shock, and Download was almost able to usurp control of his body. The pastel theme was continued here, and dried flowers hung on the walls and sat on skeletal shelves and narrow, geometrical tables.

"The furniture's different," Frisco said. Her emotion made his voice hushed and tense. "And I never had a vanity." She approached the table and looked into the neatly stocked drawers at the combs, brushes, and makeup kits. "These aren't mine. Dammit, these aren't mine!"

Pictures lined the vanity's mirror, tucked between the glass and the wood. Download counted twenty of them as Frisco leaned on the vanity and stared. Most of the photos featured a small girl and a red-haired woman with the man whose picture hung on the living room wall. There were other scenes, taken at the beach, at office functions, at parties. But the man, woman, and girl were always the center of attention.

In the reflection in the mirror, Download saw that he was crying. She'd pulled the hood back, revealing the wires tapped into his brain. Tears leaked down his stubbled face.

"I know her," she said.

"Who is she?"

"Madelyn Dunnigan. She's another assistant district attorney working in my husband's office." Frisco pushed away from the mirror, circling the room like a caged panther.

"It's been a year."

"She was my friend."

"Maybe," Download said with feeling, "if you were still around, she still would be."

She came to a stop in front of a framed document. "They're married."

Download read the date. "Less than a month old. They're still newlyweds."

Without warning, Frisco started laughing. Out of control, she had to sit on the bed. As she laughed, tears coursed down his cheeks. Download felt them, warm and wet, and tasted their salt.

"You've got all the tact of a rampaging water buffalo," she said after a bit. "I'll bet you're fantastic on dates."

Not knowing what to say, Download remained silent. He could feel the fracture in his mind. The part of him that was Eden Frisco was continuing to slip away. He reached out for his hand and managed to curl the fingers for just a moment, then his hand wasn't his again.

"What are we doing here?" he asked.

"A pilgrimage to a private hell, I suppose." Frisco got up and went to the closet and opened it. She ran his hand across the dresses and women's business suits. "I never really counted on coming back from the dead. What the hell am I supposed to do?"

"Let it lie."

"The hell with that! Do you know what I feel like right now?"

"Yes." And Download did. At least a part of it. The sense of loss and pain was almost overwhelming.

"Everything I ever loved, everything I ever lived for, has been taken away from me, and there's not a damn thing I can do about it."

"Walk away from it," Download said.

"I can't."

He made his voice harsh. "What are you going to do, Eden? Hang around and rattle chains? Try to break up your husband's new marriage?"

"Does that sound so bad?"

"Yes, it does. You don't know what he went through when he lost you. Don't you imagine that it was at least as bad as what you're going through now?"

"Turn around!"

It took a moment for Download and Frisco to realize that neither of them had spoken, and it was actually a third voice coming from behind them.

Frisco turned slowly, coming face-to-face with the mustached man in all the pictures. He looked deadly and intent, and he held a .38 S&W Bodyguard in his clenched fists.

15

Chicago, Illinois   *10:39 a.m. CST*
Great Lakes Authority (GLA)   *1639 Greenwich Mean*
87.7 degrees W Longitude   *October 24, 2023*
41.8 degrees N Latitude   *Tuesday*
                    Assignment: Pearl Jam
                    Tactical Ops: Exfiltration
                    Status: Code Green

Jimmy Conrad stared out over the placid blue of Lake Michigan and tried to pretend he didn't feel doubtful. However, Marsha Martini had known him far too long to let him off the hook so easily.

"Think of yourself as a pirate," the pert little blonde said enthusiastically. She was dressed in royal blue coveralls that had grease stains on the elbows and knees. The patch over her left breast identified her as "Ralph" of Murrays Dock Salvage. The logo showed a snake curled around an outboard motor. She also wore a cap cocked to one side, and had grease smudges on her cheeks.

"I don't want to be a pirate." Conrad looked nervously back down the docks, just knowing the salvage company they'd stolen the coveralls from was going to come for them at any time.

Bright sunlight hung over the business marina, sending dancing diamonds across the blue waves. Sport boats bobbed and cut through the water, the bright sails looking like triangular balloons escaping the beach. Farther north, the public beaches held a few diehard beachcombers despite the fact that the summer season had closed on Labor Day. Riffs of music drifted over them. A dozen workout junkies wore cyberhelmets and performed recorded routines while a camera crew filmed them. The experience of all the athletes were also being recorded for playback in virtual reality mode for people who wanted to exercise during their sleep cycle by having different muscle groups worked by computer-assist.

"Jean Lafitte," Martini said, taking the lead.

As usual, Conrad found himself following her before he knew he was in motion. The dented and faded toolbox in his right hand was heavy and unwieldy. "I wish it were night."

"Most pirates attacked during the day," Martini said. "It was too risky attacking at night because they didn't have enough light."

Conrad was surprised. Of the two, he was the reader. "And just how did you come by that bit of knowledge?"

"It's just that in all the pirate movies you see, the battles are always in the daytime."

"Movies?"

She glanced at him, not breaking stride along the marina, her booted feet clumping against the boards. "Yeah, movies. Errol Flynn. Tyrell Power."

"Tyrone."

"Whatever. Those guys."

Conrad looked at her, amazed. "Did you ever stop to think that maybe those movies had daylight sea battles because the directors didn't have the means to film them at night?"

"No. But it doesn't matter. We're going in, getting Refit, and getting the hell back out again." Matrix had contacted them with Refit's location less than a half hour ago.

Conrad just nodded, though he felt stirrings of trepidation. Despite the differences in their natures, they'd been friends all their lives. They shared a birthday, and most of the years since. Martini had always had a knack for getting into trouble, and Conrad had dedicated himself to getting her out of it. Still, it was her aggressiveness that had enabled them to make a living on the streets, usually by one scam or another, and they'd maintained a lively lifestyle even before joining FREELancers.

Their metability, Dr. Rhand felt, had its roots in a defective batch of inoculation viruses they were exposed to as children. As a result, they'd always been able to get strength from and give strength to each other. When one of Martini's scams fell apart in South Chicago and a phased wave explosion was only part of the production, they'd found those powers amplified. Vampiric to a degree in nature, the skill and strength transference abilities became phenomenal, allowing them to boost each other to superhuman level, and added to it was the ability to blast targets with telepathic force while they were in physical contact with each other.

Even now, Conrad couldn't imagine a life without Martini, though romance was never in the picture. If there was any one person in the world he trusted, it was Martini. And he knew she felt the same way.

As usual, her confidence in the scam she'd concocted was convincing, even if the plan wasn't. Conrad shifted the weight of the toolbox. Under the coveralls he was wearing bulletproof armor and carrying a Taurus 9mm semiautomatic loaded with Para-bullets. He refused to kill, and had shot only two people during his brief career with FREELancers. If the pistol had been loaded with lethal ammunition, he didn't know if he would pull the trigger to save himself. To save Martini, he would, and maybe to save others.

"Jean Lafitte," he repeated.

"Or Blackbird." Martini walked toward the freighter, taking the narrow ramp leading up onto the ship.

"Blackbeard," Conrad corrected.

"*Whatever.*"

"Okay, I'm a pirate, and when they catch us, they're going to hang me from the yardarm." Conrad paused. "Fine, I'm really comfortable with that."

"We could always go back to Plan A," Martini pointed out, throwing a leg over the top and stepping onto the deck. "Plan A was much more exciting."

"No. This is fine." Plan A was Martini's first idea for rescuing Refit, involving scuba gear, a hole in the side of the freighter, and pulling the FREELancer agent from a sinking ship while avoiding his captors. Plan B relied on guile and charm. Pulling a Rockford, as Martini termed it. Underhill hadn't been impressed with Plan A either. So Plan B was born. Conrad felt better knowing that Scratchbuilt was out in the lake submerged, waiting to offer assistance.

The freighter was the *Windcutter*, a transport ship that regularly worked the channel locks on the Great Lakes. Matrix had turned up all the background information on it. The *Windcutter* had been dry-docked for over a week, leading Underhill to speculate that Deadline had known a week ahead of time that FREELancer agents would be kidnapped and when. Matrix had found Refit's homing bug through the cellular phone towers by altering the frequency and triangulating the signal.

Rust had collected on the ship's surfaces, and the wooden deck was scuffed and stained. It appeared to be deserted, until a big man in a peacoat, watch cap, and baggy pants came up from belowdecks.

"Hey," the guy called suspiciously, "what the hell are you guys doing on board? This here's private property."

"Showtime," Martini whispered, turning to face the approaching man.

Conrad stood back, letting her handle the guy. His hand was near his coveralls opening, out of sight of the man, ready to grab the 9mm from the shoulder holster.

"Murrays Dock Salvage," Martini said with a smile. "Here to look at the electronics repairs aboard ship."

"Gillman Tech is doing the repairs," the man said.

"Most of them," Martini corrected with the smile in place. "They subcontracted the electrical part out to us." She took a sheaf of papers from her coveralls and handed them over. Matrix had arranged the dummied orders after getting into Gillman Tech's files and copying macros of their billing and contracts paperwork.

Scowling, the man looked over the work orders. "I don't know nothing about this."

"Give your boss a call," Martini suggested.

Conrad knew the guy probably wouldn't call Deadline.

"That's not possible," the man said, handing the paperwork back. "You'll have to come back."

Martini shrugged. "Fine with me, but I need you to sign this." She handed him another paper.

"What's this?"

"A bill."

"For what?"

"Look," she said in exasperation, "we came out, prepared to do the job we hired on to do, but we couldn't because you won't let us. My boss still expects to be paid. All we have to sell is time, and nobody gets a free ride."

The man looked at the bill. The amount was pretty staggering. He thought for a moment. "If you're supposed to work on the ship, where're your spare parts?"

Martini passed the first series of papers back. "We're here for estimates. We start doing replacements, you're going to see trucks out on that dock and maybe a small army of electricians."

The man folded all the papers up and handed them back. "Okay, go ahead with your estimate. But make it snappy. My orders are to not let anyone aboard."

Martini put the papers away and started for the hold.

"Hey," the man said.

Martini turned.

"I just needed to get your name for my shift report . . . *Ralph?*"

The man was starting to reach under his peacoat when Conrad took out his silenced pistol and shot him twice. Without a word, the guy slumped to the deck.

Fisting the unconscious man's collar, Conrad dragged the dead weight into the wheelhouse and closed the door. He kept the pistol in his hand as he joined Martini at the hold. "Pirates," he whispered as they started down. "I don't even want to think about what might have gone wrong with Plan A."

Chicago, Illinois   10:41 a.m. CST

"Eric," Eden Frisco said, taking a step forward.

"Don't," Download cautioned. "He doesn't *know* you like this. You're going to get me killed."

"Who are you?" her widower demanded. "And what the hell are you doing in my home?"

Frisco froze, raising her hands above her head as Download reached past her control and moved his body again. "You married Madelyn," she said.

The man's eyes narrowed. "Who are you?"

"Eden," she said.

"You're sick," he responded angrily. "Eden's dead. I saw her buried." He reached for the phone with one hand, the gun never wavering.

Surging past the woman's weakened defenses, Download took over his body completely. "Before you make that call," he said, "we need to talk."

Recognition dawned in Eric Frisco's eyes. "You're one of the FREELancers. What are you doing here?"

"It's about your wife."

Eden Frisco accessed his vocal cords. "Eric, please listen to him."

Download knew the man was confused. To him, both

voices sounded the same.

"Madelyn?" Eric Frisco asked.

"Eden," Download said.

The man's features blanched. "She's dead. Killed in the line of duty. A year ago."

"I know," Download replied, "but something's happened." He could feel Eden inside him now, shrinking, her renewed time playing out.

"You're the guy who caused Heath Muldoon so many problems," Eric Frisco said.

Last year, Download had used a skill-disk containing the abilities of a well-known race car driver named Heath Muldoon, who'd been a champion in Grand Prix racing. Muldoon had been paid for his time in the computer lab at FREELancer headquarters, but hadn't known everything he was getting himself in for.

After using the skill-disk on assignment, Download had experienced one of his traumatic flashbacks. After the assignment and return to headquarters, Scott had waited three days, then grabbed a bus to Ft. Wayne, Indiana and confronted Celia Muldoon with her husband's infidelity. The counselors who'd worked with Download after that episode had filed reports to Davison and Underhill that Muldoon's personality had been so strong and the guilt that Scott felt had been so urgent, that the FREELancer agent had forgotten who he truly was and thought he was Muldoon. Only he couldn't live with the race car driver's guilt. His confession had resulted in a messy divorce that had hit the international papers and taken half of Muldoon's considerable holdings. Before the divorce had really started, FREELancers had been sued by Muldoon. Although the case had been thrown out of court—Celia Muldoon could have hired a private investigator to acquire the same information for her, and Download had been after no personal gain—the bad publicity had hung on for months.

"Yeah, I guess I am."

"Then . . . then Eden is alive?" The gun lowered, but the

man didn't put it away.

"No. Maybe." Download was frustrated. "To tell you the truth, I don't know. But a piece of her is here now."

"Can I see her?"

"No. It doesn't work like that." The emotional exhaustion slammed into Download all at once. He leaned back tiredly against the wall. "How familiar were you with the Download project your wife agreed to with FREELancers, Inc?"

The man was silent for a moment, thinking. "She'd agreed to have her marksman skills put on some kind of computer program."

"Right. But it wasn't done until the day she died."

Eric Frisco's face grayed. "In the operating room?"

"Yeah. Not all of her died that day," Download said. "I used that disk this morning and found part of her there."

"Oh, my god." His grip tightened on the gun. "This can't be real. This is too much."

Download agreed. "Maybe you could put the gun away."

The man didn't seem comfortable with that.

Eden Frisco whispered in the back of his mind. "Tell him that I remember our honeymoon. Tell him I remember how he helped me eat a triple fudge sundae even though he was allergic to chocolate but had never told me."

Passing the information on, Download studied the man, watching confused emotions race across his face.

"We went to the horse races on our honeymoon," Eric Frisco said. "Tell me the name of the horse I bet on in the first race."

"She says it's a trick question," Download replied. "You stayed in bed too long that morning, and didn't make it to the track till the third race."

"Either you're the most informed trickster I've ever seen," Eric Frisco said, "or you're for real. But that's impossible."

Download remained silent despite Eden Frisco's pleas to say something. The man had to work it out for himself.

"Assuming that what you say is true," Eric Frisco said,

"what are we supposed to do?"

"There's something she wants to give to Emily," Download said.

"Our daughter," the man said. "At the time she was killed, Eden and Emily were going through that tough time a mother always has with her daughter. Emily was bucking authority, trying to find her own place in the scheme of things—she was so lost when Eden died, felt so much guilt. I know it still weighs on her."

"Ask him where the family Bible is," Eden Frisco said.

Lowering the pistol, Eric Frisco led the way into the living room. He went to a cedar chest in the corner supporting a half dozen potted plants and reached inside, bringing out a Bible.

Eden Frisco talked to Download as he accepted the Bible. He opened it, then slid a thumbnail along the inside back cover. The seam opened. Reaching inside, he brought out a 3.5 floppy disk. A white label across the top read: For Emily, From Mom.

"What's that?" Eric Frisco asked as Download handed it over.

"Not quite a diary," the FREELancer agent answered. "More along the lines of letters she wrote to Emily during those times when she really didn't know what to say after an argument. Maybe it will help answer some of your daughter's questions about her mother and erase some of the guilt."

The man's eyes reddened as he pocketed the disk. "There's no way I can talk to Eden?"

Download shook his head. "She's barely there for me now."

"Tell her for me that I loved her very much. I married Madelyn, but there was never anything between us before. When I was grieving over Eden, when I needed help with Emily, Madelyn was there for me. For us. If Eden were still alive, she'd be here for all of us. We didn't intend to fall in love, but it happened."

"Tell him I understand," Eden Frisco whispered.

Download did, but he knew whatever was left of the

woman was more hurt and confused than understanding.

The conversation turned awkward. None of them was pre-pared for any of the events that had just happened. Download excused himself, knowing Eden Frisco didn't want to leave.

"Let her know," Eric Frisco said, "that I still think about her."

Download nodded, then got out of the apartment. A melancholy settled over him as he made his way to the eleva-tor. When the doors came together in front of him, he saw Eden Frisco in the polished chrome of the door surfaces.

"Thanks," she told him, barely visible against the smooth, silvery sheen. "If you use my disk again, I'll be there for you. I owe you." She disappeared.

Washed out from the morning and the emotions, his body and mind craving sleep, Download leaned against the elevator wall, barely aware of when the arrival bell went off.

Chicago, Illinois   **10:44 a.m. CST**
Assignment: Pearl Jam, cont'd.
Tactical Ops: Exfiltration, Second Unit
Status: Code Red

It was the thought of seventy feet of water separating him from the surface that made John-Michael DeChanza uneasy. As far down as he was, not much light penetrated the water, so he used the sonar systems he'd designed into the armor. Where most MAPS were only terrain-based attack vehicles, he'd made the Scratchbuilt armor adaptable. Ballast tanks were built into the legs, and the arms held high-pressure jets to release compressed air that could be used to power the armor into motion. The MAPS could function just as easily on land, under the sea, or in space. Though the latter he'd never had the chance to prove.

Using a computer-enhanced thermal imager he'd added on, he tracked Tandem 1 and Tandem 2 aboard the *Windcutter*. Their ID signature was made independent of the other people

aboard the freighter by the homing bugs Doc Random had
invented. Refit had the same type, so DeChanza was able to
verify that the patchwork giant was on board.

The image on the monitor was murky at first. He upgraded
the ultrasound detector, bringing in a clearer picture. In seconds, he'd identified it with the help of the on-board computer as a mini-sub with military design for special forces.
Eighteen feet long and nine feet in diameter, the Capricorn-
class mini-sub was used for undersea delivery of SEAL warriors as well as limited engagements. The usual arsenal on
board a Capricorn-class consisted of four Mk48 torpedoes firing from two tubes.

Working smoothly, DeChanza accessed the nav-net, finding out almost immediately that the mini-sub wasn't showing up.

It also was headed for the *Windcutter.*

Unable to contact the Tandems by the Burris transceiver due
to the freighter's hull, DeChanza tried the com-link to FREE-
Lancers headquarters along a specially scrambled channel.

16

Chicago, Illinois   *10:51 a.m. CST*
Great Lakes Authority (GLA)   *1651 Greenwich Mean*
87.7 degrees W Longitude   *October 24, 2023*
41.8 degrees N Latitude   *Tuesday*
FREELancers Base

"You set up the meeting with Robeson?" Lee Won Underhill asked, seated behind her desk and facing Agent Prime. C4 sat in a chair beside the blond warrior.

"No. I was waiting to talk with you first."

"You think they're ready to deal?"

"They've got a hole. I offered to help patch it up."

"By giving them Addison Bysse?"

"As an hors d'oeuvre. I sat on Nix."

The phone rang while the FREELancers administrator was considering the ramifications. She picked it up.

"Incoming from the Pearl Jam Assignment," Philip Kent said. "Scratchbuilt."

"Put him on." Underhill waited for the transfer, working out the pros and cons on the possibility of an agreement with WEBTWO. The organization was decidedly criminal. After the beating FREELancers was presently taking in the media, getting tied to WEBTWO could be tantamount to professional suicide.

In terse sentences, DeChanza let her know about the mini-sub approaching the freighter.

"Can you take it down?" Underhill asked.

"I believe so," DeChanza said.

"Do it." She listened to him break the connection, then went back to Kent. "As soon as something breaks on this, let me know. And add a name to the SEARCH file in the media and police broadcasts. Bysse, Addison." Underhill spelled it. "When are Contact and her group due back?"

"Three and a half hours."

Underhill mentally logged the time. "Get them prepped as soon as possible. Buzz me ten minutes before they arrive because I want to deal with Proudelk myself. And get Contact a full PR blitz package."

"I've done better than that," Kent said. "I've got a scrambled mainline feed coming out of GLA media outlets beaming straight out to the Lear."

"Good." Underhill cradled the phone, changing her focus back to Prime. "How much can you trust Robeson?"

"I've met him twice. Done business with him maybe seven or eight times. The best you do is break even."

"If you give him Nix, what do we get?"

"A peek at the files of the agents we went up against this morning," C4 replied, acting unimpressed.

"If that's all we're getting, I don't know if I'm interested. Risk of exposure is high on something like that, for a very small payoff."

"I agree," Prime said. "What I'm looking at is getting Charm inside WEBTWO." Prime leaned back in his chair. "We set up the meet. During that time we create some confusion and Charm jumps ship and becomes one of theirs. Once inside, he may turn up more than what Robeson will give us."

Underhill considered the proposition, checking the angles

for chinks. "Do it," she said. "Let me know what you need."

Prime nodded and pushed himself up out of the chair. Before he could reach the door, it opened and Download walked in.

"Where have you been?" Underhill asked.

"Taking care of business," Download said. "I just got back." He eased around C4 and took an empty chair.

The phone rang and Underhill answered it. Kent was brief and to the point. Hanging up, the administrator looked at Prime. "The police bomb squad just answered a call in the North Avenue Beach area. Apparently Addison Bysse was just blown to smithereens in his own apartment."

Prime nodded. "WEBTWO's working fast. Means they're desperate."

"You knew they'd kill him," C4 said.

The warrior looked at Kesselring without emotion. "Eventually, yeah. Didn't expect it this fast. It was the litmus test. They didn't get close to Bysse and sweat him because Robeson's waiting on my call." He smiled coldly at Underhill. "If we don't work a deal, he's going to want to buy the information from me."

"Set it up for this afternoon," Underhill said, "and work with Matrix to get Charm prepped."

He tossed her a salute and led C4 out of the room.

"You want my opinion," Download said, "the man exhibits definite sociopathic tendencies."

She looked at him, saw how gaunt and hollow-eyed he appeared. His skin was waxy and he looked feverish. "What happened?"

Download spun a disk onto the desktop and it came to a rest against the phone. He lifted his feet, then dropped them on the corner of the desk. "I spent this morning with a dead woman who tried to take over my body, such as it is. It appears that the other ghouls who work for you are getting totally callous about how they get material." He told her about Eden Frisco and the encounter with her widower.

When he was finished, Underhill said, "You had no business going there."

He swore with great skill and passion. "Dammit, Lee, I've told you and Doc Random, and every damn shrink you've set me up with that that these disks often contain personalities, and that some of them are stronger than others. I've never experienced any of them as strong as that woman was this morning. One of these times I'm going to flip a disk in the Octopus and it's going to be me wandering around lost inside my own mind."

"Then get rid of the Download device," Underhill said. Her words hung between them.

"Maybe I will," he said softly. "Maybe this time I will." He dropped his feet to the floor. "I'm going to show myself to the door."

"Scott." She made her voice hard.

"Yeah." He turned to look at her.

"Either get rid of the Download device, or be ready for assignment at three o'clock today." Underhill returned his flat gaze full measure.

"Sure." He opened the door and let himself out.

Letting out a controlled breath, she got out of the chair and walked to the window overlooking Lake Michigan. Out there to the north, the Tandems and Scratchbuilt were fighting for the life of Refit, and maybe for their own lives as well. She'd endangered them all, just as she'd risked Jefferson Scott's shaky grip on sanity.

The Cyborgs Izz Us advertising zeppelin floated lazily over the lake, offering the latest discount on plastic surgery. On one of the buildings, she saw a commercial for next week's Monday Night Football game, broadcast in limited virtual reality on pay-per-view, followed immediately by a blanket denial of responsibility by an insurance group. Virtu-viewing was at the viewer's own risk.

Underhill knew she could have asked Prime to step in to help with Refit's rescue, but by the time he'd gotten there, it would have been too late. Behind her, she felt her father's holo take shape.

"Dad," she said without looking, "I'd really like to be alone for just a little while."

"Okay." And the pressure of the holo in the room went away.

Chicago, Illinois   10:53 a.m. CST
Assignment: Pearl Jam, cont'd.
Tactical Ops: Exfiltration, First Unit
Status: Code Red

Klaxons screamed in warning and, trapped between the bulkheads of the freighter, nearly deafened Jimmy Conrad as he trailed Martini. She gave him an angry glance, then shouted above the din, "You tripped something!"

"Me? You were leading!" Conrad gripped his pistol tighter and stepped up his pace, following the girl closely.

A man, carrying a silenced machine pistol walked out of a doorway. Martini was on him before he saw her. With her first flurry of martial arts blows, she stripped the weapon away from him, then knocked him out with a roundhouse kick. She dashed through the opening.

Trailing her, Conrad picked off another man who tried to shoot her. The Para-bullets sent the gunner spinning away, out on his feet.

The room held an array of diagnostic equipment, and four men who quickly pulled guns. Beyond them was a wall of glass overlooking Refit, who was belted onto a hospital bed.

"Oh, jeez, Louise," Conrad groaned as he hurled himself toward a cramped hiding place behind a surgical table under a high-intensity light. Martini was already there. Bullets thudded off the bulkhead walls and smashed into the diagnostic machines, creating sparks and smoke.

"Okay, Deadeye," Martini said, holding out her hand, "do you really want to shoot it out with these guys?"

"Deadeye? I thought I was a pirate."

"Want to hang from the yardarm?"

"No." Conrad took her hand.

"Now!" Martini yelled. They wheeled around the table together, the telepathic power already surging from them. As soon as their targets were located, rays of force lashed out.

Martini swore the telepathic forces looked like fists as they flew, but Conrad always saw them as spinning, colored triangles. In a heartbeat, the four gunners had been knocked out and lay sprawled across the deck.

Taking the lead, Martini rushed through the door into the darkened room that held Refit. She slipped a stiletto from her boot and slashed at the straps that held the patchwork giant.

"Can you walk?" she asked.

"Ain't going to be no Fred Astaire," Refit said as he forced himself to his feet. "Where's the cavalry?"

"We're it," Conrad said, taking a defensive position in the doorway.

"You guys?" Refit's scarred face looked incredulous.

"Everybody else is busy," Martini said. "But if you want, we can come back at a more convenient time."

"I'll pass."

Despite his front, Conrad knew the big man was hurting. He took point, holding his pistol in both hands. Pausing at the next doorway, he watched Martini hunker under Refit's injured arm and try to support him. The big man bent down and took up one of the silenced machine pistols, going through an unconscious man's clothing till he found two more magazines for the weapon.

"You see Deadline on your way through?" Refit asked.

"No," Martini said.

Refit worked the action on the machine pistol and smiled. With the scars, the smile looked positively gruesome and predatory. "Now," he said in a stronger voice, "I'm ready for anything."

A high-pitched keening vibrated through the hull of the

ship as they reached the corridor.

"Are you ready for torpedoes?" Conrad asked. He recognized the sound from a computer game he'd played for a time. The keening came from the screws that drove the torpedoes.

Before Refit could reply, a massive force slammed into the aft end of the freighter, shaking it from stem to stern. Then a wall of water came hurtling down the corridor, letting Conrad know the hull had been breached.

"We're sinking!" he yelled to Martini, reaching out to her as the water swirled around them. Tight as he tried to hold on to her, the swirling water pulled them apart, then he was fighting for his life.

Chicago, Illinois   *10:55 a.m. CST*
Assignment: Pearl Jam, cont'd.
Tactical Ops: Exfiltration, Second Unit
Status: Code Red

DeChanza watched the first torpedo speed toward the docked freighter, unable to bring his weapons systems up fast enough to prevent the strike. It was his fault; he hadn't been expecting an attack from outside, or having to work at a distance.

The torpedo arced gently under the water, leaving a curving trail in its wake that the armor picked up on sonar. It connected solidly with the freighter's steering section, and DeChanza watched as the big ship started floundering at once, taking on a huge amount of water.

He kicked on the underwater floodlights and brought the StarTron system on line. Even down in the murk, the StarTron ability picked up the Capricorn mini-sub. But it also made him highly visible.

The mini-sub looked like a sea turtle as it wobbled in the water and came about. Another torpedo belched out of one of the forward tubes, this one arcing out much farther. Then the IR-lock systems activated and brought it around like a Frisbee thrown into the wind.

<Warning! Attacker has achieved a target-lock! Weapon is an Mk48 torpedo that may pack a warhead big enough to injure this unit!>

His wrists and ankles already surrounded by the sensor cuffs, DeChanza thrust his hands into the weapons-response gloves. The firing studs were at his fingers and under his palms. "Can't hurt us if they can't touch us," he gritted.

Lifting the powersuit's left arm, he fired the specially modified United Weapons Anaconda net gun. Built three times as large as a normal Anaconda, the net spread was thirty feet by thirty feet. Instead of nylon, the strands were made of steel cables, allowing it the heaviness to surge through the water to a maximum distance of forty feet. DeChanza had visualized using it in a rescue effort when working underwater, either for people or hardware. With the ballast tanks built into the Scratchbuilt armor, he could easily bring four times his weight to the surface in short order.

The ball of netting sped toward the approaching torpedo, flaring out in four directions. The net had almost reached maximum spread twenty feet away when the Mk48 slammed into it.

Water roiled as it was displaced by the explosion. A concussive wave surged from the impact area and ripped the armor from its feet. Inside the powersuit, DeChanza felt the impact and struggled to stay in control of the systems.

Disoriented, he knew he had a few seconds before the team aboard the Capricorn could reload the torpedo tubes. But he'd lost the mini-sub.

<Searching> the on-board computer responded. <Suggest switching off the floodlights.>

DeChanza ignored the advice even though he'd programmed the computer himself from military consultation software. The armor settled into the silt again. He swept the area with the sensor array and armed the weapons pod on his right shoulder.

<Aqua-Stingers are on-line and armed.>

"Come on, big guy," DeChanza whispered. "Find them and let's kick butt." He turned as quickly in the water as he could, aware of the slippery footing beneath the armor's feet and the fact that the MAPS was lit up like a Christmas tree.

<Contact. Enemy craft is at heading two-seven-five. Their weapons systems have been armed.>

DeChanza whirled in time to meet the twin rush of the torpedoes. Immediately, he brushed his thumb across the firing switch for the weapons pod. A flurry of Aqua-Stingers left the pod like a swarm of bumblebees, turning the water white as they passed.

Controlling them through the wire-guided systems on board, DeChanza worked the trackball control against his palm. In response, the Aqua-Stingers spread out enough to intercept both torpedoes. The double explosions tore debris loose from the lake floor and created a brownish fog.

"Find them," DeChanza ordered.

<Tracking> the computer replied.

DeChanza watched the monitors. The picture wavered as successive bars sped from top to bottom, clearing the image more each time.

<Lock is secure.>

"Their weapons systems?"

<Disarmed. Escape imminent.>

"I don't think so," DeChanza said. He strode through the water, advancing on the Capricorn mini-sub as it rose from the lake floor. "What about the freighter?"

<Still sinking.>

"Tandem 1 and 2 and Refit?"

<Tracking. Their signals are blurred.>

"Find them." DeChanza vectored in on the mini-sub. If its crew had had time to properly power up, he knew he'd never have been able to catch it. But hemmed in as the sub was by the Lake Michigan marina and working around a preset escape path that would be protected from harbor sensors, they had to work more slowly.

The powersuit's massive feet sank a full yard into the soft bottom as he broke into an awkward, lunging run, narrowly avoiding one of the robot-guided BottomFeeders designed and run to help stave off the accumulated pollution in the harbor. He moved his arms out, snaring the mini-sub in Scratchbuilt's grasp.

The Capricorn struggled like a fish. The effort to break free sent shivers up the MAPS's arms. Hanging on, DeChanza hit the toggle to blow the ballast tanks in the powersuit's legs. Bubbles erupted around him, and he felt the buoyancy take hold. Scratchbuilt's six fingers were dug into the metal skin of the mini-sub. The floodlights, magnified by the StarTron system, displayed the buckled surface of the Capricorn. Screaming in protest, the gyros managed to keep the mini-sub overhead as the powersuit's feet left the lake floor and it launched toward the surface.

<Attacker's hull integrity has been breached. Performing evacuation maneuvers.>

Even through the confusion of bubbles streaming around him, DeChanza found the escape latch. He slid the armor's left hand over and covered it with a thumb.

<Escape route has been successfully blocked. Estimate through IR scans that Capricorn mini-sub is thirty-eight percent filled with lake water. Electronics systems have shorted out. Only threat remaining is possible small arms fire once the surface is reached.>

Riding the buoyancy inherent in the MAPS and enhanced by the ballast tanks, the Scratchbuilt armor erupted from the lake holding the mini-sub above its head. Checking the sensor array, DeChanza found the beach less than a hundred yards away. Ropes surrounded it, marking the rocky area as unsafe for swimmers. Dead brown grass crowned the top.

Accessing the gyro stabilization and the lifting hydraulics of the armor, DeChanza threw the mini-sub toward the beach. Made of high-impact polymers with a tensile strength that approached that of steel, the Capricorn weighed less than two tons. The effort wasn't easy, especially when balancing against the water, but the mini-sub sailed toward the beach like a spinning clam shell.

The immense force he'd used shoved DeChanza deep beneath the surface again, and the murk closed over him. He lowered his arms to his sides, calculating the thrust and the distance, and the angle he needed. Then he triggered the compressed-air jets in his arms.

The g-force shoved him back in the command seat. "C'mon, big guy," he said as he worked the controls. "You're the most impressive piece of hardware I've ever made. Show me what you can do."

Angling through the water, gaining momentum, the powersuit broke the lake surface less than forty yards from the beach. Utilizing the buoyancy and the built-up thrust of the compressed-air jets, Scratchbuilt came out of the water like a nuclear attack submarine.

Released from the drag of the water, the armor sailed through the air at a thirty-degree angle, then dropped toward the beach. The internal gyros kicked in and brought the powersuit's feet under it. DeChanza made a standing stop only a few yards from the wreckage of the mini-sub. The impact caused tremors that sent loose rock tumbling into the water.

"Yes!" he howled in triumph, clenching a fist and pulling it down in a pumping motion.

<Tracking of FREELancers agents aboard *Windcutter* has been completed> the computer relayed.

"Where?" Turning the armor, DeChanza looked to where the freighter had been. Pandemonium had taken hold on the beach and on the lake. Two patrol boats, lights flashing and sirens keening, were speeding toward him, and three Chicago PD patrol cars were parked at the railing above while a half-dozen uniformed officers were sliding and running down the embankment in full riot gear.

<Bearing one-one-nine.>

DeChanza spotted three figures across the dock where the

freighter had been. Only the ship's prow remained above the waterline. A red newscopter suddenly flashed by overhead, then began circling the scene.

Activating the enhancement circuitry, DeChanza magnified the images of the three people the computer had indicated. He saw Refit first, partially aided by Martini, with Conrad bringing up the rear, a bloody cut on his forehead.

DeChanza accessed the Burris transceiver frequency. "Everybody okay?"

Refit took Martini's collar and pulled it to his mouth. "Yeah, kid. Looks like you're gonna have a hell of a fish story to tell. Can you get a call out to Underhill?"

"Sure."

"Do it," Refit said, "and let's see how much red tape she can cut. I don't feel like being arrested again."

"Me neither," DeChanza said with feeling. As he accessed the FREELancers scrambled frequency, the uniformed police officers surrounded him. He ignored their commands to cease and desist because they weren't equipped to handle the Scratchbuilt armor. Kneeling, he grabbed the mini-sub again and broke it in half like an egg, following fault lines that had already been established.

Four men were inside. While he talked to Underhill and outlined the situation, he triggered the armor's recording equipment and photographed the mini-sub's team.

17

Chicago, Illinois   *11:21 a.m. CST*
Great Lakes Authority (GLA) *1721 Greenwich Mean*
87.7 degrees W Longitude   *October 24, 2023*
41.8 degrees N Latitude   *Tuesday*
FREELancers Base

Jefferson Scott grabbed the wires of the Download device in one shaking fist as he stared into the mirror. His reflection was wan and waxy, and his hazel eyes held only a hint of green. His short brown hair was matted and uncombed. Beads of perspiration trickled through the stubble on his cheeks. He was naked to the waist.

And he was certain he was as mad as a hatter.

"I can do this," he told the cold, insectoid gaze of the Octopus resting possessively on his right shoulder. The machine had no eyes, but he knew it was looking at him. Despite Dr. Rhand's insistence that the Download device was merely a machine, Scott knew it held a cruel intelligence. He was also sure it was predatory in nature, sending its taps into a person's brain, then sucking the soul out byte by byte.

The wires felt cold and thin in his hand.

He was in the small bathroom off his suite of rooms in the FREELancers building. As with every other room in his private dwelling area, the bathroom was cluttered with magazines and books and clothing. Once a week, Underhill sent in a maid to clean the rooms and supply fresh clothing in the closets, but by that same night any evidence of cleaning was gone.

He closed his eyes. Alcohol and drugs had ruled his mind and body for eleven years before he'd volunteered for the Download Project. That had been almost three years ago.

He'd been nothing before Underhill had drafted him for the Download device. In college where they'd met, he'd been one of the best students, able to grasp material a professor presented with ridiculous ease. He was even good at stage productions as an actor, and intramural sports as an all-around athlete.

It wasn't until he'd graduated and moved into business circles that he realized a gift for mimicry wasn't going to bring him the success he craved. After being fired from a succession of high-paying jobs his academic record had made him seem the perfect candidate for, he'd started on the drugs and the booze, managing to bury himself. He had scars from before his time with the FREELancers, from drunken brawls where he'd been shot, stabbed, and battered. In a good year, he spent more time out of jail than in, but there hadn't been many of those.

Then Underhill had found him.

At first he'd thought it was because of the relationship they'd had in college, some misplaced sense of responsibility. She'd been older than him. She'd started college at twenty-four the same year he was seventeen.

She'd disappeared several times during their relationship, and later he'd understood it was on FREE agency business for her father. After school, after the first of his rejections from employers, she'd disappeared from his life completely for years. He'd thought it was because he was a failure, never dreaming that the work she was doing for the espionage agency had reached critical mass.

When she'd offered him the Download Project, he'd thought it was because she felt sorry for him. But he'd gone because there'd been nowhere else to go, and because she'd pulled him out of the Cook County jail, where he was serving a seven-month tour for aggravated assault.

Now he felt like she was trying to kill him.

And the Octopus was going to be the means of execution.

He flexed his hand and took a tighter grip on the fiber-optic leads from the Octopus. "Do it," he challenged himself in a rough whisper. He remembered the pain of Eden Frisco in his mind, told himself that the next time he downloaded a skill, things could be even worse.

What if there's nothing left if you do? a voice whispered in his mind. *Jefferson Scott's just a shell, a housing for someone new.*

Scott trembled as he stared at his reflection. The voice wasn't his. Unbidden, a dark future rolled before him, walking through a succession of mirrors. Images of bars and gutters, of jails and angry policemen not afraid to hit him after he'd been cuffed took shape in his mind.

He knew he couldn't go back to that. His life would be worthless. As Download, he meant something. Even to himself.

He released the fiber-optics and let out a pent-up breath he didn't know he'd been holding. There had to be something more—if he had the strength to find it.

Leaning forward, he turned on the tap, threw a handful of water on his face, scrubbed viciously for a moment, then rinsed his mouth out. Stumbling back to the bedroom, across the discarded clothes and abandoned books and magazines and movie disks, he queued the Octopus to wake him at two-thirty and fell into bed. Sleep came at once.

Chicago, Illinois   11:26 a.m.

At her desk, Lee Won Underhill watched Download go to sleep. She'd had his room, like those of the other agents, wired with spy cameras. Everyone else had found them and either confronted her about it or quietly rendered them inoperable. Even John-Michael DeChanza had removed the bugs.

No one blamed her for the security measures, though some resented it. FREELancers attracted some who were purely mercenary at heart. C4 was a prime example and Underhill knew it. Usually agents like that were of only limited use and duration, and as long as that suited the FREELancers administrator's purposes, that was fine.

Jefferson Scott was different.

She drew her hand back from the small control pad that was held recessed in the desk. She'd held her thumb poised over one of the buttons while Scott had been in the bathroom. There was no telling what type of risk forcible disconnection from the Octopus would trigger.

Once, when attempting to use Dr. Rhand's own Rolling Savant Syndrome metability, Download had gone into a two-month coma.

The button Underhill had been prepared to use would have flooded the bathroom with anesthetic gas and knocked Download out before he could seriously damage himself. She was glad he'd stopped. Pressing another button, she watched the monitor go blank, then pull it and the control pad into the inside of the desk, leaving only a smooth surface behind.

Her phone rang and she answered it, leaving the vid-link off because the call came from the building's switchboard.

"Refit, Scratchbuilt, and the Tandems have been released by the Chicago PD," Kent said. "Pending investigation. They've been told not to leave town. Also, I've received a call regarding a possible meeting between you and a prospective client."

"I told you we wouldn't be doing any new business until we clear up the current situation," Underhill stated.

"I know that, but you might want to change your mind with this guy. It's Ambassador Masohiro Kinoshita, of the Detroit Embassy of Japan."

Underhill sipped her tea and thought about it. FREE-Lancers hadn't ever done any work for the Japanese. When Contact had recruited GlowStar, the odds against that happening had seemed to increase. Unofficially, the Japanese Diet had a price on GlowStar's head for the theft of embarrassing political documents regarding cooperation between economic interests and the Yakuza, nominally naming Sun Andoc.

"I'll see him," she said. "When's he due to arrive?"

"An hour. Will that give you enough time?"

Underhill looked at the notes scattered across the desktop. Contact and her group were en route, and the telethon crew had been put on yellow alert. Everyone else was either at headquarters or near enough that they were safe.

"No. Hold him off till three-thirty."

Kent said he would and hung up.

A sparkle started in the center of the room, then George Anthony Underhill's holo formed. "The Japanese," he breathed with interest. Her father lifted himself on his toes, then let himself slowly back down. "They don't usually let themselves get in an indefensible position."

"There is the matter of the *Rinji 8*," Underhill pointed out. She'd heard the story on CNN. "Maybe they're looking to cover all bases."

"What were they working on up there?"

Underhill leaned back in her chair and tried to get comfortable, then gave up. Too much was on her mind. "I had Matrix run an intel scan on the Yukiko Corporation, but the only thing of interest that she came up with was Grant DiLuca's name."

"Who's he?"

"A computer chip designer. He works for Yukiko Corporation and has created some role-playing games for the company that has made a considerable fortune in the toy business. Also, he's designed software for industrial use that's enhanced production lines and made them more safe."

"Losing them doesn't seem all that threatening."

"I agree."

"Then why the visit from Kinoshita?"

"Could be they think the attack on their space station was based in the United States. If you rule out the Japanese Space Service, that leaves—"

"NASA."

"And Lone Star Space," Underhill said. "FREELancers would possibly be better equipped to rove around the state alliances than Japanese investigators."

George Underhill snorted. "You mean the Yakuza. No matter what, those killers will be stalking the shadows."

"Yes."

"So what are you going to tell Kinoshita?"

"I'm going to take a pass. Politely, and offer to help where I can, but without putting a team on it. Until we figure out how we were set up, I don't want to divide our forces."

"You're probably turning down good money."

Underhill nodded. "But our coffers are doing pretty well at the moment. One thing about our line of business, we're never short of work. As long as we keep our reputation clean."

"Kinoshita's a good man, but very loyal to his government. He won't betray you. However, he won't tell you everything."

"In this case," Underhill said, "it's not going to matter."

The phone rang.

"I've got something," Matrix said, sounding like an automaton, telling Underhill that she'd been on the computers for a long time. "Some of the money deposited into the Cayman Island accounts was in the form of bearer bonds. I managed to get into the computer files, but the information's been erased."

"By whom?"

"My guess is Barnaby Maitland, because the override codes belonged to bank officials. He's the vice president who was in charge of setting up the account."

"Where is he now?"

"He quit yesterday without notice. I took the liberty of hiring a private investigator down in the Caymans to check out his home. He's not there, and from what the woman told me, it looks like he's not planning on coming back."

"Can you find him?"

"I'm working on a couple of angles. When I raided the personnel files from the Cayman International Bank, Inc., I found out that Maitland is a stamp collector. The bank authorized loans on certain stamps during his years with them. He paid them all off. Last week, according to paperwork I found in his file, he cleaned out a safe deposit box and had it shipped by Worldwide Security Services. I figure it was the stamps."

"Sounds logical. Do you know where it was sent?"

"Not yet. I've been trying to hack into their systems for the last hour. They're pretty good. Also, Maitland closed out a couple of accounts when he left."

"Cash back?"

"In part. There was another account that the bank people must not have known about. Under another name, and it was closed out at the same time. It was all handled through electronic deposit."

"How much money are we talking about?"

"Two million dollars and change."

"Where did it go?"

"So far? Miami, Florida to Perth, Australia to Berlin, Germany to Reykjavik, Iceland. At the moment it's sitting in Buenos Aires, Argentina, but I'm expecting that to change. Once I get a lock on the contents of the safe deposit box, I figure when the money meets the stamps, I've found our guy. He may be able to play games with the banking systems, but Worldwide Security Services is going to be a one-way trip."

Underhill cradled the phone and looked at her father's holo. "Did you copy that?"

He nodded. "Money's the root of all evil. Crime can't exist without it, because money's the only means of keeping score.

Get hold of the root, and you'll find out everything you need to know."

"If we have enough time," Underhill said. Like her father, she believed in the FREELancers. The world, despite the best efforts of the state alliances, was coming apart at the seams. Anarchy was at times only a stone's throw away. If they were disbanded by court order, a great number of people, unable to go anywhere for the help they needed, would be hurt.

"There's a pattern forming out there." George Underhill reached out a hand and flexed it. "You've got the WEBTWO connection, the Maitland guy down in the Caymans, the money, and the tie to Deadline. Once you get the parameters defined, filling in the missing pieces is going to be easy."

"That reminds me," Underhill said. "I've got to make a phone call." She got an outside line, dialed a number from memory, and switched on the vid-link because she wanted to see the other party's face.

The switchboard operator had obviously been prepped to expect Underhill's call because he transferred her to Crystal Young's office immediately.

Deadline leaned back in a plush office chair and maintained a neutral facade. "Ah, Ms. Underhill, how may I help you?"

"Just wanted you to know that Refit's back home," Underhill said.

"How very good for you," Deadline said. "But I wasn't aware that he had wandered off."

Underhill knew the woman was covering herself from legal repercussion. As it was, only Refit's word placed Deadline at the freighter. It wouldn't be enough to interest the Chicago district attorney because YoungLife, Inc. put too much money into business and politics in the GLA to warrant anything less than an open-and-shut case. "I'll see you in court," the FREE-Lancers administrator said. "Soon." Then she broke the connection, cutting off whatever response Deadline might have made. It was petty, but it felt good.

Springfield, Illinois   *12:01 p.m. CST*
Great Lakes Authority (GLA)   *1801 Greenwich Mean*
89.6 degrees W Longitude   *October 24, 2023*
39.8 degrees N Latitude   *Tuesday*
Assignment: Showstopper
Tactical Ops: Community PR
Status: Code Green

Clad in her skintight, one-piece red uniform with silver piping, Shirae Yoshiko vaulted onto the stage in front of all the television cameras. Silver gloves that belled at the forearms and calf-high boots that folded over like a freebooter's covered her hands and feet. Her upper face was covered by a red domino mask. Silver throwing stars studded her belt, arms, and legs. Somewhere offstage, a canned drumroll crashed, ringing inside the stage area. The lights were breathtaking, hot and intense. Perhaps two hundred strong, the studio audience started chanting her code name.

"GlowStar! GlowStar! GlowStar!"

Still in motion, she performed a floor exercise that would have shamed an Olympic athlete. A series of cartwheels turned into handsprings, then into a leap that allowed her to twirl into a one-and-a-half gainer with a twist. Effortlessly, she landed on her feet facing her audience, her arms held out at her sides. Red roses landed all around her, thrown by the male members of the audience, who were largely between the ages of fifteen and twenty-five. The catcalls made her blush.

At five-feet-two and a hundred pounds, Glowstar possessed a slim figure with demure curves. Her black hair was cropped squarely around her head in street-punk fashion. Her eyes were deep hunter green.

Holding a wireless microphone, the emcee stepped onto the stage. Wyatt Sanders was tall and lanky, with a neatly trimmed red beard and long red hair that made him look like one of King Arthur's Knights of the Round Table out of uniform. Yoshiko knew the man was too old for her. He was an

ex-tennis pro turned talk show host, and well into his forties.
She was twenty-one and an ex-thief removed from the back
alleys of Tokyo less than eight months ago. But still, she liked
to watch the way he moved.

Sanders clapped enthusiastically. "Yeah! Now that was
something, wasn't it?" He paused as the clapping died away.
"In case you've just joined us, this is the Springfield Annual
Telethon for the Association for Prevention of Life-threaten-
ing Illnesses in Neo-Natal Children. And this lovely lady is
GlowStar, the newest member of FREELancers, Inc."

The applause renewed for a moment.

Yoshiko bowed. Over the recent months, she'd learned to
like the spotlight just a little.

"And now," Sanders said, "GlowStar is going to give us a
demonstration of her incredible abilities. During this time,
don't forget our panel of volunteers waiting to take your
pledges. The money really helps, folks, and many children are
saved every year through your donations."

Glancing around the crowd, Yoshiko felt a cool feeling
ghost across the back of her neck. Centaur had told her about
Underhill's phone calls and the havoc that was going on in
Chicago. The warning didn't touch her lightly. Back in
Tokyo, she'd paid heed to them, and sometimes they'd saved
her life.

She'd lived by her wits then, as a very successful thief. But
she'd kept her needs, and therefore her risks, small, making
just enough to live on. The world had been a very small place
to her then, only getting larger when she started tackling
international hotels and stalking her chosen victims. She'd
learned then about the software designs, secret accounts, and
back-door dealings that were worth infinitely more than she
was accustomed to earning by dealing in currency, jewelry,
and hardware.

As she'd grown more successful, she'd taken on the responsibility of a number of street kids living in Tokyo's slums. No
one else looked out for them, and government subsidies were

almost nonexistent. She knew because she'd grown up in the slums. Her mother, a geisha, had unknowingly witnessed a scandal that could have ended the career of a prominent corporate exec, resulting in her murder.

Five years had passed before Yoshiko could achieve revenge, revenge that had almost cost her own life. Posing as a prostitute to get into the man's suite, she'd stolen some very valuable documents. She'd used her metability on the exec's guards, killing for the first time in her life because the money she could get for the papers would feed a lot of the street children. But the documents had been more valuable than she'd thought, and tied deeply into some of the Japanese Diet's dealings with the Yakuza. A price had been put on her head. If Summer Davison hadn't interceded and whisked her out of the country, Yoshiko was convinced she'd be dead now.

She looked about the room; nothing appeared amiss. The studio crowd was enthusiastic, and security seemed tight enough.

Out of sight of the crowd, awaiting their turn on the stage, Centaur and Captain Ares looked on and smiled encouragement. Centaur was a strange-looking one. His real name was Mathew Fine. He'd lost his legs to a land mine during his US Nicaraguan peacekeeping days in 2010. Over the next several years, using his expertise as a mechanical engineer, he'd developed a special prosthetic harness because he'd hated wheelchairs and the bulky bionic replacements that didn't look or sound human.

Giving up on having a bipedal structure, Fine had created the Centaur unit, a horse-shaped body that weighed a ton when he was finished with it. His legless torso was harnessed in where the neck and head would go, giving him the appearance of a half-man/half-horse from Greek mythology. The Centaur unit was silver with red racing stripes and a number of hidden surprises. The cybernetics systems hooked in through Fine's spinal cord at the base of his back.

Although towering nine feet seven inches in the Centaur

harness, Fine otherwise looked normal. His prematurely gray hair was pulled back in a ponytail, and his one-eighth Cherokee blood showed in his nose and the high cheekbones. His gaze was a brilliant blue, hard and direct. He wore a red tunic with gray piping over his upper body.

Captain Ares, on the other hand, stood six feet tall and had a weightlifter's build, heavy shoulders, broad chest, muscular upper arms, and thick thighs. He wore white tights with a matching ram's-head cowl. Silver stars on his collarbone on either side of his squared-off chin held the crimson cape in place so that it stuck up like a cloak. His boots and gloves were the same shade of crimson, likewise the big letter **A** centered on his chest. His blond hair was cropped to medium length but still held a hint of sun-kissed curls.

Captain Ares scared Yoshiko to a degree. Most of the other FREELancers she could figure out. Fine believed in righting injustices, but he also believed in exposing the Centaur rig he'd designed with the hopes of selling it. Refit was gruff, but it was because he needed his space while he tried to deal with everything that happened to his body and whether or not anything about him could be considered normal instead of monstrous.

Every one of the FREELancers had their own reasons for working at the agency, most of them money-related, although there was a need to see justice done to a degree also. But Captain Ares wanted to be a genuine superhero, even maintaining his identity secret from the others even though they all knew what he looked like under the mask. No one, not even Charm with all his powers of persuasion, had managed to get more out of the Captain than that he worked at FREELancers to help provide for his ailing aunt.

The ailing aunt story was an old one to Yoshiko. She'd used it on the subways when thievery wasn't necessary and she could subsist on begging alone. Of course, she'd also used ailing uncles, fathers, mothers, grandparents, and siblings.

"Ready?" Sanders asked.

She nodded, focusing her energies and her attention.

"Go!" Sanders yelled as the drumroll picked up intensity.

Yoshiko ran, drumming her feet hard against the stage. She gave two handsprings, then hurled herself high, looking for her targets as her internal radar went to work.

Across the stage, a half-dozen brightly colored balloons were released from traps set into the stage floor. Filled with helium, they instantly streaked for the ceiling. The drumroll came to an abrupt stop.

Turning her body in a series of flips, Yoshiko grabbed the throwing stars from her belt, arms, and legs and threw with both hands. Her metability guided her aim, energizing the stars and instilling her poltergeist ability within them.

Instead of simply striking each target before it touched the twenty-foot-high ceiling, Yoshiko imprinted each throwing star to veer and spin sharply, inscribing six different arcs before exploding the balloons. The energized throwing stars glowed a lambent green, leaving twisting trails almost a yard long and looking like comets.

By the time she flipped a final time and landed on her feet, not a target remained in existence. The audience came to its feet, roaring approval. She bowed, then gave a final telekinetic tug on the throwing stars where they were embedded in the walls and ceiling, and brought them spinning back toward her. She snatched them out of the air with apparent ease.

"Great show," Fine said as he galloped on stage and joined her.

"Thanks," she said.

Captain Ares took his place on the other side of her, waving to the crowd. "It's good to do this," he said in his orator's voice. "Children need to be shown positive role models in order to grow up and become responsible adults. Perhaps you'd have benefited from it yourself."

"Right," Yoshiko said, then gave a brief shrug to Fine, who flashed her a knowing smile.

"Okay," Sanders said, stepping forward, "this is the

moment a lot of you have been waiting for: the chance to
meet some of the FREELancers face-to-face. If you'll come on
down, we're setting up tables now so you can get their autographs—for a small donation toward our cause. After that,
Captain Ares, Centaur, and GlowStar will help out on our
phone lines for the next hour."

Yoshiko walked down into the roped-off area to the right of
the stage, conscious of the cameras following the trio of
FREELancers. She took her seat as the line formed to the left.

She barely registered Matthew DiLuca's name as he presented his autograph book to her five minutes later, working
his way down the table. She signed it, wishing her hand
wouldn't cramp so soon, then passed the book to Captain
Ares.

"My," the Captain said as he started to sign, "but you're a
fine-looking lad." He shook the boy's hand, eliciting a grin.

Yoshiko supposed Matthew DiLuca was. Slender and gangly, with a slight overbite, pale blue eyes, and unruly auburn
hair, he looked like a hundred other preteens she'd seen at PR
events. No matter what went on in the real world, kids liked
heroes.

"You're my favorite FREELancer," Matthew DiLuca confided in a shy voice. "I really like your costume."

"Thanks," the Captain said, mirroring the bashful, boyish
smile. "But I think evil should have a symbol to fear and
respect. Dark things should shun the light."

The boy nodded happily.

Cupping her mouth behind her hand, Yoshiko whispered
to Fine while waiting on the next autograph book, "Give him
a few more years and the right hormones, he's going to think
C4 has got the best costume."

Fine covered his laugh with a cough.

"Golly," Captain Ares said, shaking his pen, "it seems my
pen has just run out of ink."

"That's okay, Captain," Matthew DiLuca said, opening his
backpack and taking a pen from under the notebook com-

puter inside. "You can use mine."

Just as Captain Ares was about to put pen to paper, an armed group of men burst through both doors of the studio.

Reacting with superhuman reflexes, Yoshiko wrapped her arms around the kids in front of her and brought them to the ground just as the attackers started firing.

18

Springfield, Illinois
Great Lakes Authority
89.6 degrees W Longitude
39.8 degrees N Latitude

12:11 p.m. CST
1811 Greenwich Mean
October 24, 2023
Tuesday

They came spilling down the aisles with guns drawn.

When Captain Ares saw that Matt wasn't going to move, he reached out and pulled him over the table, setting him down on the floor behind him. A hail of bullets smacked into the bulletproof cape and tights.

Flattened bullets dropped to the floor at the Captain's booted feet. Matt reached out and grabbed two of them, the hot metal burning his fingers. But he refused to drop them, instead shoving them deep in his pants pocket.

"You people there!" the Captain shouted, holding his hand up like a school crossing guard. "Stop shooting! You're endangering children!"

A renewed flurry of bullets struck the FREELancer agent, causing him to cover his face with an upraised shoulder and arm. He reached for the folding table with his other hand, lifted it clear of the floor by one end, then hurled it into the crowd coming down the aisle. The attackers went down instantly as the table smashed to pieces against them.

"Awesome," Matt whispered, not wanting any of the gunmen to realize he was there. He pushed himself up on his elbows and knees, and quickly scuttled under the stage where he still had a view.

GlowStar had erupted into action and started a series of martial arts blows and kicks that cleared a space around her. Gunners tried to bring their weapons to bear, but she leaped over their heads. As they turned around, glowing green throwing stars stabbed into their faces, necks, and exposed flesh.

From his studies of the FREELancer agents, Matt knew that GlowStar used the same powerful anesthetic on her throwing stars that were in Para-bullets. The gunners dropped in a heartbeat.

Maintaining her metability as an impossible target, GlowStar filled the air with throwing stars. Lambent green comet tails streaked the battle area.

Surging from behind his table, Centaur reared up on his hind legs. Bullets sparked from the cybernetic horse body. He reached into a concealed area inside the harness and took out a specially modified rifle. The harsh cracks punctuated the auto-fire, and each time one of the attackers went spinning away. Matt knew the morally conscious and religious Centaur refused to kill. But Para-bullets put the attackers down just the same.

Captain Ares grabbed the man nearest him, then threw him at his companions, knocking them all down. "Cowardly villains," he shouted. "You show your baseness by attacking here, in a place where women and children should be safe." He picked up a chair and threw it at another man who was leveling a machine pistol. The chair caught the gunman in the chest and carried him backward dozens of feet.

Matt remembered his camera in his backpack. He shifted to get it, then came face-to-face with a Japanese man who'd been creeping up on him from under the stage.

"Enjoying the show?" the Japanese man asked in English. A hypodermic glittered in his hand.

Matt drew in his breath to scream for help, but the man clapped a hand over his mouth, then stabbed the needle into his leg through his jeans. A few seconds passed, his heart hammering in his chest, then it was as though he were swallowed up by a black ice cube.

Springfield, Illinois   **12:13 p.m. CST**
Assignment: Showstopper, cont'd.
Tactical Ops Upgrade: Community PR/Survival
Status Upgrade: Code Red

Shirae Yoshiko sucked in a ragged breath as she met her newest opponent's backswing with a checking block that bruised her forearm. Recovering instantly, she returned with a backfist that broke the man's nose and sent him stumbling backward, blood streaming from his nostrils.

She sent out her personal radar and found four of her throwing stars. Calling them to her, measuring the speed and distance required with the same kind of autonomic reflexes that kept her heart beating, she kicked the next attacker in the crotch, then leaped up above the heads of two more.

Catching the throwing stars, she flicked them toward three more targets, holding the last one till she touched ground again. A man ran toward her. She ducked, avoiding his lunge, then slammed the throwing star into his exposed bicep. He collapsed into a heap.

Wheeling, she threw three more stars and brought down more targets. Two dead security guards were stretched out in front of her. Fear touched her. Back when she'd lived in the back alleys of Tokyo, she'd avoided confrontation at every quarter.

Then, the tide turned. Abruptly their attackers recoiled and broke ranks. They ran for the doors as quickly as they'd appeared.

"After them," Captain Ares said. "They must not be allowed to get away." He ran toward the doors, his cape flowing behind him.

Yoshiko watched two of the cameras tracking on the Captain, but didn't move. More throwing stars were in her hands in case she needed them to put down any of the people around her who weren't through fighting.

No one moved.

"You okay?" Fine asked. His hooves clicked against the floor as he walked toward her, the sound odd and echoing now that the gunfire had died away.

"Yeah. You?" Yoshiko stared at the carnage, not believing what she saw. The audience had been scattered by the violence. Some had been injured, some had been killed, and some were simply stunned. It was going to take an army of hospital and emergency medical people to sort them out.

Fine nodded. Then the wailing of a small child drew their attention.

The frightened cries came from a little red-haired girl who didn't look over two years old. She clung desperately to the back of a chair.

Fine went forward, towering over her in the Centaur harness. He stopped in front of her, folded the front legs under him, then leaned down and gathered the little girl in his arms. Regaining his feet, he held her tenderly till she stopped crying.

At the far end of the studio, the doors opened and the Captain reentered. He slammed one big fist into his palm. "Drat! They escaped," he explained. Beige-uniformed security officers filed into the room after him, working quickly to divide the victims into areas of differing needs.

Glancing to her right, Yoshiko found Sanders talking quietly in front of a television camera, gesturing out over the crowd. She didn't try to overhear his words. She recognized an opportunist when she saw one. From telethon host to news anchor, all in one easy step.

"Hey," Captain Ares said, looking around. "Where's that boy I saved? The one who was getting the autographs?"

Yoshiko helped him look, even getting down on her knees to peer under the stage, fearing the worst. Five minutes later, they still hadn't found him. By then his parents had noticed he was missing, and the confusion grew even worse.

Boston, Massachusetts   **1:41 p.m. EST**
Megastate of Greater   **1841 Greenwich Mean**
Massachusetts (MGM)   **October 24, 2023**
70.9 degrees W Longitude   **Tuesday**
42.4 degrees N Latitude

"And how was lunch, Ms. Nakeshita?"

Seated in the back of her personal limousine, Ruriko Nakeshita glanced back at the four-star hotel she'd just quitted. A proto-copy of Digital Magick, Inc.'s latest wonders was in the false bottom of her purse. Her driver was Irish, a shrewd and intelligent man who, because of past indiscretions, could not return to his native Belfast for a few years yet.

"Very productive, Torrence," she replied, then applied lipstick. Her hair was still damp from the shower, and her body tingled from more than just the past success. The young vice president had worked very hard to prove himself.

Strident ringing issued from the phone in the back of the luxury sedan. The limousine cruised like an electric blue ghost through the narrow streets of Little Italy. Nakeshita picked up the handset, slid off her earring with the other hand, then switched on the scrambler. "Nakeshita," she said, knowing no one called her on this line unless it was very important.

"It is Hideo, Mistress. We have the boy. Do you want us to bring him there?"

Nakeshita considered that, then decided against it. "Find a place in Detroit," she ordered. "That way, if things do not work out favorably to us, I can turn him over to Kinoshita or a representative of Sun Andoc with minimal fuss and maybe maximum profit."

"As you wish. I'll call you when we arrive."

Nakeshita hung up. With the DiLuca boy in hand, all she needed was access to Grant DiLuca. She smiled. All in all, it was promising to be a very profitable day.

Chicago, Illinois   *12:51 p.m.*

"I'm sorry I don't have more time to give you a guided tour of the building and corporation," Lee Won Underhill said as they traveled upstairs in the elevator.

"It's okay," Gitano Proudelk said.

"No," she replied, "actually it's not. I like things done a certain way, and I do a number of them myself because I want to make sure this corporation makes the right first impression. But we have something of a situation here."

"I've been following it on the news." His handsome features didn't reveal anything of what he was thinking.

Underhill knew the media was filled with the day's misadventures. The elevator bell sounded, and they got off on one of the apartment floors. The corridor was neat and stark, with few paintings on the wall. Security cameras openly monitored the area. "For the time," she said, "these will be your quarters. After a few days, when things get less hectic, if you find another suite you'd rather stay in, we'll get you moved."

"Three weeks," Proudelk said. "That's what I told Davison."

Underhill turned to face him. "I'm betting we can interest you in more than that."

"I doubt it." Proudelk hitched up his jeans. "My grandfather may be entranced by the big-screen TV in the room, but that'll wear off in a couple days."

Underhill paused by the suite door. "Your uniform's inside."

"How?"

"The maids."

Proudelk nodded. "Maids."

"Once a week," Underhill said. "Other than that, you're expected to clean your own room. It's one of the perks provided by the corporation. They also attend to meals downstairs in the cafeteria, and to your laundry."

"The easy life," Proudelk said as he slid the electronic key through the slot.

"Till it gets you dead," Underhill replied coldly. "The work you do is important and very dangerous. You can get inured to it to a degree, but the most important weapon in your arsenal will be your recognition that you could die at any second. You let go of that edge, you're an accident waiting to happen."

Proudelk waved her into the suite, and she took the lead. It was large and lavish, with three bedrooms, a formal dining room, and a complete kitchen. Having a whole building to work with, space wasn't a problem. "After a morale-building speech like that," Proudelk said, "I'm surprised you're not turning away applicants by the dozens."

"You'd be surprised at how many people we do turn away." Underhill walked into the main bedroom after giving a small wave to Virgil Foxfoot seated on the pit group in front of the big television. A cowboy movie was on the screen.

"*Shane*," Proudelk said. "One of his favorites. I'll get to hear about honor and duty again tonight over dinner."

"If you're here."

He looked at her. "What do you mean?"

"There's a meeting at three o'clock. You need to attend. If things go the way I think they will, there'll be an assignment."

"I just got here," Proudelk protested. "What happened to the part where I get to 'pass go and collect two hundred dollars'?"

Underhill returned his gaze full measure. "Paymaster's office is on the third floor. You can call the switchboard, and they'll give you directions. I've already set up an account for

you. As a first-year agent, your living and travel expenses are
paid for, you earn sixty-five hundred a month, plus you get a
percentage of whatever recovered cash this agency gets to
keep or bonuses that are paid out. You can make a draw
against that if you like."

"Just like that." Proudelk snapped his fingers.

Nodding, Underhill said, "Just like that." She opened the
closet and reached in for the uniform the PR department had
designed for him.

The uniform was blood-red, separated into a shirt and
pants. On the left chest a FREELancers logo was held in the
fierce claws of a hawk with a full wingspread stitched in
white.

"Most of the agents, despite my wishes for them not to,
have a habit of making their uniforms unique," Underhill
said. "If you come up with something else, let the PR department know, and they'll work on it for you."

Proudelk tapped the shirt with a forefinger. "Why a bird?"

"Not just a bird," Underhill said. "That's a hawk. Your
code name is Nighthawk."

He showed her a crooked grin. "I guess nobody around here
gets code-named Bob."

"You want Bob," Underhill said, "it's yours."

He waited to see if she would laugh or smile.

Underhill did neither.

"I'll stick with Nighthawk," Proudelk said.

"Fine. The computer will alert you about the meeting fifteen minutes before it's time, and you'll be given directions
then. Come in uniform."

"Sure."

Leaving him then, Underhill showed herself out. She
hated being so stretched out she didn't have time to better
assess a new recruit. Not that it mattered. Most of them
stayed or went on their own choosing, not really influenced
by what FREELancers had to offer. She and her father had
known from the beginning that they were looking for a

select few, a breed of special warriors that stood apart from other metables.

In the elevator again, on her way up to her office, the phone rang. She answered it.

"Matrix," the woman said. "The stamps just showed up."

"Where?"

"New Orleans, registered in the name of Joren Beaudreaux. I accessed the Louisiana DMV and got a picture of Beaudreaux. It's Maitland. I got the address from a bill of lading from the Worldwide Security Services delivery."

"Print it out for me in my office." Five minutes later, she was sure Matrix had found their missing banker. She lifted the phone and called Kent. "Get a plane ready to take Tandems 1 and 2 to New Orleans. I want it in the air in twenty minutes and at New Orleans no later than three-thirty."

"That's going to be close even for the boosted Sabreliner."

"It can be done. The CT-39 cruises at six hundred miles an hour. Have the pilot push it." She turned in her chair and looked out over the skyline. The sun was behind her now, setting in the west, and viewing was much easier. Her eyes felt grainy from lack of sleep, and her muscles ached from built-up fatigue. More than anything she wanted to jog a couple miles downstairs on the inside track in the gym, then grab a few hours of sleep.

She clicked on the television and saw that CNN was running the footage from the telethon, then added the chip recorder. The event was a shambles, but at least the FREE-Lancers came off as heroic.

On screen, she saw Centaur holding the scared little girl against his chest. The image was so striking that it wouldn't leave her mind even after the footage moved on. She switched off the TV function, turned on the chip recorder, and flipped back through the recorded footage on the chip. Another button on the remote, and it was printing out on the color printer beside her desk.

She lifted the phone and called Davison, who was working away in her office. "Have you heard about the telethon in Springfield?"

"Yeah. As near as the Springfield PD can figure, the group belonged to a GENEcologists cell from Sioux City, Iowa. One of the major sponsors of the telethon for the last eight years has been Roberts Pharmaceuticals in Sioux City. The GENE-cologists have stood against the testing that company does on animals, and threats were mailed in prior to the airing of the show."

Underhill knew about the GENEcologists. Young and fanatical, the ecological terrorists actively fought against what they considered to be oppressive and world-damaging technology. Full-scale battles were nothing new to them. "The police don't think FREELancers had anything to do with it?"

"For now, the PD just figures GENEcologists chose that time to attack because the appearances of Centaur, GlowStar, and Captain Ares was the pinnacle of the show." Davison sighed tiredly. "And after all the advertising I designed and paid for, they should have been. Now it could potentially be another black eye for us."

Underhill flipped her fax machine on. "Not necessarily. In fact, I think I have something here you'll like. I'm going to fax it to you."

"Just a second, let me boot up." A pause. "Okay."

Underhill fed the printout into the fax and watched it cycle through with a heavy hum, spitting out the original on her desktop.

"Oh, wow," Davison said. "I'm looking at it now. Centaur looks great, holding the little girl and everything. This will look fantastic with the ad campaign I've designed for next quarter. And with the exposure on the media, people are going to know it's not posed. Do you know who the girl is?"

"No."

"Don't worry about it. I'll find out. I'm going to need a model release form from her and her parents."

Leaving Davison with it, Underhill cradled the phone and got up. She had to figure out a way to make sure Davison got another quarter to worry about.

19

Atlanta, Georgia   *2:41 p.m. EST*
South Atlantic States   *1941 Greenwich Mean*
Directive (SASD)   *October 24, 2023*
84.4 degrees W Longitude   *Tuesday*
33.7 degrees N Latitude
Dekalb Peachtree Airport

Aramis Tadashi made the phone call from the airport lobby and paid the extra amount for the vid-link. He waited patiently for the overseas call to be placed. In the row of seats just across from him, a man in a suit wore a virtu-dream headset and moved jerkily. The chip case beside him advertised *Muhammad Ali's Greatest Fights.*

NASA was a short jet ride away. Louis Lassiter had been filled with questions, but Tadashi hadn't answered any of them. Security had been tight at the landing strip, but Tadashi knew he wouldn't go unnoticed. Lassiter ran a tight operation with NASA these days, but greed poked holes in the most secure holdings.

His team, joined by another dozen men, stuck out in the airport lobby. But corporate executives were expected to travel with a large security retinue. Grant DiLuca sat quietly in a chair, flanked by Saito and another man equally as intimidating, and kept his face buried in his hands. The bustle of travelers, wearing everything from winter clothes to Bermuda shorts, flowed around them, hardly noticing. Huge tri-dee billboards along the waiting room walls advertised Atlanta Falcons Football, Independent Operators International (complete with the organization's flashiest metable, Jade Ghost, with a sarcastic smile on her lips and holding a severed head in one dainty hand), and the current stock quotes on body parts, from both the deceased and living.

The vid-link flared to life and Tadashi stepped so he was fully facing it.

The woman who answered the call was beautiful, crisp and efficient. "Kaori Enterprises," she said in Japanese. "How may I help you?" The corporation was the main thrust of Family Andoc's legitimate investments.

"I need to speak with Sun Andoc," Tadashi said.

"Do you have an appointment?"

He thought he saw a flicker of recognition in her eyes. "No, but he will speak with me."

"I, too, think so. Hold while I transfer you. Andoc-san is not here at the moment." The vid blanked.

"Fine." Tadashi motioned Kerrick forward, and she plugged her notebook computer modem into the pay phone. If any attempts were made to trace them, she would know and could reroute the signal. He looked at her. "I'm being transferred. Can you get a fix on him?"

"Given time, sure." Kerrick worked the keyboard.

Less than two minutes later, the vid cleared again, letting Sun Andoc's harsh features surface like continents on a cooling planet. Over eighty years old, his flesh had shrunk to the bone and his skin looked like ancient parchment. His silver hair looked polished, pulled up on top in a Samurai knot while the rest flowed past his shoulders. A wispy mustache and goatee surrounded his thin slash of a mouth.

"You betrayed your master, Tadashi," he said, leaving off the respectful term of san. "Even a cur knows better than to bite the hand that feeds it."

Stung, Tadashi struggled to control the angry retort that almost flew from his lips. "I am no cur."

"I found you in an alley, feeding off scraps like a cur."

"You found me in a bar," Tadashi said, "taking what I wanted with the strength of my arms and the cunning of my brain. I learned from you how to take even more than my hands could hold. You should be proud."

"I should be shamed. Perhaps I am. But your death will erase that shame."

"If you were strong enough to do that, I would fear you at this moment."

"Yet you do not?"

"No." Tadashi wasn't hesitant. "You know what I have done. I have DiLuca's work, and I know that no other copies of it exist. You taught me that. A common thief steals objects that anyone would want: cars, jewelry, money. But these things are not unique. A successful thief takes something from a man that is one of a kind, then threatens him with never seeing it again. The robbed man will give much more than a fence will for the stolen object."

"Is that what this is?" Andoc asked. "The ransoming back of the Fusuma Project software?"

"In simple terms, yes." At Tadashi's side, Kerrick nodded, letting him know Andoc's people were trying to trace the call.

"And what do you hope to get for it? Money? You'll never have enough to run and hide successfully forever."

Tadashi laughed. "You don't realize how much I have grown, old man. I have no intentions of running. I want a kingdom laid at my feet."

On the screen, Andoc leaned back in his papa-san chair, his hands working up and down the polished length of his cherrywood cane. "Just where do you propose to find this kingdom?"

"I want your end of the action in Detroit. I want all of the Yakuza activity surrounding the Japanese embassy and their corporations."

"You're mad," Andoc said.

"As hell," Tadashi agreed. "You've gotten fat and lazy. There needs to be some new blood here in America, someone with new vision."

"You?" Andoc's sarcasm was cutting.

"Yes." Tadashi met the man's gaze without fear. He had planned well. Andoc would know how well very soon.

"Do you expect the people I have handpicked in those areas to simply go to work for you?" the old man demanded.

"Some will, some won't," Tadashi said.

"None of them will!" Andoc roared. "Those people are mine! I own them!"

"As you once thought you owned me." Tadashi paused. "The Yakuza in America are just a facet of business. Japanese interests over here can't exist without them. But now the corporate people know you're losing control. I am proof of that. They will see that you are spread too far, and remember that your home will always be Tokyo. In order to be effective against other outside interests, they need to have someone who lives here."

"You expect to blackmail me?" Andoc asked.

"No," Tadashi said. "I'm merely serving you notice. After tonight, I will own Detroit's illegal business, and I will be backed by the Japanese corporate world, here and in Tokyo."

"When the assassin's bullet or knife takes your life," Andoc promised, "it will be by my hand."

"If that happens," Tadashi said, "copies of the Fusuma Project will be turned over to every state alliance in the US, and every country in the world. I don't think that's what Yukiko Corporation and Yoshio Nishida want. The Japanese Diet has invested heavily in Yukiko stock."

Andoc stared at him coldly, slitted eyes filled with hatred.

"And I think they're going to *not* want that bad enough to end their business arrangements with you. At least in the United States." Tadashi smiled, knowing he had the upper hand. "I'm being generous. If the research is everything they believe it to be, it's possible that I could take Japan as well. But I leave that in your capable hands." He tagged the phone's switch hook and ended the conversation, then looked at Kerrick.

"No sweat," she said. "His people never even got close to us."

"Where is he?"

She punched keys, paused, then said, "Detroit."

Tadashi considered that, feeling the tightness in his stomach. Sun Andoc possibly had proven more clever than he'd believed the man to be. But then, given the circumstances, Detroit was a logical neutral meeting ground for an extortion attempt.

He punched in his next number and was quickly passed on to Yoshio Nishida, the number one man in the Japanese Diet. When the man's face filled the vid-screen, Tadashi's grin was the epitome of confidence. Andoc was reacting out of anger, which blinded him to the reality of the situation. Nishida was a businessman and could tolerate acceptable losses.

Chicago, Illinois   1:59 p.m. CST

"How are you feeling?"

Sluggish still from the anesthetic, Refit forced his eyes open and turned his head enough to see John-Michael DeChanza lounging in one of the hospital room's chairs. "With my fingers, kid. Same as always." He lifted his left arm and saw unblemished skin, four fingers and a thumb at the end of it. "With somebody else's fingers anyway."

He reached for the triangular support bar hanging above him, then pulled himself into a sitting position. Black spots whirled in his vision for a few seconds, and he felt the tightness in his chest from the new lungs. He surveyed his made-over body.

Besides the new arm and lungs and heart, he'd been outfitted with new legs. As a bonus, they looked like they'd come from the same person.

"Hey," DeChanza said, standing, "I thought you weren't supposed to move around for another hour. The docs just finished the transplants an hour and a half ago."

Usually a transplant took only two hours to heal up after being performed. Refit's rogue immune system allowed total acceptance of massive tissue replacement, but wouldn't heal it. Once an organ or limb was damaged, it had to be replaced or it stayed damaged until it quit functioning.

"Let me worry about that," Refit said. "I been doing this a lot longer than you." He turned around and put his bare feet on the floor. The white tile was cold against his skin. "The meeting with Underhill still at three o'clock?"

"Yeah."

Struggling against the trembling that filled his legs and stomach, Refit made himself stand.

DeChanza started forward.

"Sit," Refit commanded. Reluctantly, the young man dropped back into his chair. He wore a maroon Minnesota Twins sweatshirt with the sleeves ripped out, jeans, a Mickey Mouse ball cap, and tennis shoes that looked more broken down than broken in.

"What are you doing here anyway?" Refit asked.

DeChanza shrugged, as if unsure whether he was going to get yelled at. "Wanted to make sure you were okay."

"Me and this room are old friends," Refit said, referring to the room he usually occupied on the medical floor of the FREELancers building. He grinned mirthlessly and held out his replaced arm. "I go to sleep, and wake up feeling like a new man. Or part of one anyway."

The new scars were pink and shiny, but he knew from experience that they'd gray out in the next couple of days, till they looked like reworked leather.

DeChanza was quiet. Then, "I just wanted you to know someone was thinking about you."

The honest emotion touched Refit. So many people looked at him and figured the transplants, grafts, and scars didn't mean anything to him. On the street, little kids called him monster behind his back, never meaning anything by it, just scared. He walled off the emotion before it could blossom into anything more. All of it was just meat, and it didn't mean anything.

"The day comes and they wheel me in here and can't put me back together, that'll be the day to worry. But not today. You really want to be a help, see if they got any clothes for me in that closet. What size feet do you think these are?"

"Nines, nine-and-a-halfs," DeChanza said as he went through the closet and came out with a standard FREELancer uniform.

"Christ, I would get a small-footed guy. How the hell's a big guy like me supposed to juke and move when I got no foundation? First week on these legs, I'll probably get fallen arches."

He took the uniform from the younger agent, then ripped off the shirt sleeves and pulled the seams out of the pantlegs.

The door opened and a white-smocked woman walked in with a clipboard in her hands and a stethoscope draped around her neck. Professional and compact, Dr. Martine Llewellyn took one look at Refit, ignored the fact that he was standing there naked, and said, "You're supposed to be in bed."

Refit gave DeChanza a lewd wink. "Take a hint, kid. She wants us to be alone."

"In your dreams," Llewellyn said, consulting the chart on the clipboard.

"Got things to do," Refit said. "Bad guys to catch, worlds to save. I'll take a raincheck on the love-in, though." He started for the bathroom in the corner, walking stiffly, getting used to the new meat.

"No way am I letting you go," the doctor said. "You talk to me like that, I know you're still delusional. Where are you going?"

"Bathroom." Refit halted at the door and gave her his best inquisitive look, not thinking about what the crisscrossing scars on his face rendered it as. "Don't I have one of those weight-limitations or something? Ten pounds, something like that?" He glanced down. "Hell, I may need you to come help me."

Llewellyn wrote on the clipboard, saying, "Brain damage, coupled with a lack of size perception."

Looking back up, Refit glanced at DeChanza. "Scram, kid. I'll catch you at the meeting with Underhill. Once I get past Nurse Ratchett."

DeChanza nodded, still not looking sure of himself.

"Kid," Refit said, wanting to say something more, but not trusting himself. If he let too much touch him, he'd start thinking the meat actually meant something and wasn't just a tool.

DeChanza looked at him.

"Back at the lake," Refit said. "You did good. Never saw a mini-sub put down quite like that. Get you on World Wrestling or something. You'll be a contender."

"Yeah." DeChanza grinned and let himself out.

Stepping into the bathroom, Refit closed the door and closed down the feelings as well. He gazed into the mirror, studying the scars that tracked across his face and neck and upper body. He cared about DeChanza. He was a good kid.

He turned away from the reflection in the mirror. Today he was lucky to be among the survivors.

When he returned to the hospital room, Llewellyn was waiting on him. "There's a message here for you."

"Underhill? Probably to let me know how much she's going to charge for my rescue."

"No. Somebody named Risa."

Refit's mind focused on the name, remembering the EMT

in the ambulance that morning. "She okay?"

The doctor looked up. "Underhill had her and the Chicago detective checked out. Bumps and bruises for the most part. Haddonfield will be sore for a while where his Kevlar vest stopped a slug, but it's nothing serious."

"Good." Refit stepped into his pants.

"She wants you to call her, let her know you're okay."

"You can do that."

"Maybe you should do that."

Refit gave the woman a hard glance. "I'll buzz my social secretary, have her get right on it."

"Might not hurt."

"Doc, take my pulse and give me my hall pass. I may have to go buy some new cowboy boots." There was no way he was going to call.

Chicago, Illinois   2:03 p.m. CST

"So you think a metable was responsible for this?" Lee Won Underhill asked as she studied the holo of the *Rinji 8* floating only inches above one of Doc Random's work desks.

"Part of it." His real name was Dr. Andrew J. Rhand, and he had phoned with more bad news.

Rhand had degrees from Oxford, Purdue, Cambridge, the Sorbonne, UCLA, MIT, and Carnegie-Mellon, and an ego the size of the Waldorf. He was tall and broadly built, heavyset and ham-handed. His skin was a burnished ebony, making the white-gold skull earring in his left ear stand out even more. A receding hairline seemed to push the short Afro cut back on top of his head. He wore a white lab smock over his gray business suit.

"What makes you think that?" Underhill asked.

"The satellite we used had a number of data collectors aboard it," Rhand said. He took a telescoping pointer from his pocket and pointed it into the third deck of the space station. "There were unusually high concentrations of magnetic activity in this area. Actually shoved quite deep into the steel." He indicated the scraps of metal stuck against the deck surfaces.

Underhill peered at the holo. Inside it, tiny space-suited figures clambered about, sorting through the wreckage. The holo covered a time-loop of about five minutes. As she watched, the image wavered, then started over just as the space-suited figures started crawling into the remains of the third deck. "Does the JSS say anything about it?"

"Not in the files Matrix has hacked her way in to. They're keeping quiet about this." Rhand put the pointer away. "Unless the raiding party managed to get a huge electromagnet up there, then learned how to make it become a concussive force strong enough to explode a space station designed to withstand limited meteor impact, I can't think of any other explanation."

Thinking of possibilities and impossibilities, theoretical and otherwise, was Rhand's job at FREELancers. He was an expert on metabilities as well, having one of the most unusual and unique of the powers that had shown up. He called it the Rolling Savant Syndrome. The metability made him an expert in any number of fields, even ones he hadn't studied. But the drawback was that as soon as he went to sleep, the current knowledge he was working with faded, and the morning brought a new—and most times—unrelated understanding and interest. He'd invented the Download device during a week without sleep.

On the subjects of science and metabilities, Underhill was willing to trust Rhand's instinct. At the exorbitant rates FREELancers was paying to have him, she knew she'd be a fool not to.

"This person would have to be one of the most powerful metables we've gone up against," she said. "What did you find out about Grant DiLuca?"

He sighed. When she'd asked him to check through associates he had in scientific circles, he'd protested, saying he was near the end of a project that he desperately wanted to finish before the need for sleep vanquished him.

"His last studies," Rhand said, "were in the field of Savantism."

"Regarding what?"

Rhand held a screwdriver and pliers out in frustration. "Lee, I don't know. That's why they call it secret research, because nobody knows what it is. I got you more than Matrix was able to get."

"DiLuca is a software designer," Underhill said. "How does that correlate with savantism?"

"As far as I know, it doesn't. But it has to. DiLuca was a software designer, but he'd been researching heavily into savantism. When you rule out the possible, what remains—no matter how impossible—has got to be the truth."

"Whatever it is," Underhill said, "it's worth a lot of money."

Rhand pointed the screwdriver toward one of the corpses floating just outside the wrecked space station. "Somebody thinks so."

20

"His name is Aramis Tadashi," Matrix said in a flat voice.

Underhill stood in the small, dark computer room and watched Matrix accessing the equipment. Pictures, some still and some moving, filled six monitors. "You're sure he's the one who hit the *Rinji 8*?" She'd asked the computer expert to start surveillance on NASA as soon as she'd heard about Kinoshita's expected arrival. Louis Lassiter was one of a small group that the FREELancers administrator tried to keep tabs on, and the main one for business in space.

"As sure as I can be," Matrix affirmed, "given the parameters you stated. Look at monitor four."

Underhill did, and saw a space shuttle touch down in an effortless glide on a long stretch of tarmac. A digital readout in the upper left corner gave the date. The location was given as NASA, and the time was 1:37 p.m. EST.

"What do you see?" Matrix asked. The ruby-lensed bubble-goggles reflected the glare from the monitors.

"I see a NASA shuttle returning from a flight," Underhill said.

"That's not a NASA shuttle." Matrix worked the keyboard and the landing repeated itself, the image magnifying and enhancing.

Underhill looked at the shuttle more closely, seeing the markings and ID. "Tell me what I'm looking at, then."

"A Japanese shuttle that's been mocked-up to resemble a NASA shuttle called the *Lemuria*." Matrix froze the images. "See . . . here, here, and here? You can see that plates have been spot-welded over the Japanese numbers, then overlaid with NASA ones. They probably worked it in space, either before or after raiding the *Rinji 8*."

"No one else caught this?" Underhill asked.

"No." Matrix continued working the keyboard. "I first noticed it because this shuttle was four feet nine-point-two inches shorter than the real *Lemuria*. I designed a program to pick out irregularities of known shuttles flying in and out of NASA for the next few weeks. I hit this awhile ago, but I wanted to be certain."

"I'm convinced."

"Let me show you the clincher."

The monitors cleared. When the pictures resumed, they were shots of the crew debarking from the shuttle, still in the bulky space suits.

"Third man out," Matrix said softly. "I took these with an overhead satellite, so the angle is a little awkward and takes some getting used to."

The third man wiped his forehead with one hand, carrying his helmet with the other.

"There." Matrix hit the keyboard and froze the image, zooming in on the helmet's face mask. An image was reflected in the polarized plastic. "It took some reinterpretation on my part. Wait a moment."

The reflected image popped onto another monitor, dark and slightly distorted. Then the picture lightened up, turning the dark shadows into flesh tones, straightening out the misshapen features.

"Grant DiLuca," Underhill whispered.

"Right. And here, giving orders then shaking hands with Louis Lassiter, is Aramis Tadashi."

Onscreen, the Asian male Matrix pointed out did just as she announced. A heartbeat later, a profile shot of him, then a full frontal of him, popped onto different monitors.

"Have you got anything on him?" Underhill asked.

"Plenty," Matrix replied. "He worked with Family Andoc in Japan, one of Sun Andoc's handpicked lieutenants."

"Get me the file," Underhill said. "I've got a briefing session in half an hour and I need to be prepared. Have you found where Maitland's money came from?"

"No."

"Tandem 1 and Tandem 2 will be in New Orleans soon," Underhill said. "We'll know more then." The phone on the wall rang and she picked it up automatically, knowing it was for her.

"Prime and Charm just made Seattle," Kent said.

"Fine," Underhill said. "Keep me apprised." She felt good; everything was rolling smoothly, and she had more of the pieces than she'd expected.

Seattle, Washington   **12:31 p.m. PST**
The Pacific Coast   **2031 Greenwich Mean**
122.4 degrees W Longitude   **October 24, 2023**
47.5 degrees N Latitude   **Tuesday**
Assignment: Blue Smoke
Tactical Ops: Covert Infiltration
Status: Code Green

Agent Prime sat in the back of the altered limousine and looked at Simon Drake. The changes the ex-actor had affected were nothing short of miraculous. He held up an eight-by-ten glossy photograph of the man Charm was going to impersonate in order to infiltrate WEBTWO.

"Satisfied?" Drake asked, smirking.

"Got lucky that you looked so much like this guy to begin with," Prime said.

Drake shook his head. "Luck had nothing to do with it. Five guys to choose from, I had to look like somebody." His cheeks were fatter now, moved out by pads inside his mouth. Facial prosthetics took care of the rest of it, but they were kept at a minimum. For all intents and purposes, Drake was a WEBTWO agent named Raymond Sender. He even knew the man's background, adding mannerisms to his repertoire from canned film on the agent from FBI and CIA files he'd viewed on the two-hour trip from Chicago aboard the military Rockwell B-1 jet.

"Yeah, well keep out of sight when we pop the cap on the ball, mate," Prime advised, "or you might get your arse shot off by mistake."

"Terrific. That's a really positive thought."

Prime checked the traffic, seeing the two other cars of combat operatives he'd brought with him from Chicago. The driver made two more turns, bringing the Space Needle into view for just an instant before threading its way back into the older industrial part of the city. Warehouses lined the blocks. With the earthquakes that had wiped out so much of the California coastline in 2008 and caused the radioactive cloud from the broken nuclear reactor site, shipping was even more important in Seattle.

"We're there," Prime said.

Drake nodded, then pressed against the back of the seat, working the trick locks that allowed him entrance through a hidden door into the spacious trunk. Another door awaited him in there, where he could slip out when signaled.

"Prime," the Burris transceiver called out.

"Go," Prime responded.

"Our company is waiting on us," the combat operative said.

"Let's hope they don't get excited and jump the gun."

The "company" Prime had been expecting was a group of Millenniests. Originally, the anarchic terrorists had stated their belief that the world was going to end in the year 2000, but since that hadn't happened, most of them agreed that the calendars had been screwed up over the centuries and that it was probably only a couple more years away.

Opposed to all types of government that didn't reflect Millennial thought, the radical faction staged raids against governments and corporations all along the Pacific Coast. Sometimes they resorted to stealing toxic waste on its way to the dumps in Oregon and blackmailed nearby towns and cities, threatening to dump it in the precious water supplies.

Prime had purposefully leaked information about the meeting with the WEBTWO agents to a cybernetic spy network that worked for the Millenniests, letting them think a huge payoff was going down at the Brooks & Keith warehouse.

WEBTWO agents in street clothes were strung out along the street but didn't look too obvious to the untrained eye.

The doors of the warehouse opened smoothly and the driver passed through them, flicking his lights on to light up the dim interior.

Prime was dressed in a sports shirt and jeans, but carried a Detonics Scoremaster .45 in a shoulder rig under his jacket. He'd purposefully loaded it with hardball ammunition because he didn't care for Millenniests and didn't see anything wrong with killing two birds with one stone. Or as many as he could get. What Underhill didn't know, as long as it didn't conflict with the mission parameters, wouldn't hurt her.

Maxwell Robeson, looking tan and fit and well dressed in a dark blue suit, stood in front of a trio of expensive cars. He was thin and compact, with short dark hair, a long nose, and a crooked devil-may-care smile. He held his hands in front, one over the other. Six men flanked him, all of them openly carrying machine pistols.

Prime got out easy, opening his jacket to show he was carrying the .45.

Some of the WEBTWO agents shifted, but Robeson waved them down, still smiling. "You didn't come alone," Robeson said, nodding toward the two cars that followed him into the warehouse.

"No. Did you expect me to?"

"Not really. But one has to play out the familiar games."

Prime shrugged. He was conscious of his men spreading out behind him. Scanning the WEBTWO agents, he spotted the real Raymond Sender standing to the left. He tapped the Burris transceiver, using an abbreviated Morse code to let the black bag team know where Sender was. A long buzz against his wrist let him know they had the target in their sights.

"How do you want to handle the switch?" Robeson asked.

"I'll give you the name," Prime said, "then you give me the files."

Robeson was amused. "You're going to trust me?"

Prime shrugged. "As you said, I didn't come alone."

A hard light shone in the WEBTWO agent's eyes. "All right, give me the name."

"Greg Nix."

Robeson nodded. "I had him figured for it, but—unfortunately—Bysse wasn't able to confirm it."

"I heard he got real broken up over things," Prime said dryly.

Robeson laughed. "He didn't know I'd talked to you. He thought if he stayed quiet, I'd try to wait him out. He didn't last as long as he thought he could, and he died before my men got the information. The bomb was just to add insult to injury."

"The files?" Prime prompted.

"Of course." Robeson reached back, and a man put a slim

valise in his hand. He passed it across to Prime. "You'll find everything you wanted in there."

Prime took the valise without looking in it. He didn't ask what would become of Greg Nix because he knew.

"You want to look inside?" Robeson asked.

"Wouldn't mean anything to me," Prime said. "This is all for the intelligence branch. Paint a bulls-eye on something for me, and that's when I take over."

As if to punctuate his words, an explosion rocked the warehouse.

Prime crouched down, making a smaller target as he drew the Detonics. He glanced at Robeson and saw suspicion in the other man's eyes. Killing the WEBTWO agent might have complicated matters, but Prime was willing.

"Millenniests!" Robeson yelled to Prime, then to his men. He cupped a hand to his ear, making the radio transmission easier to understand.

Prime radioed the same information to his team, playing out the hand.

"Dammit!" Robeson roared as two off-road vehicles sped through the huge opening at the other end of the warehouse. "How could they have known about this meeting?"

"Your organization's already lousy with leaks," Prime shouted back, drawing a bead on a machine-gunner mounted on back of a converted pickup. "You can't figure it out?"

Robeson swore vehemently.

Taking up trigger slack, Prime fired a bullet through the brain of the machine-gunner. The body tumbled backward. The FREELancer agent sprinted back to the limousine. The driver held an Ingram-11 Stuttershot out and fired controlled bursts, picking off targets with Para-bullets.

The interior of the warehouse became a whirling mass of smoke-filled confusion. More grenades flew from the hands of the Millenniests, and motorcycles poured through the opening in the wall. The explosions set off the fire-suppression system twenty feet overhead, and white blots of foam drifted down like fat snowflakes, making the floor incredibly slick in a short time.

Prime killed three more men, then had to reload. While he was changing magazines in his pistol, a motorcyclist roared up over the side of the limousine, the machine coming down at Prime while the rider brought a shotgun to bear.

Setting himself, Prime lashed out with a reverse kick to the motorcycle's front wheel. The machine swiveled and threw the rider off-balance. The charge of buckshot smashed into the concrete floor.

Prime slipped the magazine into the gun butt and turned, bringing the pistol around. He fired through the face mask before the man could get away.

Then the Burris transceiver buzzed three quick bursts against his wrist, letting him know Charm had made the switch and the real Sender was in FREELancer hands. One of the modified trucks raced by him, the guy on the passenger side about to heave a grenade. Prime fired twice through the window, hitting his target both times.

The grenade fell into the truck cab and blew up an instant later. Flames leapt up behind the cracked windshield as the truck ran into a stone ceiling support.

"I'm going to leave you with it, mate," Prime yelled to Robeson.

"I don't plan on making a career of this either," the WEBTWO agent said.

Prime opened the limo's door and slid inside. He signaled to break off the attack, then picked up the TI-45p laser mounted inside the luxury sedan. He emptied most of the thirty bursts into Millenniests before they made the street.

Flames burned on the hood of the limousine as it raced through the narrow streets, but they quickly went out. Prime used the Burris to access the results of the mission and found that only five men had been wounded and none had been killed.

And Simon Drake was ensconced within the WEBTWO organization.

Chicago, Illinois   2:47 p.m. CST
Assignment: Viperstrike
Briefing

"DiLuca, huh?"

Lee Won Underhill looked along the oval table in the center of the briefing room and saw Captain Ares almost all the way down on the right. He was flipping through the files she'd had Matrix prepare on the results of Broken Goblin and the *Rinji 8* incident.

"I met a young lad at the telethon named DiLuca," the Captain said. As usual, he showed up early for the meetings. "His parents couldn't find him after the incident there. I wanted to stay and help look, but we were needed back here. I fear something might have happened to the little guy."

"You're sure it was DiLuca?" Underhill asked.

The Captain shrugged. "I think so. Wait, I'll check." He swept his cape up in one gloved fist and rummaged through the secret pockets he had there. A moment later, he took out an ink pen. Studying it, he said, "Yes. Matthew Voight DiLuca. He gave me his pen to use, and during the confusion I forgot to get it back to him. I should find out where he lives and mail it to him. A personalized pen like that, it was probably a gift."

Refit walked into the room, saw Captain Ares sitting at the table, and grimaced. Their personalities clashed all the time. The patchwork giant crossed the room to the coffee service in the corner, poured himself a cup, and lounged against the wall.

Underhill lifted the phone and called Matrix's extension. She'd learned over the years never to ignore coincidence. Sometimes events were only coincidental and didn't tie at all, but the flip side was that often events that seemed not to be related were actually cause-and-effect.

"Cross-reference the files you have on Grant DiLuca," the FREELancers administrator said. "Reference to Matthew Voight DiLuca."

"I'm running it," Matrix replied. "I've also got a prelim

finished on the agent files we received from Prime. The only common denominator I've found is that all of these agents have been assigned to Pacific Rim posts in the last three years. Usually to spy on Yakuza activity."

Underhill wrote the information down on her legal pad. WEBTWO usually didn't move into the Pacific Rim because they were able to keep abreast of things from Seattle. And spying on the Yakuza wouldn't have been healthy.

"There is a Matthew Voight DiLuca mentioned in Grant DiLuca's files," Matrix said. "The boy is his twelve-year-old nephew. He lives in Chicago."

"Do you have a picture of him?"

"Yes."

"Send it through." Underhill turned on the holo function in the room. A glowing ball nearly three feet across took shape in the air above the conference table, then flattened out into a multifaceted diamond. The lower panels became monitor screens that coalesced into the features of a preteen male.

"That's the boy from the telethon."

Underhill glanced over at the speaker and saw Shirae Yoshiko taking a seat across from the Captain, her attention riveted on the holo.

"Matthew DiLuca?"

"Yeah. Something like that."

Underhill glanced at Captain Ares.

"That's the lad," the Captain said, rubbing his impressive jawline.

"Matrix," the FREELancers administrator said, "how much contact did DiLuca have with his nephew?"

"According to the files I've filched from Yukiko Corporation, DiLuca phoned the boy regularly."

"What about from the *Rinji 8?*"

"Yes. In fact, it was a point in his contract when he went into space."

Metallic clip-clopping sounded out in the hall, then Mathew Fine entered the conference room, having to duck to get through the doorway while in the Centaur harness. He helped himself to a bottle of orange juice at the service area, then folded his four bionic legs beneath him and sat.

Underhill's mind raced. "Did Yukiko Corporation keep files on DiLuca's discussions with his nephew?"

"Yes. I found those too, with some difficulty."

Staring at the boy's face, Underhill asked, "What did they talk about?"

"Games, comics, FREELancers, family, school, and what it was like being in space."

"Nothing about what DiLuca was working on?"

"No. Unless Yukiko Corporation deleted that from these records. But I can't see any evidence of tampering within the files."

Underhill felt something was there. Familial ties were understandable, but why was DiLuca so forceful about it?

"They only had conversations?" Agatha Greywood asked from the other end of the table. Wearing a long dress, she lounged regally in the chair, her fingers steepled before her. She'd come into the room so quietly that Underhill hadn't heard her.

Underhill posed the question to Matrix, then put the conversation on speakerphone so everyone could hear.

"They spent a considerable amount of time playing computer role-playing games," Matrix answered. "The times are logged. Once or twice a week they'd play for a couple of hours."

"The corporate internal intelligence guys never found anything?" Refit asked.

"No," Matrix said.

Dervish entered the room and sat quietly, flipping rapidly through the files in front of her. C4 came in next, followed by DeChanza and Proudelk, who looked self-conscious in his new uniform.

"They were sending information back and forth?" Underhill asked.

"Yes," Matrix replied. "It is possible that DiLuca was sending more than just game information. If properly archived, he could have been sending much more."

"Like what?" DeChanza asked.

"The Fusuma Project," the FREELancer administrator said, her mind playing with the possibilities.

"But why?" Captain Ares asked.

"As self-protection," C4 answered as she worked her way through the files on the space station raid. "If Yukiko Corporation had everything they needed from DiLuca, they'd have written him off when he was taken instead of thinking of hiring the FREELancers."

"So you think the Yukiko people lost more than just a research scientist?" Refit asked.

"Yes," Underhill said with a conviction that surprised even her slightly. "With all the searching that Matrix has done, we still don't know what the Fusuma Project entailed. But Yukiko Corporation spent millions of dollars developing it."

"With no payoff along the way?" Fine asked.

"None that we could find."

"Usually there are some subsidiary benefits that can be packaged and sold before a project's completion." As designer of the Centaur harness, Fine had plenty of experience in research development and financial costs. Some of the new cybernetic systems he'd had to create had been leased out to other companies for enough money to finish the harness.

"Matrix?" Underhill said.

"Nothing. Everything about the Fusuma Project was very guarded."

"Has the boy been found?"

There was a pause, then Matrix came back. "No. The Springfield PD is still searching for him."

"But if DiLuca was sending Matthew details about his work on the Fusuma Project," Captain Ares asked, "wasn't that illegal?"

"Very," DeChanza answered.

"I'll bet the lad didn't know it," the Captain said in a confident voice. "You could tell by looking into his eyes that there wasn't a dishonest bone in his body. His uncle was using him, and if I ever see him, I'm going to take umbrage with him."

"I'll bet if he found that out," Refit said, "the poor guy would be quaking in his boots right now."

Captain Ares scowled at Refit. "Honesty is the best policy, and a young lad like Matthew is impressionable."

Ignoring the exchange, Underhill turned her attention back to Matrix. Download entered the room at one minute past three, dressed in a new uniform and freshly shaven. He wore the shiny helmet and kept to himself.

"Access the PR films that were taken of the telethon," Underhill told Matrix. "Cross-reference them with the picture of Matthew Voight DiLuca and let's see what you come up with."

Summer Davison regularly set up cameras just for FREELancers use, with provisions in the contracts she signed with various companies. Usually she used the footage in PR campaigns and advertising.

"Coming on-line now," Matrix said.

The footage spilled across the holo, showing the boy in the crowd in a few shots, then following his progress through the line to get autographs from Captain Ares, GlowStar, and Centaur. The last shot was confusing because of the battle with the GENEcologists.

"Where is he?" Underhill asked.

In response, the holo blurred as the picture magnified, then settled onto a perspective that had been in an upper corner. There, barely recognizable, his face turned in profile, was Matthew DiLuca. The boy was obviously unconscious and hung draped over the shoulder of a Japanese man. A bag was in the Japanese man's hand, hanging heavily.

"Why, the lad was kidnapped," Captain Ares said in consternation. "No wonder the police have failed to find him."

"That guy doesn't look like your typical GENEcologist,"

DeChanza said.

"He isn't," Matrix said. "According to the records I've accessed using his picture and running him through NCIC and Interpol, his name is Hideo Yamamiko. He has a record in Japan and in the US, and is currently thought to be working with Ruriko Nakeshita in Boston."

"Springfield ain't exactly in his neck of the woods," Refit commented.

"We can't let the poor lad stay in their hands," Captain Ares said, obviously disturbed by the thought. "We at least need to let the police know what has happened to him. And, if I may, I'd like to assist them."

"We're going to get him back," Underhill said. She couldn't ignore Matthew DiLuca's predicament. And the fact that the WEBTWO agents had Japanese service in their records at a time when the Japanese space station was raided was too much to simply ignore.

"How do you propose to do that?" C4 asked. "You don't know enough to know where the boy is. Unless you're planning on asking Nakeshita."

"I," Dervish said with clear emphasis, raising one eyebrow, "would not mind asking her. She's said to be a very clever and dangerous opponent. I'd like to know exactly how good she really is."

"There may be another way," Underhill said, getting up from her chair.

"You're proposing to take on the job offered by the Japanese now?" Greywood asked.

"At least for a time," Underhill said. "Until we see where it's going to take us. If it strays too far from our current problems, then we'll drop it. But for starters, we can get the boy back."

"Do you know where to find him?" C4 asked.

"Not yet." Underhill stopped in front of the Captain. "May I see the ink pen?"

"Yes. But take care of it. It doesn't belong to me." Captain

Ares passed it over.

"You've all been briefed about Nighthawk," the FREE-Lancers administrator said. "Introductions can come later." She handed Proudelk the pen. "Can you find him?"

"I can try." Nighthawk took the pen.

21

"What have you learned from the little urchin?" Ruriko Nakeshita asked.

Hideo shrugged. He was short and stocky, scarred from many battles, and had very cold eyes. "He admits he has an uncle who works for Yukiko Corporation, but nothing else."

Nakeshita stared through the one-way glass at the boy sitting on the edge of the bed in the other room. They were in a safe-house she maintained in Detroit, one that the Japanese Liberal Democratic Party did not know about. Her employers liked benefiting from her work, but they did not always want to know her methods of achieving their goals.

"Do you believe he knows nothing?" she asked.

"Hai," Hideo replied. "The boy is very afraid."

In truth, Matthew DiLuca looked quite forlorn. His eyes were red and his shoulders were tight from struggling not to cry.

"Has his computer been searched?"

"Hai. But we've found nothing. Perhaps, Mistress, it would help if we knew what we were looking for."

"If I knew what we were looking for," Nakeshita said, "I'd find it myself."

Chastised, the man nodded.

Nakeshita stepped close to the glass and watched the boy, wondering what made him so interesting to Family Andoc and Yukiko Corporation, and so necessary to the Japanese government. "Have you found out where Grant DiLuca is?"

"No, Mistress."

An intercom buzzed for attention.

Crossing the room, Nakeshita pressed the button. "Speak."

"Mistress," a woman's voice said, "the call you've been expecting from Orlando has come."

Nakeshita glanced at the desk in the corner of the room and saw the flashing light on the phone. She crossed the room, pressed the button, and lifted the phone. "Yes."

"I've got the information, but I want more money."

Anger stirred inside Nakeshita. The contact was a relatively new one, and she didn't know how firm she could be. "We've already agreed on the amount."

The man on the other end laughed nervously. "You'll find you're glad to pay for this. I think it's more than you expected."

She glanced up at Hideo, who looked at her impassively. The informant worked for NASA, one of the few people she'd cultivated inside Lassiter's organization. "How much?"

He told her.

"Can you access your bank account from where you are?"

"I'm standing beside an ATM."

"Fine. In two minutes go check your account balance, then call me back." She hung up, then called one of the dozens of banks she used and transferred money to the Orlando account. "When this is over," she said to Hideo, "I want you to take care of it personally. I want the body found. That way the other two stool pigeons I have at NASA will think twice before attempting to blackmail me."

"Hai, Mistress."

Less than two minutes later, the intercom buzzed and the woman put the informant through.

"It's there," he said with excitement. "You won't regret this."

"I know I won't," Nakeshita promised.

"Checking back through the records, I found out that a JSS shuttle landed at our strip this afternoon. The guy you told me to look for, DiLuca? Well, he was aboard. But the guy who ramrodded the whole show was a man named Aramis Tadashi. It took some digging, but a couple of the service people who took care of the shuttle overheard his name."

"That's good." Nakeshita's mind reeled with the implications. "Mention this to no one else."

"Not a problem." The man seemed hesitant. "I'm looking forward to doing business with you again."

"As I am looking forward to working with you." Nakeshita broke the connection and looked at Hideo. "I was wrong about him. He's dangerous. Do you have anyone in Orlando who can terminate him?"

"Hai."

She pushed the phone toward him. "Call them. Get them on it now. Every breath that fool breathes offends me."

Hideo lifted the handset and began punching buttons. His conversation was very brief. "It's done," he said when he hung up.

"Tadashi staged the raid on the space station," she said.

"But Sun Andoc himself is interested in where Grant DiLuca and this boy are," Hideo replied. "Family Andoc is heavily invested in the Fusuma Project."

Nakeshita nodded. "Yes. Andoc has taken a viper to his breast, and now it has struck him." She contemplated the boy in the other room for a short time, then returned to the phone, alerting her people to find out where Andoc and

Tadashi were. With the bad blood between them, she knew the two men would be drawn into a collision course. One of them would have to die.

Her only hope was that she could figure out who it would be most worth her while to join forces with in time to reap the greatest profit.

Chicago, Illinois   3:19 p.m. CST
Assignment: Viperstrike, cont'd.
Briefing

Gitano Proudelk's metability for telelocation didn't always work, and he knew it. But when he closed his hand around the pen Underhill handed him, he knew he could find the boy.

He closed his eyes, shutting out the crowd of people around him, forced himself to forget the pressure their very presence put on him. He took deep breaths in through his nose, then released them through his mouth. He relaxed and freed his mind and the special senses that made everything possible. Over the years he'd discovered that it was easier to locate young people than older ones. Their impressions were stronger, more focused.

When the contact was made, he fell through the middle of his mind, went through a chill, then struck out on his quest on eagle's wings. The wind was at his back. Through the wispy layers of clouds, he saw highways and roads that looked like concrete ribbons twisted through hills and wooded areas, and vast bodies of water that glimmered like sun-kissed mirrors. Then that gave way to a city, large and dirty and imposing, streets choked with cars and buses and Japanese advertising. Without warning, a small jet passed through Proudelk, but he didn't lose the psychic thread he followed.

He sensed the boy's fear first, then found the room in the suburban Victorian house where he was being held prisoner. For a few minutes, he hovered near the boy and looked around the room.

He tried his voice. Sometimes the contact was strong enough to permit it.

Matthew.

The boy started. "Who's there?"

A friend. I want to help you.

"How?"

Go to the window and look out. Once contact was made when it was this strong, Proudelk found himself stuck within the person's mind, unable to move.

"Okay." The boy got off the bed and walked to the window. Bars were on the other side of the glass.

Can you see a street sign?

"No."

Look harder. Proudelk felt attention on the other side of the glass wall behind the boy and knew they were under observation.

"There!" Matthew whispered excitedly. "I see it."

Proudelk looked, memorizing the street scene. The street sign held the name Gulley Road. He couldn't see the name of the cross street. *You did well. Hang on a little longer, and we'll be there.*

"Who are you?"

A friend. Proudelk remembered the footage of the autograph signing, of the boy's apparent infatuation with Captain Ares. *The Captain asked me to find you.*

"He's coming?"

Yes.

"When?"

Soon. Be patient, and be strong. You haven't been forgotten. Proudelk reached out for the boy's shoulder and gave him a reassuring squeeze with a hand that didn't really exist. Still, he could tell the boy felt something. He reached for his flesh-and-blood self, snapped back like a rubber band.

He opened his eyes, back in the conference room. Light strobed into his eyes like pinpricks. He looked up at Underhill. "I need a map."

She punched buttons on the pad built into the conference table. The holo wavered, then became a globe. "It's voice activated."

Proudelk nodded.

Captain Ares was leaning in, his burning blue gaze intent. "Just show me where to find the little guy, friend."

"North America," Proudelk said. The holo swiveled till North America came to a rest under his forefinger. "The United States." The view magnified. "Great Lakes Authority. Lake Erie, northwest. Michigan. Lake St. Clair. Detroit." The holo followed every command, coming up with a Detroit street map at the end that showed the different neighborhoods. "Dearborn Heights." Proudelk paused, letting the metability guide him. He pushed his forefinger forward, would have made contact if the holo had possessed tactile properties. "Here. Somewhere along Gulley Road. It's a big house. Victorian. He's being held on the second floor."

The Captain stood. "Then I must go to him."

"I'll go with you," C4 said.

Underhill looked at her.

"Unless there's something else you want me to do," C4 said. "Hanging around here's getting to be a drag. I could use some action."

"Fine," Underhill said. She glanced at Agatha Greywood. "I want you to head up this team. Take the Captain with you. And C4. Centaur and Nighthawk and Matrix will round out the team."

"When should we leave?" Greywood asked.

"Immediately. Take one of the jets."

Proudelk followed Greywood and felt like rebelling. Group scenes weren't something he enjoyed. But the sheer helplessness of the boy echoed in his mind, and he knew he couldn't stay behind. Maybe Summer Davison was right when she'd said the curse of some metables was that they knew they could make a difference. In this case, he couldn't imagine Greywood and the others finding the boy without him.

C4 walked up and took his arm, smiling. "C'mon, Proud-stallion. I'll give you a private lesson on the heroing biz."

"Proudelk," he corrected, wondering how to extract his arm. He'd been the object of adoration to some of the girls on the res, too. But when he'd politely declined their advances, he'd never had to worry about them making him explode. Things here were going to be very different—but only for the next month.

Detroit, Michigan   4:24 p.m. EST

Aramis Tadashi, dressed in a new Italian suit, walked through the hallway with an air of predatory confidence. He was flanked by his handpicked bodyguards, and Kerrick and Cydney were a half step behind him on either side.

"All hail the conquering hero," Kerrick said softly. She looked more feminine in the clinging blue silk dress that started at her throat, left her arms bare, dropped to her ankles, and hugged every curving inch of her on the way down. Pearls glittered at her throat, and her white high heels brought her almost up to Tadashi's height.

"It's not going to be that easy," Cydney growled. Like Tadashi, he wore an expensive suit of polished sharkskin. "These guys all have that look in their eyes that says they're just waiting for the opportunity to slip a knife between our ribs."

The corridor was filled with Yakuza guards dressed all in black, their eyes hidden by dark mirrorshades. Only a couple of blocks from Engawa Towers, the Cherryspire Tower was a fourteen-story structure that was all steel and glass, constructed after the Japanese had purchased Detroit. Where most Japanese business was conducted in Engawa Towers, all crime in the city went on with a benevolent nod from the people in the Cherryspire Tower. One of the floors was dedicated to bringing all the domestic street crime under Yakuza control. Prostitutes, heisters, boosters, chip runners, body jackals, and blackmailers all had to pay tribute to the dark force residing in the building.

The top floor was paneled in expensive woods, and original paintings hung on the walls. Persian carpets overlaid hard-wood floors. Double doors were at the end of the hall. Two men, faces polite and unreadable behind their mirrorshades, opened them as Tadashi neared.

Blond and svelte, the female secretary waved them through the next set of doors, pressing a button to open them. Yoshio Nishida and Sun Andoc stood inside the spacious room hold-ing drinks and talking as if nothing had changed in their worlds. Behind them, a wall of glass overlooked Mack Avenue. The center of the room was sunken at least eight inches, leaving an upper semi-oval that was divided by expen-sive furniture and a generously stocked wet bar into two office areas complete with desks and computers. In the Yakuza, even pleasure had business attached.

Sun Andoc's countenance was filled with pure, nova-intensity hatred. Two of his guards standing nearby pulled in protectively as Tadashi entered. Two others turned to face Tadashi but remained out of the group.

"I thought we were going to talk business privately," Tadashi said.

Nishida looked uncomfortable. "Andoc-san wished to be present while we discussed the situation."

"How does the Yukiko Corporation feel about this?" Tadashi asked. He was very aware that the two bodyguards hovering around Andoc had eyes like gun sights. He walked to the wet bar and made himself a drink.

"Exactly the way I tell them to," Andoc said. "I think you're forgetting who has the power around here."

"Not me," Tadashi said. "In this room, I do."

A bodyguard drew his weapon. Reacting instantly, without looking, Andoc slapped the man in the face. "But, master," the man said, "disrespect is not allowed."

"You will act only on my orders," Andoc said.

"Hai." Dropping his hand, the bodyguard bowed his head quickly, his eyes never leaving Tadashi.

"You disagree with my claim?" Tadashi asked, gazing straight at the Yakuza master.

"You're a capable opponent," Andoc said. "You've proven most resourceful in obtaining the Fusuma Project."

Tadashi bowed slightly, a smile twisting his lips. "Maybe you were right to ask Andoc-san to join us," he said to Nishida. "I like being acknowledged."

Nishida, looking like a man who wished he knew exactly what to say, didn't say anything.

"You're a pompous jaybird," Andoc said. "You were allowed to walk into this building and come up here only because my people were ordered to let you. How do you expect to get down again?"

"The elevator," Tadashi answered.

"You live only as long as I wish it," the Yakuza master said.

"And maybe you live only as long as I wish it," Tadashi responded.

White spots formed on Andoc's cheekbones.

"Where is Grant DiLuca?" Nishida asked.

"Safe," Tadashi replied.

"He was supposed to be here."

"No. *I* was supposed to be here, and *you* were supposed to be here." Tadashi smiled. "But that's okay. I think I'll enjoy watching you tell Andoc he no longer runs this operation."

Nishida looked at the floor between his feet.

"So tell him," Tadashi instructed.

"I can't," the Japanese government representative said. "I don't have that kind of authority."

Tadashi grinned and looked at Andoc. "Do you hear that? He's not going to tell you that you're dismissed because he doesn't have that kind of authority. Otherwise you'd be out of here."

Andoc said nothing.

"However," Nishida said, "I've been authorized to make a

cash settlement with you."

Laughing, Tadashi stepped up on the surrounding oval and seated himself on one of the luxurious desks. "Cash, even if I lived to spend it, would soon be gone. Then what?" He shook his head. "No. I've already stated my price. Either ante up, or I'll find someone else willing to pay for the Fusuma Project."

"Insolent pup!" Andoc snarled.

Tadashi ignored him, concentrating on Nishida. "You have one minute to make your choice, then I'll find someone else to deal with."

Andoc snapped his fingers. The wall to his left suddenly slid away, revealing a dozen ninjas armed with short swords and machine pistols. "You'll deal with us," the Yakuza master said.

A wolfish grin thinned Tadashi's lips as he searched inside himself and grabbed the metability. The power surged, as malleable as clay and as deadly as an explosive. "Very well, I will." He reached under his jacket and removed the Colt Government Model .45 from the shoulder rig.

The two men closest to Andoc stood in front of their master and brought up their guns.

Lifting his other hand, Tadashi sent green-tinged yellow rays licking out to touch their weapons. The control, even though there were four targets in all, came easily. He magnetized the bullets in the chambers.

"Do not kill him!" Andoc roared.

The hammers clicked against the firing pins and the gunpowder detonated. Then the barrels blew up because the bullets were frozen in place. In quick succession, Tadashi shot each of the four men through the head. As their victims' bodies dropped, the ninjas rushed forward.

Involuntarily, Cydney backed away, fumbling for his weapon. Kerrick stood her ground and took an H&K VP70Z from her purse. She fired without hesitation.

At one with the forces he'd raised within himself, Tadashi focused on the metal weapons held naked in the hands of the

ninjas, and on the ones hidden within their clothing. He
shoved with nearly as much force as he'd used on the space
station. Lifted from their feet, the ninjas exploded through
the floor-to-ceiling window facing Mack Avenue, then
dropped on the afternoon traffic below. A few seconds later,
car horns started up and became a constant noise, though
weak and distant.

Tadashi reveled in his power. With quick flicks of the magnetic force, he sealed the door, activating the lock and magne-
tizing the steel plate, concealed under the wood veneer, to the
jamb. Then he picked up the bodies of the men he'd slain and
hurled them through the broken window.

Kerrick coolly reloaded and kept her weapon out.

Nishida had gone ashen.

Tadashi turned to face Andoc. "Your time here is over, old
man. You can't stop me." He paused, then caused two short
swords that had been dropped by men Kerrick had shot to
rise, in glittering arcs, from the floor. They spun hypnotically,
then came to a rest on either side of the Yakuza master's
throat. "It is *you* who can't leave this building—unless I
choose to let you."

Hatred glowed in Andoc's eyes as he fisted the hafts of the
floating swords. "Then kill me, cur."

Gesturing, Tadashi caused the swords to lift, their hafts
crossed like a giant scissors, but didn't allow the blades to
break Andoc's skin. The Yakuza master gripped the sword
hafts involuntarily and struggled to keep from getting hurt.
His shoes floated two feet above the ground.

"No," Tadashi said. "I don't want you dead. I want you to
live and to know my power."

With a shrill cry of rage, Andoc lunged forward and tried
to cut his throat on the **Y** of the joined blades.

Already expecting Andoc to try to take the way out that
would permit him to save face, Tadashi flicked the blades
away. Andoc fell, then reached beneath his jacket and brought
out a small silver pistol. Tadashi used his power again, feeling

a slight headache oozing up from his shoulders. Instantly, the pistol in Andoc's fist flew into a dozen pieces as the parts repelled each other.

"No," Tadashi said, closing in. Andoc stayed on his knees, glaring up at the younger man. "You're going to live. If you were dead, a dozen others would rise and try to fill your shoes. With you alive, no one will challenge you. When you say I am to be left alone, they will listen to you."

"And why would I let you live?"

"Because if there are any attempts on my life that I think come from you, I'll have one member of your family killed for each attempt." Tadashi paused. "And now you know I can do that."

Andoc pushed himself to his feet but didn't say anything. Across the room, hands and feet thudded against the door as people tried to break in. The wind swirled in through the broken window.

Tadashi turned to Nishida. "I'm waiting for your answer."

Without much hesitation, the Diet representative bowed deeply. "We'll be happy to accede to your terms. When may we have the Fusuma Project?"

"Soon. First I want to settle into my new headquarters." Tadashi turned to Andoc. "To begin with, you'll order the people here to recognize my authority. Gradually, I'll replace them with my own staff."

Slowly, the Yakuza master nodded.

Flicking the power out again, Tadashi caused the door to open. "You may leave," he said to both men.

Andoc strode across the room regally, and the security men shoving their way inside took their cue from him and backed away.

"But the Fusuma Project . . ." Nishida protested.

Crossing the room, Tadashi seated himself in a big leather chair behind one of the desks. "It will wait," he said. "The *Rinji 8* no longer exists. And it will take eight months to ready another space station."

Reluctantly, Nishida bowed and left the room.

Kerrick seated herself at the other desk and used the computer. A few minutes later, she said, "All the bugs and hidden cameras to the top floor have been turned over to us. No one else can access them."

"Good." Tadashi looked out over the city, enjoying the feel of his new position. "Have the maintenance people come up and fix this glass and replace the carpet." Blood stains were grouped in patches.

Kerrick nodded and turned back to the keyboard. "How much time do you think we have?"

"A few days at the outside." Tadashi glanced up at Cydney. "Have there been any changes regarding the DiLuca boy?"

"The Springfield police are still searching for him."

"Get whatever footage you can of the telethon. If the boy has been missing this long, something has to have happened to him."

The phone rang and Kerrick answered it. After a moment, she looked up at Tadashi. "It's for you."

Leaning forward, Tadashi lifted the phone and punched the flashing extension. He gave his name.

"I have something you want," a woman said.

"Who is this?" Tadashi demanded.

"Ruriko Nakeshita. Congratulations on your recent promotion. I hope you live long enough to enjoy it."

Tadashi had heard of the woman but had never done business with her. Whatever dealings Family Andoc had had with her over the years had been handled by Sun Andoc alone. "And what is it I could possibly want?"

"Grant DiLuca's nephew," Nakeshita said. "I had him kidnapped from the Springfield telethon. I know you and Family Andoc are looking for him. And I know you're responsible for the raid on *Rinji 8*. My guess is that you need the boy to leverage Grant DiLuca's cooperation."

The tightness in Tadashi's stomach lessened. For once, the woman didn't know the value of the property she held. He was willing to pay anything.

He settled down to haggle, a warlord who'd just placed himself on dangerous ground with enemies at every quarter.

22

New Orleans, Louisiana   **3:28 p.m. CST**
Ohio-Lower Mississippi Basin   **2128 Greenwich**
Cooperative (OLMBC)   **Mean**
90.2 degrees W Longitude   **October 24, 2023**
29.9 degrees N Latitude   **Tuesday**
Assignment: Glass Hobbit
Tactical Ops: Soft Probe, Fact-finding
Status: Code Green

"Can't you imagine zombies living there?"

Jimmy Conrad finished surveying the gabled house tucked back in a thick copse of magnolias and looked over his shoulder at Marsha Martini. "Zombies?"

"Yeah," Martini said. She held up her arms and hands in mock claws to illustrate. "The living dead. Voodoo, that kind of thing. They have a lot of it down here, you know."

They were both dressed in dark clothes to blend in with the dense, swampy forest that surrounded them. The house was less than a hundred yards away, looking a couple hundred years old. Three stories tall and painted white, it stood out against the forest background. A low stone fence ran around the main estate, but bushes and trees threatened to camouflage it. Recent gardening and landscaping had left piles of brush near the narrow blacktop road that led to the house. A circle drive covered in broken blue shale dipped near the three-car garage that was a separate structure. Servants' quarters were on the other side of that, a small house that probably had four or five bedrooms, dwarfed by the immensity of the main house.

Conrad watched the house. They knew Barnaby Maitland was inside. The burgundy Cadillac Cibola licensed to him was parked in the circle drive.

"Do zombies ever go on a diet?" asked Conrad.

"What?"

"If they don't, you're safe."

"Very funny."

Conrad shook his head. "You're an expert on pirates and zombies all in the same day. How are you on alien abductions and Elvis sightings?"

"Together, or separate? Quiet," Martini cautioned, slinking deeper into the brush. "Maitland's coming out."

Maitland was a beefy man, barely thirty years old, with wispy blond hair. He wore glasses and a new suit. Two men, both in good physical condition, accompanied him to the car. One slid behind the wheel and the other took the shotgun seat while Maitland sat in the back.

Conrad took out his binoculars and surveyed the Cadillac as it took off for the massive wrought-iron gates.

"Armored?" Martini asked.

He shook his head. "No. It's riding too high. When they got in, they made a difference. New house alarm systems, though. Bodyguards. But he's only recently come into wealth. Probably more afraid of going broke than being found." Conrad pushed himself to his feet. "Let's go."

He took the lead, running through the brush, following the falling land. The road from the gabled house curved back around their present position, cutting through the wooded area again just below them. Less than two minutes later, he broke through the final layer of brush to the pile of rocks where they'd set up their ambush. The Isuzu Trooper they'd rented sat safely hidden behind trees.

He opened the rear deck and took out the Savage bolt-action .30-30. The rifle was short and light, perfect for the bush area, but he knew it would have a hell of a kick.

"They're coming," Martini said.

Conrad threw himself on top of the rocks and lined up his shot. He removed the plastic caps from the powerful scope. In the distance he heard the smooth purr of the Cadillac's engine. Relaxing, keeping his arms loose, he spotted the flash of red that signaled the car's approach. He found the front tire in his scope, let out half a breath, and squeezed the trigger.

The Savage impacted roughly against his shoulder and he rode out the recoil as best as he could. The echo of the percussion cracked and rolled over the land around him. He was working the bolt action when he heard Martini tell him he'd shot the tire. Feeling good about his marksmanship, he sighted the other front tire. This time it took him two shots because the Cadillac was wobbling terribly. Then the other front tire deflated and the driver lost it entirely.

The Cibola crashed into a stand of trees less than fifty yards down the hill from their position.

Conrad reached into a pants pocket and took out the other three-round clip he had ready for the rifle. He slipped the first clip out, worked the bolt action, and chambered the first round of the new clip. These were Para-bullets and wouldn't do permanent damage.

"Maitland's coming out," Martini said.

Conrad ignored the ex-banker as the man ran from the back door, blood staining his forehead. For a moment, he stood frozen in indecision. Passing on the driver, Conrad picked up the passenger on the other side of the car because the man had more room to hide or take cover. Now used to the recoil of the Savage, he fired.

The Para-bullet caught the man in the upper chest and threw him backward. Working the bolt action, Conrad sighted in on the driver as he sprinted for the woods. He led the man slightly, aware that Martini was in motion in front of him, streaking toward Maitland.

The other bodyguard saw her break cover and came around with a pistol in his hand. Conrad yelled a warning, then took up trigger slack. The Savage kicked into his shoulder and a heartbeat later the driver went down, his machine pistol raking leaves from the trees overhead.

Abandoning the rifle, Conrad ran down the hill and drew the 9mm pistol from shoulder leather. He'd lost Martini in the confusion, didn't know if she'd been hit.

Then he saw her bolting across the street to bring Maitland down in a flying tackle. By the time he arrived, she had the situation well in hand. Martini sat astride him, holding both of his hands up behind his back.

"I don't know what you think you're doing," the beefy man said. "You've got the wrong guy."

"Wrong, zombie-breath," Martini said. "We've got the right guy. We're FREELancers, and we know you helped set us up with those accounts in the Cayman International Bank." She showed him her ID card. "You're going to tell us what we want to know, or we're going to turn you into swamp mulch."

"Okay," Maitland said, staring wildly from behind the cracked lenses of his glasses. "Just don't hurt me."

"Get up," Conrad ordered, motioning with the pistol. He had to help Maitland to his feet. Martini got behind him and slipped a pair of plastic disposable cuffs around his wrists, trapping his arms behind him.

Conrad pushed their prisoner ahead of them, knowing someone at the big house could have heard the shots and might come to investigate.

"We did pretty good, didn't we?" Martini asked. "Two assignments in one day, and we aced them both. Maybe when we get back to Chicago I'm going to hit Underhill up for a raise. There's a new stereo system I've had my eye on."

"Zombie-breath?" Conrad whispered to her. "Swamp mulch? Jeez, how lame can you get?"

"Hey," she said. "You want to start thinking up snappy retorts, fine by me. But in the hero biz, we've got an image to uphold."

He shook his head. "Somehow I can't see Captain Ares calling someone zombie-breath."

"No, he'd probably say 'Zowie.' Zombie-breath is a definite improvement. More hard-edged twenty-first century."

Conrad glanced at her. "Oh, yeah," he said.

Chicago, Illinois   3:30 p.m. CST
Assignment: Viperstrike, cont'd.
Tactical Ops: Information Retrieval
Status: Code Green

Lee Won Underhill entered the conference room briskly. Masohiro Kinoshita, wearing a dark, elegant suit, sat at ease in one of the plush chairs in front of an inlaid desk. The room's motif was early nineteenth century exploration, with charts and compasses and astrolabes hung on the walls. A pith helmet hung beside a Nitro Express elephant gun mounted on the wall behind the desk.

Kinoshita rose when he saw her. "Ms. Underhill," he said in English.

"Ambassador Kinoshita." The FREELancers administrator took her seat behind the desk. "Would you care for something to drink? I have a good range of teas."

"No," he said, sitting. "I know you're pressed for time, so I'll be brief with my business. My government wishes to retain the services of the FREELancers."

Underhill leaned back in her chair, studying the man. "In what capacity?"

Kinoshita leaned back in his chair, obviously not used to

the defensive position he suddenly found himself in. "There has been an incident. Something was taken from my government. We wish to have it recovered."

"From whom?"

"We're not certain."

Underhill considered that. It was possible her investigation was ahead of that of the Japanese. When it came to the space program, they were generally considered bedmates with Lassiter. With that being the case, their spying network at NASA could have been circumvented. "What was taken?"

"Experimental research. Computer programming." Kinoshita made direct eye contact with her. "I find myself in an untenable position. My government has a policy of maintaining its secrets, as does yours, yet I find myself revealing them to you. It is most difficult."

Nodding, Underhill knew that the ambassador would reveal only as many of those secrets as he had to.

"You're aware of the accident that happened on board the *Rinji 8*?"

"Yes."

"There was research going on aboard the space station."

"Dr. Grant DiLuca's," she prompted, letting him know she was versed with the events so that he wouldn't try to hide too much. Kinoshita, uncertain about the depth of her knowledge, would realize he was walking a tightrope if he tried to lie to her about too many things.

"Yes. It is called the Fusuma Project and is very important in our business circles."

"What is it?"

"It is research on computer chip development." Kinoshita spread his hands. "More than that I, myself, do not know."

Figuring that was possible, and even if it wasn't that it was an acceptable lie, Underhill said, "The people who went to so much trouble to acquire this research might not give it up so easily. What then?"

"At that point," the ambassador replied, "your team can

turn them over to our negotiators, and we will work on them."

Underhill had no illusions about how that "work" would be conducted. If they had to, Japanese military specialists would take the minds of the guilty parties apart piece by piece. The phone rang. She excused herself and answered it, knowing Kent wouldn't have bothered her unless it was significant.

"The Tandems just called from New Orleans with the names on the bearer bonds" Kent said. "I checked them out. They came from a Pacific Rim company called Kabuki Productions, an investments business. Checking back, I turned up Sun Andoc's name, but the manager of record of the accounts for the last few years has been Aramis Tadashi. It was Tadashi's name on the bearer bonds."

"Get me a jacket on this guy." Underhill watched Kinoshita, knowing the man was listening to her though acting like he wasn't.

"No prob. I'm adding to the one Matrix started. One curious aspect about the bearer bonds, though, is that they were moved into the Caymans through Stride Consultation."

The name rang a bell for Underhill immediately. Stride Consultation was a fringe business that trafficked internationally in shady deals. Though they'd worked for months to prove who ultimately owned Stride Consultation, her investigators had never been able to connect Crystal Young to the corporation.

"And there's one other thing. Guess who was PR director for Kabuki Productions up until six weeks ago? If you say Skyler Deshane, you get the brass ring."

"Work that one up too." Underhill hung up. "Sorry."

Kinoshita waved the apology away. "I know this is a bad time for you."

She guessed that it was his way of letting her know he was aware of the problems facing FREELancers.

"Perhaps news of our alliance will help," Kinoshita said.

The expressed opinion transgressed polite conduct but Underhill didn't let it faze her. It was possible that a show of faith on behalf of the Japanese government might tilt the scales in the media somewhat. After all, they owned a fair percentage of the major outlets. "Do you know who attacked the space station?"

Kinoshita lifted his shoulders a fraction of an inch, then dropped them. "Regretfully, no. If we did, our security people would take care of the problem."

"But you suspect that the people responsible are in the United States?"

"Your country is the largest space-faring nation in the world," the ambassador said. "And you have more satellites in orbit than anyone else. It is felt that we would be fools to ignore that."

"I agree." If the conversation was to be a tennis match, Underhill figured she was going to try for a service ace. "What can you tell me about Aramis Tadashi?"

For a moment, Kinoshita was silent. "I do not know if I've ever heard the name."

Underhill nodded, realizing the ambassador knew full well who Tadashi was. With Tadashi tied in to the space station raid and the public smear of FREELancers, she knew she wasn't going to turn away from the proffered Japanese employment. "At this point, I'm ready to enter into a preliminary contract with your government regarding FREELancers recovering the Fusuma Project."

Kinoshita nodded.

The phone rang and Underhill answered.

"I've got an emergency call here for the ambassador," Kent said.

"Point of origin?"

"Detroit."

"The caller?"

"Yoshio Nishida."

The politician was Kinoshita's superior in the Diet. Underhill said, "Give him five minutes, then try it again."

"Right." Kent hung up.

"Sorry," the FREELancers administrator said. Standard operating procedures meant that Kent would let the call go through in ten minutes, doubling the vocalized amount so the listener wouldn't bridge the omission so easily. "Let's talk about the contract."

"Of course."

Underhill dropped a thumb on a button, alerting one of the secretaries outside. "Our standard recovery contract for a person or property recovery is an agreed-upon amount at signing, plus an additional fifteen percent of the person or property's worth."

"I'll have to seek confirmation on the amounts."

Lacing her fingers together in front of her, Underhill said, "Mr. Ambassador, beating around the bush is only going to waste time. The Fusuma Project has been in what I can only think of as enemy hands for hours. How much damage can be done in that amount of time, I have no idea." She paused to let her words sink in. "If the Japanese Diet had wanted to merely broach the subject of employing the FREELancers, they'd have sent someone else. They sent you because they're ready to deal."

As he let out his breath, Kinoshita nodded. "So where would you like to open negotiations? I can tell you already that your fifteen percent is too high."

"The advance against the percentage is nonreturnable."

Kinoshita nodded.

"Four million," the FREELancer administrator said.

"Ridiculous. I've been authorized to offer two million dollars. And that's only if we get results."

"If you can get someone for two million," Underhill said, "you should go ahead and hire them. However, anticipating a big return on the percentage, I'll agree to three-million-five."

"Two-and-a-half million," the ambassador said. "With the percentage lowered to ten—upon recovery."

"Split the difference," Underhill said. "Give us an advance of three million and we'll drop the percentage to twelve, require only half that up-front after recovery, and we'll pay our own medical expenses."

Kinoshita examined the offer thoughtfully.

Outwardly at ease, Underhill watched the clock. Only seven minutes remained of the time she'd asked from Kent.

Finally, the ambassador nodded. "We have a deal."

Underhill flipped the intercom switch. "Joyce, bring in the contract." The secretary entered from a side door, bearing legal documents. There were three copies. Underhill quickly checked off the particulars for Kinoshita.

"Will a check be sufficient?" the ambassador asked, drawing a checkbook and pen from his jacket.

"Very." Underhill handed the check and signed copies of the contract to the secretary, who left. The phone rang.

"It seems we have a new wrinkle," Kent said. "Aramis Tadashi just got himself named as the new head of the Cherryspire Tower."

"His predecessor?"

"Bowed out."

"Willingly?"

"Anything but, from what I've heard from the covert intelligence we've got in that building."

The only insider Underhill had ever managed to get into the Cherryspire Tower was now one of the PR staff there, which did not get her very near the truth of what was going on behind the concrete-and-glass walls. "How did it happen?"

"Tadashi cut a deal with Nishida that ousted Andoc only minutes ago. Now you know everything I do. Also, I'm now holding that call for Ambassador Kinoshita. Want me to ring you back?"

"Yes." A moment later the phone rang and she passed it to the Japanese ambassador.

Kinoshita spoke for only a moment, as cryptically as she

had, then hung up. "It appears that my government's decision to hire you was premature."

Underhill raised an eyebrow.

"The Fusuma Project has been returned to us."

"How fortunate for you," Underhill said.

Kinoshita nodded. "I'm sorry to have taken up your time."

"You'll be billed for the consultation."

"Of course. I would expect nothing less." The ambassador hesitated uncomfortably. "Might I suggest we take care of the matter now."

"Sure. Let me get your check back to you, and we can make the adjustment." Underhill called the secretary, asking for the check.

"I'm sorry," the secretary responded over the speakerphone, "but I deposited that in the bank through the computers. It's already been cleared."

Underhill acted a little surprised, though she'd given the secretary orders to consummate the transaction at once. She looked at Kinoshita. "I'm sorry, but I make it a policy here that deposits are to be handled immediately. May I write you a check for the difference?"

Kinoshita obviously wasn't happy about the situation, but good manners prevented him from saying so. "That would be fine."

Taking a checkbook from the desk drawer, Underhill wrote a check on one of the accounts she maintained in Chicago. She blew the ink dry, then handed it over.

"It's for the full amount," Kinoshita observed. "You haven't taken out for today."

"I'll see that you're billed," Underhill said. After a few minutes of polite conversation while her mind dealt with everything she'd just learned, she ushered the Japanese ambassador to the door.

Once he was gone, the FREELancers administrator called the bank that held the account the check was drawn on and issued a stop-payment order. Kinoshita wouldn't realize he was holding nothing but bad paper until he was back in Detroit.

In any event, Underhill fully intended to earn out the advance, and get as much of the percentage as she could.

23

Seattle, Washington   **1:43 p.m. PST**
The Pacific Coast   **2143 Greenwich Mean**
122.4 degrees W Longitude   **October 24, 2023**
47.5 degrees N Latitude   **Tuesday**
Assignment: Mirrors
Tactical Ops: Covert Probe
Status: Code Green

"You know, I'd never have picked Nix as a turncoat," Wyndom Amakyn said as he watched a sort program working on the computer monitor in front of him.

"You never know about people," Simon Drake said. "Everyone has their secrets." He sat on the corner of the man's small desk, drinking coffee he hated and still managing to tweak the metability inside himself to reach the WEBTWO computer tech with confidentiality and friendliness.

"And what secret do you have?" Amakyn asked, gazing up from the monitor. He was young and earnest, blond hair spiky and short. They were seated in the computer room of the WEBTWO base. Security was loose and freewheeling. The organization owned city blocks in all four directions. The cybernetic nerve center was disguised as a travel bureau, with information tendrils into most of the major European cities.

"Me?" Drake replied. "I'm a spy." And he grinned.

Amakyn laughed. "Aren't we all?" He tapped commands on the keyboard and the perspective of the different monitors changed, funneling intelligence from dozens of BBSs across the globe. Then he squirmed uncomfortably.

Drake glanced at his watch, knowing the diuretic he'd laced the man's coffee with would be kicking in. Since his arrival at the WEBTWO base he'd familiarized himself with as much of the everyday ops as he could while Robeson filed his reports concerning the deal with Agent Prime and the Millenniests, and took steps to deal with the traitor, Nix. As Raymond Sender, the man he was disguised as, Drake had already shut down his ops field for the next hour. It was all the maneuvering room he figured he had.

"How much do you know about these computers?" Amakyn asked.

Drake shrugged. "They're Hunter Js, a derivative of the new Cray Fours."

"Do you feel okay watching them for just a minute?"

"Sure. The way I understand it, you don't have to be a rocket scientist to get around on them."

"Yeah." Amakyn stood. "I buzzed my relief, but he must be busy, and I'm about to bust a kidney here."

Actually, Drake had disconnected the buzzer wire under the table with wire cutters. "I don't mind."

"Lucky you were in the neighborhood," Amakyn said. "Otherwise every piece of equipment in the room might have been flooded out." He left.

Working quickly, knowing he had only minutes at his disposal, Drake lifted the phone, got an outside line, and punched in one of the junction numbers that connected him with FREELancers Base without tracing back. He held the receiver on his shoulder while he flipped through the menus. An earlier check had revealed Greg Nix's files, though he

hadn't been able to get to them. From the real Raymond
Sender's office, he'd put together a program that flagged Nix's
files and would chain them when he was on the master
boards.

He accessed the prepped program, activated it, and
watched the screens fill with information. When Philip Kent
came on-line, he said, "Charm. I'm ready to transmit."

"Go."

Drake tagged the button, then watched the information
trek across the screens as it was absorbed by FREELancers
computers.

"What the hell are you doing?"

Turning around, Drake found the relief guy suddenly
standing in the doorway, outfitted in WEBTWO's purple
one-piece uniform.

"Get away from that computer," the WEBTWO man
ordered, reaching for the pistol sheathed on his hip.

Drake dropped his hand into his pocket, then came out
with the telescoping Wilkinson StunSabre. When he flicked
the ten-inch haft, thirty-six inches of Toledo steel shot out.
The half-cup quillon folded over his fingers to protect them.
The blue light in the pommel showed the weapon had a full
charge, set on stun-burst.

The pistol came up quickly.

A pirate's grin on his face, Drake said, "Ho, knave, thou
shalt never shed the life's blood of a prince of the realm." His
execution was flawless as he demonstrated the skill he'd
brought to the stage as Cyrano.

The first flashing sweep of the sword knocked the pistol
from his attacker's grasp, then he slashed the tip toward the
man's chest, made contact, and thumbed the firing stud. The
smell of electricity filled the air as the WEBTWO member
jerked once, then slumped to the floor, unconscious.

Another shout let Drake know the battle hadn't escaped
notice. A pair of bullets slammed through the glass inset in
the door, sending shards raining to the floor. The FREELancers

agent dropped his hand into his jacket, found a pair of small explosive devices, flipped the activating toggles, then hurled them toward the computers. In addition to stealing whatever information he could, he'd decided to add mayhem to the occasion.

He bolted through the other door in the back of the room, barely making it out before the concussive waves filled the computer lab. A pair of WEBTWO agents stood in the corridor before him, their weapons drawn.

The StunSabre was a spark of light as he wove a net of defense before him. It flicked out, made contact with one weapon's barrel, and shot electricity through the metal to shock the wielder into insensibility. Before the first man dropped, Drake scored with a lunge to the other man's neck, shorting out his consciousness as well.

Fleeing down the corridor he'd already chosen as his emergency escape route, Drake dropped a hand on the fire alarm. Harsh, strident ringing swept confusion through the buildings as WEBTWO agents tried to figure out what was going on. Turning a corner, he glanced down the hallway and saw the emergency fire chute extending from the building. Ground level was three stories below.

Using his free hand, Drake swept the fire hose from the rack inside the space built into the wall, flung it out onto the carpeted floor, then turned the valve. Water gushed at once, flooding the carpet.

Over his shoulder, Drake saw the fire chute was almost at full extension. Then the first wave of his pursuers caught up to him. They raised their weapons, and he knew that prisoners were an option rather than a requirement.

Adjusting the StunSabre to its highest setting to totally drain the charge in one burst, Drake shoved the point against the wet carpet. The charge slithered through a half dozen WEBTWO agents caught standing in the water, dropping them in their tracks.

"Sorry to fight and run," Drake said, offering a mock salute to his vanquished foes. Then he turned and ran, throwing himself down the fire chute.

He turned in midslide and landed on his feet, breaking into a flat-out run immediately. He collapsed the StunSabre and put it away, then dropped into a well of descending stairs where the frenetic strains of heavy metal music issued from behind a heavy wooden door with a gryphon carved on it, the eyes made from cut glass the color of honey with sunburst designs.

Before he reached it, the door flew open and five young men and two women dressed in similar black tee shirts and jeans walked out of the tavern, obviously disgruntled.

"Look," a tall, lean guy with shocking green hair said, "if Bishop can't come up with the money to pay us, then he can stick with the Moose and Squirrel band. We don't need this crap. We just turned a record deal." His shirt advertised Fried Crimson Silk Kisses.

A heavyset man with a fierce mustache and a totally bald head glared at the band from the doorway. "Record deals for you don't pay the gate in this place. The offer's on the table. Take it or leave it, McBain."

McBain waved a hand. "We're leaving it. You change your mind, call me in Nacogdoches."

Knowing the WEBTWO people were hot on his heels but drawn into the conversation, Drake stepped forward. "Maybe I can be of help," he said. "The name's Lansdale."

"Who're you?" the mustached man demanded.

"An agent." Drake offered a card, stepping into their group.

"Already got an agent," McBain said.

"I know," Drake replied. "He got you a record deal. But I'm thinking maybe he's not considering exposure enough. You guys are going to go national with an album, you got to be seen." He glanced at the mustached man. "What's your name?"

"Barrett."

"Fine. Barrett, how're you fixed for cameras inside the place?" Drake asked.

The man lifted his shoulders and dropped them.

"Why don't we go take a look?"

McBain seemed reluctant. "Don't need an agent. We've been getting gigs like this for years."

"Yeah," Drake said smoothly, accessing the metability, "but you're about to hit the big time, my friend. Tell you what, if I can't do you any good, I won't take one thin dime. And if I can't increase this guy's gate, I'm not doing any of us any good."

Two of the other band members opted to try, saying that their present agent wasn't concerned with their nightly gigs, which had been paying their bills for years. Before anyone knew exactly what was going on, Drake had them herded back inside the tavern and into the office, and was cutting a deal that none of them had thought possible.

Seated comfortably behind the manager's desk, talking effortlessly to a local news station, he watched through the one-way glass as WEBTWO agents worked their way through the afternoon crowd searching for him. By the time they cleared out, he'd already nailed down two human-interest spots on the local networks.

Chicago, Illinois   *3:54 p.m. CST*
Assignment: Viperstrike, cont'd.
Tactical Ops: Intelligence Recovery
Status: Code Green

Refit, John-Michael DeChanza, GlowStar, Dervish, and Download were all waiting in the conference room when Lee Won Underhill arrived. She wasted no time.

"Charm scored with his end of the operation in Seattle," the FREELancers administrator said. "The accounts used by the ex-WEBTWO agents were part of the Kabuki Productions network the Tandems uncovered."

Dervish looked at her from the end of the table where she sat in a full lotus position, her scimitar haft poking up over her shoulder. "All of these events are related?"

"Yes," Underhill said. "Tadashi, on the surface, used the holding company that Deadline owns to work the deals."

"So maybe she helped set up the Gibney kidnappings," DeChanza said.

Underhill nodded. "Whether she bartered with Tadashi to frame us, or if it was part of his plan all along, we may never know. But he's become our target." She activated the holo and brought up the limited footage Matrix and Kent had been able to find on the man. What they knew of Tadashi's career was quickly laid out.

"I guess," Refit said when they finished, "this means we're going to Detroit."

"I've got a jet standing by," the FREELancers administrator said. "It'll leave as soon as we're on board."

Download looked at her, his arms crossed over his chest. But he didn't say anything.

Refit, Dervish, and DeChanza were already headed for the door.

"I didn't know you involved yourself personally with missions," GlowStar said.

"As a general rule," Underhill admitted, "I don't. But Tadashi has made this personal. I'm not about to walk away from that." She gazed at the frozen image on the holo. "Nobody harms this organization and walks away scot-free. He's going to find that out. In spades."

24

Detroit, Michigan   **9:41 p.m. EST**
Great Lakes Authority (GLA)   **0241 Greenwich Mean**
83.1 degrees W Longitude   **October 24, 2023**
42.3 degrees N Latitude   **Tuesday**
      Assignment: Viperstrike, cont'd.
        Tactical Ops: Forcible Recovery
           Status: Code Green

"That's the house I saw," Gitano Proudelk said. He gazed through the windshield of the Plymouth Voyager van at the dark Victorian sitting on the corner of Gulley Road and Puckett Street. A fear ran through him, cold and deep. He'd never experienced anything like it before. When he'd rescued Edward Sharpnose, he'd had no doubts about recovering the boy safely.

"Is he inside now?" Agatha Greywood asked from behind the steering wheel.

Gripping the pen that linked him to Matthew DiLuca, Proudelk said, "Yes. He's afraid. He's on the second floor."

"Can you tell how many people are guarding him?"

"No. My metability doesn't work like that."

Greywood activated her Burris transceiver, letting the rest of the team know.

"We need to go to the lad now," Captain Ares insisted when she finished.

"Agreed," Greywood said, "but we'll have to push the odds as much in his favor as we can before we breach their security."

"I can get up on the building," Proudelk said. "I'll figure out where he is."

"They have a good security system on the windows and doors of the house," Matrix said from the back. She sat beside the wooden crate holding one of Greywood's stone golems. Her crimson-lensed glasses shone darkly. "It's a Wexler. With time I could get past it."

"We'd still have to nullify the team inside," Greywood said. "No, I think Gitano's right. We'll stand a better chance if we can get to the boy quickly and try to remove him from the scene." In short, terse sentences she laid out the attack scenario. While Nighthawk tackled the rooftops, Captain Ares would take the front door. Golem would take the rear, with Centaur floating in a loose perimeter farther out, and C4 watching over the garage. Matrix would remain in the van, maintaining the link with Underhill's group, who had also arrived in Detroit and were setting up on the Cherryspire Tower downtown.

When the signal was given, Proudelk slipped from the van, opened the rear door, and eased the crate with the Golem out, watching as nails groaned when the stone figure inside pushed its way free, operated by Greywood's mind. Then he sped for the shadows. Around him, he knew two other FREE-Lancers vehicles were disgorging metables. C4 and the Captain had come by sedan, while Centaur had driven a specially modified van that housed the harness.

Proudelk moved quietly, reaching out with his metability to quiet dogs that ran in backyards of nearby houses. He let them know that friends moved among them tonight. Less than two minutes later, he was at the rear of the Victorian climbing a drainpipe that hung down from the gutter.

Finding footing on the first-floor roof, he left the drainpipe and crossed the shingles quietly till he was at the window to the room he knew housed Matthew DiLuca. He accessed the Burris transceiver and let the team know he was in place.

Tense seconds ticked by, then the whole house seemed to shiver as Captain Ares forced his way into the dwelling. Gunshots and hoarse yells followed instantly.

Ignoring the violence that suddenly swirled around him, Proudelk seized the edges of the window in both fists, concentrated on his metable strength, and yanked. With a groaning shudder, the bars pulled free.

He was aware of figures going into motion around the boy on the bed. Three men rushed for Matthew DiLuca while trying to bring weapons into play.

Proudelk grabbed the man closest to him by the arm, then flipped him toward the bedroom's other window. The man flailed, then struck the bars and ripped them from their moorings, dropping onto the rooftop and rolling away. One of the other men got off a shot. A foot-long muzzle flash licked out for the young AmerInd, then he felt the crash against his chest as the Kevlar armor stopped the bullet.

Still in motion, he backhanded the shooter in the face and sent him smashing through the closet door. The remaining man had been reaching for the boy in the bed, then realized the threat that stood before him.

Proudelk was on him while he still had his hand on the shoulder holster, digging for the pistol. He gave the man a forearm shiver that bounced him off the wall and dropped him in a heap.

The boy blinked at him owlishly, obviously terrified. Crashing thunder sounded below.

"Matthew," Proudelk said easily. "I'm a friend."

The boy swallowed hard. "I talked to you. Earlier."

"Yes. Now we're getting out of here. Okay?"

"Okay."

"Where's your computer?"

The boy pointed to the bag at the foot of the bed.

Proudelk grabbed the boy and tossed him over his shoulder, then fisted the straps of the bag. "Keep your head down." He stepped out of the room just as the bedroom door exploded inward. Bullets crashed through the glass behind him. "Hang on."

With long strides, he ran across the steep roof and leapt from the edge. The ground came up at him, but he handled it easily, listening to the soft *chuff* of the DiLuca boy's breath come out of his lungs. He broke into a run at once, streaking for the alley they'd agreed upon. Accessing the Burris, he said, "This is Nighthawk. We're clear."

"I'm on my way," Matrix called back.

"Break off the assault," Greywood ordered.

Pausing at the alley's mouth, Proudelk glanced back at the Victorian. Flames and shadows, intermingled in savage violence, could be seen through the windows. The Golem pushed its way through the rear wall, bullets bouncing from the stone skin. Then Captain Ares strode through the wreckage of the front door with a man's shirt wadded in each fist, shaking the wearers fiercely.

"The Captain," Matthew DiLuca breathed.

"Yeah." And Proudelk had to admit, seeing Captain Ares against the backdrop of the burning Victorian was awe-inspiring. Nothing like it back on the res. Centaur galloped like a flesh-and-steel ghost across the landscaped yard, hooves throwing clods as he took deadly aim with the pistols in both fists. A Lincoln Towncar barreled through the closed garage doors, sending wood splinters and metal hardware flying.

"Where the hell is C4?" Centaur demanded over the radio-link.

The expensive sedan fishtailed out in the street, and the lights swept over Proudelk and the boy. The AmerInd turned at once and sprinted deeper into the alley. Matrix was supposed to be waiting on the other side.

"Nighthawk!"

The shout brought Proudelk up short. He turned to face C4, looking like a white-bikinied wraith against the shadows of the three-story home behind her.

"Give me the boy," she said, reaching out.

"I've got him," Proudelk said. "You were supposed to cover the garage."

The Lincoln Towncar sped toward them. Centaur galloped to head it off, unaware of the figures in the alley.

"Give me the boy," C4 ordered. "Now!"

Proudelk put the boy down behind him, shielding him with his body. "I don't think so." He felt just as he had when he'd recovered Edward Sharpnose. He was responsible for the boy. He didn't know if that was heroic or not, but he knew the FREELancers team wouldn't have found Matthew DiLuca without his help. Suddenly he wasn't so sure where that responsibility ended.

"You're a fool," C4 told him. "We're on the same side."

"Then let me do my job."

Power sparked between her hands in orange-and-yellow waves. Then it leaped for him, flicking across the Burris transceiver. The explosion plunged Proudelk into a black pit, and he lost consciousness.

Detroit, Michigan   ***9:49 p.m. EST***
Assignment: Viperstrike II
Tactical Ops: Hard Probe, Subject: Tadashi
Status: Code Green

Cloaked in the darkness at the side of the Cherryspire Tower, dressed in a long coat and a snap-brim hat that shadowed his scarred features, Refit slipped the bootlegged smartcard through the magnetic locks of the door. Immediately, the latches disengaged with electronic bleeps and metallic snicks.

He stepped inside, never once letting himself believe his entrance had escaped detection. All he'd succeeded in doing was bypassing traditional security and moving up into the kill zone. But he was providing Tadashi's people with a target while the rest of the team moved into their positions.

The security teams would know he wasn't alone, but he was going to make it too costly to ignore him. Doffing the trench coat and hat, he reached into his chest pack and took out a HE-bomb.

The building records Underhill's intelligence people had found were surprisingly accurate. He swept the Ingram Stutter-shot from his hip holster and jogged down the corridor. Two security people moved out of the shadows, never realizing the threat till he was among them. He swept the Ingram across them in a blazing figure eight, using the weapon's eye-tracking scanner and on-board computer chips to aid his aim. Underhill had okayed the use of hardball ammunition for the operation. People that went down under the FREELancers guns during this operation were going to stay down—permanently.

The basement door was locked. He kicked three times before his great strength shattered the mechanisms holding it. On the other side of the leaning door, emergency lights lit up the small railed platform that led to stairs descending to the basement. Car odors filled this level. Beyond the railing, a phalanx of vehicles sat silently.

He started down, then froze as a dark-uniformed figure flipped and came to a landing a few steps beneath his position. Steel whickered out, long and gleaming and deadly, in semigloved hands. Above the mask and below the cowl, the ninja's eyes were like steel bearings. The attack came at once. The blade licked out like a living thing, echoed by the robot canine-thing that was the other part of the Cy-9 team.

Lunging to one side, unable to totally escape the sword thrust, Refit felt the blade give him a long, smooth kiss along his side, under the Kevlar vest. Blood surged warm and thick down his hip. The cyber-canine, wired to work in tandem with its flesh-and-blood partner, grabbed Refit's leg in its jaws.

"Damn pest," the patchwork giant snarled as he brought

up the Ingram and fired at the place where the head was joined to the cyber-canine's shoulders. Bullets spit in all directions, but tore the creature's head away and rendered it inert. Then Refit swept the Stuttershot up at the ninja.

The bullets caught the ninja and threw him backward, his body coming to a rest on the lower steps.

Reloading the machine pistol, Refit went on, stepping over the downed ninja. Below, the door to the building's power station was illuminated by a small light above the entrance. A red-and-black sign advertised DANGER! HIGH VOLTAGE!

A rustle of clothing warned Refit only a second before he would have been decapitated. He ducked and spun, coming around with the ninja's sword point close enough to nick his chin.

"Damn!" Refit swore as he raised the Ingram and barely managed to deflect a swing directed at his throat. Sparks flew from the metal on contact; he knew the ninja wore body armor under the loose clothing.

The ninja's blade, flashing at him again and again, was unrelenting.

"Just meat," Refit reminded himself quietly. "Only thing you got to worry about is if you run out of it." He grabbed for the ninja and tucked the HE-bomb inside the man's clothing.

Taking advantage of the situation, the ninja swung the sword. The keen edge took off Refit's left ear, then cleaved into his collarbone.

While the blade was trapped in the collection of blood, muscle, and bone, Refit slammed the Ingram's barrel alongside the ninja's head. The impact was terrific, and the Yakuza assassin went limp in Refit's grasp. Without pause, the patchwork giant stumbled down the stairs, ignoring the pain in his head and shoulder. He used the forged smart-card on the power room door to open it.

Holding the ninja in one hand and dragging him across the floor, Refit opened the power-room door. Machinery occupied the room from floor to ceiling. According to the specs Underhill had turned up, the power room was the heart of the Cherryspire Tower. Once it was down, the building lived only through backup lights. The computers would stay on-line because of emergency generators.

As the ninja started to come to, Refit tripped the HE-bomb he'd placed inside the man's clothes. A short blade materialized in the ninja's hand and swept toward Refit's face. Before it could reach him, Refit threw the man inside the power room and slammed the door shut.

The explosive went off a heartbeat later, ripping the door from its hinges and sending it into the concrete wall across from it. Whole blocks blew out of the wall housing the power room. Fragmented holes peered out over the stairs as blue lightnings chased themselves around the hulks of machinery, then flickered out. Darkness, held at bay only by clusters of emergency lights, fell over the building.

Refit used the Burris. "Mission accomplished," he said needlessly.

"What kind of shape are you in?" Underhill demanded.

"I'm walking," Refit answered as he placed bandages over the wound in his side and over his shoulder to hold things together for the moment. He didn't let the hovering trauma touch him. It was only borrowed meat, and he was the machine that drove it.

"What about the elevator?" Underhill asked.

"I'm on it." Refit made his way back up the stairs. With the power knocked out, only one elevator remained operable in the building. Unless Tadashi and his people chose to take the fire escape, it was the only way down. "Download, how's that elevator coming?"

"It's not even breathing hard yet," Download replied, then he gave a short, wheezy laugh that belonged to a much older man.

"Terrific."

"It's on your floor. You say the word, and I'll power you up again."

Refit returned to the first floor and came out behind a man armed with a combat shotgun that had a flashlight taped to the barrel, who was searching the hallway. Though weakened from his wounds, he came up behind the man noiselessly, grabbed his chin in one hand and wrenched quickly, breaking the man's neck.

He holstered the Ingram and picked up the shotgun. If he got to where he couldn't function with the computer circuitry of the Stuttershot, the 12-gauge would be an asset. A brief check through the dead man's clothes turned up a bandolier of shells, which he draped across his chest.

The private elevator was off the main foyer in a security office. Two men, marked by special glow-in-the-dark armbands, stood beside the defunct security systems.

Swinging around the door, Refit raised the shotgun and fired point-blank, then racked the slide and fired again. When he stepped into the office, he was the only man alive.

Shoving his fingers into the elevator doors, he forced them open. The shaft was empty, but he spotted the cage four floors above him. He accessed the Burris. "Download."

With a jerk, the elevator cage went into motion. Refit kept his thumb over the "up" button as it dropped toward him. When it arrived, he stepped inside and punched the button for the top floor. As it rose, he fed more shells into the shotgun and tried to ignore the fact that he was probably bleeding to death on the carpeted floor.

Detroit, Michigan   **9:53 p.m. EST**

"You reneged on our deal."

Aramis Tadashi, seated in the plush chair behind the big desk, smiled at Crystal Young, whose café-au-lait features were edged with anger visible even on the vid-screen. "I don't see it that way," he said.

"The hell you say. In exchange for my help, you were supposed to take out the FREELancers."

"I gave you one of them," Tadashi pointed out. "You should have killed him immediately. Instead, you chose to use him as bait and ended up losing him."

"But you haven't moved against the others since."

"Give me time," Tadashi said. "They are involved in this. It won't be long before they are once more in my sights."

"Let me remind you," Deadline said, "that your reign there in Cherryspire Tower as the Japanese Diet's new crime czar could be brief without help from the right people."

Tadashi grew irritable. With all the successes of the day, he refused to bend under the thumb of someone else. "That remains to be seen."

Deadline's eyes hardened. Whatever retort she had planned was lost as the lights went out and the phone lines went dead.

Tadashi glanced at Kerrick and Cydney. "What happened?"

"We're under attack," Kerrick said, looking at her computer. An icon indicating that the system was now running on reserve power took shape in the upper corner. "The power-supply room just crashed."

"How?"

"I don't know."

Then a tremble thrilled up the core of the building.

"Explosion," Cydney answered. The tremors went away.

"Andoc's people?" Tadashi demanded.

Cydney shook his head, gazing at a security monitor while he worked the keyboard beside it. The scenes shifted rapidly, then focused on a figure coming in through a side door. When the image was blown up and enhanced, the scarred features were unmistakable. "The FREELancers," Cydney said.

"Find them," Tadashi ordered. He shoved himself up from the desk. "Find them and let me know where they are." His mind flooded with questions, wondering how Underhill had gotten on to him so quickly, and how she had found him at Cherryspire Tower. Then he shoved the thoughts out of his mind. None of it mattered. It mattered only that they were taken care of. And he was sure, no matter how much the mercenary leader had researched him, that she didn't know everything about him.

He reflected wryly as he walked toward the building's private elevator that Deadline's complaints were about to be addressed.

25

Detroit, Michigan   *10:01 p.m. EST*
Great Lakes Authority (GLA)   *0301 Greenwich Mean*
83.1 degrees W Longitude   *October 24, 2023*
42.3 degrees N Latitude   *Tuesday*
Assignment: Viperstrike II, cont'd.
Tactical Ops: Enemy Computer Interface
Status: Code Red

Streaming with sweat inside the electrical service conduit under the building, worn out from his half-mile crawl along its length, Download worked with the maze of electrical wires with a speed and a skill that surprised him in spite of everything he'd done before.

Marley Crowder, the electronic security sysops who'd been the resource for the present skill-disk in the Octopus, was a genius when it came to computer systems. But he'd always wanted to be a stand-up comedian. As Download worked, the ghost in his mind kept up a steady patter of ancient vaudevillian jokes and didn't seem to mind that his captive audience didn't laugh. Crowder laughed along at the appropriate places all on his own. His thin, raucous guffaws punctuated every punchline.

Download had already decided that if the guy was still alive, he never wanted to meet the man. But he was a wizard when it came to the systems.

"Uh-oh," Crowder said.

" 'Uh-oh' what?" Download demanded.

"You've got a slaved circuit there."

"Where?"

Crowder pointed with Download's finger.

"What does it do?"

Crowder poked at it. "Judging from the placement and the other tie-ins, I have to assume it works along the phone lines."

"So?"

"So, you bring up the phone lines later for your people to use, that slaved circuit is going to do exactly what it's supposed to do."

"And what is that?" Download demanded.

"Let's find out. You mind?"

"Not me," Download said, offering up his hands.

Expertly, Crowder used his hands to sort through the wires, strip some of the plastic cover off with a box-knife, then affix new leads into the wiring harness with a crimping tool. A moment later, he plugged the harness into the notebook computer Download had packed into the tunnel.

"It's a disbursement rigging," Crowder said as the specs came up on the computer screen. "If the phone lines go up, it'll call these locations and download a database that's already been put into place."

Download looked at the list on the notebook's monitor. All of them were high-tech development corporations scattered across the globe. "What's the database?"

"Can't say," Crowder admitted.

"Maybe I know someone who can." Download patched into a phone servo that he'd left active. Scanning other information available on the computer, he saw that Refit had almost reached the top of the building.

"Matrix," the woman's voice answered, still and distant. In the background, violence erupted.

Download identified himself. "I've got something for you."

"What?" Tires shrilled.

"A database. I need you to tell me what it is."

"Send it. I'll get back to you over the Burris."

Download sent the huge file, then broke the connection. The rewiring was finished. He put the tools away and readied himself for the one-hundred yard climb that would take him into Cherryspire Tower.

"You know," Crowder said, stretching inside Download's mind, "this set-up ain't too bad. 'Course, some folks would probably think you're talking to yourself if they heard you."

"Yeah, but for now we're going to have to be quiet," Download pointed out. "Unless you want to get shot."

"Nope. Mum's the word."

Download had to resist the impulse to zip his lips with his fingers. He kept crawling, ignoring the ache in his back, neck, and knees.

Detroit, Michigan   *10:09 p.m. EST*
Assignment: Viperstrike II, cont'd.
Tactical Ops: Troop Deployment
Status: Code Red

Strapped into the copilot's seat in the BirdSong JK91 heligyro, Lee Won Underhill surveyed the Cherryspire Tower. Only the dim glow of the emergency lights illuminated the building. Against the bright panoply of the other structures around it in downtown Detroit, it looked like an abscessed and rotting tooth.

The hammering of the rotors would have made hearing impossible if it weren't for the headsets. Dervish occupied one of the rear seats amid a team of Agent Prime's combat ops. The strike team was dressed in gray and red, their chests bulky with armor and extra pockets. They all carried assault rifles and wore headgear that allowed them to switch from light-amplifying mode to infrared. Dervish looked svelte and deadly when compared to them.

Underhill wore a red-and-gray jumpsuit festooned with hidden pockets containing a deadly arsenal. Her hair was pulled back in a braid. She carried a Beretta Nova laser pistol on her hip, and a conventional Government Model .45 in a boot holster. Ammunition for the .45 hung from the recharging belt for the laser.

She hit the transmit button on the Burris. "Scratchbuilt. GlowStar." She already knew where Refit and Download were.

"We're in place," DeChanza radioed back.

"Affirmative," GlowStar chimed in.

"Take down your targets." Underhill dropped out of the com-loop, studying the building intently. The two other members were underground, following up an escape tunnel that led to Lake St. Clair.

"Trouble," the pilot said, pointing.

Underhill followed his line of sight as he started juking the BirdSong JK91. A gun emplacement on the twelfth floor shed the mock wall that had covered it. An instant later, tracers filled the air, whipping for the heligyro.

"What do you want to do?" the pilot asked.

"Get me a shot," Underhill said, reaching for the controls for the 30mm cannon mounted on the belly of the craft. The waldoes felt comfortable on her hands as the tracking screen lit up.

The pilot heeled the BirdSong over, letting the reinforced armor along the belly of the heligyro absorb the brunt of the .50-cal bullets that found them. Sparks leaped from the whirling rotor blades.

"Can't take much of this," the pilot said.

Underhill, intent on getting a target-lock on the gun emplacement, didn't reply. The crosshairs flared bright when

it was achieved, and she rolled her thumb over on the firing
stud. The heligyro bucked as the 30mm cannon fired ten
rounds in less than two seconds. The gun emplacement disin-
tegrated, leaving a gaping hole in the side of the building.

"Get us over there," Underhill directed, releasing the waldoes. The heligyro pilot nodded and brought the craft down
in a quick dip that left the interior pulling negative Gs for a
few seconds. Once stability had been achieved, Underhill
unbuckled from her seat and walked to the rear of the Bird-
Song.

Two combat ops were already in place with a rope ladder.
She nodded, and they kicked it out. Spinning rapidly, it
dropped beside the building, listing slowly in the wind created by the whirling rotor blades.

One of the men climbed down while two others swung the
ladder close to the building. When he made contact, it took
him only a few seconds to secure it, leaving enough slack that
the BirdSong JK91 could fluctuate slightly.

Underhill made the climb, then dropped onto the cracked
floor of the twelfth story. Dervish was at her side in one lithe
move, scimitar in one hand and a wavy dagger in the other.

As the rest of the strike force continued to deploy into the
building, the FREELancers administrator took the lead. She
drew the Beretta Nova and flicked off the safety. Blueprints of
the building filled her mind as she charged out of the office.

A roving, two-man security team spotted her and fired
immediately, letting her know Tadashi was aware of the
FREELancers red-and-gray uniforms on the premises. "Down!"
she yelled to the team. She dived to the floor with the Nova
thrust before her as auto-fire raked the walls. She fired three
times, and the laser blasts incinerated the attackers.

As she got to her feet, three ninjas hurled themselves from
the shadows, naked blades in their fists. Backing away,
Underhill, unable to bring the laser pistol into play, engaged
the first one. She used her free arm like a sword, and swatted
away the sword along the flat of the blade, making no contact

with the keen edge. Then she delivered a roundhouse kick that caught the man in the face. Before her opponent could rise, she burned a hole through his chest with the Nova.

When she looked around, she saw that Dervish had accounted for the other two ninjas. A dim memory of steel on steel at her back hummed in her mind. The combat ops flanked them. She gave Dervish a brief nod that was returned, then took up the lead again.

The Burris buzzed for attention.

"Underhill."

"The magnetic activity in that building just went off the scale," Dr. Rhand said without preamble. "If we're right, and Tadashi has a metability involving magnokinesis, it's stronger than anything we've ever encountered before."

"I know," Underhill said. Rhand faded out of the com-link. At the fire escape, Underhill paused, uncertain which direction to head. Then Refit broke in over the Burris.

"I just reached the fourteenth floor. Nobody's home."

Tense minutes later, Underhill spotted the glowing green-tinged yellow nimbus that floated from above. Before it touched the metal stairway below it, the steps tore free of the wall and careened downward. The FREELancers administrator almost lost her head to the avalanche of metal.

Detroit, Michigan   *10:13 p.m. EST*
Assignment: Viperstrike, cont'd.
Subassignment: Fang-puller
Tactical Ops: Termination
Status: Code Red

Running through the darkness of the alley, Agent Prime paused only an instant beside Gitano Proudelk. Superficial burns on the young AmerInd's face and chest seemed to be the only result of the exploding Burris transceiver. Proudelk was already coming around.

"You'll be okay, mate," he said gruffly, then set off in pursuit of C4. The CO_2-powered crossbow was heavy at the end of his arm, but it was a weight he was accustomed to.

C4 had taken an offshoot from the main alley. He saw her ahead of him, dashing across the legs of burnt-out wire-heads GLA Social Services hadn't tracked down and institutional-ized yet, or turned over to the organ recovery division. The woman had the boy thrown over her shoulder, but she wasn't handling the weight as easily as Proudelk had.

"Traitoress!" he yelled when he'd narrowed the distance to forty yards.

She came around instantly. The end of the alley was scarcely twenty yards farther on, and the headlights of a wait-ing car glared into the alley.

"Prime!" C4 dropped the backpack with the computer in it, but maintained her hold on the boy.

"Surprised to see me, sheila?" Prime asked, standing his ground. "Think maybe I'd still be in Seattle?"

She smiled wryly.

"Appears that you didn't fool Underhill as much as you thought you did," Prime said. "She's suspected you were working for Deadline for a few months now, and your volun-teering for this leg of the mission didn't set well with her. Me, I figured I just didn't like you. Now I know my feelings were justified." He took a slow step forward. "She asked me to come check on you."

"Stay there," C4 commanded the boy as she lowered him. Matthew DiLuca dropped to the ground and stayed put.

"Easy or hard, sheila," Prime said, "you name the tune. I'd prefer it if you resisted."

She laughed. "You of all people should fear me. How many pieces do you think I can blow you into?"

"Not many," Prime admitted. "I came prepared for you." He raised the crossbow, a red-fletched bolt already in place.

An orange-and-yellow ray jumped for him from C4's hands but didn't make contact.

Nothing incendiary was included in Prime's equipment: no

bullets, no grenades, no chemicals. He held only the crossbow and a half-dozen knives secreted on his body.

Yelling her rage, C4 turned her metability toward the walls of the buildings.

Aware of the gas lines that ran through the buildings, Prime knew he was still in big trouble. He raised the crossbow to his shoulder and aimed by instinct. His finger caressed the trigger, then the butt stock shoved against his shoulder.

The orange-and-yellow rays from C4's hands evaporated. Limned by the moonlight, Prime saw that the quarrel had suddenly appeared as if by magic between the woman's eyes. She dropped forward on her knees, swaying for just a moment before falling facedown onto the asphalt surface of the alley.

Prime pumped another quarrel into the breech and started for the boy and the backpack. He kept his eyes focused on the waiting headlights, looking for movement.

Instead, the car backed away in a semicircle that left it pointed out toward the street. For an instant moonlight fell across the rear window, and Prime recognized Ruriko Nakeshita.

"Another time, wench," he said softly. "Another time. You can't keep walking the tightrope forever without falling." He leaned down and helped Matthew DiLuca up.

"Are you okay, lad?" Captain Ares asked as he bounded down the alley. He gathered the boy in his arms, then draped his cape over him so he couldn't see C4's body. "We'll get you out of here. You're safe now."

Prime ignored the other agent and gathered the backpack straps in one fist. Police sirens were already screaming in the distance when he returned to the van and handed the computer to Matrix.

"You feeling okay, mate?" Prime asked Proudelk as the young AmerInd came forward. "That was quite a wallop you took back there."

"I'll be fine. I thought she was on our side."

"This old world," Prime said, "most people tend to be on their own side. You find a few who look at life with some of the common interests you have, you should stick by them."

"I'll keep that in mind. But this isn't a business I think I want to invest much time in."

Prime nodded, but his eyes were focused down the street where the Captain was climbing into the rear of a sedan with Matthew DiLuca. "Understand your feeling, mate. But there's some rewards you get in this line of work that you just don't get anywhere else."

"I know," Proudelk said softly.

Prime noticed the younger agent's eyes on the boy as well. It was like he'd told Underhill before when arguing about what Prime considered excessive recruitment: being a FREE-Lancer was a calling. Members couldn't just be drafted into the ranks.

And he was certain young Gitano Proudelk was going to have a hard time resisting that siren call.

Detroit, Michigan   10:17 p.m. EST
Assignment: Viperstrike II, cont'd.
Tactical Ops: Blockade
Status: Code Red

John-Michael DeChanza came up out of the lake water into an airlock under the Cherryspire Tower. The Scratchbuilt armor almost reached the ceiling overhead. Emergency lights filled the area with a pleasant yellow glow, bathing the cut-stone walls.

"God, but that water was cold."

Looking down, DeChanza saw GlowStar, dressed in a clinging thermal swimsuit that echoed her own uniform's color scheme, stride up from the waterline. Every delicious curve was outlined, and DeChanza was suddenly thinking that she really wasn't that much older than he was.

She dropped the diving helmet at her side and shook out

her hair.

The outlet for the airlock was over fifty feet below the lake's surface, allowing for a secret sub base where contraband could be delivered or shipped out. Information about the port hadn't been contained in the blueprints Underhill had found, but she'd surmised its existence from coastal reports on the lake's water currents. With the Japanese ownership of Detroit, it was easy to see how they could allow secret transactions to happen without alerting the US Coast Guard farther out.

To the right was a small docking area with a Capricorn-class mini-sub already tethered. A warehouse area sat up on the concrete pillars, a green cargo-Exo sitting by idly. Pallets containing crated boxes were lined up neatly.

Underhill had figured that if Tadashi could break free of the cordon they were setting up around the building, the underground airlock would probably be the first place he'd head. Scratchbuilt and GlowStar's job was to see to it that no one left by the airlock.

"Makes me feel guilty for being inside here," DeChanza said, referring to the armor.

"If things were reversed," GlowStar assured him as she checked her suit for the throwing stars that had been specially made for the mission, "I wouldn't feel guilty for a minute."

<Warning> the on-board computer suddenly buzzed. <This unit has been successfully target-locked.>

DeChanza sank into the cyberveil's sensory input as he brought the MAPS around. "We're not alone here," he said.

Then a rocket swirled out of the shadows at the far end of the airlock and exploded against the Scratchbuilt suit's upper chest.

<Warning! This unit's gyro stabilizers are unable to conform to the changed demands. All systems down to ninety-three percent. Renewed target-lock being searched for.>

"Bring up the weapons systems," DeChanza ordered as he

fell backward. "Identify attacker." He watched the monitor
screens even as his perspective changed.

<Weapons systems on-line. Right shoulder laser cannon.
Left shoulder .50-caliber heavy machine gun. Right wrist
flamethrower.>

Then water closed over the Scratchbuilt unit. DeChanza
flailed for equilibrium, knowing GlowStar had been left to
face the unseen attacker alone. Once he got his feet under
him, he pushed up, coming out of the water with the
flamethrower leveled before him.

<Attackers identified: three MAPS units. All in full attack
mode. Armament as follows.>

Seventeen feet tall, looking like walking skulls with legs
and arms, the MAPS units crossed the pier toward Glow-
Star. Using her agility and speed, she flipped out of their
way and flung her throwing stars with unerring accuracy.
Specially magnetized, the stars stuck to the metallic figures.
Seconds after adhering, they exploded, causing damage but
not disabling the units. Lines of machine gun fire raced after
GlowStar.

<Target-lock achieved. Fire flamethrower.>

DeChanza dropped his thumb over the firing stud. A blanket of napalm dropped over the MAPS unit farthest from
GlowStar. Flames wreathed it instantly, the smoke obscuring
visibility in the airlock. Below lake level, the airlock
depended on vents to recycle the atmosphere. It took only
seconds for the MAPS unit to fry, then collapse into an inert
heap. Flames licked at the soot-covered surface.

GlowStar, still on the move, threw more stars. This time
she aimed for the more vulnerable joints of the powersuits.
When the explosions came, they blew one of the legs off
the MAPS closest to her last position. It rolled over on its
back and strained like an overturned turtle to get erect
again.

<Warning! Target-lock being sought by surviving MAPS
unit.>

Turning his attention to the third armored suit, DeChanza brought up the laser cannon as 80mm missiles slammed into the Scratchbuilt armor.

<Suit efficiency down to seventy-six percent.>

"Yeah, yeah," DeChanza said. "I built this thing to take abuse." The target-lock flashed on the laser cannon. Firing, he cut the MAPS into two pieces.

Working the perimeter of the fallen suit still trying to get to its remaining foot, GlowStar threw more stars. When they exploded, wrecking the drive systems, the MAPS unit froze.

Suddenly, a large group of men, armed with conventional weapons and pulsers, entered the airlock from the tunnel leading back into the building.

<Warning! Hostile group—>

"I see them," DeChanza said, working the waldoes and taking in everything the cyberveil had to offer. He brought the .50-cal machine gun on-line and raked a vicious line of fire across the new attackers. They took defensive positions along the pier.

<Enemy targets are in possession of rocket launchers.>

"I see them," DeChanza said. He brought the flamethrower on-line as well and sprayed pools of flame along the dock. The Yakuza line broke.

"Cover me," GlowStar said, taking shelter behind one of his massive legs.

Keeping an eye on her, DeChanza worked the weapons waldoes. If a concerted effort was being made to clear the FREE-Lancer agents from the airlock, it had to be because an escape effort was being made in that direction. GlowStar was ready in seconds, bringing out more throwing stars.

"Ready," she said, then exploded out from him in a series of flips that took her across the floor in a blur of motion. Twice she flipped a half-dozen stars from her fingers, finding targets among their attackers. The anesthetic on the sharp edges acted quickly.

Figuring that removing the only objective in the airlock that the Yakuza soldiers were interested in would probably result in a full rout, DeChanza took two huge strides that brought him next to the Capricorn mini-sub. He slid to his knees, straightened the fingers of his right hand, and drove them through the mini-sub's hull. The craft started taking on water at once.

<Damage report upgrade. Extensive damage done to unit's right hand. Backup systems will be able to deliver only forty-seven percent efficiency at half speed.>

"It was worth it," DeChanza said. He swiveled his view and watched the line of attackers retreat. Using the .50-cal machine gun, he hastened their departure.

GlowStar used the Burris, and DeChanza picked up the broadcast on the armor's radio. Before she could make contact with Underhill, the water out in the middle of the airlock erupted.

<Danger> the on-board computer shrilled. <Possible enemy craft approaching.>

DeChanza pushed the powersuit to its feet and scanned the roiling water coming toward the pier in waves. "Identify."

<Accessing sonar capabilities. Verification imminent.>

A tri-cannon surfaced first, its three long barrels looking impossibly huge. Then the deck followed, smooth and dark and forbidding, looking like a kraken breaking from the water.

<Identification: Jupiter-class, streamlined attack sub, military complement. Target-locks are being focused on this unit.>

"No guano," DeChanza said as he worked the weapons waldoes. Tadashi hadn't been heading for the airlock for the mini-sub. His objective had been the war sub. Before DeChanza could get off a single round, the tri-cannon fired.

Two impacts scored in the chest area of the Scratchbuilt unit. The impact drove the powersuit from its feet and slammed it against the wall. DeChanza's senses swam as he struggled to hold on to consciousness.

<Suit efficiency down to thirty-eight percent. Enemy craft is vectoring for another shot. Estimated firing time, twenty-two seconds. Twenty-one, twenty . . .>

Unable to hold on, DeChanza's mind filled with blackness.

26

Detroit, Michigan   **10:19 p.m. EST**
Great Lakes Authority (GLA)   **0319 Greenwich Mean**
83.1 degrees W Longitude   **October 24, 2023**
42.3 degrees N Latitude   **Tuesday**
          Assignment: Viperstrike, cont'd.
          Tactical Ops: Information Retrieval
                    Status: Code Green

Deep within the Savant state, Matrix was dimly aware of
the motion and people around her. She knew, in a distant
part of her mind, that her team was racing for the Cherryspire Tower across town, and that it would take nearly
twenty minutes at best to get there. They would probably
arrive too late to have a positive effect on the events tran-
spiring there now.

But the program designed by Grant DiLuca and called
Project Fusuma was fascinating. She marveled at its com-
plexities, at the twists and turns of logic. In her mind, it
appeared as blue and green lines of power warping through
blackest space. Yet, instead of three dimensions, it somehow existed in four, linking into a spatial plane that she'd

never before encountered. Maybe it was the sheer dynamics of the design, because every part she took time to examine took her into another wrinkle that existed as a cosmos of its own, worthy of days if not weeks of study. And maybe it was because the chip had been designed and structured to be made in zero-gravity, which had been allowed for in the programming. It was something that she'd never seen.

The part of her that was Irene Domino rebelled. She knew she was trapped by the Savant personality inside her and probably wouldn't break out of the hypnotic trance until her physical body passed out from lack of water and food. The thought chilled her human side.

Then a voice somehow found her.

Irene.

She gathered cognizance, allowing her to pull away from the hypnotic lure of the programming for a second.

It's time to come back. Let me help you.

A figure stretched forth a hand, and she took it. Gently, she was pulled away from the programming. When she blinked her eyes, she saw the new metable, Nighthawk, leaning down over her. She was lying in the rear seat of the van. "Did you do that?" she asked.

"Yeah."

Then she noticed the burns across his face and hands, and she remembered where they were and what they were doing. She forced herself to sit up. "I've got to talk to Underhill."

"Did you get it?" Greywood asked from the driver's seat. Before her, through the windshield, the urban landscape had given way to the city and whipped by at dangerous speeds.

"Yes." Matrix activated the Burris, calling for the FREE-Lancers administrator. "It's terrible. She's got to destroy it."

Detroit, Michigan   **10:21 p.m. EST**
        Assignment: Viperstrike II, cont'd.
         Tactical Ops: Search and Destroy
              Status: Code Red

Holding the shotgun canted up before him, Refit took cover behind the corner of the corridor as bullets thunked into the wall. His assessment to Underhill of total evacuation of the upper floor was obviously premature. He'd discovered that on his way to the fire escape. Since no one had come down the elevator, the fire escape was the only means of getting down inside the building. He'd heard GlowStar's frenzied report of the war sub waiting in the airlock below, then she'd gone off-line when a huge explosion—bigger than the one he'd used to destroy the power-supply room—had shuddered through Cherryspire Tower. The probable fate of John-Michael DeChanza up against the firepower of a war sub worried him. He didn't like thinking the kid wouldn't make it out of this one alive.

As soon as the firing in the hallway paused, he whirled around the corner and dropped the shotgun to waist-level. He squeezed the trigger, aiming for the four men scattered across the hallway.

His first round caught a Yak in the face and spilled the corpse backward. He racked the slide and fed another round into the chamber, the empty plastic cartridge whirling by his head as the stink of gunpowder filled his nostrils. Bullets slammed into his Kevlar vest, rocking him, but he rode out the impacts and concentrated on his targets. He fired quickly, working through all seven rounds.

When the din of firing died away, he was the only living thing in the hallway. And he had two holes in his left thigh and one in his calf. Luckily, none of them had hit bone and his leg was more or less intact.

He made the meat move, pushing it to its limits as he sprinted for the fire escape. His fingers automatically fed more shells into the shotgun. When he reached the fire escape door, he fired a round. The pellets shattered the glass window inset high on the door and a man screamed. Knowing the ferocity of his attack was one of his main offensive weapons, he charged the door, kicking it open.

Five men and one woman were inside the stairwell. One of the men was down on the floor, clutching at his wounded face.

Without hesitation, Refit attacked the two nearest him. Blood coursed down from his wounds, and the ear that had been sliced off had filled, deafening him on that side. He thrust the shotgun into the face of the nearest man and pulled the trigger. The corpse was blown over the side of the stairwell.

The second man brought a sword around in a blurring arc. Refit sidestepped the blow, then butt-stroked the guy on the side of the head with the shotgun, crushing his skull.

When he turned to face the surviving trio, he recognized Aramis Tadashi. The other man and woman were unknown to him. The Japanese crime lord held a pistol.

Refit grinned. "If I was you, I'd give up. That popgun's only going to slow me down—*if* I decide to try to bring you in alive." He pointed the shotgun's muzzle at the man. "And that ain't exactly my first choice."

"Nor mine," Tadashi said. He raised the hand that didn't hold the pistol.

Refit fired at once, intending to shoot the man in the legs and knock him down. Green sparks jumped from the yellow field that shimmered into being in front of Tadashi. The man stood unharmed behind it. Unbelieving, Refit stared at the spread of buckshot frozen in the yellow field inches from Tadashi.

"Fool," the man snarled. "You don't even know the kind of power you're up against." He gestured with the free hand.

Shrieking sharply, metal snapped. Bars lining the railing yanked free and heeled over in the air. Then they came at Refit like thrown spears. He leaped to one side, but three of them still caught him. Two skewered him through the abdomen, and one punched through his lower chest and came out his back. He fell heavily to the ground, stunned. Under-hill had said that Tadashi might have metabilities, but her warning hadn't prepared him for this.

"Enjoy your death," Tadashi said. "I hope you're in considerable agony the whole time." He stepped onto the stairs joining Cydney and Kerrick. Green-tinged yellow power raced from his whole body, then the stairway shivered and pulled free of its moorings. Another pulse of power, and the lower part of the stairway sheared away, leaving Tadashi and company standing on the top platform plate, complete with railing on two sides. It hovered effortlessly.

Then Tadashi directed a force beam at the stairs below him. As Refit reached for the shotgun, he heard the rending metal scream in protest. Without warning, Tadashi's improvised sled dropped down the stairwell shaft.

Groaning curses, the patchwork giant reached for the first of the bars transfixing him. He pulled it out with difficulty, the slick blood making it hard to get a grip. It clanged to the floor when he released it. The other two followed it as the growl of shifting metal continued echoing up the shaft.

Dizzy, he forced himself to his feet. As long as the meat still worked, he meant to be in the fight. And he intended to collect his pound of flesh.

Detroit, Michigan   **10:23 p.m. EST**
Assignment: Viperstrike II, cont'd.
Tactical Ops: Search and Destroy
Status: Code Red

Lee Won Underhill stared out at the platform that went floating rapidly down the fire escape shaft and recognized Aramis Tadashi, Rochelle Kerrick, and Hilario Cydney aboard it. A glowing green-and-yellow nimbus surrounded them, obviously emanating from Tadashi. She lifted the .45 from her boot holster because the laser was still exhausted and hadn't recharged. She squeezed the trigger as soon as she had it up, firing from the point.

The bullets sparked as they touched the glowing nimbus, then stopped inches from Tadashi's face and chest. An instant later, one of Dervish's wavy knives came to a rest beside them.

Tadashi gestured, and the nimbus flared, giving off sunspots.

Instinctively, Underhill withdrew. On the other side of the door, Dervish did the same. The repelled bullets and knife struck the walls beside them and the ceiling over their heads, ripping much more deeply into the concrete than normally possible.

Once the fusillade had died away, Underhill cautiously peered back down into the fire escape shaft. The glowing nimbus had dropped lower.

The Burris buzzed for attention.

"Underhill," she answered, watching Dervish shake a length of nylon cord with a grappling hook from her uniform.

"It's Matrix." The woman's voice sounded tired, spent. "We rescued the boy and we got the computer."

Dervish set the grappling hook and started down the cord. Underhill followed her, letting the nylon slip through her gloves as she kicked out from the wall. The air inside the fire escape shaft seemed thick, hard to breathe. "What's Project Fusuma?"

"You've got to destroy it," Matrix replied. "If it works, it's one of the most dangerous things ever created."

Two floors below where she'd started, Underhill asked, "What is it?"

"A computer chip designed to interface with latent Savant metables," Matrix said. "If it does what it's supposed to do, it'll enhance Savant metabilities in people who are borderline, and open those portions of the mind that haven't been tapped by the latents. It's also possible that the computer chips can be designed so the Savant metability can be channeled in certain fields."

"So the designer can choose the type of Savant ability the user is able to access?" Underhill asked, her breath coming hard now as her legs absorbed the shock of another rappelling jump.

"Exactly."

"Lee," Dr. Rhand interrupted, letting her know he was still monitoring the mission, "if the Japanese get their hands on that kind of technology, this country and every other country on the face of the earth is going to become a technological wasteland. We could never hope to catch up to them enough to compete in the markets."

"I know." She made another jump.

"We could keep it," Rhand said. "Study it."

"And control it for ourselves?" Matrix asked derisively. "It's evil. It'll destroy lives."

"DiLuca, if he's still alive, will only duplicate his research," Rhand said. "You can't avoid progress."

Underhill came to a rest on a portion of a surviving stairwell with Dervish. Three combat ops stood near her, their weapons ready, while others clung to projections along the wall above her. Tadashi was out of sight. They were at the fourth floor. Dervish shook the grappling hook free and reeled it in as it spun in the open space.

The FREELancer administrator's mind filled with the implications of the research. Even as Dervish set the grappling hook again, she reached her decision. There'd be no time for recriminations if anything went wrong. She accessed the Burris. "Download."

"Here."

"Do you still have access to the slaved circuitry you found?"

"Yeah."

"Matrix," Underhill said, starting down the rappelling line after Dervish.

"Yes."

"Link up with Download's computer and give him the missing programming. Make it a single, complete unit."

"Okay."

Underhill's mind was already turning to ways to deal with Tadashi's immense power. "When it's done, Download, I want you to reactivate the slaved circuitry."

"You want this program to go out to all those different places?"

"Yes. Get it done." Underhill broke out of the com-link. Her arms, legs, and back ached from the effort of the descent, and she still didn't know how she was going to contain Tadashi or how many of her team remained alive.

Detroit, Michigan   **_10:24 p.m. EST_**
          Assignment: Viperstrike II, cont'd.
          Tactical Ops: Search and Destroy
                  Status: Code Red

<Target-lock secured. Prepare for damage.>

"No!" John-Michael DeChanza roared as his senses returned. He felt dulled, used up, and his head pounded incessantly. Rolling, he worked to stand, feeling the power-suit's huge feet dig into the concrete of the pier. His back scraped along the cut stone walls.

<Enemy craft is firing> the on-board computer warned.

Evidently the war sub hadn't been able to set itself properly for the first rounds from the cannon. The recoil had briefly submerged it and turned it sideways.

Working the weapons waldoes, DeChanza accessed the .50-cal machine gun. He saw the explosive rounds belch from the tri-cannon. Using his computer-assisted laser sighting, he targeted the rounds themselves. Over halfway to his position, the .50-cal bullets hammered into the cannon rounds and detonated them. The concussive wave slapped him back against the wall.

<Armor operating at thirty-one percent efficiency.>

The war sub jockeyed for another salvo.

"Get me some stress readings on this airlock," DeChanza ordered. "With all the firepower cutting loose in here, the structure's bound to have taken some damage."

<Computing. Seismographic search commencing.>

Aware of GlowStar down near his feet, DeChanza cut loose
with the laser cannon. The pink beam bathed the top of the
war sub, causing the water to boil around it. It caught an
explosive round coming out one of the mouths of the tri-
cannon and exploded it, rupturing the barrel beyond use. The
other two rounds escaped the .50-cal bullets DeChanza fired
at them, but the war sub's weapons ops didn't have target-
lock either. The rounds exploded against the nearby wall,
gouging out huge craters.

<Seismographic search finished.>

"Show me." DeChanza knew he was running dangerously
low on .50-cal ammunition, and the laser would take too
long to be of any real use against the war sub's refractive
surface.

On one of the monitors, a computer-generated simulation
of the airlock took shape. Fault lines in the rock were marked
in glowing violet. According to the figures he was looking at,
the impact point he needed was almost directly overhead,
well within his reach.

"Give me everything the suit has left," DeChanza said. "I
want it put behind this one blow."

<Warning. To carry that out may seriously endanger this
unit and the human operator.>

"If I had a choice," DeChanza said, "I'd act on it, get it
done."

<Parameters of instructions complied. Systems are go.>

DeChanza accessed the Burris. "GlowStar!"

"Yes."

"Get down. Now!"

As the war sub came around again, the young woman
dropped to the ground beside him. He covered her with one
of the armor's huge hands, making both a prison and a shield
of the steel fingers.

<Target-lock secure. Estimate probability of survival at

nineteen percent.>

DeChanza made a fist of the suit's other hand and slammed it into his chosen point of impact. The steel fingers crumpled, and sparks jumped from wrecked servos.

Overhead, a fissure opened in the ceiling as the impact rattled along the stress lines in the rock. Then an avalanche of rock came raining down over everything inside the airlock. DeChanza saw the war sub broken apart by huge boulders as he leaned the suit against the wall, taking as much shelter as he could.

In seconds, it was over. A pile of rock out in the water marked the war sub's grave. As he watched, the water level started to climb as the lake flooded in, no longer held at bay by air pressure.

Working carefully, the suit's power almost depleted except for emergency survival circuits, DeChanza dug the hand shielding GlowStar from the fallen rock. Anxious, he lifted his fingers.

Slowly, she got to her feet. "Wow," she said in a small voice.

"Yeah," DeChanza said, trying not to let the pent-up emotions he felt sound in his voice. He gazed up and saw the hole gaping in the street almost forty yards up. "Let's get out of here."

He offered her his hand, and she stepped up into it. He lifted her carefully to the Scratchbuilt armor's neck and told her to her hang on. Then he began the climb to the street.

27

Detroit, Michigan   **10:27 p.m. EST**
Great Lakes Authority (GLA)   **0327 Greenwich**
                                                    Mean
83.1 degrees W Longitude   **October 24, 2023**
42.3 degrees N Latitude   **Tuesday**
Assignment: Viperstrike II, cont'd.
Tactical Ops: Terminate with Extreme Prejudice
Status: Code Red

On the basement level, Lee Won Underhill dropped the final few feet to the floor and landed gracefully. The Colt Government Model .45 was in her hand. Dervish held her scimitar in both fists. The combat ops team landed a minute later, making hardly any noise at all.

The greenish-yellow nimbus was ahead of them, the glow more powerful than the emergency lights on the walls.

The lower level was primarily storage area for the computer mainframes and weapons stores of the Yakuza. At the other end, it also held vehicles and a ramp leading up to a garage at street level.

Underhill guessed Tadashi knew the war sub that had been

waiting in the airlock below no longer existed. She went forward, walking counterpoint to Dervish as they passed banks of computer hardware.

"Lee," Download transmitted.

"Go."

"Your slaved circuit's back together, hidden even better than it was before. Once power is returned to this building, those calls will be made." He paused. "I sure hope you know what you're doing."

Underhill didn't reply. Sometimes her actions were never measured for effect until after the smoke cleared. She'd made mistakes before.

Dervish waved her back, drew the scimitar into position, then engaged the ninja who swung suddenly around the doorway. Metal rang on metal for a moment, then the black-clad figure dropped, holding his stomach. A fresh sheen of blood was on Dervish's blade.

Following the woman through the door, Underhill saw that they were in the underground garage. The glowing nimbus was nowhere to be seen. Dark hulks of cars and sports utility vehicles were silhouette cutouts in the darkness.

"He hasn't left," Dervish whispered in a taut voice, "and we are not alone."

That was the only warning Underhill received before all hell broke loose. Auto-fire lit up the battlefield. At least three 5.56mm rounds slammed into the FREELancer administrator's protective body armor. She flung herself to the ground, her .45 thrust out at the line of figures that rushed at her.

Rolling on the ground toward a concrete support pillar, she fired the entire magazine, making all seven rounds body shots even though she figured the Yak attackers would be wearing body armor as well. Still, the impact from the huge slugs knocked her targets from their feet.

She came up with her back against the support pillar. Bullets streaked for her vulnerable flesh, spanging off the pillar. Concrete splinters dug into her left cheek as she shook the empty magazine free of the pistol. A pink laser beam drilled into a nearby car's gas tank and ignited it, causing an explosion that rolled it dangerously near her position.

The vehicle came to a rest on its side, flaming now, but providing more cover.

Underhill slammed home a fresh magazine and worked the slide to snap the first round into the firing chamber. A ninja, moving silent and swift, came over the burning car in a flip, his sword aimed at the FREELancer administrator's face.

She fired at almost point-blank range, hitting the man in the forehead. The body went limp and fell behind her. Moving again, firing when she had targets, dropping two more ninjas, she saw Dervish as a whirling slash of naked steel.

The woman had penetrated Yak lines and was causing the attackers to fall back to defend themselves against a shadow that could not be touched.

Finding the outside perimeter of the underground garage, Underhill made her way around the battle zone. It was impossible to tell who was winning. She fired twice from hiding, cutting down snipers who were attempting to kill her combat ops from hiding.

"Lee," Download radioed.

"Go."

"I'm on my way up to you."

Underhill didn't respond. His statement had sounded almost too personal, and it made her uncomfortable. Movement alerted her and she dove for cover as bullets snapped against the concrete wall where she'd just been. She rolled and came up holding the pistol in both hands, bracing on her elbows.

Two Yakuza holding assault rifles swept the barrels toward her.

She fired rapidly, and the crash of detonations filled the air around her. The two gunners were driven backward by her bullets, stopped by a station wagon with company markings on the sides.

While she was reloading, the nimbus reappeared, glowing brighter than ever. Tadashi could barely be seen within it. Abruptly, part of the nimbus shifted and formed an elongated segment that slammed into a van and two cars parked ahead of it. The vehicles tumbled end over end like a child's toys till they punched their way halfway through the wall where the FREELancers team had entered.

"Underhill!" Tadashi screamed. The nimbus shifted again and swatted away more cars and trucks, leaving the man standing in the middle of the underground garage. Sparks testified to the fact that FREELancer guns were being fired on him, but the bullets dropped to the concrete floor. "Come out from wherever you're hiding and let's end this charade."

Quietly, the FREELancer administrator closed the distance, staying in the shadows. She couldn't see Dervish, but she knew the woman was around.

"There's nothing you can do to stop me," Tadashi taunted. "Granted, you seem to have screwed things up here, but that can be fixed. I still have DiLuca and the Fusuma Project. The Japanese government will have to deal with me."

"You're no longer the sole owner of the Fusuma Project," Underhill said. "My people lifted it from your computers. And we got the missing piece from the boy."

Tadashi turned toward her, the nimbus pulsing like a live thing. "Then I'll have to see to it that you erase those files."

"I won't." Underhill took up a defensive position. From the corner of her eye, she saw Download moving along the shadows. Most of the gunfire had quieted, and she guessed that whatever Yakuza assassins hadn't gone down under FREE-Lancer guns had elected to fight another day.

"I can make you," Tadashi said. He lifted an arm and made a fist. In response, the nimbus curled a tendril, mirroring the movement. "You have that gun now only because I allow it."

Still behind the concrete pillar, Underhill fired from a modified Weaver stance, intending to give Download and Dervish more time to move without being noticed. All three bullets sped straight at Tadashi's face.

The sparks made green-hued arcs over the surface of the nimbus. But they penetrated almost to Tadashi's eyes.

Feeling encouraged, Underhill fired again, finishing off the four rounds remaining in the magazine. These stopped only inches from Tadashi's left cheek. The FREELancer administrator reloaded. "Maybe you're burning out using that much power. How much more can you take before a bullet gets through? And it's only going to take one. I promise."

Tadashi laughed. With one hand, he knocked the swarm of bullets away from his face. They gained incredible speed and knocked holes that were inches across in the wall around Underhill. "And maybe I was only showing off my control."

The elevator, less than twenty feet behind Tadashi, suddenly opened. Refit stepped through, looking like a blood-covered creature from a nightmare of violence. He held what looked like a mop handle in his hand.

"Hey, tough guy," the patchwork giant said, "since you're so keen on metal objects, I thought maybe you'd like something a little different." He threw the mop handle like a spear, and Underhill noticed the end was now a jagged shard. "You can call me Captain Ahab."

A green-tinged yellow tendril snaked toward the slim projectile, but had no effect. No metal remained in it. A heartbeat later, it impacted against Tadashi's shoulder with an audible *thunk*.

Tadashi screamed in pain as the impromptu wooden spear sank into his flesh. He dropped to his knees, the nimbus popping like a soap bubble.

Refit lunged forward and launched himself at the man, growling savagely. Before he could reach his target, though, a yellow glow surrounded Tadashi. A half-dozen green spikes of energy shot out and made contact with the patchwork giant. Their impacts sounded like slaps of wet flesh.

When she saw Refit suddenly stumble back, gaping holes in his chest, Underhill knew Tadashi had caused some of the

spent bullets around him to slice through the FREELancer
agent. "No!" she yelled as Tadashi forced himself to his feet.
She raised the pistol and emptied the clip.

"Yes!" Tadashi screamed.

Beside him, Kerrick stepped forward coolly and fired her
machine pistol at Refit, driving him back against the closed
elevator doors. She stopped suddenly, as a dagger materialized
in her throat. With a surprised look on her face, she turned to
Tadashi and grasped the handle of the wickedly curved knife.

Tadashi caught the woman with his good arm, but she died
before he could do anything.

While he was distracted, Underhill reloaded and shifted
her aim to Cydney, who had suddenly realized he was standing out in the open. Both her shots caught him in the back
and sent him tumbling.

"Damn you!" Tadashi roared. "This ends now!" He ripped
the wooden spear from his shoulder and flung it aside, then
whirled toward the line of cars to his left. Molten green-yel-
low beams leaped from his fingers, then the cars tumbled like
leaves caught in a hurricane.

Before Dervish could leave her hiding place, the cars flew
toward her. Tremendous crashes sounded, then she was buried
under tons of metal.

"You're powerless before me!" Tadashi screamed. The nimbus grew again, chasing away the darkness inside the underground garage. Curved hooks of green energy raced toward
Underhill.

She couldn't avoid them. The gun flipped from her hands,
then she found herself elevated, lifted by the metal snaps,
buckles, and catches in her uniform and body armor. She
struggled as she floated toward Tadashi.

He held her aloft less than six feet from him, and she struggled against the clothing and armor that held her trapped.
"You've lost," he said.

Mustering her reserves, Underhill reached inside one of her
pockets and pulled out a plastic explosive with a timer

attached. She held it in her fist and hit the timer. "Then nobody wins," she said in a cold voice.

Detroit, Michigan   10:32 p.m. EST
Assignment: Viperstrike II, cont'd.
Tactical Ops: Terminate with Extreme Prejudice
Status: Code Red

As he saw the gun fly from Underhill's hands and watched her lifted from her feet by the magnetic force beams, Download knew he had no choice. No other skill disk he had on him would help. He was forty yards out and just as vulnerable because of his armor as Underhill was.

He reached into his vest pocket and extracted the skill disk. Instinctively he fed it into the Octopus mounted on his shoulder. Blue lightning bounced inside his mind as he pulled the Beretta Nova laser pistol from the counterterrorist drop holster on his right thigh.

Then *she* filled his mind.

He ignored the fears because it was Lee who was about to die, whether by Tadashi's hand or her own. He couldn't let it happen.

"Hello," she said, already in possession of everything he knew.

"Hello, Eden," Download said. "Time to move."

"Let's do it."

Her confidence, her expertise, filled him as he broke cover and raised the Beretta Nova. "Hey, hairball," he yelled.

Tadashi turned to look. So did Underhill.

Abruptly a car swept toward him, sparks shooting out when the metal scraped the concrete floor. Download leaped to the side, feeling like he was back on the obstacle shooting course he was familiar with but had never seen. He pulled the Nova's trigger and five quick laser bursts burned holes through Tadashi's head.

Underhill dropped, off-balance.

"Lee!" Download yelled. "The bomb! Throw it!" He tried to bring himself to a stop, but slipped in blood from an earlier victim.

The FREELancer administrator tossed the bomb into the air, and it hung suspended for just a moment before it started to fall.

"It's okay," Eden Frisco said in Download's mind even though he was sliding and he knew that the bomb was enough to level the basement section of the building. "I told you I'd be here for you. Now make the damn shot."

He drew on her skill, focused on the white rectangular shape, breathed out to relax his arm, and fired.

The plastic explosive, without the arming device to set off the chemical reaction, simply evaporated, without detonating, in the laser beam.

"Thanks," Download said to the ghost.

But she walked away from him, walling herself away in a section of his mind that he knew he'd never be able to reach again.

Slowly, he got to his feet, the Nova still held before him. Underhill crossed the room to where Refit lay in front of the elevator doors.

"Good shooting."

Download turned and found Dervish standing beside him, her face scratched and bleeding. "I thought you were dead," he said.

"No," she said. "But it was a close thing."

He turned his attention to Underhill and crossed the room.

"Refit's still alive," the FREELancer administrator said, "but barely. Stay with him while I get some help in here."

Download nodded and dropped to his knees beside the patchwork giant.

"Jefferson . . ." Underhill said.

He looked up at her.

She tried, but no words came out.

"I know," he said softly. "Go on."

She turned, once more the Dragon Lady, cold and calculating.

"Hard woman," Refit wheezed, looking up at him with unfocused eyes.

"Yeah," Download said. "But if she were any other way, she wouldn't be able to do the things she does." And he knew it was true.

Refit was quiet for a moment. Then, "You and her really used to have a thing going?"

Download looked down at the other man. "Careful," he advised. "I can always tell her you died before the medical team arrived."

"Right. Forget I asked."

In spite of the situation, Download chuckled. The reaction seemed insane at the time, but he was used to that. It was where he lived.

Epilogue

Chicago, Illinois   *10:14 a.m. CST*
Great Lakes Authority (GLA)   *1614 Greenwich Mean*
87.7 degrees W Longitude   *October 27, 2023*
41.8 degrees N Latitude   *Friday*
              FREELancers Base

Lee Won Underhill entered her office and saw her father's holo standing at the window looking down. "Good morning," she told him, dropping her jacket on her chair behind the desk. With the morning's hectic schedule, she hadn't had time to speak with him earlier.

"Good morning." George Anthony Underhill turned to face her. "How'd it go with the Japanese?"

"They're paying."

"So easily?"

She made a cup of tea and sat at the desk, managing the television remote control with one hand and switching on CNN. "Reluctantly." She kept the sound on mute, checking the news story, finding it was still on the international scene, and glanced at the list of things to do she'd outlined on the legal pad. She turned to face him, noticing the small smile on his face. "What's up?"

He shrugged. "Were there any problems with them?"

"They were upset that we hadn't found the slaved circuitry that forwarded the Fusuma Project to the other companies. Of course, they didn't mention Tadashi's threats to us either."

"They don't suspect you or FREELancers of being responsible for the dissemination of that research?"

"As far as I could tell, no. Anyway, I hired this company out to return the Fusuma Project. I never guaranteed that it would remain uncopied."

"You could have maintained the integrity of it," her father pointed out.

Underhill sipped her tea. "Yes, and possibly doomed the struggling international economy."

"So you feel no remorse over the course of action you chose?"

"Not one bit," she replied emphatically. "If the Japanese had gotten the Savant chip all to themselves, assuming it even works—which we still don't know—there's no telling how many nations might not have survived the sudden shift in the balance of power."

"Including a certain mercenary organization."

"Yes."

"You could have kept it for this company."

"And do what with it? We're not set up to deal with something like the Savant chip. It's going to affect nations and decades. Probably history. FREELancers is set up for the here-and-now, for problems that can be solved with direct action." Underhill looked at him. "Why the twenty questions routine?"

He paused for a moment. "I wanted to tell you how proud I am of you. You snatched victory from the jaws of defeat. A few days ago, the future of the corporation looked bleak. Now everything's back the way it should be. According to the figures I looked at, we're getting more calls now than ever."

"Most of that has to do with Contact. Her operations with media resources have been nothing short of phenomenal."

"She blackmailed them with potential lawsuits."

Underhill shrugged and smiled. "Possibly a few of them."

"You did good, Lee."

"Thank you."

George Anthony Underhill went back to window watching. "How's Refit?"

"Up and around since yesterday. He checked himself out of the medical center."

"Of course. What about Charm?"

"He hasn't turned up," Underhill said. "Yet. But he will. I think he's on another of his sojourns. I put Nighthawk and Greywood on him. They'll find him soon enough."

"Aramis Tadashi won't be the last of them," her father said. "Other men, other metables, will rise up. These are troubled times."

"Times that try the souls of men?"

He smiled. "Nothing as clichéd as that, yet that sums up the truth of the matter succinctly enough. A gathering darkness is hovering out there, and not many will be able to stand against it."

A chill touched Underhill. The world had changed, becoming leaner and meaner, like a hungry predator that would feast on its own young if it had to. She watched her father continue his window browsing. "What's so interesting out there?"

"Come see."

She crossed the room and stood at his side. When she looked down, she saw a brand new billboard facing the city, the colors clean and bright and honest. With a long brush, a man on a hanging scaffold was putting the finishing touches on the surface.

On the billboard was a picture of Centaur with the girl from the telethon in his arms, his image nothing less than heroic and noble. On the billboard was the wording: NEED HELP? CALL FREELANCERS.

"That should be worth a few points on the stock exchange

this morning," she said softly. But she knew that wasn't all the sign represented. It spoke of heroes, men and women who would champion lost causes across a terrifying world. For a price. For some it would offer hope. For others it would be an open threat. A torch in the face of the oppressor.

And that was what Lee Won Underhill was proudest of.

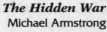